Winter's Tales

Isak Dinesen is the pseudonym of Karen Blixen,
born in Denmark in 1885. After her marriage in 1914
to Baron Bror Blixen, she and her husband lived
in British East Africa, where they owned a coffee
plantation. She was divorced from her husband
in 1921 but continued to manage the plantation for
another ten years, until the collapse of the coffee
market forced her to sell the property and return
to Denmark in 1931. There she began to write in
English under the *nom de plume* Isak Dinesen.
Her first book, and literary success, was *Seven
Gothic Tales*. It was followed by *Out of Africa, The
Angelic Avengers* (written under the pseudonym
Pierre Andrézel), *Winter's Tales, Last Tales, Anecdotes
of Destiny, Shadows on the Grass* and *Ehrengard*. She
died in 1962.

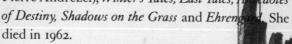

V I N T A G E

INTERNATIONAL

ALSO BY *Isak Dinesen*

Winter's Tales

ISAK DINESEN

Vintage International

VINTAGE BOOKS

A DIVISION OF RANDOM HOUSE, INC.

NEW YORK

First Vintage International Edition, July 1993

Copyright © 1942 by Random House, Inc.

Copyright renewed 1970 by Johan Philip Thomas Ingerslev

Library of Congress Cataloging-in-Publication Data
Dinesen, Isak, 1885–1962.
[Vinter-eventyr. English]
Winter's tales/Isak Dinesen.—1st Vintage International ed.
p. cm.
ISBN 0-679-74334-0
1. Dinesen, Isak, 1885–1962 Translations into English.
I. Title
PT8175.B545V513   1993
839.8′1372—dc20   92-50615
CIP

Manufactured in the United States of America

10 9 8 7 6 5

CONTENTS

THE YOUNG MAN
WITH THE CARNATION

THREE-QUARTERS of a century ago there lay in Antwerp, near the harbour, a small hotel named the Queen's Hotel. It was a neat, respectable place, where sea captains stayed with their wives.

To this house there came, on a March evening, a young man, sunk in gloom. As he walked up from the harbour, to which he had come on a ship from England, he was, he felt, the loneliest being in the world. And there was no one to whom he could speak of his misery, for to the eyes of the world he must seem safe and fortunate, a young man to be envied by everyone.

He was an author who had had a great success with his first book. The public had loved it; the critics had been at one in praising it; and he had made money on it, after having been poor all his life. The book, from his own experience, treated the hard lot of poor children, and it had brought him into contact with social reformers. He had been enthusiastically received within a circle of highly cultivated, noble men and women. He had even married into their community, the daughter of a famous scientist, a beautiful young woman, who idolized him.

He was now going to Italy with his wife, there to finish his next book, and was, at the moment, carrying the manuscript in his port-manteau. His wife had preceded him by a few days, for she wanted to visit her old school in Brussels on the way. "It will do me good," she had said, smiling, "to think and talk of other things than you." She was now waiting for him at the Queen's Hotel, and would wish to think and talk of nothing else.

All these things looked pleasant. But things were not what they looked. They hardly ever were, he reflected, but in his case they were even exactly the opposite. The world had been turned upside down upon him; it was no wonder that he should feel sick, even to death, within it. He had been trapped, and had found out too late.

For he felt in his heart that he would never again write a great book. He had no more to tell, and the manuscript in his bag was nothing but a pile of paper that weighed down his arm. In his mind he quoted the Bible, because he had been to a Sunday School when he was a boy, and thought: "I am good for nothing but to be cast out and be trodden under foot by men."

How was he to face the people who loved him, and had faith in him: his public, his friends and his wife? He had never doubted but that they must love him better than themselves, and must consider his interests before their own, on account of his genius, and because he was a great artist. But when his genius had gone, there were only two possible future courses left. Either the world would despise and desert him, or else it might go on loving him, irrespective of his worthiness as an artist. From this last alternative, although in his thoughts he rarely shied at anything, he turned in a kind of *horror vaccui;* it seemed in itself to reduce the world to a void and a caricature, a Bedlam. He might bear anything better than that.

The idea of his fame augmented and intensified his despair. If in the past he had been unhappy, and had at times contemplated throwing himself in the river, it had at least been his own affair. Now he had had the glaring searchlight of renown set on him; a hundred eyes were watching him; and his failure, or suicide, would be the failure and the suicide of a world-famous author.

And even these considerations were but minor factors in his misfortune. If worse came to worst, he could do without his fellow-creatures. He had no great opinion of them, and might see them go, public, friends and wife, with infinitely less regret than they would ever have suspected, as long as he himself could remain face to face, and on friendly terms, with God.

The love of God and the certainty that in return God loved him beyond other human beings had upheld him in times of poverty and adversity. He had a talent for gratitude as well; his recent good luck had confirmed and sealed the understanding between God and him. But now he felt that God had turned away from him. And if he were not a great artist, who was he that God should love him? Without his visionary powers, without his retinue of fancies, jests and tragedies, how could he even approach the Lord and implore Him to redress him? The truth was that he was then no better than other people. He might deceive the world, but he had never in his life deceived himself. He had become estranged from God, and how was he now to live?

His mind wandered, and on its own brought home fresh material for suffering. He remembered his father-in-law's verdict on modern literature. "Superficiality," the old man had thundered, "is the mark of it. The age lacks weight; its greatness is hollow. Now your own noble work, my dear boy . . ." Generally the views of his father-in-law were to him of no consequence whatever, but at the present moment he was so low in spirits that they made him writhe a little. Superficiality, he thought, was the word which the public and the critics would use about him, when they came to know the truth— lightness, hollowness. They called his work noble because he had moved their hearts when he described the sufferings of the poor. But he might as well have written of the sufferings of kings. And he had described them, because he happened to know them. Now, that he had made his fortune, he found that he had got no more to say of the poor, and that he would prefer to hear no more of them. The word "superficiality" made an accompaniment to his steps in the long street.

While he had meditated upon these matters he had walked on. The night was cold, a thin, sharp wind ran straight against him. He looked up, and reflected that it was going to rain.

The young man's name was Charlie Despard. He was a small, slight person a tiny figure in the lonely street. He was not yet thirty, and looked extraordinarily young for his age; he might have been a boy of seventeen. He had brown hair and skin, but blue eyes, a narrow face and a nose with a faint bend to one side. He was extremely light of movement, and kept himself very straight, even in his present state of depression, and with the heavy portmanteau in his hand. He was well dressed, in a havelock, all his clothes had a new look on him, and were indeed new.

He turned his mind towards the hotel, wondering whether it would be any better to be in a house than out in the street. He decided that he would have a glass of brandy when he came there. Lately he had turned to brandy for consolation; sometimes he found it there and at other times not. He also thought of his wife, who was waiting for him. She might be asleep by now. If only she would not have locked the door, so that he should have to wake her up and talk, her nearness might be a comfort to him. He thought of her beauty and her kindness to him. She was a tall young woman with yellow hair and blue eyes, and a skin as white as marble. Her face would have been classic if the upper part of it had not been a little short and narrow in proportion to the jaw and chin. The same peculiarity was repeated in her body; the upper part of it was a little too short and slight for the hips and legs. Her name was Laura. She had a clear, grave, gentle gaze, and her blue eyes easily filled with tears of emotion, her admiration for him in itself would make them run full when she looked at him. What was the good of it all to him? She was not really his wife; she had married a phantom of her own imagination, and he was left out in the cold.

He came to the hotel, and found that he did not even want the brandy. He only stood in the hall, which to him looked like a grave, and asked the porter if his wife had arrived. The old man told him that Madame had arrived safely, and had informed him that Monsieur would come later. He offered to take the traveller's portmanteau upstairs for him, but Charlie reflected that he had better bear his own burdens. So he got the number of the room from him, and walked up the stairs and along the corridor alone. To his surprise he found the double door of the room unlocked, and went straight in. This seemed to him the first slight favour that fate had shown him for a long time.

The room, when he entered it, was almost dark; only a faint gas-jet burned by the dressing-table. There was a scent of violets in the air. His wife would have brought them and would have meant to give them to him with a line from a poem. But she lay deep down in the pillows. He was so easily swayed by little things at the present time that his heart warmed at his good luck. While he took off his shoes he looked round and thought: "This room, with its sky-blue wallpaper and crimson curtains, has been kind to me; I will not forget it."

But when he got into bed he could not sleep. He heard a clock in the neighborhood strike the quarter-stroke once, and twice, and three times. He felt that he had forgotten the art of sleeping and would have to lie awake for ever. "That is," he thought, "because I am really dead. There is no longer any difference to me between life and death."

Suddenly, without warning, for he had heard no steps approaching, he heard somebody gently turning the handle of the door. He had locked the door when he came in. When the person in the corridor discovered that, he waited a little, then tried it once more. He seemed to give it up, and after a moment softly drummed a little tune upon the door, and repeated it. Again there was a silence; then the stranger lowly whistled a bit of a tune. Charlie became

deadly afraid that in the end all this would wake up his wife. He
got out of bed, put on his green dressing-gown and went and
opened the door with as little noise as possible.

The corridor was more clearly lighted than the room, and there
was a lamp on the wall above the door. Outside, beneath it, stood
a young man. He was tall and fair, and so elegantly dressed that
Charlie was surprised to meet him in the Queen's Hotel. He had
on evening clothes, with a cloak flung over them, and he wore in a
buttonhole a pink carnation that looked fresh and romantic against
the black and white. But what struck Charlie the moment he
looked at him was the expression in the young man's face. It was
so radiant with happiness, it shone with such gentle, humble, wild,
laughing rapture that Charlie had never seen the like of it. An
angelic messenger straight from Heaven could not have displayed
a more exuberant, glorious ecstasy. It made the poet stare at him for
a minute. Then he spoke, in French—since he took it that the distinguished young man of Antwerp must be French, and he himself
spoke French well, for he had in his time been apprenticed to a
French hairdresser. "What is it you want?" he asked. "My wife is
asleep and I very much want to sleep myself."

The young man with the carnation had appeared as deeply surprised at the sight of Charlie as Charlie at the sight of him. Still, his
strange beatitude was so deeply rooted within him that it took him
some time to change his expression into that of a gentleman who
meets another gentleman. The light of it remained on his face,
mingled with bewilderment, even when he spoke and said: "I beg
your pardon. I infinitely regret to have disturbed you. I have made
a mistake." Then Charlie closed the door and turned. With the
corner of his eye he saw that his wife was sitting up in her bed. He
said, shortly, for she might still be only half awake: "It was a

gentleman. I believe he was drunk." At his words she lay down again, and he went back to bed himself.

The moment he was in his bed he was seized by a tremendous agitation; he felt that something irreparable had happened to him. For a while he did not know what it was, nor whether it was good or bad. It was as if a gigantic, blazing light had gone up on him, passed, and left him blinded. Then the impression slowly formed and consolidated, and made itself known in a pain so overwhelming that it contracted him as in a spasm.

For here, he knew, was the glory, the meaning and the key of life. The young man with the carnation had it. That infinite happiness which beamed on the face of the young man with the carnation was to be found somewhere in the world. The young man was aware of the way to it, but he, he had lost it. Once upon a time, it seemed to him, he too had known it, and had let go his hold, and here he was, forever doomed. O God, God in Heaven, at what moment had his own road taken off from the road of the young man with the carnation?

He saw clearly now that the gloom of his last weeks had been but the foreboding of this total perdition. In his agony, for he was really in the grip of death, he caught at any means of salvation, fumbled in the dark and struck at some of the most enthusiastic reviews of his book. His mind at the next moment shrank from them as if they had burnt him. Here, indeed, lay his ruin and damnation: with the reviewers, the publishers, the reading public, and with his wife. They were the people who wanted books, and to obtain their end would turn a human being into printed matter. He had let himself be seduced by the least seductive people in the world; they had made him sell his soul at a price which was in itself a penalty. "I will put enmity," he thought, "between the author and the readers, and between thy seed and their seed; thou shalt bruise their heel, but they shall bruise thine head." It was no wonder that God had ceased to love him, for he had, from his own free will, exchanged the things of the Lord—the moon, the sea, friendship, fights—for the words that describe them. He might now sit in a room and write down these words, to be praised by the critics, while outside, in the corridor, ran the road of the young man with the carnation into that light which made his face shine.

He did not know how long he had lain like this; he thought that he had wept, but his eyes were dry. In the end he suddenly fell asleep and slept for a minute. When he woke up he was perfectly calm and resolved. He would go away. He would save himself, and he would go in search of that happiness which existed somewhere. If he were to go to the end of the world for it, it did not signify; indeed it might be the best plan to go straight to the end of the world. He would now go down to the harbour and find a ship to take him away. At the idea of a ship he became calm.

He lay in bed for an hour more; then he got up and dressed. The while he wondered what the young man with the carnation had thought of him. He will have thought, he said to himself: "Ah, le pauvre petit bonhomme à la robe de chambre verte." Very silently he packed his portmanteau; his manuscript he first planned to leave behind, then took it with him in order to throw it into the sea, and witness its destruction. As he was about to leave the room he bethought himself of his wife. It was not fair to leave a sleeping woman, forever, without some word of farewell. Theseus, he remembered, had done that. But it was hard to find the word of farewell. In the end, standing by the dressing-table he wrote on a sheet from his manuscript, "I have gone away. Forgive me if you can." Then he went down. In the loge the porter was nodding over a paper. Charlie thought: "I shall never see him again. I shall never again open this door."

When he came out the wind had lowered, it rained, and the rain was whispering and murmuring on all sides of him. He took off his hat; in a moment his hair was dripping wet, and the rain ran down his face. In this fresh, unexpected touch there was a purport. He went down the street by which he had come, since it was the only street he knew in Antwerp. As he walked, it seemed as if the world was no longer entirely indifferent to him, nor was he any longer absolutely lonely in it. The dispersed, dissipated phenomena of the universe were consolidating, very likely into the devil himself, and the devil had him by the hand or the hair.

Before he expected it, he was down by the harbour and stood upon the wharf, his portmanteau in his hand, gazing down into the water. It was deep and dark, the lights from the lamps on the quay played within it like young snakes. His first strong sensation about it was that it was salt. The rainwater came down on him from above; the salt water met him below. That was as it should be. He stood here for a long time, looking at the ships. He would go away on one of them.

The hulls loomed giant-like in the wet night. They carried things in their bellies, and were pregnant with possibilities; they were porters of destinies, his superiors in every way, with the water on all sides of them. They swam; the salt sea bore them wherever they wanted to go. As he looked, it seemed to him that a kind of sympathy was going forth from the big hulks to him; they had a message for him, but at first he did not know what it was. Then he found the word; it was superficiality. The ships were superficial, and kept to the surface. Therein lay their power; to ships the danger is to get to the bottom of things, to run aground. They were even hollow, and hollowness was the secret of their being; the great depths slaved for them as long as they remained hollow. A wave of happiness heaved Charlie's heart; after a while he laughed in the dark.

"My sisters," he thought, "I should have come to you long ago. You beautiful, superficial wanderers, gallant, swimming conquerors of the deep! You heavy, hollow angels, I shall thank you all my life. God keep you afloat, big sisters, you and me. God preserve our superficiality." He was very wet by now; his hair and his havelock were shining softly, like the sides of the ships in the rain. "And now," he thought, "I shall hold my mouth. My life has had altogether too many words; I cannot remember now why I have talked so much. Only when I came down here and was silent in the rain was I shown the truth of things. From now on I shall speak no more, but I shall listen to what the sailors will tell me, the people who are familiar with the floating ships, and keep off the bottom of things. I shall go to the end of the world, and hold my mouth."

He had hardly made this resolution before a man on the wharf came up and spoke to him. "Are you looking for a ship?" he asked. He looked like a sailor, Charlie thought, and like a friendly monkey as well. He was a short man with a weather-bitten face and a neck-beard. "Yes, I am," said Charlie. "For which ship?" asked the sailor. Charlie was about to answer: "For the ark of Noah, from the flood." But in time he realized that it would sound foolish. "You see," he said, "I want to get aboard a ship, and go for a journey." The sailor spat, and laughed. "A journey?" he said. "All right. You were staring down into the water, so that in the end I believed that you were going to jump in." "Ah, yes, to jump in!" said Charlie. "And so you would have saved me? But there it is, you are too late to save me. You should have come last night, that would have been the right moment. The only reason why I did not drown myself last night," he went on, "was that I was short of water. If the water had come to me then! Here lies the water—good; here stands the man—good. If the water comes to him he drowns himself. It all goes to prove that the greatest of poets make mistakes, and that one should never become a poet." The sailor by this time had made up his mind that the young stranger was drunk. "All right, my boy," he said, "if you have thought better about drowning yourself, you may go your own way, and good night to you." This was a great disappointment to Charlie, who thought that the conversation was going extraordinarily well. "Nay, but can I not come with you?" he asked the sailor. "I am going into the inn of La Croix du Midi," the sailor answered, "to have a glass of rum." "That," Charlie exclaimed, "is an excellent idea, and I am in luck to meet a man who has such ideas."

They went together into the inn of La Croix du Midi close by, and there met two more sailors, whom the first sailor knew, and introduced them to Charlie as a mate and a supercargo. He himself was captain of a small ship riding at anchor outside the harbour. Charlie put his hand in his pocket and found it full of the money which he had taken with him for his journey. "Let me have a bottle of your best rum for these gentlemen," he said to the waiter, "and a pot of coffee for myself." He did not want any spirits in his present mood. He was actually scared of his companions, but he found it difficult to explain his case to them. "I drink coffee," he said, "because I have taken"—he was going to say: a vow, but thought better of it—"a bet. There was an old man on a ship—he is, by the way, an uncle of mine—and he bet me that I could not keep from drink for a year, but if I won, the ship would be mine." "And have you kept from it?" the captain asked. "Yes, as God lives," said Charlie. "I declined a glass of brandy not twelve hours ago, and what, from my talk, you may take to be drunkenness, is nothing but the effect of the smell of the sea." The mate asked: "Was the man who bet you a small man with a big belly and only one eye?"

"Yes, that is Uncle!" cried Charlie. "Then I have met him myself, on my way to Rio," said the mate, "and he offered me the same terms, but I would not take them."

Here the drinks were brought and Charlie filled the glasses. He rolled himself a cigarette, and joyously inhaled the aroma of the rum and of the warm room. In the light of a dim hanging-lamp the three faces of his new acquaintances glowed fresh and genial. He felt honoured and happy in their company and thought: "How much more they know than I do." He himself was very pale, as always when he was agitated. "May your coffee do you good," said the captain. "You look as if you had got the fever." "Nay, but I have had a great sorrow," said Charlie. The others put on condolent faces, and asked him what sorrow it was. "I will tell you," said Charlie. "It is better to speak of it, although a little while ago I thought the opposite. I had a tame monkey I was very fond of; his name was Charlie. I had bought him from an old woman who kept a house in Hongkong, and she and I had to smuggle him out in the dead of midday, otherwise the girls would never have let him go, for he was like a brother to them. He was like a brother to me, too. He knew all my thoughts, and was always on my side. He had been taught many tricks already when I got him, and he learned more while he was with me. But when I came home the English food did not agree with him, nor did the English Sunday. So he grew sick, and he grew worse, and one Sabbath evening he died on me." "That was a pity," said the captain compassionately. "Yes," said Charlie. "When there is only one person in the world whom you care for, and that is a monkey, and he is dead, then that is a pity."

The supercargo, before the others came in, had been telling the mate a story. Now for the benefit of the others he told it all over. It was a cruel tale of how he had sailed from Buenos Aires with wool.

When five days out in the doldrums the ship had caught fire, and the crew, after fighting the fire all night, had got into the boats in the morning and left her. The supercargo himself had had his hands burnt; all the same he had rowed for three days and nights, so that when they were picked up by a steamer from Rotterdam his hand had grown round his oar, and he could never again stretch out the two fingers. "Then," he said, "I looked at my hand, and I swore an oath that if I ever came back on dry land, the Devil take me and the Devil hold me if ever I went to sea again." The other two nodded their heads gravely at his tale, and asked him where he was off to now. "Me?" said the supercargo. "I have shipped for Sydney."

The mate described a storm in the Bay, and the captain gave them a story of a blizzard in the North Sea, which he had experienced when he was but a sailor-boy. He had been set to the pumps, he narrated, and had been forgotten there, and as he dared not leave, he had pumped for eleven hours. "At that time," he said, "I too, swore to stay on land, and never to set foot on the sea again."

Charlie listened, and thought: "These are wise men. They know what they are talking about. For the people who travel for their pleasure when the sea is smooth, and smiles at them, and who declare that they love her, they do not know what love means. It is the sailors, who have been beaten and battered by the sea, and who have cursed and damned her, who are her true lovers. Very likely the same law applies to husbands and wives. I shall learn more from the seamen. I am a child and a fool, compared to them."

The three sailors were conscious, from his silent, attentive attitude, of the young man's reverence and wonder. They took him for a student, and were content to divulge their experiences to him. They also thought him a good host, for he steadily filled their glasses, and ordered a fresh bottle when the first was empty. Charlie, in return for their stories, gave them a couple of songs. He had a sweet voice and tonight was pleased with it himself; it was a long time since he had sung a song. They all became friendly. The captain slapped him on the back and told him that he was a bright boy and might still be turned into a sailor.

But as, a little later, the captain began to talk tenderly of his wife and family, whom he had just left, and the supercargo, with pride and emotion, informed the party that within the last three months two barmaids of Antwerp had had twins, girls with red hair like their father's, Charlie remembered his own wife and became ill at ease. These sailors, he thought, seemed to know how to deal with their women. Probably there was not one of them so afraid of his wife as to run away from her in the middle of night. If they knew that he had done so, he reflected, they would think less well of him.

The sailors had believed him to be much younger than he was; so in their company he had come to feel himself like a very young man, and his wife now looked to him more like a mother than a mate. His real mother, although she had been a respectable trades-woman, had had a drop of gypsy blood in her, and none of his quick resolutions had ever taken her by surprise. Indeed, he reflected, she kept upon the surface through everything, and swam there, ma-jestically, like a proud, dark, ponderous goose. If tonight he had gone to her and told her of his decision to go to sea, the idea might very well have excited and pleased her. The pride and gratitude which he had always felt towards the old woman, now, as he drank his last cup of coffee, were transferred to the young. Laura would understand him, and side with him.

He sat for some time, weighing the matter. For experience had taught him to be careful here. He had, before now, been trapped as by a strange optical delusion. When he was away from her, his wife took on all the appearance of a guardian angel, unfailing in sympathy and support. But when again he met her face to face, she was a stranger, and he found his road paved with difficulties.

Still tonight all this seemed to belong to the past. For he was in power now; he had the sea and the ships with him, and before him the young man with the carnation. Great images surrounded him. Here, in the inn of La Croix du Midi he had already lived through much. He had seen a ship burn down, a snowstorm in the North Sea, and the sailor's homecoming to his wife and children. So potent did he feel that the figure of his wife looked pathetic. He remembered her as he had last seen her, asleep, passive and peaceful, and her whiteness, and her ignorance of the world, went to his heart. He suddenly blushed deeply at the thought of the letter he had written to her. He might go away, he now felt, with a lighter heart, if he had first explained everything to her. "Home," he thought, "where is thy sting? Married life, where is thy victory?"

He sat and looked down at the table, where a little coffee had been spilled. The while the sailors' talk ebbed out, because they saw that he was no longer listening; in the end it stopped. The consciousness of silence round him woke up Charlie. He smiled at them. "I shall tell you a story before we go home. A blue story," he said.

"There was once," he began, "an immensely rich old Englishman who had been a courtier and a councillor to the Queen and who now, in his old age, cared for nothing but collecting ancient blue china. To that end he travelled to Persia, Japan and China, and he was everywhere accompanied by his daughter, the Lady Helena. It happened, as they sailed in the Chinese Sea, that the ship caught fire on a still night, and everybody went into the lifeboats and left her. In the dark and the confusion the old peer was separated from his daughter. Lady Helena got up on deck late, and found the ship quite deserted. In the last moment a young English sailor carried her down into a lifeboat that had been forgotten. To the two fugitives it seemed as if fire was following them from all sides, for the phosphorescence played in the dark sea, and, as they looked up, a falling star ran across the sky, as if it was going to drop into the boat. They sailed for nine days, till they were picked up by a Dutch merchantman, and came home to England.

"'The old lord had believed his daughter to be dead. He now wept with joy, and at once took her off to a fashionable watering-place so that she might recover from the hardships she had gone through. And as he thought it must be unpleasant to her that a young sailor, who made his bread in the merchant service, should tell the world that he had sailed for nine days alone with a peer's daughter, he paid the boy a fine sum, and made him promise to go shipping in the other hemisphere and never come back. 'For what,' said the old nobleman, 'would be the good of that?'

"When Lady Helena recovered, and they gave her the news of the Court and of her family, and in the end also told her how the young sailor had been sent away never to come back, they found that her mind had suffered from her trials, and that she cared for nothing in all the world. She would not go back to her father's castle in its park, nor go to Court, nor travel to any gay town of the continent. The only thing which she now wanted to do was to go, like her father before her, to collect rare blue china. So she began to sail, from one country to the other, and her father went with her.

"In her search she told the people, with whom she dealt, that she was looking for a particular blue colour, and would pay any price for it. But although she bought many hundred blue jars and bowls, she would always after a time put them aside and say: 'Alas, alas, it is not the right blue.' Her father, when they had sailed for many years, suggested to her that perhaps the colour which she sought did not exist. 'O God, Papa,' said she, 'how can you speak so wickedly? Surely there must be some of it left from the time when all the world was blue.'

"Her two old aunts in England implored her to come back, still to make a great match. But she answered them: 'Nay, I have got to sail. For you must know, dear aunts, that it is all nonsense when learned people tell you that the seas have got a bottom to them. On the contrary, the water, which is the noblest of the elements, does, of course, go all through the earth, so that our planet really floats in the ether, like a soap-bubble. And there, on the other hemisphere, a ship sails, with which I have got to keep pace. We two are like the reflection of one another, in the deep sea, and the ship of which I speak is always exactly beneath my own ship, upon the opposite side of the globe. You have never seen a big fish swimming underneath a boat, following it like a dark-blue shade in the water. But in that way this ship goes, like the shadow of my ship, and I draw it to and fro wherever I go, as the moon draws the tides, all through the bulk of the earth. If I stopped sailing, what would those poor sailors who make their bread in the merchant service do? But I shall tell you a secret,' she said. 'In the end my ship will go down, to the centre of the globe, and at the very same hour the other ship will sink as well—for people call it sinking, although I can assure you that there is no up and down in the sea—and there, in the midst of the world, we two shall meet.'

"Many years passed, the old lord died and Lady Helena became old and deaf, but she still sailed. Then it happened, after the plunder of the summer palace of the Emperor of China, that a merchant brought her a very old blue jar. The moment she set eyes on it she gave a terrible shriek. 'There it is!' she cried. 'I have found it at last. This is the true blue. Oh, how light it makes one. Oh, it is as fresh as a breeze, as deep as a deep secret, as full as I say not what.' With trembling hands she held the jar to her bosom, and sat for six hours sunk in contemplation of it. Then she said to her doctor and her lady-companion: 'Now I can die. And when I am dead you will cut out my heart and lay it in the blue jar. For then everything will be as it was then. All shall be blue round me, and in the midst of the blue world my heart will be innocent and free, and will beat gently, like a wake that sings, like the drops that fall from an oar blade.' A little later she asked them: 'Is it not a sweet thing to think that, if only you have patience, all that has ever been, will come back to you?' Shortly afterwards the old lady died."

The party now broke up, the sailors gave Charlie their hands and thanked him for the rum and the story. Charlie wished them all good luck. "You forgot your bag," said the captain, and picked up Charlie's portmanteau with the manuscript in it. "No," said Charlie, "I mean to leave that with you, till we are to sail together." The captain looked at the initials on the bag. "It is a heavy bag," he said. "Have you got anything of value in it?" "Yes, it is heavy, God help me," said Charlie, "but that shall not happen again. Next time it will be empty." He got the name of the captain's ship, and said good-bye to him.

As he came out he was surprised to find that it was nearly morning. The long spare row of street lamps held up their melancholy heads in the grey air.

A thin young girl with big black eyes, who had been walking up and down in front of the inn, came up and spoke to him, and, when he did not answer, repeated her invitation in English. Charlie looked at her. "She too," he thought, "belongs to the ships, like the mussels and seaweeds that grow on their bottoms. Within her many good seamen, who escaped the deep, have been drowned. But all the same she will not run aground, and if I go with her I shall still be safe." He put his hand in his pocket, but found only one shilling left there. "Will you let me have a shilling's worth?" he asked the girl. She stared at him. Her face did not change as he took her hand, pulled down her old glove and pressed the palm, rough and clammy as fish-skin, to his lips and tongue. He gave her back her hand, placed a shilling in it, and walked away.

For the third time he walked along the street between the harbour and the Queen's Hotel. The town was now waking up, and he met a few people and carts. The windows of the hotel were lighted. When he came into the hall there was no one there, and he was about to walk up to his room, when, through a glass door, he saw his wife sitting in a small, lighted dining room next to the hall. So he went in there.

When his wife caught sight of him her face cleared up. "Oh, you have come!" she cried. He bent his head. He was about to take her hand and kiss it when she asked him: "Why are you so late?" "Am I late?" he exclaimed, highly surprised by her question, and because the idea of time had altogether gone from him. He looked at a clock upon the mantelpiece, and said: "It is only ten past seven." "Yes, but I thought you would be here earlier!" said she. "I got up to be ready when you came." Charlie sat down by the table. He did not answer her, for he had no idea what to say. "Is it possible," he thought, "that she has the strength of soul to take me back in this way?"

"Will you have some coffee?" said his wife. "No, thank you," said he, "I have had coffee." He glanced round the room. Although it was nearly light and the blinds were up, the gas lamps were still burning, and from his childhood this had always seemed to him a great luxury. The fire on the fireplace played on a somewhat worn Brussels carpet and on the red plush chairs. His wife was eating an egg. As a little boy he had had an egg on Sunday mornings. The whole room, that smelled of coffee and fresh bread, with the white tablecloth and the shining coffee-pot, took on a sabbath-morning look. He gazed at his wife. She had on her grey travelling cloak, her bonnet was lying beside her, and her yellow hair, gathered in a net, shone in the lamplight. She was bright in her own way, a pure light came from her, and she seemed enduringly fixed on the sofa, the one firm object in a turbulent world.

An idea came to him: "She is like a lighthouse," he thought, "the firm, majestic lighthouse that sends out its kindly light. To all ships it says: 'Keep off.' For where the lighthouse stands, there is shoal water, or rocks. To all floating objects the approach means death." At this moment she looked up, and found his eyes on her. "What are you thinking of?" she asked him. He thought: "I will tell her. It is better to be honest with her, from now, and to tell her all." So he said, slowly: "I am thinking that you are to me, in life, like a lighthouse. A steady light, instructing me how to steer my course." She looked at him, then away, and her eyes filled with tears. He became afraid that she was going to cry, even though till now she had been so brave. "Let us go up to our own room," he said, for it would be easier to explain things to her when they were alone.

They went up together, and the stairs, which, last night, had been so long to climb, now were so easy, that his wife said: "No, you are going up too high. We are there." She walked ahead of him down the corridor, and opened the door to their room.

The first thing that he noticed was that there was no longer any smell of violets in the air. Had she thrown them away in anger? Or had they all faded when he went away? She came up to him and laid her hand on his shoulder and her face on it. Over her fair hair, in the net, he looked round, and stood quite still. For the dressing-table, on which, last night, he had put his letter for her, was in a new place, and so, he found, was the bed he had lain in. In the corner there was now a cheval-glass which had not been there before. This was not his room. He quickly took in more details. There was no longer a canopy to the bed, but above it a steel-engraving of the Belgian Royal family that till now he had never seen. "Did you sleep here last night?" he asked. "Yes," said his wife. "But not well. I was worried when you did not come; I feared that you were having a bad crossing." "Did nobody disturb you?" he asked again. "No," she said. "My door was locked. And this is a quiet hotel, I believe."

As Charlie now looked back on the happenings of the night, with the experienced eye of an author of fiction, they moved him as mightily as if they had been out of one of his own books. He drew in his breath deeply. "Almighty God," he said from the bottom of his heart, "as the heavens are higher than the earth, so are thy short stories higher than our short stories."

He went through all the details slowly and surely, as a mathematician sets up and solves an equation. First he felt, like honey on his tongue, the longing and the triumph of the young man with the carnation. Then, like the grip of a hand round his throat, but with hardly less artistic enjoyment, the terror of the lady in the bed. As if he himself had possessed a pair of firm young breasts he was conscious of his heart stopping beneath them. He stood perfectly still, in his own thoughts, but his face took on such an expression of rapture, laughter and delight that his wife, who had lifted her head from his shoulder, asked him in surprise: "What are you thinking of now?"

Charlie took her hand, his face still radiant. "I am thinking," he said very slowly, "of the Garden of Eden, and the cherubim with the flaming sword. Nay," he went on in the same way, "I am thinking of Hero and Leander. Of Romeo and Juliet. Of Theseus and Ariadne, and the Minotaur as well. Have you ever tried, my dear, to guess how, upon the occasion, the Minotaur was feeling?"

"So you are going to write a love story, Troubadour?" she asked, smiling back upon him. He did not answer at once, but he let go her hand, and after a while asked: "What did you say?" "I asked you if you were going to write a love story?" she repeated timidly. He went away from her, up to the table, and put his hand upon it.

The light that had fallen upon him last night was coming back, and from all sides now—from his own lighthouse as well, he thought confusedly. Only then it had shone onward, upon the infinite world, while at this moment it was turned inwards, and was lightening up the room of the Queen's Hotel. It was very bright; it seemed that he was to see himself, within it, as God saw him, and under this test he had to steady himself by the table.

While he stood there the situation developed into a dialogue between Charlie and the Lord.

The Lord said: "Your wife asked you twice if you are going to write a love story. Do you believe that this is indeed what you are going to do?" "Yes, that is very likely," said Charlie. "Is it," the Lord asked, "to be a great and sweet tale, which will live in the hearts of young lovers?" "Yes, I should say so," said Charlie. "And are you content with that?" asked the Lord.

"O Lord, what are you asking me?" cried Charlie. "How can I answer yes? Am I not a human being, and can I write a love story without longing for that love which clings and embraces, and for the softness and warmth of a young woman's body in my arms?" "I gave you all that last night," said the Lord. "It was you who jumped out of bed, to go to the end of the world from it." "Yes, I did that," said Charlie. "Did you behold it and think it very good? Are you going to repeat it on me? Am I to be, forever, he who lay in bed with the mistress of the young man with the carnation, and, by the way, what has become of her, and how is she to explain things to him? And who went off, and wrote to her: 'I have gone away. Forgive me, if you can." "Yes," said the Lord.

"Nay, tell me, now that we are at it," cried Charlie, "am I, while I write of the beauty of young women, to get, from the live women of the earth, a shilling's worth, and no more?" "Yes," said the Lord. "And you are to be content with that." Charlie was drawing a pattern with his finger on the table; he said nothing. It seemed that the discourse was ended here, when again the Lord spoke.

"Who made the ships, Charlie?" he asked. "Nay, I know not," said Charlie, "did you make them?" "Yes," said the Lord, "I made the ships on their keels, and all floating things. The moon that sails in the sky, the orbs that swing in the universe, the tides, the generations, the fashions. You make me laugh, for I have given you all the world to sail and float in, and you have run aground here, in a room of the Queen's Hotel to seek a quarrel."

"Come," said the Lord again, "I will make a covenant between me and you. I, I will not measure you out any more distress than you need to write your books." "Oh, indeed!" said Charlie. "What did you say?" asked the Lord. "Do you want any less than that?" "I said nothing," said Charlie. "But you are to write the books," said the Lord. "For it is I who want them written. Not the public, not by any means the critics, but ME!" "Can I be certain of that?" Charlie asked. "Not always," said the Lord. "You will not be certain of it at all times. But I tell you now that it is so. You will have to hold on to that." "O good God," said Charlie. "Are you going," said the Lord, "to thank me for what I have done for you tonight?" "I think," said Charlie, "that we will leave it at what it is, and say no more about it."

His wife now went and opened the window. The cold, raw morning air streamed in, with the din of carriages from the street below, human voices and a great chorus of sparrows, and with the smell of smoke and horse manure.

When Charlie had finished his talk with God, and while it was still so vivid to him that he might have written it down, he went to the window and looked out. The morning colours of the grey town were fresh and delicate, and there was a faint promise of sunshine in the sky. People were about; a young woman in a blue shawl and slippers was walking away quickly; and the omnibus of the hotel, with a white horse to it, was halting below, while the porter helped out the travellers and took down their luggage. Charlie gazed down into the street, a long way under him.

"I shall thank the Lord for one thing all the same," he thought. "That I did not lay my hand on anything that belonged to my brother, the young man with the carnation. It was within my reach, but I did not touch it." He stood for a while in the window and saw the omnibus drive away. Where, he wondered, amongst the houses in the pale morning, was now the young man of last night?

"O the young man," he thought. "Ah, le pauvre jeune homme à l'œillet."

SORROW-ACRE

THE LOW, undulating Danish landscape was silent and serene, mysteriously wide-awake in the hour before sunrise. There was not a cloud in the pale sky, not a shadow along the dim, pearly fields, hills and woods. The mist was lifting from the valleys and hollows, the air was cool, the grass and the foliage dripping wet with morning-dew. Unwatched by the eyes of man, and undisturbed by his activity, the country breathed a timeless life, to which language was inadequate.

All the same, a human race had lived on this land for a thousand years, had been formed by its soil and weather, and had marked it with its thoughts, so that now no one could tell where the existence of the one ceased and the other began. The thin grey line of a road, winding across the plain and up and down hills, was the fixed materialisation of human longing, and of the human notion that it is better to be in one place than another.

A child of the country would read this open landscape like a book. The irregular mosaic of meadows and cornlands was a picture, in timid green and yellow, of the people's struggle for its daily bread; the centuries had taught it to plough and sow in this way. On a distant hill the immovable wings of a windmill, in a small blue cross against the sky, delineated a later stage in the career of bread. The blurred outline of thatched roofs—a low, brown growth of the earth—where the huts of the village thronged together, told the history, from his cradle to his grave, of the peasant, the creature nearest to the soil and dependent on it, prospering in a fertile year and dying in years of drought and pests.

A little higher up, with the faint horizontal line of the white cemetery-wall round it, and the vertical contour of tall poplars by its side, the red-tiled church bore witness, as far as the eye reached, that this was a Christian country. The child of the land knew it as a strange house, inhabited only for a few hours every seventh day, but with a strong, clear voice in it to give out the joys and sorrows of the land: a plain, square embodiment of the nation's trust in the justice and mercy of heaven. But where, amongst cupular woods and groves, the lordly, pyramidal silhouette of the cut lime avenues rose in the air, there a big country house lay.

The child of the land would read much within these elegant, geometrical ciphers on the hazy blue. They spoke of power, the lime trees paraded round a stronghold. Up here was decided the destiny of the surrounding land and of the men and beasts upon it, and the peasant lifted his eyes to the green pyramids with awe. They spoke of dignity, decorum and taste. Danish soil grew no finer flower than the mansion to which the long avenue led. In its lofty rooms life and death bore themselves with stately grace. The country house did not gaze upward, like the church, nor down to the ground like the huts; it had a wider earthly horizon than they, and was related to much noble architecture all over Europe. Foreign artisans had been called in to panel and stucco it, and its own inhabitants travelled and brought back ideas, fashions and things of beauty. Paintings, tapestries, silver and glass from distant countries had been made to feel at home here and now formed part of Danish country life.

The big house stood as firmly rooted in the soil of Denmark as the peasants' huts, and was as faithfully allied to her four winds and her changing seasons, to her animal life, trees and flowers. Only its interests lay in a higher plane. Within the domain of the lime trees it was no longer cows, goats and pigs on which the minds and the talk ran, but horses and dogs. The wild fauna, the game of the land, that the peasant shook his fist at, when he saw it on his young green rye or in his ripening wheat field, to the residents of the country houses were the main pursuit and the joy of existence.

The writing in the sky solemnly proclaimed continuance, a worldly immortality. The great country houses had held their ground through many generations. The families who lived in them revered the past as they honoured themselves, for the history of Denmark was their own history.

A Rosenkrantz had sat at Rosenholm, a Juel at Hverringe, a Skeel at Gammel-Estrup as long as people remembered. They had seen kings and schools of style succeed one another and, proudly and humbly, had made over their personal existence to that of their land, so that amongst their equals and with the peasants they passed by its name: Rosenholm, Hverringe, Gammel-Estrup. To the King and the country, to his family and to the individual lord of the manor himself it was a matter of minor consequence which particular Rosenkrantz, Juel or Skeel, out of a long row of fathers and sons, at the moment in his person incarnated the fields and woods, the peasants, cattle and game of the estate. Many duties rested on the shoulders of the big landowners—towards God in heaven, towards the King, his neighbour and himself—and they were all harmoniously consolidated into the idea of his duties towards his land. Highest amongst these ranked his obligation to uphold the sacred continuance, and to produce a new Rosenkrantz, Juel or Skeel for the service of Rosenholm, Hverringe and Gammel-Estrup.

Female grace was prized in the manors. Together with good hunting and fine wine it was the flower and emblem of the higher existence led there, and in many ways the families prided themselves more on their daughters than on their sons.

The ladies who promenaded in the lime avenues, or drove through them in heavy coaches with four horses, carried the future of the name in their laps and were, like dignified and debonair caryatides, holding up the houses. They were themselves conscious of their value, kept up their price, and moved in a sphere of pretty worship and self-worship. They might even be thought to add to it, on their own, a graceful, arch, paradoxical haughtiness. For how free were they, how powerful! Their lords might rule the country, and allow themselves many liberties, but when it came to that supreme matter of legitimacy which was the vital principle of their world, the centre of gravity lay with them.

The lime trees were in bloom. But in the early morning only a faint fragrance drifted through the garden, an airy message, an aromatic echo of the dreams during the short summer night.

In a long avenue that led from the house all the way to the end of the garden, where, from a small white pavilion in the classic style, there was a great view over the fields, a young man walked. He was plainly dressed in brown, with pretty linen and lace, bareheaded, with his hair tied by a ribbon. He was dark, a strong and sturdy figure with fine eyes and hands; he limped a little on one leg.

The big house at the top of the avenue, the garden and the fields had been his childhood's paradise. But he had travelled and lived out of Denmark, in Rome and Paris, and he was at present appointed to the Danish Legation to the Court of King George, the brother of the late, unfortunate young Danish Queen. He had not seen his ancestral home for nine years. It made him laugh to find, now, everything so much smaller than he remembered it, and at the same time he was strangely moved by meeting it again. Dead people came towards him and smiled at him; a small boy in a ruff ran past him with his hoop and kite, in passing gave him a clear glance and laughingly asked: "Do you mean to tell me that you are I?" He tried to catch him in the flight, and to answer him: "Yes, I assure you that I am you," but the light figure did not wait for a reply.

The young man, whose name was Adam, stood in a particular relation to the house and the land. For six months he had been heir to it all; nominally he was so even at this moment. It was this circumstance which had brought him from England, and on which his mind was dwelling, as he walked along slowly.

The old lord up at the manor, his father's brother, had had much misfortune in his domestic life. His wife had died young, and two of his children in infancy. The one son then left to him, his cousin's playmate, was a sickly and morose boy. For ten years the father travelled with him from one watering place to another, in Germany and Italy, hardly ever in other company than that of his silent, dying child, sheltering the faint flame of life with both hands, until such time as it could be passed over to a new bearer of the name. At the same time another misfortune had struck him: he fell into disfavour at Court, where till now he had held a fine position. He was about to rehabilitate his family's prestige through the marriage which he had arranged for his son, when before it could take place the bridegroom died, not yet twenty years old.

Adam learned of his cousin's death, and his own changed fortune, in England, through his ambitious and triumphant mother. He sat with her letter in his hand and did not know what to think about it.

If this, he reflected, had happened to him while he was still a boy, in Denmark, it would have meant all the world to him. It would be so now with his friends and schoolfellows, if they were in his place, and they would, at this moment, be congratulating or envying him. But he was neither covetous nor vain by nature; he had faith in his own talents and had been content to know that his success in life depended on his personal ability. His slight infirmity had always set him a little apart from other boys; it had, perhaps, given him a keener sensibility of many things in life, and he did not, now, deem it quite right that the head of the family should limp on one leg. He did not even see his prospects in the same light as his people at home. In England he had met with greater wealth and magnificence than they dreamed of; he had been in love with, and made happy by, an English lady of such rank and fortune that to her, he felt, the finest estate of Denmark would look but like a child's toy farm.

And in England, too, he had come in touch with the great new ideas of the age: of nature, of the right and freedom of man, of justice and beauty. The universe, through them, had become infinitely wider to him; he wanted to find out still more about it and was planning to travel to America, to the new world. For a moment he felt trapped and imprisoned, as if the dead people of his name, from the family vault at home, were stretching out their parched arms for him.

But at the same time he began to dream at night of the old house and garden. He had walked in these avenues in dream, and had smelled the scent of the flowering limes. When at Ranelagh an old gypsy woman looked at his hand and told him that a son of his was to sit in the seat of his fathers, he felt a sudden, deep satisfaction, queer in a young man who till now had never given his sons a thought.

Then, six months later, his mother again wrote to tell him that his uncle had himself married the girl intended for his dead son. The head of the family was still in his best age, not over sixty, and although Adam remembered him as a small, slight man, he was a vigorous person; it was likely that his young wife would bear him sons.

Adam's mother in her disappointment lay the blame on him. If he had returned to Denmark, she told him, his uncle might have come to look upon him as a son, and would not have married; nay, he might have handed the bride over to him. Adam knew better. The family estate, differing from the neighbouring properties, had gone down from father to son ever since a man of their name first sat there. The tradition of direct succession was the pride of the clan and a sacred dogma to his uncle; he would surely call for a son of his own flesh and bone.

But at the news the young man was seized by a strange, deep, aching remorse towards his old home in Denmark. It was as if he had been making light of a friendly and generous gesture, and disloyal to someone unfailingly loyal to him. It would be but just, he thought, if from now the place should disown and forget him. Nostalgia, which before he had never known, caught hold of him; for the first time he walked in the streets and parks of London as a stranger.

He wrote to his uncle and asked if he might come and stay with him, begged leave from the Legation and took ship for Denmark. He had come to the house to make his peace with it; he had slept little in the night, and was up so early and walking in the garden, to explain himself, and to be forgiven.

While he walked, the still garden slowly took up its day's work. A big snail, of the kind that his grandfather had brought back from France, and which he remembered eating in the house as a child, was already, with dignity, dragging a silver train down the avenue. The birds began to sing; in an old tree under which he stopped a number of them were worrying an owl; the rule of the night was over.

He stood at the end of the avenue and saw the sky lightening. An ecstatic clarity filled the world; in half an hour the sun would rise. A rye field here ran along the garden; two roe-deer were moving in it and looked roseate in the dawn. He gazed out over the fields, where as a small boy he had ridden his pony, and towards the wood where he had killed his first stag. He remembered the old servants who had taught him; some of them were now in their graves.

The ties which bound him to this place, he reflected, were of a mystic nature. He might never again come back to it, and it would make no difference. As long as a man of his own blood and name should sit in the house, hunt in the fields and be obeyed by the people in the huts, wherever he travelled on earth, in England or amongst the red Indians of America, he himself would still be safe, would still have a home, and would carry weight in the world.

His eyes rested on the church. In old days, before the time of Martin Luther, younger sons of great families, he knew, had entered the Church of Rome, and had given up individual wealth and happiness to serve the greater ideals. They, too, had bestowed honour upon their homes and were remembered in its registers. In the solitude of the morning half in jest he let his mind run as it listed; it seemed to him that he might speak to the land as to a person, as to the mother of his race. "Is it only my body that you want," he asked her, "while you reject my imagination, energy and emotions? If the world might be brought to acknowledge that the virtue of our name does not belong to the past only, will it give you no satisfaction?" The landscape was so still that he could not tell whether it answered him yes or no.

After a while he walked on, and came to the new French rose garden laid out for the young mistress of the house. In England he had acquired a freer taste in gardening, and he wondered if he could liberate these blushing captives, and make them thrive outside their cut hedges. Perhaps, he meditated, the elegantly conventional garden would be a floral portrait of his young aunt from Court, whom he had not yet seen.

As once more he came to the pavilion at the end of the avenue his eyes were caught by a bouquet of delicate colours which could not possibly belong to the Danish summer morning. It was in fact his uncle himself, powdered and silk-stockinged, but still in a brocade dressing-gown, and obviously sunk in deep thought. "And what business, or what meditations," Adam asked himself, "drags a connoisseur of the beautiful, but three months married to a wife of seventeen, from his bed into his garden before sunrise?" He walked up to the small, slim, straight figure.

His uncle on his side showed no surprise at seeing him, but then he rarely seemed surprised at anything. He greeted him, with a compliment on his matunality, as kindly as he had done on his arrival last evening. After a moment he looked to the sky, and solemnly proclaimed: "It will be a hot day." Adam, as a child, had often been impressed by the grand, ceremonial manner in which the old lord would state the common happenings of existence; it looked as if nothing had changed here, but all was what it used to be.

The uncle offered the nephew a pinch of snuff. "No, thank you, Uncle," said Adam, "it would ruin my nose to the scent of your garden, which is as fresh as the Garden of Eden, newly created." "From every tree of which," said his uncle, smiling, "thou, my Adam, mayest freely eat." They slowly walked up the avenue together.

The hidden sun was now already gilding the top of the tallest trees. Adam talked of the beauties of nature, and of the greatness of Nordic scenery, less marked by the hand of man than that of Italy. His uncle took the praise of the landscape as a personal compliment, and congratulated him because he had not, in likeness to many young travellers in foreign countries, learned to despise his native land. No, said Adam, he had lately in England longed for the fields and woods of his Danish home. And he had there become acquainted with a new piece of Danish poetry which had enchanted him more than any English or French work. He named the author, Johannes Ewald, and quoted a few of the mighty, turbulent verses.

"And I have wondered, while I read," he went on after a pause, still moved by the lines he himself had declaimed, "that we have not till now understood how much our Nordic mythology in moral greatness surpasses that of Greece and Rome. If it had not been for the physical beauty of the ancient gods, which has come down to us in marble, no modern mind could hold them worthy of worship. They were mean, capricious and treacherous. The gods of our Danish forefathers are as much more divine than they as the Druid is nobler than the Augur. For the fair gods of Asgaard did possess the sublime human virtues; they were righteous, trustworthy, benevolent and even, within a barbaric age, chivalrous." His uncle here for the first time appeared to take any real interest in the conversation. He stopped, his majestic nose a little in the air. "Ah, it was easier to them," he said.

"What do you mean, Uncle?" Adam asked. "It was a great deal easier," said his uncle, "to the northern gods than to those of Greece to be, as you will have it, righteous and benevolent. To my mind it even reveals a weakness in the souls of our ancient Danes that they should consent to adore such divinities." "My dear uncle," said Adam, smiling, "I have always felt that you would be familiar with the modes of Olympus. Now please let me share your insight, and tell me why virtue should come easier to our Danish gods than to those of milder climates." "They were not as powerful," said his uncle.

"And does power," Adam again asked, "stand in the way of virtue?" "Nay," said his uncle gravely. "Nay, power is in itself the supreme virtue. But the gods of which you speak were never all-powerful. They had, at all times, by their side those darker powers which they named the Jotuns, and who worked the suffering, the disasters, the ruin of our world. They might safely give themselves up to temperance and kindness. The omnipotent gods," he went on, "have no such facilitation. With their omnipotence they take over the woe of the universe."

They had walked up the avenue till they were in view of the house. The old lord stopped and ran his eyes over it. The stately building was the same as ever; behind the two tall front windows, Adam knew, was now his young aunt's room. His uncle turned and walked back.

"Chivalry," he said, "chivalry, of which you were speaking, is not a virtue of the omnipotent. It must needs imply mighty rival powers for the knight to defy. With a dragon inferior to him in strength, what figure will St. George cut? The knight who finds no superior forces ready to hand must invent them, and combat wind-mills; his knighthood itself stipulates dangers, vileness, darkness on all sides of him. Nay, believe me, my nephew, in spite of his moral worth, your chivalrous Odin of Asgaard as a Regent must take rank below that of Jove who avowed his sovereignty, and accepted the world which he ruled. But you are young," he added, "and the experience of the aged to you will sound pedantic."

He stood immovable for a moment and then with deep gravity proclaimed: "The sun is up."

The sun did indeed rise above the horizon. The wide landscape was suddenly animated by its splendour, and the dewy grass shone in a thousand gleams.

"I have listened to you, Uncle," said Adam, "with great interest.

But while we have talked you yourself have seemed to me pre-occupied; your eyes have rested on the field outside the garden, as if something of great moment, a matter of life and death, was going on there. Now that the sun is up, I see the mowers in the rye and hear them whetting their sickles. It is, I remember you telling me, the first day of the harvest. That is a great day to a landowner and enough to take his mind away from the gods. It is very fine weather, and I wish you a full barn."

The elder man stood still, his hands on his walking-stick. "There is indeed," he said at last, "something going on in that field, a matter of life and death. Come, let us sit down here, and I will tell you the whole story." They sat down on the seat that ran all along the pavilion, and while he spoke the old lord of the land did not take his eyes off the rye field.

"A week ago, on Thursday night," he said, "someone set fire to my barn at Rødmosegaard—you know the place, close to the moor—and burned it all down. For two or three days we could not lay hands on the offender. Then on Monday morning the keeper at Rødmose, with the wheelwright over there, came up to the house; they dragged with them a boy, Goske Piil, a widow's son, and they made their Bible oath that he had done it; they had themselves seen him sneaking round the barn by nightfall on Thursday. Goske had no good name on the farm; the keeper bore him a grudge upon an old matter of poaching, and the wheelwright did not like him either, for he did, I believe, suspect him with his young wife. The boy, when I talked to him, swore to his innocence, but he could not hold his own against the two old men. So I had him locked up, and meant to send him in to our judge of the district, with a letter.

"The judge is a fool, and would naturally do nothing but what he thought I wished him to do. He might have the boy sent to the convict prison for arson, or put amongst the soldiers as a bad character and a poacher. Or again, if he thought that that was what I wanted, he could let him off.

"I was out riding in the fields, looking at the corn that was soon ripe to be mowed, when a woman, the widow, Goske's mother, was brought up before me, and begged to speak to me. Anne-Marie is her name. You will remember her; she lives in the small house east of the village. She has not got a good name in the place either. They tell as a girl she had a child and did away with it.

"From five days' weeping her voice was so cracked that it was difficult for me to understand what she said. Her son, she told me at last, had indeed been over at Rødmose on Thursday, but for no ill purpose; he had gone to see someone. He was her only son, she called the Lord God to witness on his innocence, and she wrung her hands to me that I should save the boy for her.

"We were in the rye field that you and I are looking at now. That gave me an idea. I said to the widow: 'If in one day, between sunrise and sunset, with your own hands you can mow this field, and it be well done, I will let the case drop and you shall keep your son. But if you cannot do it, he must go, and it is not likely that you will then ever see him again.'

"She stood up then and gazed over the field. She kissed my riding boot in gratitude for the favour shown to her."

The old lord here made a pause, and Adam said: "Her son meant much to her?" "He is her only child," said his uncle. "He means to her her daily bread and support in old age. It may be said that she holds him as dear as her own life. As," he added, "within a higher order of life, a son to his father means the name and the race, and he holds him as dear as life everlasting. Yes, her son means much to her. For the mowing of that field is a day's work to three men, or three days' work to one man. Today, as the sun rose, she set to her task. And down there, by the end of the field, you will see her now, in a blue head-cloth, with the man I have set to follow her and to ascertain that she does the work unassisted, and with two or three friends by her, who are comforting her."

Adam looked down, and did indeed see a woman in a blue head-cloth, and a few other figures in the corn.

They sat for a while in silence. "Do you yourself," Adam then said, "believe the boy to be innocent?" "I cannot tell," said his uncle. "There is no proof. The word of the keeper and the wheel-wright stand against the boy's word. If indeed I did believe the one thing or the other, it would be merely a matter of chance, or maybe of sympathy. The boy," he said after a moment, "was my son's playmate, the only other child that I ever knew him to like or to get on with." "Do you," Adam again asked, "hold it possible to her to fulfill your condition?" "Nay, I cannot tell," said the old lord. "To an ordinary person it would not be possible. No ordinary person would ever have taken it on at all. I chose it so. We are not quibbling with the law, Anne-Marie and I."

Adam for a few minutes followed the movement of the small group in the rye. "Will you walk back?" he asked. "No," said his uncle, "I think that I shall stay here till I have seen the end of the thing." "Until sunset?" Adam asked with surprise. "Yes," said the old lord. Adam said: "It will be a long day." "Yes," said his uncle, "a long day. But," he added, as Adam rose to walk away, "if, as you said, you have got that tragedy of which you spoke in your pocket, be as kind as to leave it here, to keep me company." Adam handed him the book.

In the avenue he met two footmen who carried the old lord's morning chocolate down to the pavilion on large silver trays.

As now the sun rose in the sky, and the day grew hot, the lime trees gave forth their exuberance of scent, and the garden was filled with unsurpassed, unbelievable sweetness. Towards the still hour of midday the long avenue reverberated like a soundboard with a low, incessant murmur: the humming of a million bees that clung to the pendulous, thronging clusters of blossoms and were drunk with bliss.

In all the short lifetime of Danish summer there is no richer or more luscious moment than that week wherein the lime trees flower. The heavenly scent goes to the head and to the heart; it seems to unite the fields of Denmark with those of Elysium; it contains both hay, honey and holy incense, and is half fairy-land and half apothecary's locker. The avenue was changed into a mystic edifice, a dryad's cathedral, outward from summit to base lavishly adorned, set with multitudinous ornaments, and golden in the sun. But behind the walls the vaults were benignly cool and sombre, like ambrosial sanctuaries in a dazzling and burning world, and in here the ground was still moist.

Up in the house, behind the silk curtains of the two front windows, the young mistress of the estate from the wide bed stuck her feet into two little high-heeled slippers. Her lace-trimmed nightgown had slid up above her knee and down from the shoulder; her hair, done up in curling-pins for the night, was still frosty with the powder of yesterday, her round face flushed with sleep. She stepped out to the middle of the floor and stood there, looking extremely grave and thoughtful, yet she did not think at all. But through her head a long procession of pictures marched, and she was unconsciously endeavouring to put them in order, as the pictures of her existence had used to be.

She had grown up at Court; it was her world, and there was probably not in the whole country a small creature more exquisitely and innocently drilled to the stately measure of a palace.

By favour of the old Dowager Queen she bore her name and that
of the King's sister, the Queen of Sweden: Sophie Magdalena.
It was with a view to these things that her husband, when he
wished to restore his status in high places, had chosen her as a
bride, first for his son and then for himself. But her own father,
who held an office in the Royal Household and belonged to the
new Court aristocracy, in his day had done the same thing the
other way round, and had married a country lady, to get a foothold within the old nobility of Denmark. The little girl had her
mother's blood in her veins. The country to her had been an
immense surprise and delight.

To get into her castle-court she must drive through the farm
yard, through the heavy stone gateway in the barn itself, wherein
the rolling of her coach for a few seconds re-echoed like thunder.
She must drive past the stables and the timber-mare, from which
sometimes a miscreant would follow her with sad eyes, and might
here startle a long string of squalling geese, or pass the heavy,
scowling bull, led on by a ring in his nose and kneading the earth
in dumb fury. At first this had been to her, every time, a slight
shock and a jest. But after a while all these creatures and things,
which belonged to her, seemed to become part of herself. Her
mothers, the old Danish country ladies, were robust persons, un-
dismayed by any kind of weather; now she herself had walked in
the rain and had laughed and glowed in it like a green tree.

She had taken her great new home in possession at a time when
all the world was unfolding, mating and propagating. Flowers,
which she had known only in bouquets and festoons, sprung from
the earth round her; birds sang in all the trees. The new-born
lambs seemed to her daintier than her dolls had been. From her
husband's Hanoverian stud, foals were brought to her to give
names; she stood and watched as they poked their soft noses into

their mothers' bellies to drink. Of this strange process she had till now only vaguely heard. She had happened to witness, from a path in the park, the rearing and screeching stallion on the mare. All this luxuriance, lust and fecundity was displayed before her eyes, as for her pleasure.

And for her own part, in the midst of it, she was given an old husband who treated her with punctilious respect because she was to bear him a son. Such was the compact; she had known of it from the beginning. Her husband, she found, was doing his best to fulfill his part of it, and she herself was loyal by nature and strictly brought up. She would not shirk her obligation. Only she was vaguely aware of a discord or an incompatibility within her majestic existence, which prevented her from being as happy as she had expected to be.

After a time her chagrin took a strange form: as the consciousness of an absence. Someone ought to have been with her who was not. She had no experience in analysing her feelings; there had not been time for that at Court. Now, as she was more often left to herself, she vaguely probed her own mind. She tried to set her father in that void place, her sisters, her music master, an Italian singer whom she had admired; but none of them would fill it for her. At times she felt lighter at heart, and believed the misfortune to have left her. And then again it would happen, if she were alone, or in her husband's company, and even within his embrace, that everything round her would cry out: Where? Where? so that she let her wild eyes run about the room in search for the being who should have been there, and who had not come.

When, six months ago, she was informed that her first young bridegroom had died and that she was to marry his father in his place, she had not been sorry. Her youthful suitor, the one time she had seen him, had appeared to her infantile and insipid; the father would make a statelier consort. Now she had sometimes thought of the dead boy, and wondered whether with him life would have been more joyful. But she soon again dismissed the picture, and that was the sad youth's last recall to the stage of this world.

Upon one wall of her room there hung a long mirror. As she gazed into it new images came along. The day before, driving with her husband, she had seen, at a distance, a party of village girls bathe in the river, and the sun shining on them. All her life she had moved amongst naked marble deities, but it had till now never occurred to her that the people she knew should themselves be naked under their bodices and trains, waistcoats and satin breeches, that indeed she herself felt naked within her clothes. Now, in front of the looking-glass, she tardily untied the ribbons of her nightgown, and let it drop to the floor.

The room was dim behind the drawn curtains. In the mirror her body was silvery like a white rose; only her cheeks and mouth, and the tips of her fingers and breasts had a faint carmine. Her slender torso was formed by the whalebones that had clasped it tightly from her childhood; above the slim, dimpled knee a gentle narrowness marked the place of the garter. Her limbs were rounded as if, at whatever place they might be cut through with a sharp knife, a perfectly circular transverse incision would be obtained. The side and belly were so smooth that her own gaze slipped and glided, and grasped for a hold. She was not altogether like a statue, she found, and lifted her arms above her head. She turned to get a view of her back, the curves below the waistline were still blushing from the pressure of the bed. She called to mind a few tales about nymphs and goddesses, but they all seemed a long way off, so her mind returned to the peasant girls in the river. They were, for a few minutes, idealized into playmates, or sisters even, since they belonged to her as did the meadow and the blue river itself. And within the next moment the sense of forlornness once more came upon her, a *horror vaccui* like a physical pain. Surely, surely someone should have been with her now, her other self, like the image in the glass, but nearer, stronger, alive. There was no one, the universe was empty round her.

A sudden, keen itching under her knee took her out of her reveries, and awoke in her the hunting instincts of her breed. She wetted a finger on her tongue, slowly brought it down and quickly slapped it to the spot. She felt the diminutive, sharp body of the insect against the silky skin, pressed the thumb to it, and triumphantly lifted up the small prisoner between her fingertips. She stood quite still, as if meditating upon the fact that a flea was the only creature risking its life for her smoothness and sweet blood.

Her maid opened the door and came in, loaded with the attire of the day—shift, stays, hoop and petticoats. She remembered that she had a guest in the house, the new nephew arrived from England. Her husband had instructed her to be kind to their young kinsman, disinherited, so to say, by her presence in the house. They would ride out on the land together.

In the afternoon the sky was no longer blue as in the morning. Large clouds slowly towered up on it, and the great vault itself was colourless, as if diffused into vapours round the white-hot sun in zenith. A low thunder ran along the western horizon; once or twice the dust of the roads rose in tall spirals. But the fields, the hills and the woods were as still as a painted landscape.

Adam walked down the avenue to the pavilion, and found his uncle there, fully dressed, his hands upon his walking-stick and his eyes on the rye field. The book that Adam had given him lay by his side. The field now seemed alive with people. Small groups stood here and there in it, and a long row of men and women were slowly advancing towards the garden in the line of the swath.

The old lord nodded to his nephew, but did not speak or change his position. Adam stood by him as still as himself.

The day to him had been strangely disquieting. At the meeting again with old places the sweet melodies of the past had filled his senses and his mind, and had mingled with new, bewitching tunes of the present. He was back in Denmark, no longer a child but a youth, with a keener sense of the beautiful, with tales of other countries to tell, and still a true son of his own land and enchanted by its loveliness as he had never been before.

But through all these harmonies the tragic and cruel tale which the old lord had told him in the morning, and the sad contest which he knew to be going on so near by, in the corn field, had re-echoed, like the recurrent, hollow throbbing of a muffled drum, a redoubtable sound. It came back time after time, so that he had felt himself to change colour and to answer absently. It brought with it a deeper sense of pity with all that lived than he had ever known. When he had been riding with his young aunt, and their road ran along the scene of the drama, he had taken care to ride between her and the field, so that she should not see what was going on there, or question him about it. He had chosen the way home through the deep, green wood for the same reason.

More dominantly even than the figure of the woman struggling with her sickle for her son's life, the old man's figure, as he had seen it at sunrise, kept him company through the day. He came to ponder on the part which that lonely, determinate form had played in his own life. From the time when his father died, it had impersonated to the boy law and order, wisdom of life and kind guardianship. What was he to do, he thought, if after eighteen years these filial feelings must change, and his second father's figure take on to him a horrible aspect, as a symbol of the tyranny and oppression of the world? What was he to do if ever the two should come to stand in opposition to each other as adversaries?

At the same time an unaccountable, a sinister alarm and dread on behalf of the old man himself took hold of him. For surely here the Goddess Nemesis could not be far away. This man had ruled the world round him for a longer period than Adam's own lifetime and had never been gainsaid by anyone. During the years when he had wandered through Europe with a sick boy of his own blood as his sole companion he had learned to set himself apart from his surroundings, and to close himself up to all outer life, and he had become insusceptible to the ideas and feelings of other human beings. Strange fancies might there have run in his mind, so that in the end he had seen himself as the only person really existing, and the world as a poor and vain shadow-play, which had no substance to it.

Now, in senile wilfullness, he would take in his hand the life of those simpler and weaker than himself, of a woman, using it to his own ends, and he feared of no retributive justice. Did he not know, the young man thought, that there were powers in the world, different from and more formidable than the short-lived might of a despot?

With the sultry heat of the day this foreboding of impending disaster grew upon him, until he felt ruin threatening not the old lord only, but the house, the name and himself with him. It seemed to him that he must cry out a warning to the man he had loved, before it was too late.

But as now he was once more in his uncle's company, the green calm of the garden was so deep that he did not find his voice to cry out. Instead a little French air which his aunt had sung to him up in the house kept running in his mind.—"*C'est un trop doux effort . . ."* He had good knowledge of music; he had heard the air before, in Paris, but not so sweetly sung.

After a time he asked: "Will the woman fulfill her bargain?" His uncle unfolded his hands. "It is an extraordinary thing," he said animatedly, "that it looks as if she might fulfill it. If you count the hours from sunrise till now, and from now till sunset, you will find the time left her to be half of that already gone. And see! She has now mowed two-thirds of the field. But then we will naturally have to reckon with her strength declining as she works on. All in all, it is an idle pursuit in you or me to bet on the issue of the matter; we must wait and see. Sit down, and keep me company in my watch." In two minds Adam sat down.

"And here," said his uncle, and took up the book from the seat, "is your book, which has passed the time finely. It is great poetry, ambrosia to the ear and the heart. And it has, with our discourse on divinity this morning, given me stuff for thought. I have been reflecting upon the law of retributive justice." He took a pinch of snuff, and went on. "A new age," he said, "has made to itself a god in its own image, an emotional god. And now you are already writing a tragedy on your god."

Adam had no wish to begin a debate on poetry with his uncle, but he also somehow dreaded a silence, and said: "It may be, then, that we hold tragedy to be, in the scheme of life, a noble, a divine phenomenon."

"Aye," said his uncle solemnly, "a noble phenomenon, the noblest on earth. But of the earth only, and never divine. Tragedy is the privilege of man, his highest privilege. The God of the Christian Church Himself, when He wished to experience tragedy, had to assume human form. And even at that," he added thoughtfully, "the tragedy was not wholly valid, as it would have become had the hero of it been, in very truth, a man. The divinity of Christ conveyed to it a divine note, the moment of comedy. The real tragic part, by the nature of things, fell to the executors, not to the victim. Nay, my nephew, we should not adulterate the pure elements of the cosmos. Tragedy should remain the right of human beings, subject, in their conditions or in their own nature, to the dire law of necessity. To them it is salvation and beatification. But the gods, whom we must believe to be unacquainted with and incomprehensive of necessity, can have no knowledge of the tragic. When they are brought face to face with it they will, according to my experience, have the good taste and decorum to keep still, and not interfere.

"No," he said after a pause, "the true art of the gods is the comic. The comic is a condescension of the divine to the world of man; it is the sublime vision, which cannot be studied, but must ever be celestially granted. In the comic the gods see their own being reflected as in a mirror, and while the tragic poet is bound by strict laws, they will allow the comic artist a freedom as unlimited as their own. They do not even withhold their own existence from his sports. Jove may favour Lucianos of Samosata. As long as your mockery is in true godly taste you may mock at the gods and still remain a sound devotee. But in pitying, or condoling with your god, you deny and annihilate him, and such is the most horrible of atheisms.

"And here on earth, too," he went on, "we, who stand in lieu of the gods and have emancipated ourselves from the tyranny of necessity, should leave to our vassals their monopoly of tragedy, and for ourselves accept the comic with grace. Only a boorish and cruel master—a parvenu, in fact—will make a jest of his servants' necessity, or force the comic upon them. Only a timid and pedantic ruler, a *petit-maître*, will fear the ludicrous on his own behalf. Indeed," he finished his long speech, "the very same fatality, which, in striking the burgher or peasant, will become tragedy, with the aristocrat is exalted to the comic. By the grace and wit of our acceptance hereof our aristocracy is known."

Adam could not help smiling a little as he heard the apotheosis of the comic on the lips of the erect, ceremonious prophet. In this ironic smile he was, for the first time, estranging himself from the head of his house.

A shadow fell across the landscape. A cloud had crept over the sun; the country changed colour beneath it, faded and bleached, and even all sounds for a minute seemed to die out of it.

"Ah, now," said the old lord, "if it is going to rain, and the rye gets wet, Anne-Marie will not be able to finish in time. And who comes there?" he added, and turned his head a little.

Preceded by a lackey a man in riding boots and a striped waistcoat with silver buttons, and with his hat in his hand, came down the avenue. He bowed deeply, first to the old lord and then to Adam.

"My bailiff," said the old lord. "Good afternoon, Bailiff. What news have you to bring?" The bailiff made a sad gesture. "Poor news only, my lord," he said. "And how poor news?" asked his master. "There is," said the bailiff with weight, "not a soul at work on the land, and not a sickle going except that of Anne-Marie in this rye field. The mowing has stopped; they are all at her heels. It is a poor day for a first day of the harvest." "Yes, I see," said the old lord. The bailiff went on. "I have spoken kindly to them," he said, "and I have sworn at them; it is all one. They might as well all be deaf."

"Good bailiff," said the old lord, "leave them in peace; let them do as they like. This day may, all the same, do them more good than many others. Where is Goske, the boy, Anne-Marie's son?" "We have set him in the small room by the barn," said the bailiff.

"Nay, let him be brought down," said the old lord; "let him see his mother at work. But what do you say—will she get the field mowed in time?" "If you ask me, my lord," said the bailiff, "I believe that she will. Who would have thought so? She is only a small woman. It is as hot a day today as, well, as I do ever remember. I myself, you yourself, my lord, could not have done what Anne-Marie has done today." "Nay, nay, we could not, Bailiff," said the old lord.

The bailiff pulled out a red handkerchief and wiped his brow, somewhat calmed by venting his wrath. "If," he remarked with bitterness, "they would all work as the widow works now, we would make a profit on the land." "Yes," said the old lord, and fell into thought, as if calculating the profit it might make. "Still," he said, "as to the question of profit and loss, that is more intricate than it looks. I will tell you something that you may not know: The most famous tissue ever woven was ravelled out again every night. But come," he added, "she is close by now. We will go and have a look at her work ourselves." With these words he rose and set his hat on.

The cloud had drawn away again; the rays of the sun once more burned the wide landscape, and as the small party walked out from under the shade of the trees the dead-still heat was heavy as lead; the sweat sprang out on their faces and their eyelids smarted. On the narrow path they had to go one by one, the old lord stepping along first, all black, and the footman, in his bright livery, bringing up the rear.

The field was indeed filled with people like a market-place; there were probably a hundred or more men and women in it. To Adam the scene recalled pictures from his Bible: the meeting between Esau and Jacob in Edom, or Boas' reapers in his barley field near Bethlehem. Some were standing by the side of the field, others pressed in small groups close to the mowing woman, and a few followed in her wake, binding up sheaves where she had cut the corn, as if thereby they thought to help her, or as if by all means they meant to have part in her work. A younger woman with a pail on her head kept close to her side, and with her a number of half-grown children. One of these first caught sight of the lord of the estate and his suite, and pointed to him. The binders let their sheaves drop, and as the old man stood still many of the onlookers drew close round him.

The woman on whom till now the eyes of the whole field had rested—a small figure on the large stage—was advancing slowly and unevenly, bent double as if she were walking on her knees, and stumbling as she walked. Her blue head-cloth had slipped back from her head; the grey hair was plastered to the skull with sweat, dusty and stuck with straw. She was obviously totally unaware of the multitude round her; neither did she now once turn her head or her gaze towards the new arrivals.

Absorbed in her work she again and again stretched out her left hand to grasp a handful of corn, and her right hand with the sickle in it to cut it off close to the soil, in wavering, groping pulls, like a tired swimmer's strokes. Her course took her so close to the feet of the old lord that his shadow fell on her. Just then she staggered and swayed sideways, and the woman who followed her lifted the pail from her head and held it to her lips. Anne-Marie drank without leaving her hold on her sickle, and the water ran from the corners of her mouth. A boy, close to her, quickly bent one knee, seized her hands in his own and, steadying and guiding them, cut off a gripe of rye. "No, no," said the old lord, "you must not do that, boy. Leave Anne-Marie in peace to her work." At the sound of his voice the woman, falteringly, lifted her face in his direction.

The bony and tanned face was streaked with sweat and dust; the eyes were dimmed. But there was not in its expression the slightest trace of fear or pain. Indeed amongst all the grave and concerned faces of the field hers was the only one perfectly calm, peaceful and mild. The mouth was drawn together in a thin line, a prim, keen, patient little smile, such as will be seen in the face of an old woman at her spinning-wheel or her knitting, eager on her work, and happy in it. And as the younger women lifted back the pail, she immediately again fell to her mowing, with an ardent, tender craving, like that of a mother who lays a baby to the nipple. Like an insect that bustles along in high grass, or like a small vessel in a heavy sea, she butted her way on, her quiet face once more bent upon her task.

The whole throng of onlookers, and with them the small group from the pavilion, advanced as she advanced, slowly and as if drawn by a string. The bailiff, who felt the intense silence of the field heavy on him, said to the old lord: "The rye will yield better this year than last," and got no reply. He repeated his remark to Adam, and at last to the footman, who felt himself above a discussion on agriculture, and only cleared his throat in answer. In a while the bailiff again broke the silence. "There is the boy," he said and pointed with his thumb. "They have brought him down." At that moment the woman fell forward on her face and was lifted up by those nearest to her.

Adam suddenly stopped on the path, and covered his eyes with his hand. The old lord without turning asked him if he felt incommoded by the heat. "No," said Adam, "but stay. Let me speak to you." His uncle stopped, with his hand on the stick and looking ahead, as if regretful of being held back.

"In the name of God," cried the young man in French, "force not this woman to continue." There was a short pause. "But I force her not, my friend," said his uncle in the same language. "She is free to finish at any moment." "At the cost of her child only," again cried Adam. "Do you not see that she is dying? You know not what you are doing, or what it may bring upon you."

The old lord, perplexed by this unexpected animadversion, after a second turned all round, and his pale, clear eyes sought his nephew's face with stately surprise. His long, waxen face, with two symmetrical curls at the sides, had something of the mien of an idealized and ennobled old sheep or ram. He made sign to the bailiff to go on. The footman also withdrew a little, and the uncle and nephew were, so to say, alone on the path. For a minute neither of them spoke.

"In this very place where we now stand," said the old lord, then, with hauteur, "I gave Anne-Marie my word."

"My uncle!" said Adam. "A life is a greater thing even than a word. Recall that word, I beseech you, which was given in caprice, as a whim. I am praying you more for your sake than for my own, yet I shall be grateful to you all my life if you will grant me my prayer."

"You will have learned in school," said his uncle, "that in the beginning was the word. It may have been pronounced in caprice, as a whim, the Scripture tells us nothing about it. It is still the principle of our world, its law of gravitation. My own humble word has been the principle of the land on which we stand, for an age of man. My father's word was the same, before my day."

"You are mistaken," cried Adam. "The word is creative—it is imagination, daring and passion. By it the world was made. How much greater are these powers which bring into being than any restricting or controlling law! You wish the land on which we look to produce and propagate; you should not banish from it the forces which cause, and which keep up life, nor turn it into a desert by dominance of law. And when you look at the people, simpler than we and nearer to the heart of nature, who do not analyse their feelings, whose life is one with the life of the earth, do they not inspire in you tenderness, respect, reverence even? This woman is ready to die for her son; will it ever happen to you or me that a woman willingly gives up her life for us? And if it did indeed come to pass, should we make so light of it as not to give up a dogma in return?"

"You are young," said the old lord. "A new age will undoubtedly applaud you. I am old-fashioned, I have been quoting to you texts a thousand years old. We do not, perhaps, quite understand one another. But with my own people I am, I believe, in good understanding. Anne-Marie might well feel that I am making light of her exploit, if now, at the eleventh hour, I did nullify it by a second word. I myself should feel so in her place. Yes, my nephew, it is possible, did I grant you your prayer and pronounce such an amnesty, that I should find it void against her faithfulness, and that we would still see her at her work, unable to give it up, as a shuttle in the rye field, until she had it all mowed. But she would then be a shocking, a horrible sight, a figure of unseemly fun, like a small planet running wild in the sky, when the law of gravitation had been done away with."

"And if she dies at her task," Adam exclaimed, "her death, and its consequences will come upon your head."

The old lord took off his hat and gently ran his hand over his powdered head. "Upon my head?" he said. "I have kept up my head in many weathers. Even," he added proudly, "against the cold wind from high places. In what shape will it come upon my head, my nephew?" "I cannot tell," cried Adam in despair. "I have spoken to warn you. God only knows." "Amen," said the old lord with a little delicate smile. "Come, we will walk on." Adam drew in his breath deeply.

"No," he said in Danish. "I cannot come with you. This field is yours; things will happen here as you decide. But I myself must go away. I beg you to let me have, this evening, a coach as far as town. For I could not sleep another night under your roof, which I have honoured beyond any on earth." So many conflicting feelings at his own speech thronged in his breast that it would have been impossible for him to give them words.

The old lord, who had already begun to walk on, stood still, and with him the lackey. He did not speak for a minute, as if to give Adam time to collect his mind. But the young man's mind was in uproar and would not be collected.

"Must we," the old man asked, in Danish, "take leave here, in the rye field? I have held you dear, next to my own son. I have followed your career in life from year to year, and have been proud of you. I was happy when you wrote to say that you were coming back. If now you will go away, I wish you well." He shifted his walking-stick from the right hand to the left and gravely looked his nephew in the face.

Adam did not meet his eyes. He was gazing out over the land-scape. In the late mellow afternoon it was resuming its colours, like a painting brought into proper light; in the meadows the little black stacks of peat stood gravely distinct upon the green sward. On this same morning he had greeted it all, like a child running laughingly to its mother's bosom; now already he must tear himself from it, in discordance, and forever. And at the moment of parting it seemed infinitely dearer than any time before, so much beautified and solemnized by the coming separation that it looked like the place in a dream, a landscape out of paradise, and he wondered if it was really the same. But, yes—there before him was, once more, the hunting-ground of long ago. And there was the road on which he had ridden today.

"But tell me where you mean to go from here," said the old lord slowly. "I myself have travelled a good deal in my days. I know the word of leaving, the wish to go away. But I have learned by experience that, in reality, the word has a meaning only to the place and the people which one leaves. When you have left my house—although it will see you go with sadness—as far as it is concerned the matter is finished and done with. But to the person who goes away it is a different thing, and not so simple. At the moment that he leaves one place he will be already, by the laws of life, on his way to another, upon this earth. Let me know, then, for the sake of our old acquaintance, to which place you are going when you leave here. To England?"

"No," said Adam. He felt in his heart that he could never again go back to England or to his easy and carefree life there. It was not far enough away; deeper waters than the North Sea must now be laid between him and Denmark. "No, not to England," he said. "I shall go to America, to the new world." For a moment he shut his eyes, trying to form to himself a picture of existence in America, with the grey Atlantic Ocean between him and these fields and woods.

"To America?" said his uncle and drew up his eyebrows. "Yes, I have heard of America. They have got freedom there, a big waterfall, savage red men. They shoot turkeys, I have read, as we shoot partridges. Well, if it be your wish, go to America, Adam, and be happy in the new world."

He stood for some time, sunk in thought, as if he had already sent off the young man to America, and had done with him. When at last he spoke, his words had the character of a monologue, enunciated by the person who watches things come and go, and himself stays on.

"Take service, there," he said, "with the power which will give you an easier bargain than this: That with your own life you may buy the life of your son."

Adam had not listened to his uncle's remarks about America, but the conclusive, solemn words caught his ear. He looked up. As if for the first time in his life, he saw the old man's figure as a whole, and conceived how small it was, so much smaller than himself, pale, a thin black anchorite upon his own land. A thought ran through his head: "How terrible to be old!" The abhorrence of the tyrant, and the sinister dread on his behalf, which had followed him all day, seemed to die out of him, and his pity with all creation to extend even to the sombre form before him.

His whole being had cried out for harmony. Now, with the possibility of forgiving, of a reconciliation, a sense of relief went through him; confusedly he bethought himself of Anne-Marie drinking the water held to her lips. He took off his hat, as his uncle had done a moment ago, so that to a beholder at a distance it would seem that the two dark-clad gentlemen on the path were repeatedly and respectfully saluting one another, and brushed the hair from his forehead. Once more the tune of the garden-room rang in his mind:

"Mourir pour ce qu'on aime
C'est un trop doux effort ..."

He stood for a long time immobile and dumb. He broke off a few ears of rye, kept them in his hand and looked at them.

He saw the ways of life, he thought, as a twined and tangled design, complicated and mazy; it was not given him or any mortal to command or control it. Life and death, happiness and woe, the past and the present, were interlaced within the pattern. Yet to the initiated it might be read as easily as our ciphers—which to the savage must seem confused and incomprehensible—will be read by the schoolboy. And out of the contrasting elements concord rose. All that lived must suffer; the old man, whom he had judged hardly, had suffered, as he had watched his son die, and had dreaded the obliteration of his being. He himself would come to know ache, tears and remorse, and, even through these, the fullness of life. So might now, to the woman in the rye field, her ordeal be a triumphant procession. For to die for the one you loved was an effort too sweet for words.

As now he thought of it, he knew that all his life he had sought the unity of things, the secret which connects the phenomena of existence. It was this strife, this dim presage, which had sometimes made him stand still and inert in the midst of the games of his playfellows, or which had, at other moments—on moonlight nights, or in his little boat on the sea—lifted the boy to ecstatic happiness. Where other young people, in their pleasures or their amours, had searched for contrast and variety, he himself had yearned only to comprehend in full the oneness of the world. If things had come differently to him, if his young cousin had not died, and the events that followed his death had not brought him to Denmark, his search for understanding and harmony might have taken him to America, and he might have found them there, in the virgin forests of a new world. Now they have been disclosed to him today, in the place where he had played as a child. As the song is one with the voice that sings it, as the road is one with the goal, as lovers are made one in their embrace, so is man one with his destiny, and he shall love it as himself.

He looked up again, towards the horizon. If he wished to, he felt, he might find out what it was that had brought to him, here, the sudden conception of the unity of the universe. When this same morning he had philosophized, lightly and for his own sake, on his feeling of belonging to this land and soil, it had been the beginning of it. But since then it had grown; it had become a mightier thing, a revelation to his soul. Some time he would look into it, for the law of cause and effect was a wonderful and fascinating study. But not now. This hour was consecrated to greater emotions, to a surrender to fate and to the will of life.

"No," he said at last. "If you wish it I shall not go. I shall stay here."

At that moment a long, loud roll of thunder broke the stillness of the afternoon. It re-echoed for a while amongst the low hills, and it reverberated within the young man's breast as powerfully as if he had been seized and shaken by hands. The landscape had spoken. He remembered that twelve hours ago he had put a question to it, half in jest, and not knowing what he did. Here it gave him its answer.

What it contained he did not know; neither did he inquire. In his promise to his uncle he had given himself over to the mightier powers of the world. Now what must come must come.

"I thank you," said the old lord, and made a little stiff gesture with his hand. "I am happy to hear you say so. We should not let the difference in our ages, or of our views, separate us. In our family we have been wont to keep peace and faith with one another. You have made my heart lighter."

Something within his uncle's speech faintly recalled to Adam the misgivings of the afternoon. He rejected them; he would not let them trouble the new, sweet felicity which his resolution to stay had brought him.

"I shall go on now," said the old lord. "But there is no need for you to follow me. I will tell you tomorrow how the matter has

ended." "No," said Adam," I shall come back by sunset, to see the
end of it myself."

All the same he did not come back. He kept the hour in his mind,
and all through the evening the consciousness of the drama, and
the profound concern and compassion with which, in his thoughts,
he followed it, gave to his speech, glance and movements a grave
and pathetic substance. But he felt that he was, in the rooms of the
manor, and even by the harpsichord on which he accompanied his
aunt to her air from *Alceste,* as much in the centre of things as if
he had stood in the rye field itself, and as near to those human
beings whose fate was now decided there. Anne-Marie and he were
both in the hands of destiny, and destiny would, by different ways,
bring each to the designated end.

Later on he remembered what he had thought that evening.

But the old lord stayed on. Late in the afternoon he even had an
idea; he called down his valet to the pavilion and made him shift
his clothes on him and dress him up in a brocaded suit that he had
worn at Court. He let a lace-trimmed shirt be drawn over his head
and stuck out his slim legs to have them put into thin silk stockings
and buckled shoes. In this majestic attire he dined alone, of a frugal
meal, but took a bottle of Rhenish wine with it, to keep up his
strength. He sat on for a while, a little sunk in his seat; then, as the
sun neared the earth, he straightened himself, and took the way
down to the field.

The shadows were now lengthening, azure blue along all the
eastern slopes. The lonely trees in the corn marked their site by
narrow blue pools running out from their feet, and as the old man
walked a thin, immensely elongated reflection stirred behind him
on the path. Once he stood still; he thought he heard a lark singing
over his head, a spring-like sound; his tired head held no clear per-

ception of the season; he seemed to be walking, and standing, in a kind of eternity.

The people in the field were no longer silent, as they had been in the afternoon. Many of them talked loudly among themselves, and a little farther away a woman was weeping.

When the bailiff saw his master, he came up to him. He told him, in great agitation, that the widow would, in all likelihood, finish the mowing of the field within a quarter of an hour.

"Are the keeper and the wheelwright here?" the old lord asked him. "They have been here," said the bailiff, "and have gone away, five times. Each time they have said that they would not come back. But they have come back again, all the same, and they are here now." "And where is the boy?" the old lord asked again. "He is with her," said the bailiff. "I have given him leave to follow her. He has walked close to his mother all the afternoon, and you will see him now by her side, down there."

Anne-Marie was now working her way up towards them more evenly than before, but with extreme slowness, as if at any moment she might come to a standstill. This excessive tardiness, the old lord reflected, if it had been purposely performed, would have been an inimitable, dignified exhibition of skilled art; one might fancy the Emperor of China advancing in like manner on a divine procession or rite. He shaded his eyes with his hand, for the sun was now just beyond the horizon, and its last rays made light, wild, many-coloured specks dance before his sight. With such splendour did the sunset emblazon the earth and the air that the landscape was turned into a melting-pot of glorious metals. The meadows and the grasslands became pure gold; the barley field near by, with its long ears, was a live lake of shining silver.

There was only a small patch of straw standing in the rye field, when the woman, alarmed by the change in the light, turned her head a little to get a look at the sun. The while she did not stop her work, but grasped one handful of corn and cut it off, then another, and another. A great stir, and a sound like a manifold, deep sigh, ran through the crowd. The field was now mowed from one end to the other. Only the mower herself did not realize the fact; she stretched out her hand anew, and when she found nothing in it, she seemed puzzled or disappointed. Then she let her arms drop, and slowly sank to her knees.

Many of the women burst out weeping, and the swarm drew close round her, leaving only a small open space at the side where the old lord stood. Their sudden nearness frightened Anne-Marie; she made a slight, uneasy movement, as if terrified that they should put their hands on her.

The boy, who had kept by her all day, now fell on his knees beside her. Even he dared not touch her, but held one arm low behind her back and the other before her, level with her collar-bone, to catch hold of her if she should fall, and all the time he cried aloud. At that moment the sun went down.

The old lord stepped forward and solemnly took off his hat. The crowd became silent, waiting for him to speak. But for a minute or two he said nothing. Then he addressed her, very slowly.

"Your son is free, Anne-Marie," he said. He again waited a little, and added: "You have done a good day's work, which will long be remembered."

Anne-Marie raised her gaze only as high as his knees, and he understood that she had not heard what he said. He turned to the boy. "You tell your mother, Goske," he said, gently, "what I have told her."

The boy had been sobbing wildly, in raucous, broken moans. It took him some time to collect and control himself. But when at last he spoke, straight into his mother's face, his voice was low, a little impatient, as if he were conveying an everyday message to her. "I am free, Mother," he said. "You have done a good day's work that will long be remembered."

At the sound of his voice she lifted her face to him. A faint, bland shadow of surprise ran over it, but still she gave no sign of having heard what he said, so that the people round them began to wonder if the exhaustion had turned her deaf. But after a moment she slowly and waveringly raised her hand, fumbling in the air as she aimed at his face, and with her fingers touched his cheek. The cheek was wet with tears, so that at the contact her fingertips lightly stuck to it, and she seemed unable to overcome the infinitely slight resistance, or to withdraw her hand. For a minute the two looked each other in the face. Then, softly and lingeringly, like a sheaf of corn that falls to the ground, she sank forward onto the boy's shoulder, and he closed his arms round her.

He held her thus, pressed against him, his own face buried in her hair and head-cloth, for such a long time that those nearest to them, frightened because her body looked so small in his embrace, drew closer, bent down and loosened his grip. The boy let them do so without a word or a movement. But the woman who held Anne-Marie, in her arms to lift her up, turned her face to the old lord. "She is dead," she said.

The people who had followed Anne-Marie all through the day kept standing and stirring in the field for many hours, as long as the evening light lasted, and longer. Long after some of them had made a stretcher from branches of the trees and had carried away the dead woman, others wandered on, up and down the stubble, imitating and measuring her course from one end of the rye field to the other, and binding up the last sheaves, where she had finished her mowing.

The old lord stayed with them for a long time, stepping along a little, and again standing still.

In the place where the woman had died the old lord later on had a stone set up, with a sickle engraved in it. The peasants on the land then named the rye field "Sorrow-Acre." By this name it was known a long time after the story of the woman and her son had itself been forgotten.

THE HEROINE

THERE WAS a young Englishman, named Frederick Lamond, who was the descendant of a long line of clergymen and scholars, and himself a student of religious philosophy, and who when he was twenty years old attracted his teacher's attention by his talent and tenacity. In the year of 1870 he got a travelling legacy, and went away to Germany. He meant to write a book upon the doctrine of atonement, and had his mind all filled with his subject.

Frederick had lived a seclusive life amongst books; now every day brought him new impressions. The world itself, like a big old book, fell open, and slowly, on its own, turned one leaf after another. The first great phenomenon that met him within it was the art of painting. One day he went up into the gallery of Das Altes Museum to look at Venusti's picture of Christ on the Mount of Olives, of which a friend had told him. He was amazed to find himself surrounded by paintings connected with his study. He had not known that there were so many pictures in the world. He returned to see them again, and from the sacred paintings he turned to the profane work of the great masters. He was a simple young man. He had nobody to guide him, and no illusions as to his own knowledge of art; he came back to the pictures because he was happy amongst them. In the end he felt at home in the galleries. He recognized most Biblical characters by sight, and stood in a friendly relation to the mythological and allegorical figures as well. These indeed were the people of Berlin whom he knew best, for outside the galleries he was slow in making acquaintances.

While he was thus wandering in his own thoughts, the world of hard facts round him was not standing still, but was, on the contrary, moving with feverish haste. A great war was about to break out.

71

The situation was first made clear to him on a hot day in July, when he met a young man from the manor by his father's rectory, who greeted him proudly with a quotation from *Hamlet*: "Upon my life, Lamond!" and went on to unburden to him his wild young mind, all seething with rumours of the coming Franco-Prussian war. This young man had a brother at the Embassy in Paris, and he explained to Frederick that there was not a button lacking in a gaiter in the French army, and that in Paris the crowds were crying: "*À Berlin!*" Frederick now realized that he had already for some time known of all this, from talk in the cafés where he dined, but only, as it were, with the surface of his mind. He also found that his sympathies were with France. "I had better get out of Berlin," he thought.

He collected his manuscripts and packed his clothes. Then he went to say good-bye to the pictures, and prayed that the coming siege and storm of Berlin might not affect them. And so he made for the frontier. But he had not gone far before he found that he had been too slow. By this time travelling was difficult; he could get neither forward nor back. He changed his plans and decided to go to Metz, where he knew people, but he could not get to Metz either. In the end he had to content himself on being allowed to stay in a small town, named Saarburg, near the border.

In the modest hotel of Saarburg there were many stranded French travellers. Amongst them was an old priest, who came from a college in Bavaria, and two old nuns from a convent school, a widow who kept a hotel in a provincial town, a rich wine-grower, and a commercial traveller. All these people were in the greatest agitation of mind. The optimists amongst them hoped to get permission to pass the frontier of the Duchy of Luxembourg and to get to France that way; the pessimists repeated alarming tales of how Frenchmen were accused of espionage, and shot. The landlord of the hotel was unkindly disposed towards his guests, for some of them had hurried from their homes without luggage or money, and besides he was an atheist, and disliked the Church.

The refugees now found a kind of sedative in the unconcerned-ness of the young English scholar; they came and talked to him of their troubles. He and the old priest, to pass the time, carried on long theological discussions. The old man confided to him that he had, in his young days, composed a treatise upon the denial of Peter. At that, Frederick translated bits of his manuscript to him.

Within the last days of July the air and ground of Saarburg began to boil and smoke with coming events. It was rumoured that German troops would arrive here on their way to France. In the foreshadow of their mightiness the landlord hardened in his man-ner to the Frenchmen; he made the two old nuns weep, and the widow, after a great scene with him, fainted, and went to bed. The rest of the party lay as low as they could.

In the midst of these trials a French lady, with her maid, arrived at the hotel from Wiesbaden, and immediately became the central figure of its small world.

She bore a name which to Frederick had all the sound of heroic French history. He first read it on a number of boxes and trunks in the hall of the hotel, and expected to see an old majestic lady, like a spectre out of the grand past. But when she appeared she was as young as himself, flourishing like a rose, a great beauty. He thought: "It is as if a lioness had calmly walked among a flock of sheep." She had been, he reflected, so slow to leave Wiesbaden because she had it not in her to believe that any inconvenience could ever hit her personally; she refused to believe so now. She was not in the least afraid. She met the anxiety of the pale assembly of the hotel with undaunted forbearance, as if she realized that they must needs have been looking forward in suspense to her arrival. Confronted with the danger of the moment, the timidity of the little group and the hostility of its surroundings, she became still more heraldic, like a lioness in a coat of arms. In spite of her youthfulness and fragility, to Frederick she seemed, from hour to hour, and even as to her carriage, mien and speech, to grow into the orthodox and ideal figure of a *"dame haute et puissante,"* and an embodiment of ancient France.

The refugees took shelter behind her. She wafted the landlord out of existence, changed the servants' manners, and improved the table. She had the bills paid, and sent for a doctor for Madame Bellot. In these matters she had need of a courier, and thus she and Frederick became acquainted.

If Frederick had met this lady six months earlier, before he left England, he would have felt shy and embarrassed in her society. Now he was familiar, if not with herself, at least with sisters and kinswomen of hers. For although she was so elegantly modern, she had all the looks of the goddesses of Titian and Veronese. Her long silky curls shone with the same pale golden tint as their tresses; her carriage had that female majesty with which they sit enthroned or dance, and her flesh had the mysterious freshness and lustre of their flesh.

She had on a small chasseur hat with a pink ostrich feather, a dove-grey silk dress of unbelievable voluminousness, long suede gloves, and round her white throat a narrow black velvet ribbon. She had pearls in her ears and on her neck, and diamond rings on her fingers. He had never seen anything the least like her in real life, but she might well have sat within a gold frame in the gallery of Das Altes Museum. He learned that she was a widow, having been married very young, but not much more about her. But he knew, without being told, where she had spent the years till they now met: amongst the luminous marble columns, in the sweet verdure, in front of the burning blue sea and the silvery and coral-line clouds, which he had seen in the paintings. Perhaps she had had a small Negro servant to wait on her. At times his thoughts would wander, and he would see her in divinely negligent attitudes —yes, in the attire of Venus herself. But these fancies of his were candid and impersonal; he would not offend her for the world.

She was kind to him in an elder-sisterly way, but was at times a little curt, as if impatient with a world so much less perfect than herself. Frederick reflected that he and she had got something in common. They agreed in overlooking many facts of existence, which to other people were of the greatest importance. Only in his case this disregard arose from a sense of remoteness from, or estrangement to, the world in general. "While with her," he thought, "it springs from the circumstance that she masters the world, and will stand no nonsense from it. She is the descendant, and the rightful heiress, of conquerors and commanders, even of tyrants, of this world." Her Christian name, he learned from the trunks, was Heloïse.

In the consciousness of Madame Heloïse's power the refugees of the hotel lived through one or two happy days. In the end they all somewhat overdid their gallant assurance. At supper, over a roast chicken and some excellent wine, they talked freely and hopefully, and the commercial traveller, who was a small, timid man, but had a sweet voice, gave them a number of songs. There was a piano in the dining room, and the old priest accompanied him on it. At last the whole party joined in the hymn of: *"Partant pour la Syrie."* In the midst of a verse there was a knocking, like thunder, on the door. They did not mind, they sang on, and parted for the night confidently. The next day the German troops made their entry into Saarburg, in a storm of excitement and triumph, and in the afternoon the refugees of the hotel, with the exception of

Madame Bellot, who was still in bed, were arrested, and brought before the magistrate.

To his surprise Frederick learned that he was, together with the old priest, accused of espionage, and that their long talks, and his manuscript and notes, formed the material for the accusation. The magistrate would have it that his quotations from Isaiah, 53.8: "For the transgression of my people" had reference to the hour, date and month of the German advance. Frederick reflected that he had, before now, heard Isaiah interpreted to strange purposes, and patiently tried to reason with the magistrate. But he found this gentleman obsessed by the great emotions of the hour, and inaccessible to arguments. The old priest would not, or could not, speak.

Slowly, in the course of the day, it became clear to Frederick that he might in very earnest be shot before night. The certitude gave him a strange, deep tremor. "I shall know now," he thought, "if there is a life after death." He realized that the priest would know it as soon as he. The idea was difficult to conceive; the old man had been such a doctrinairian. But by sunset the magistrate himself grew tired of the case, and had both the accused brought before a party of officers, who were in residence in a big villa outside the town, from which the owners had fled in fear of a French invasion. They found the rest of the group from the hotel here.

The atmosphere of the villa was very different from that of the municipality office. The three German officers had found it convenient to dine in the ease of the salon, which was richly done up in crimson brocade, with heavy curtains and large paintings on the walls. Their dessert and wine were still on the table before them. They were flushed with wine, but even more with triumph, for they had, an hour ago, had news of the action of Wissenburg, and the telegram lay by their glasses.

One of the three was an erect, grey-haired man with a lean face, another seemed to be the leading spirit, or the spoiled child, amongst them. He was left a free hand in the cross-examination of the prisoners, for he spoke French better than the others, and amused them by his exuberant vitality. He was quite young, a giant in stature, and strikingly fair, with a fullness, or heaviness, that gave him the appearance of a young god. He met the people from the hotel with laughing surprise and disdain, and seemed to fear neither God nor the Devil—and still less any Frenchman— until he caught sight of Madame Heloïse. From then the case became a matter between him and her.

Frederick could see that much. But he was no judge of this kind of warfare; and, although after the first glance she did not once look at the man, while his light, protruding eyes did not for a moment leave her face or figure, he could not have decided whether, in very truth, the offensive lay with him or with her.

The two were alike, and might have been brother and sister. They were obviously afraid of one another. As the interview proceeded the German sweated with dread, and she grew pale, still nothing could have held them apart. Frederick was certain that they met here for the first time; all the same it was an old feud which was about to be settled in the salon of the villa. Was it, he wondered, a hereditary national combat, or would he have to go further back, and deeper down, to discover the root of it?

The young German began by stating that he now hardly found it worth his while to proceed to Paris. He asked her how she had got into her present company, and whether she considered her compeers to be more dangerous than herself? She replied curtly, her chin lifted. Frederick was aware that his own fate, with that of his fellows, now rested with her. He reflected that no human being, and least of all this young soldier, would for long put up with her look and manner, and still in his heart he applauded the fine display of insolence that she gave them. It was inevitable that in the end the German should come up close to her; as he held a paper up for her inspection he spoke straight into her face. At that, in a gentle movement, she swept back the ample skirt of her dress, so that it should get in no contact with him.

He stopped short in the midst of his speech, and gasped for breath. "I am not, Madame," he said very slowly, "going to touch your dress. I am going to make you a proposal. I shall write out the passport for you and your friends to get into Luxembourg, which you want from me. You may come and fetch it in half an hour. But you will have to come without that skirt, which you do, rightly, take such trouble to keep away from me. You will, in fact, have to come for your passports dressed like the goddess Venus. That is," he added after a moment's breathless silence, "at any rate, a handsome proposition, Madame." At his own words he suddenly blushed dark crimson.

Frederick's heart ceased to beat for a moment, with disgust or horror, and with sadness. The sentence was a distortion of his own beautiful fancies about Heloïse. The blasphemy made of the world a place of nauseating baseness, and of him an accomplice.

As to Heloïse herself, the insult changed her as if it had set fire to her. She turned straight upon the insulter, and Frederick had never seen her so abundant in vitality or arrogance; she seemed about to laugh in her adversary's face. The sordidness of the world, he thought with deep ecstatic gratitude, did not touch her; she was above it all. Only for a moment her hand went up to the collar of her mantilla, as if, choking under the wave of her disdain, she must free herself of it. But again the next moment she stood still; her hand sank down, and with it the blood from her cheeks; she became very pale. She turned to her fellow-prisoners, and slowly let her gaze run over their white, horrified faces.

The two older officers stirred in their chairs. The young man wafted his paper at them. "Why!" he cried. "He was wounded for our transgressions! For the transgressions of my people we are stricken! With chapter and verse to it! We have a whole gang of spies before us, Sirs, with her—" he pointed a shaking finger at Heloïse, "at the head of them. Why must she come here of all places? Could she not have left us, at any rate, alone?"

He spoke to her again; he could not let go his hold of her. "Are you sure you have understood me?" he screamed. "No, I am not sure," said she. "The French language will lend itself badly to your proposition. Will you please repeat it in German?" This was difficult for him to do; still he did it. Heloïse took off her hat, so that her golden hair shone in the lamplight. During the rest of the interview she kept it in her hands behind her slim waist, and it gave her a look of having her hands tied upon her back.

"Why do you ask me?" she said. "Ask those who are with me. These are poor people, hard-working, and used to hardships. Here is a French priest," she went on very slowly, "the consoler of many poor souls; here are two French sisters, who have nursed the sick and dying. The two others have children in France, who will fare ill without them. Their salvation is, to each one of them, more important than mine. Let them decide for themselves if they will buy it at your price. You will be answered, by them, in French."

The old priest took a step forward. He had been given to long speeches, in the hotel, but here he did not say a word. He only stretched his right arm upwards, and waved it to and fro. The one old nun threw herself back towards the wall, as if already facing the fusillading squad. She lifted both arms and cried: "No!" The other nun burst into terrible sobs, her legs gave way under her, she fell down upon her knees and repeated: "No. No. No."

It was the commercial traveller who made a speech. He took a long step towards the young officer, looked up to his great height and said: "You believe that we are afraid of you? Yes, so we are. We are afraid ever to come to look as you do." Frederick did not speak; he looked the officer in the face, and could not help smiling a little.

The German stared down at the commercial traveller, and then over his head at Heloïse. He cried out: "Then away with you. Let it have an end. Away with you all!" He called on two soldiers from the adjoining room. "Take these people down," he commanded, "into the courtyard. For further orders." And once more he cried to the prisoners: "You will have it your own way now. Let me have peace. Let me have peace only." The last thing that Frederick saw in the room was his face, as Heloïse passed him and looked at him. The whole party was rushed down the stairs, and out of the house.

As they came down in the courtyard the night was clear and the stars began to show in the sky. There was a low wall running along the one side of the court, fencing the garden of the villa; from the other side of it came the smell of stock. One by one the tired refugees, ignorant of their fate, went and took their place by this wall. Heloïse, who stood bareheaded in the court, looked up to the sky, then after a while said to Frederick: "There was a falling star. You might have wished."

When they had stood in the courtyard for half an hour three soldiers came out of the house; one of them carried a lamp. One of the others, who seemed to be a superintendent, looked round at the prisoners, went up to the old priest and handed him a paper. "This is your permission to go to Luxembourg," he said. "It is for all of you. The trains are filled up; you will have to get a carriage in town. You had better leave at once."

As soon as he had finished, another of the soldiers stepped forward and addressed himself to Heloïse, and they were surprised to see that he was holding a big bouquet of roses, which had been upon the table of the salon. He made a military salute. "The Colonel," he said, "asks Madame to accept these. With his compliments. To a heroine." Heloïse took the bouquet from him as if she did not see either him or it.

They managed to get carriages at the hotel. While they were kept waiting for them they had a hurried, spare meal of bread and wine, for none of them had eaten anything since morning. It was no renewal of their gallant supper of last night; it seemed to have no connection with it. Their existence, since then, had been set on another plane. They held one another's hands, each of them owed his life to each of the others.

Heloïse was still the central figure of their communion, but in a new way, as an object infinitely precious to them all. Her pride, her glory was theirs, since they had been ready to die for it. She was still very pale; she looked like a child amongst the old people, and laughed at what they said to her. As she insisted on taking all her trunks and boxes with her, evidently regarding them as part of herself and not to be left in the hands of the enemy, and as Frederick had to load them up, he and she came to drive together, behind the others, and in a small fiacre, to the frontier.

Frederick all his life remembered this drive, even to the curves of the road. The moon was up, and the stretch of sky between her and the low horizon was as if powdered with gold-dust. When the dew fell, Heloïse drew her shawl over her head; within its dark folds she looked like a village-girl, and still she sat enthroned, like a muse, by his side. He had read in books, before now, of heroics and heroines; the episode he had lived through and the young woman beside him were like the books, and all the same she was so gently and simply vivid, like no book in the world. Her silent, triumphant happiness was as sweet to him as the smell of the ripe cornfield through which they drove. All of a sudden she took his hand.

It was early when they passed the frontier and came to the small station of Wasserbillig, where they found the rest of their party. While they waited for the train, which was to take them into France, and once more turned their faces to Paris, his French friends, Frederick felt, became like one family, to which he no longer belonged. When the train at last came in, they seemed almost ignorant of his existence.

But at the last moment Heloïse gave him a long, deep, tender glance. It followed him from behind the window of her compartment. Then suddenly she was gone.

Frederick stood on the platform and watched the train disappear in a dim morning landscape. He felt that the curtain had gone down upon a great event in his life. His heart was aching both with happiness and with woe. The lately born artist within him, Venusti's friend, received the adventure in a humble, ecstatic spirit, and *"Domine, non sum dignus"* was his response to it. But when he was once more alone, the searcher and inquirer, his old self of the universities of England took hold, craved for more than that, and demanded to be enlightened, to know and understand. There was, within the phenomena of the heroic mind, still something left uncomprehended, an unexplored, a mysterious area.

It would be, he reflected, this moment of incompleted investigation and unobtained insight, which now caused him to stand at the station of Wasserbillig with an almost choking feeling of loss or privation, as if a cup had been withdrawn from his lips before his thirst was quenched.

The true seeker is sometimes helped to his end by the hand of fate. So was Frederick in his research on the heroic mind. He only had to wait for a while.

In England he went back to his books. He finished his treatise on the doctrine of atonement, and later on wrote another book. With time he strolled from the area of religious philosophy to that of history of religion in general. He was holding a good position amongst the young men of letters of his generation, and was engaged to a girl, whom he had known from the time when they were both children, when, five or six years after his adventure at Saarburg, he had to go to Paris to attend a course of lectures by a great French historian.

He looked up an old friend there, a brother of the boy who, in Berlin, had first given him news of the war. This young man's name was Arthur, and he was still, as then, in the same office at the Embassy. Arthur was at a loss to know how to entertain a student of theology in Paris. He invited Frederick out to dine at a select restaurant, and, while they were dining, asked him how he liked Paris, and what he had been seeing there. Frederick answered that he had seen a multitude of beautiful things, and had been to the museums of the Louvre and Luxembourg. They talked for some time of classic and modern art. Then suddenly Arthur exclaimed: "If you like to look at beautiful things I know what we will do. We will go and see Heloïse." "Heloïse?" said Frederick. "Not a word more," said Arthur. "It cannot be described; it shall be seen."

He took Frederick to a small, select and exquisite music hall. "We are just in time," he said. Then he laughed and added: "Although you really ought to have seen her at the time of the Empire. Some people have it that she is as stupid as a goose, but you cannot believe it when you look at her legs. *La jambe c'est la femme!* They also tell me that her private life is quite respectable. I do not know."

The show which they were to see was called *Diana's Revenge* and affected the classic style, but was elegantly modern in its details. A great number of lovely young dancers danced and posed, as nymphs in a forest, and were all very scantily dressed. But the climax of the whole performance was the appearance of the goddess Diana herself, with nothing on at all.

As she stepped forward bending her golden bow, a noise like a long sigh went through the house. The beauty of her body came as a surprise and an ecstasy even to those who had seen her before; they hardly believed their eyes.

Arthur regarded her in his opera-glasses, then generously handed them on to Frederick. But he noticed that Frederick did not make use of them, and, after a moment, that he had become very still. He wondered if he was shocked. *"C'est une chose incroyable,"* he said, *"que la beauté de cette femme.* What do you say?"

"Yes," said Frederick. "But I know her. I have seen her before now." "But not in this thing?" said Arthur. "No. Not in that," said Frederick. After a little while he added: "Perhaps she will remember me. I shall send up my card." Arthur smiled. The page who had taken up Frederick's card came back with a small letter for him. "Is that from her?" Arthur asked. "Yes," said Frederick. "She remembers me. She will come and see us when the performance is over." "Heloïse?" exclaimed Arthur. "Well, you English professors of religious philosophy! When did you meet her? Was it when you were writing upon the mysteries of the Egyptian Adonis?" "No, I was writing on another theme then," said Frederick. Arthur ordered a table and wine and a big bouquet of roses.

Heloïse came into the theatre, and made all heads turn towards her, like a bed of sunflowers towards the sun. She was in black, with a long train and long gloves, ostrich feathers and pearls. "All that black," sighed the house in its heart, "to cover up all that white!"

She was perhaps a little fuller of bosom, and thinner in the face, than she had been six years ago, but she still moved in the same way, like one of the great Felidae, and had, in her countenance and mien, that brevity or impatience which had then charmed Frederick. Frederick rose to greet her, and Arthur, who had thought him sadly awkward amongst the elegant public of the theatre, was struck by his friend's dignity, and, as he and Heloïse looked at each other, by the completely identical expression of deep happy earnestness in their two faces. They gave him the impression that they would have liked to kiss as they met, but were held back by something other than the presence of people round them. They kept standing up, as if they had forgotten the human faculty of sitting down.

Heloïse beamed on Frederick. "I am so happy that you have come to see me," she said, with his hand in hers. Frederick at first could not find a word to say; in the end he asked a stupid question. "Have any of the others," he asked, "been here to see you?" "No," said Heloise. "No, none of them." Here Arthur succeeded in making them sit down, opposite each other, by his table. "You know," said Heloïse, "that poor old Father Lamarque has died?" "No!" said Frederick. "I have not been in touch with any of them." "Yes, he died," said Heloïse. "When he came to Paris, then, he asked to be sent to the army. He did wonders there; he was a hero! But he got wounded, later, here in Paris, by the soldiers of Versailles. When I heard of it I ran to the hospital, but alas, it was too late."

To make up for his countryman's silence Arthur poured out the champagne to her with a compliment.

"Oh, they were good people," she cried, taking her glass. "What a fine time it was! The two old sisters, too, how good they were! And so were all of them.

"But they were not exactly very brave," she added, setting down the glass again. "They were all in a deadly funk that night at the villa. They were already seeing the muzzles of the German rifles, pointing at them. And, good God, they were running a risk then, too, and a worse one than they ever knew themselves."

"How do you mean?" Frederick asked.

"Yes, a worse risk to them," said Heloïse. "For they would have made me do as the German demanded. They would have made me do it, to save their lives, if he had put it straight to them at first, or if they had been left to themselves. And then they would never have got over it. They would have repented it all their lives, and have held themselves to be great sinners. They were not the people for that kind of business, they, who had never before done a mean thing in their life. That is why it was a sad thing that they should have been so badly frightened. I tell you, my friend, for those people it would have been better to be shot than to live on with a bad conscience. They were not used to that, you see; they would not have known how to live with it."

"How do you know all that?" asked Frederick.

"Oh, I know that kind of people well," said Heloïse. "I was brought up amongst poor, honest people myself. My grandmother had a sister who was a nun, and it was an old poor priest, like Father Lamarque, who taught me to read."

Frederick put his elbow on the table, and his chin in his hand, and sat and looked at her. "Then your triumph afterwards," he said very slowly, "was really all on our behalf? Because we had behaved so well?" "You did behave well, did you not?" said she, smiling at him. "So you were a greater heroine, even," said Frederick in the same way, "than I knew at the time." "My dear friend!" said she.

He asked her, "Did you believe, at the moment, that you might really be shot?" "Yes," said she. "He might very well have had me shot, and all of you with me. That might well have been his fashion of making love. And all the same," she added thoughtfully, "he was honest, an honest young man. He could really want a thing. Many men have not got that in them."

She drank, had her glass refilled, and looked at Frederick. "You," she said, "you were not like the others. If you and I had been alone there, everything would have been different. You might have made me save my life, in the way he told me, quite simply, and have thought nothing of it afterwards. I saw it, at the time. And when we drove together to the frontier, and you did not say a word, I knew it, in that fiacre. I liked it in you, and I do not know where you have learned it, seeing that after all you are an Englishman." Frederick thought her words over. "Yes," he said slowly, "if you had proposed it yourself, of your own free will." Heloïse laughed at that.

"But do you know," she suddenly cried, "what was good luck both for you and me, and for all of us? That there were no women with us at the time! A woman would have made me do it, quick, had I been ever so distressed. And where, in that case, would all our greatness have been?" "But there were women with us," said Frederick. "There were the nuns." "Nay, they do not count," said Heloïse. "A nun is not a woman in that sense. No, I mean a married woman, or an old maid, an honest woman. If Madame Bellot had not had stomach-ache with fear, she would have had everything off me in no time, I can promise you. Her I could never have talked round."

Heloïse fell into thought, with her eyes on Frederick's face, and after a minute or two said: "What a man you have become! I believe that you have grown. You were only a boy then. We were both so much younger." "Tonight," said he, "it does not seem to me a long time ago." "But it is a long time, all the same," said she, "only to you it does not matter. You are a man, a writer, are you not? You are on the upward path. You will be writing many more books, I feel that. Do you remember, now, how when we went out for a walk, in Saarburg, you told me about the books of a Jew in Amsterdam? He had a pretty name, like a woman's. I might have chosen it for myself, instead of the one I have got, which also a learned man selected for me. I suppose that only very learned people would know it at all. What was it, now?" "Spinoza," said Frederick. "Yes," said Heloïse, "Spinoza. He cut diamonds. It was very interesting. No, to you time does not matter. One is happy to meet one's friends again," she said, "and yet it is then that one realizes how time flies. It is we who feel it, the women. From us time takes away so much. And in the end: everything." She looked up at Frederick, and none of the faces which the great masters paint had ever given him such a vision of life, and of the world. "How I wish, my dear friend," she said, "that you had seen me then."

THE SAILOR-BOY'S TALE

THE BARQUE *Charlotte* was on her way from Marseille to Athens, in grey weather, on a high sea, after three days' heavy gale. A small sailor-boy, named Simon, stood on the wet, swinging deck, held on to a shroud, and looked up towards the drifting clouds, and to the upper top-gallant yard of the main-mast.

A bird, that had sought refuge upon the mast, had got her feet entangled in some loose tackle-yarn of the halliard, and, high up there, struggled to get free. The boy on the deck could see her wings flapping and her head turning from side to side.

Through his own experience of life he had come to the conviction that in this world everyone must look after himself, and expect no help from others. But the mute, deadly fight kept him fascinated for more than an hour. He wondered what kind of bird it would be. These last days a number of birds had come to settle in the barque's rigging: swallows, quails, and a pair of peregrine falcons; he believed that this bird was a peregrine falcon. He remembered how, many years ago, in his own country and near his home, he had once seen a peregrine falcon quite close, sitting on a stone and flying straight up from it. Perhaps this was the same bird. He thought: "That bird is like me. Then she was there, and now she is here."

At that a fellow-feeling rose in him, a sense of common tragedy; he stood looking at the bird with his heart in his mouth. There were none of the sailors about to make fun of him; he began to think out how he might go up by the shrouds to help the falcon out. He brushed his hair back and pulled up his sleeves, gave the deck round him a great glance, and climbed up. He had to stop a couple of times in the swaying rigging.

It was indeed, he found when he got to the top of the mast, a peregrine falcon. As his head was on a level with hers, she gave up her struggle, and looked at him with a pair of angry, desperate yellow eyes. He had to take hold of her with one hand while he got his knife out, and cut off the tackle-yarn. He was scared as he looked down, but at the same time he felt that he had been ordered up by nobody, but that this was his own venture, and this gave him a proud, steadying sensation, as if the sea and the sky, the ship, the bird and himself were all one. Just as he had freed the falcon, she hacked him in the thumb, so that the blood ran, and he nearly let her go. He grew angry with her, and gave her a clout on the head, then he put her inside his jacket, and climbed down again.

When he reached the deck the mate and the cook were standing there, looking up; they roared to him to ask what he had had to do in the mast. He was so tired that the tears were in his eyes. He took the falcon out and showed her to them, and she kept still within his hands. They laughed and walked off. Simon set the falcon down, stood back and watched her. After a while he reflected that she might not be able to get up from the slippery deck, so he caught her once more, walked away with her and placed her upon a bolt of canvas. A little after she began to trim her feathers, made two or three sharp jerks forward, and then suddenly flew off. The boy could follow her flight above the troughs of the grey sea. He thought: "There flies my falcon."

When the *Charlotte* came home, Simon signed aboard another ship, and two years later he was a light hand on the schooner *Hebe* lying at Bodø, high up on the coast of Norway, to buy herrings.

To the great herring-markets of Bodø ships came together from all corners of the world; here were Swedish, Finnish and Russian boats, a forest of masts, and on shore a turbulent, irregular display of life, with many languages spoken, and mighty fights. On the shore booths had been set up, and the Lapps, small yellow people, noiseless in their movements, with watchful eyes, whom Simon had never seen before, came down to sell bead-embroidered leather-goods. It was April, the sky and the sea were so clear that it was difficult to hold one's eyes up against them—salt, infinitely wide, and filled with bird-shrieks—as if someone were incessantly whetting invisible knives, on all sides, high up in Heaven.

Simon was amazed at the lightness of these April evenings. He knew no geography, and did not assign it to the latitude, but he took it as a sign of an unwonted good-will in the Universe, a favour. Simon had been small for his age all his life, but this last winter he had grown, and had become strong of limb. That good luck, he felt, must spring from the very same source as the sweetness of the weather, from a new benevolence in the world. He had been in need of such encouragement, for he was timid by nature; now he asked for no more. The rest he felt to be his own affair. He went about slowly, and proudly.

One evening he was ashore with land-leave, and walked up to the booth of a small Russian trader, a Jew who sold gold watches. All the sailors knew that his watches were made from bad metal, and would not go, still they bought them, and paraded them about. Simon looked at these watches for a long time, but did not buy. The old Jew had divers goods in his shop, and amongst others a case of oranges. Simon had tasted oranges on his journeys; he bought one and took it with him. He meant to go up on a hill, from where he could see the sea, and suck it there.

As he walked on, and had got to the outskirts of the place, he saw a little girl in a blue frock, standing at the other side of a fence and looking at him. She was thirteen or fourteen years old, as slim as an eel, but with a round, clear, freckled face, and a pair of long plaits. The two looked at one another.

"Who are you looking out for?" Simon asked, to say something. The girl's face broke into an ecstatic, presumptuous smile. "For the man I am going to marry, of course," she said. Something in her countenance made the boy confident and happy; he grinned a little at her. "That will perhaps be me," he said. "Ha, ha," said the girl, "he is a few years older than you, I can tell you." "Why," said Simon, "you are not grown up yourself." The little girl shook her head solemnly. "Nay," she said, "but when I grow up I will be exceedingly beautiful, and wear brown shoes with heels, and a hat." "Will you have an orange?" asked Simon, who could give her none of the things she had named. She looked at the orange and at him. "They are very good to eat," said he. "Why do you not eat it yourself then?" she asked. "I have eaten so many already," said he, "when I was in Athens. Here I had to pay a mark for it." "What is your name?" asked she. "My name is Simon," said he. "What is yours?" "Nora," said the girl. "What do you want for your orange now, Simon?"

When he heard his name in her mouth Simon grew bold. "Will you give me a kiss for the orange?" he asked. Nora looked at him gravely for a moment. "Yes," she said, "I should not mind giving you a kiss." He grew as warm as if he had been running quickly. When she stretched out her hand for the orange he took hold of it. At that moment somebody in the house called out for her. "That is my father," said she, and tried to give him back the orange, but he would not take it. "Then come again tomorrow," she said quickly, "then I will give you a kiss." At that she slipped off. He stood and looked after her, and a little later went back to his ship.

Simon was not in the habit of making plans for the future, and now he did not know whether he would be going back to her or not.

The following evening he had to stay aboard, as the other sailors were going ashore, and he did not mind that either. He meant to sit on the deck with the ship's dog, Balthasar, and to practise upon a concertina that he had purchased some time ago. The pale evening was all round him, the sky was faintly roseate, the sea was quite calm, like milk-and-water, only in the wake of the boats going inshore it broke into streaks of vivid indigo. Simon sat and played; after a while his own music began to speak to him so strongly that he stopped, got up and looked upwards. Then he saw that the full moon was sitting high on the sky.

The sky was so light that she hardly seemed needed there; it was as if she had turned up by a caprice of her own. She was round, demure and presumptuous. At that he knew that he must go ashore, whatever it was to cost him. But he did not know how to get away, since the others had taken the yawl with them. He stood on the deck for a long time, a small lonely figure of a sailor-boy on a boat, when he caught sight of a yawl coming in from a ship farther out, and hailed her. He found that it was the Russian crew from a boat named *Anna,* going ashore. When he could make himself understood to them, they took him with them; they first asked him for money for his fare, then, laughing, gave it back to him. He thought: "These people will be believing that I am going in to town, wenching." And then he felt, with some pride, that they were right, although at the same time they were infinitely wrong, and knew nothing about anything.

When they came ashore they invited him to come in and drink in their company, and he would not refuse, because they had helped him. One of the Russians was a giant, as big as a bear; he told Simon that his name was Ivan. He got drunk at once, and then fell upon the boy with a bear-like affection, pawed him, smiled and laughed into his face, made him a present of a gold watch-chain, and kissed him on both cheeks. At that Simon reflected that he also ought to give Nora a present when they met again, and as soon as he could get away from the Russians he walked up to a booth that he knew of, and bought a small blue silk handkerchief, the same colour as her eyes.

It was Saturday evening, and there were many people amongst the houses; they came in long rows, some of them singing, all keen to have some fun that night. Simon, in the midst of this rich, bawling life under the clear moon, felt his head light with the flight from the ship and the strong drinks. He crammed the handkerchief in his pocket; it was silk, which he had never touched before, a present for his girl.

He could not remember the path up to Nora's house, lost his way, and came back to where he had started. Then he grew deadly afraid that he should be too late, and began to run. In a small passage between two wooden huts he ran straight into a big man, and found that it was Ivan once more. The Russian folded his arms round him and held him. "Good! Good!" he cried in high glee, "I have found you, my little chicken. I have looked for you everywhere, and poor Ivan has wept because he lost his friend." "Let me go, Ivan," cried Simon. "Oho," said Ivan, "I shall go with you and get you what you want. My heart and my money are all yours, all yours; I have been seventeen years old myself, a little lamb of God, and I want to be so again tonight." "Let me go," cried Simon, "I am in a hurry." Ivan held him so that it hurt, and patted him with his other hand. "I feel it, I feel it," he said. "Now trust to me, my little friend. Nothing shall part you and me. I hear the others coming; we will have such a night together as you will remember when you are an old grandpapa."

Suddenly he crushed the boy to him, like a bear that carries off a sheep. The odious sensation of male bodily warmth and the bulk of a man close to him made the lean boy mad. He thought of Nora waiting, like a slender ship in the dim air, and of himself, here, in the hot embrace of a hairy animal. He struck Ivan with all his might. "I shall kill you, Ivan," he cried out, "if you do not let me go." "Oh, you will be thankful to me later on," said Ivan, and began to sing. Simon fumbled in his pocket for his knife, and got it opened. He could not lift his hand, but he drove the knife, furiously, in under the big man's arm. Almost immediately he felt the blood spouting out, and running down in his sleeve. Ivan stopped short in the song, let go his hold of the boy and gave two long deep grunts. The next second he tumbled down on his knees. "Poor Ivan, poor Ivan," he groaned. He fell straight on his face. At that moment Simon heard the other sailors coming along, singing, in the by-street.

He stood still for a minute, wiped his knife, and watched the blood spread into a dark pool underneath the big body. Then he ran. As he stopped for a second to choose his way, he heard the sailors behind him scream out over their dead comrade. He thought: "I must get down to the sea, where I can wash my hand." But at the same time he ran the other way. After a little while he found himself on the path that he had walked on the day before, and it seemed as familiar to him, as if he had walked it many hundred times in his life.

He slackened his pace to look round, and suddenly saw Nora standing on the other side of the fence; she was quite close to him when he caught sight of her in the moonlight. Wavering and out of breath he sank down on his knees. For a moment he could not speak. The little girl looked down at him. "Good evening, Simon," she said in her small coy voice. "I have waited for you a long time," and after a moment she added: "I have eaten your orange."

"Oh, Nora," cried the boy. "I have killed a man." She stared at him, but did not move. "Why did you kill a man?" she asked after a moment. "To get here," said Simon. "Because he tried to stop me.

But he was my friend." Slowly he got on to his feet. "He loved me!" the boy cried out, and at that burst into tears. "Yes," said she slowly and thoughtfully. "Yes, because you must be here in time." "Can you hide me?" he asked. "For they are after me." "Nay," said Nora, "I cannot hide you. For my father is the parson here at Bodø, and he would be sure to hand you over to them, if he knew that you had killed a man." "Then," said Simon, "give me something to wipe my hands on." "What is the matter with your hands?" she asked, and took a little step forward. He stretched out his hands to her. "Is that your own blood?" she asked. "No," said he, "it is his." She took the step back again. "Do you hate me now?" he asked. "No, I do not hate you," said she. "But do put your hands at your back."

As he did so she came up close to him, at the other side of the fence, and clasped her arms round his neck. She pressed her young body to his, and kissed him tenderly. He felt her face, cool as the moonlight, upon his own, and when she released him, his head swam, and he did not know if the kiss had lasted a second or an hour. Nora stood up straight, her eyes wide open. "Now," she said slowly and proudly, "I promise you that I will never marry anybody, as long as I live." The boy kept standing with his hands on his back, as if she had tied them there. "And now," she said, "you must run, for they are coming." They looked at one another. "Do not forget Nora," said she. He turned and ran.

He leapt over a fence, and when he was down amongst the houses he walked. He did not know at all where to go. As he came to a house, from where music and noise streamed out, he slowly went through the door. The room was full of people; they were dancing in here. A lamp hung from the ceiling, and shone down on them; the air was thick and brown with the dust rising from the floor. There were some women in the room, but many of the men danced with each other, and gravely or laughingly stamped the floor. A moment after Simon had come in the crowd withdrew to the walls to clear the floor for two sailors, who were showing a dance from their own country.

Simon thought: "Now, very soon, the men from the boat will come round to look for their comrade's murderer, and from my hands they will know that I have done it." These five minutes during which he stood by the wall of the dancing-room, in the midst of the gay, sweating dancers, were of great significance to the boy. He himself felt it, as if during this time he grew up, and became like other people. He did not entreat his destiny, nor complain. Here he was, he had killed a man, and had kissed a girl. He did not demand any more from life, nor did life now demand more from him. He was Simon, a man like the men round him, and going to die, as all men are going to die.

He only became aware of what was going on outside him, when he saw that a woman had come in, and was standing in the midst of the cleared floor, looking round her. She was a short, broad old woman, in the clothes of the Lapps, and she took her stand with such majesty and fierceness as if she owned the whole place. It was obvious that most of the people knew her, and were a little afraid of her, although a few laughed; the din of the dancing-room stopped when she spoke.

"Where is my son?" she asked in a high shrill voice, like a bird's. The next moment her eyes fell on Simon himself, and she steered through the crowd, which opened up before her, stretched out her old skinny, dark hand, and took him by the elbow. "Come home with me now," she said. "You need not dance here tonight. You may be dancing a high enough dance soon."

Simon drew back, for he thought that she was drunk. But as she looked him straight in the face with her yellow eyes, it seemed to him that he had met her before, and that he might do well in listening to her. The old woman pulled him with her across the floor, and he followed her without a word. "Do not birch your boy too badly, Sunniva," one of the men in the room cried to her. "He has done no harm, he only wanted to look at the dance."

At the same moment as they came out through the door, there was an alarm in the street, a flock of people came running down it, and one of them, as he turned into the house, knocked against Simon, looked at him and the old woman, and ran on.

While the two walked along the street, the old woman lifted up her skirt, and put the hem of it into the boy's hand. "Wipe your hand on my skirt," she said. They had not gone far before they came to a small wooden house, and stopped; the door to it was so low that they must bend to get through it. As the Lapp-woman went in before Simon, still holding on to his arm, the boy looked up for a moment. The night had grown misty; there was a wide ring round the moon.

The old woman's room was narrow and dark, with but one small window to it; a lantern stood on the floor and lighted it up dimly. It was all filled with reindeer skins and wolf skins, and with reindeer horn, such as the Lapps use to make their carved buttons and knife-handles, and the air in here was rank and stifling. As soon as they were in, the woman turned to Simon, took hold of his head, and with her crooked fingers parted his hair and combed it down in Lapp fashion. She clapped a Lapp cap on him and stood back to glance at him. "Sit down on my stool, now," she said. "But first take out your knife." She was so commanding in voice and manner that the boy could not but choose to do as she told him; he sat down on the stool, and he could not take his eyes off her face, which was flat and brown, and as if smeared with dirt in its net of fine wrinkles. As he sat there he heard many people come along outside, and stop by the house; then someone knocked at the door, waited a moment and knocked again. The old woman stood and listened, as still as a mouse.

"Nay," said the boy and got up. "This is no good, for it is me that they are after. It will be better for you to let me go out to them." "Give me your knife," said she. When he handed it to her, she stuck it straight into her thumb, so that the blood spouted out, and she let it drip all over her skirt. "Come in, then," she cried.

The door opened, and two of the Russian sailors came and stood in the opening; there were more people outside. "Has anybody come in here?" they asked. "We are after a man who has killed our mate, but he has run away from us. Have you seen or heard anybody this way?" The old Lapp-woman turned upon them, and her eyes shone like gold in the lamplight. "Have I seen or heard anyone?" she cried, "I have heard you shriek murder all over the town. You frightened me, and my poor silly boy there, so that I cut my thumb as I was ripping the skin-rug that I sew. The boy is too scared to help me, and the rug is all ruined. I shall make you pay me for that. If you are looking for a murderer, come in and search my house for me, and I shall know you when we meet again." She was so furious that she danced where she stood, and jerked her head like an angry bird of prey.

The Russian came in, looked round the room, and at her and her blood-stained hand and skirt. "Do not put a curse on us now, Sunniva," he said timidly. "We know that you can do many things when you like. Here is a mark to pay you for the blood you have spilled." She stretched out her hand, and he placed a piece of money in it. She spat on it. "Then go, and there shall be no bad blood between us," said Sunniva, and shut the door after them. She stuck her thumb in her mouth, and chuckled a little.

The boy got up from his stool, stood straight up before her and stared into her face. He felt as if he were swaying high up in the air, with but a small hold. "Why have you helped me?" he asked her. "Do you not know?" she answered. "Have you not recognised me yet? But you will remember the peregrine falcon which was caught in the tackle-yarn of your boat, the *Charlotte,* as she sailed in the Mediterranean. That day you climbed up by the shrouds of the top-gallantmast to help her out, in a stiff wind, and with a high sea. That falcon was me. We Lapps often fly in such a manner, to see the world. When I first met you I was on my way to Africa, to see my younger sister and her children. She is a falcon too, when she chooses. By that time she was living at Takaunga, within an old ruined tower, which down there they call a minaret." She swathed a corner of her skirt round her thumb, and bit at it. "We do not forget," she said. "I hacked your thumb, when you took hold of me; it is only fair that I should cut my thumb for you tonight."

She came close to him, and gently rubbed her two brown, claw-like fingers against his forehead. "So you are a boy," she said, "who will kill a man rather than be late to meet your sweetheart? We hold together, the females of this earth. I shall mark your forehead now, so that the girls will know of that, when they look at you, and they will like you for it." She played with the boy's hair, and twisted it round her finger.

"Listen now, my little bird," said she. "My great grandson's brother-in-law is lying with his boat by the landing-place at this moment; he is to take a consignment of skins out to a Danish boat. He will bring you back to your boat, in time, before your mate comes. The *Hebe* is sailing tomorrow morning, is it not so? But when you are aboard, give him back my cap for me." She took up his knife, wiped it in her skirt and handed it to him. "Here is your knife," she said. "You will stick it into no more men; you will not need to, for from now you will sail the seas like a faithful seaman. We have enough trouble with our sons as it is."

The bewildered boy began to stammer his thanks to her. "Wait," said she, "I shall make you a cup of coffee, to bring back your wits, while I wash your jacket." She went and rattled an old copper kettle upon the fireplace. After a while she handed him a hot, strong, black drink in a cup without a handle to it. "You have drunk with Sunniva now," she said; "you have drunk down a little wisdom, so that in the future all your thoughts shall not fall like raindrops into the salt sea."

When he had finished and set down the cup, she led him to the door and opened it for him. He was surprised to see that it was almost clear morning. The house was so high up that the boy could see the sea from it, and a milky mist about it. He gave her his hand to say good-bye.

She stared into his face. "We do not forget," she said. "And you, you knocked me on the head there, high up in the mast. I shall give you that blow back." With that she smacked him on the ear as hard as she could, so that his head swam. "Now we are quits," she said, gave him a great, mischievous, shining glance, and a little push down the doorstep, and nodded to him.

In this way the sailor-boy got back to his ship, which was to sail the next morning, and lived to tell the story.

THE PEARLS

ABOUT EIGHTY YEARS AGO a young officer in the guards, the youngest son of an old country family, married, in Copenhagen, the daughter of a rich wool merchant whose father had been a peddler and had come to town from Jutland. In those days such a marriage was an unusual thing. There was much talk of it, and a song was made about it, and sung in the streets.

The bride was twenty years old, and a beauty, a big girl with black hair and a high colour, and a distinction about her as if she were made from whole timber. She had two old unmarried aunts, sisters of her grandfather the peddler, whom the growing fortune of the family had stopped short in a career of hard work and thrift, and made to sit in state in a parlour. When the elder of them first heard rumours of her niece's engagement she went and paid her a visit, and in the course of the conversation told her a story.

"When I was a child, my dear," she said, "young Baron Rosenkrantz became engaged to a wealthy goldsmith's daughter. Have you heard such a thing? Your great-grandmother knew her. The bridegroom had a twin sister, who was a lady at Court. She drove to the goldsmith's house to see the bride. When she had left again, the girl said to her lover: 'Your sister laughed at my frock, and because, when she spoke French, I could not answer. She has a hard heart, I saw that. If we are to be happy you must never see her again, I could not bear it.' The young man, to comfort her, promised that he would never see his sister again. Soon afterwards, on a Sunday, he took the girl to dine with his mother. As he drove her home she said to him: 'Your mother had tears in her eyes, when she looked at me. She has hoped for another wife for you. If you love me, you must break with your mother.' Again the enamoured young man promised to do as she wished, although it cost him much, for his mother was a widow, and he was her only son. The same week he sent his valet with a bouquet to his bride. Next day she said to him: 'I cannot stand the mien your valet has when he looks at me. You must send him away at the first of the month.' 'Mademoiselle,' said Baron Rosenkrantz, 'I cannot have a wife who lets herself be affected by my valet's mien. Here is your ring. Farewell forever.'"

While the old woman spoke she kept her little glittering eyes upon her niece's face. She had an energetic nature and had long ago made up her mind to live for others, and she had established herself as the conscience of the family. But in reality she was, with no hopes or fears of her own, a vigorous old moral parasite on the whole clan, and particularly on the younger members of it. Jensine, the bride, was a full-blooded young person and a gratifying object to a parasite. Moreover, the young and the old maid had many qualities in common. Now the girl went on pouring out coffee with a quiet face, but behind it she was furious, and said to herself: "Aunt Maren shall be paid back for this." All the same, as was often the case, the aunt's admonition went deep into her, and she pondered it in her heart.

After the wedding, in the Cathedral of Copenhagen, on a fine June day, the newly married couple went away to Norway for their wedding trip. They sailed as far north as Hardanger. At that time a journey to Norway was a romantic undertaking, and Jensine's friends asked her why they did not go to Paris, but she herself was pleased to start her married life in the wilderness, and to be alone with her husband. She did not, she thought, need or want any further new impressions or experiences. And in her heart she added: God help me.

The gossips of Copenhagen would have it that the bridegroom had married for money, and the bride for a name, but they were all wrong. The match was a love affair, and the honeymoon, tech-

nically, an idyll. Jensine would never have married a man whom
she did not love; she held the god of love in great respect, and had
already for some years sent a little daily prayer to him: "Why
doest thou tarry?" But now she reflected that he had perhaps
granted her her prayer with a vengeance, and that her books had
given her but little information as to the real nature of love.

The scenery of Norway, amongst which she had her first experience of the passion, contributed to the overpowering impression of it. The country was at its loveliest. The sky was blue, the
bird-cherry flowered everywhere and filled the air with sweet and
bitter fragrance, and the nights were so light that you could see
to read at midnight. Jensine, in a crinoline and with an alpen-
stock, climbed many steep paths on her husband's arm—or alone,
for she was strong and lightfooted. She stood upon the summits,
her clothes blown about her, and wondered and wondered. She
had lived in Denmark, and for a year in a pension in Lubeck, and
her idea of the earth was that it must spread out horizontally, flat
or undulating, before her feet. But in these mountains everything
seemed strangely to stand up vertically, like some great animal
that rises on its hind legs—and you know not whether to play, or
to crush you. She was higher than she had ever been, and the air
went to her head like wine. Also, wherever she looked there was
running water, rushing from the sky-high mountains into the
lakes, in silvery rivulets or in roaring falls, rainbow-adorned. It
was as if Nature itself was weeping, or laughing, aloud.

At first all this was so new to her that she felt her old ideas of
the world blown about in all directions, like her skirts and her
shawl. But soon the impressions converged into a sensation of the
deepest alarm, a panic such as she had never experienced.

She had been brought up in an atmosphere of prudence and
foresight. Her father was an honest tradesman, afraid both to

lose his own money, and to let down his customers. Sometimes this double risk had thrown him into melancholia. Her mother had been a God-fearing young woman, a member of a pietistic sect; her two old aunts were persons of strict moral principle, with an eye to the opinions of the world. At home Jensine had at times believed herself a daring spirit, and had longed for adventure. But in this wildly romantic landscape, and taken by surprise and overwhelmed by wild, unknown, formidable forces within her own heart, she looked round for support. Where was she to find it? Her young husband, who had brought her there, and with whom she was all alone, could not help her. He was, on the contrary, the cause of the turbulence in her, and he was also, in her eyes, pre-eminently exposed to the dangers of the outward world. For very soon after her marriage Jensine realized—as she had perhaps dimly known from their first meeting—that he was a human being entirely devoid, and incapable, of fear.

She had read in books of heroes, and had admired them with all her heart. But Alexander was not like the heroes of her books. He was not braving, or conquering, the dangers of this world, but he was unaware of their existence. To him the mountains were a playground, and all the phenomena of life, love itself included, were his playmates within it. "In a hundred years, my darling," he said to her, "it will all be one." She could not imagine how he had managed to live till now, but then she knew that his life had been, in every way, different from hers. Now she felt, with horror, that here she was, within a world of undreamt of heights and depths, delivered into the hands of a person totally ignorant of the law of gravitation. Under the circumstances her feelings for him intensified into both a deep moral indignation, as if he had deliberately betrayed her, and into an extreme tenderness, such as she would have felt towards an exposed, helpless child. These two passions were the strongest of which her nature was capable; they took speed with her, and developed into a possession. She recalled the fairy tale of the boy who is sent out in the world to learn to be afraid, and it seemed to her that for her own sake and his, in self-defense as well as in order to protect and save him, she must teach her husband to fear.

He knew nothing of what went on in her. He was in love with her, and he admired and respected her. She was innocent and pure; she sprang from a stock of people capable of making a fortune by their wits; she could speak French and German, and knew history and geography. For all these qualities he had a religious reverence. He was prepared for surprises in her, for their acquaintance was but slight, and they had not been alone together in a room more than three or four times before their wedding. Besides, he did not pretend to understand women, but held their incalculableness to be part of their grace. The moods and caprices of his young wife all confirmed in him the assurance, with which she had inspired him at their first meeting, that she was what he needed in life. But he wanted to make her his friend, and reflected that he had never had a real friend in his life. He did not talk to her of his love affairs of the past—indeed he could not have spoken of them to her if he had wanted to—but in other ways he told her as much as he could remember of himself and his life. One day he recounted how he had gambled in Baden-Baden, risked his last cent, and then won. He did not know that she thought, by his side: "He is really a thief, or if not that, a receiver of stolen goods, and no better than a thief." At other times he made fun of the debts he had had, and the trouble he had had to take to avoid meeting his tailor. This talk sounded really uncanny to Jensine's ears. For to her debts were an abomination, and that he should have lived on in the midst of them without anxiety, trusting to fortune to pay up for him, seemed against nature. Still, she reflected, she herself, the rich girl he married, had come along in time, as the willing tool of fortune, to justify his trust in the eyes of his tailor himself. He told her of a duel that he had fought with a German officer, and showed her a scar from it. As, at the end of it all, he took her in his arms, on the high hilltops, for all the skies to see them, in her heart she cried: "If it be possible, let this cup pass from me."

When Jensine set out to teach her husband to fear, she had the tale of Aunt Maren in her mind, and she made the vow that she would never cry quarter, but that this should be his part. As the relation between herself and him was to her the central factor of existence, it was natural that she should first try to scare him with the possibility of losing her. She was an unsophisticated girl, and resorted to simple measures.

From now on she became more reckless than he in their climbs. She would stand on the edge of a precipice, leaning on her parasol, and ask him how deep it was to the bottom. She balanced across narrow, brittle bridges, high above foaming streams, and chattered to him the while. She went out rowing in a small boat, on the lake, in a thunderstorm. At nights she dreamed about the perils of the days, and woke up with a shriek, so that he took her in his arms to comfort her. But her daring did her no good. Her husband was surprised and enchanted at the change of the demure maiden into a Valkyrie. He put it down to the influence of married life, and felt not a little proud. She herself, in the end, wondered whether she was not driven on in her exploits by his pride and praise as much as by her resolution to conquer him. Then she was angry with herself, and with all women, and she pitied him, and all men.

Sometimes Alexander would go out fishing. These were welcome opportunities to Jensine to be alone and collect her thoughts. So the young bride would wander about alone, in a tartan frock, a small figure in the hills. Once or twice, in these walks, she thought of her father, and the memory of his anxious concern for her brought tears to her eyes. But she sent him away again; she must be left alone to settle matters of which he could know nothing.

One day, when she sat and rested on a stone, a group of children, who were herding goats, approached and stared at her. She called them up and gave them sweets from her reticule. Jensine had adored her dolls, and as much as a modest girl of the period dared, she had longed for children of her own. Now she thought with sudden dismay: "I shall never have children! As long as I must strain myself against him in this way, we will never have a child." The idea distressed her so deeply that she got up and walked away.

On another of her lonely walks she came to think of a young man in her father's office who had loved her. His name was Peter Skov. He was a brilliant young man of business, and she had known him all her life. She now recalled how, when she had had the measles, he had sat and read to her every day, and how he had accompanied her when she went out skating, and had been distressed lest she should catch cold, or fall, or go through the ice. From where she stood she could see her husband's small figure in the distance. "Yes," she thought, "this is the best thing I can do. When I come back to Copenhagen, then, by my honour, which is still my own"—although she had doubts on this point—"Peter Skov shall be my lover."

On their wedding day Alexander had given his bride a string of pearls. It had belonged to his grandmother, who had come from Germany and who was a beauty and a *bel esprit*. She had left it to him to give to his future wife. Alexander had talked much to her of his grandmother. He did, he said, first fall in love with her because she was a little like his grandmama. He asked her to wear the pearls every day. Jensine had never had a string of pearls before, and she was proud of hers. Lately, when she had so often been in need of support, she had got into the habit of twisting the string, and pulling it with her lips. "If you go on doing that," Alexander said one day, "you will break the string." She looked at him. It was the first time that she had known him to foresee disaster. "He has loved his grandmother," she thought, "or is it that you must be dead to carry weight with this man?" Since then she often thought of the old woman. She, too, had come from her own milieu and had been a stranger in her husband's family and circle of friends. She had managed to get this string of pearls from Alexander's grandfather, and to be remembered by it down through the generations. Were the pearls, she wondered, a token of victory, or of submission? Jensine came to look upon Grandmama as her best friend in the family. She would have liked to pay her a grand-daughterly visit, and to consult her on her own troubles.

The honeymoon was nearing its end, and that strange warfare, the existence of which was known to one of the belligerents only, had come to no decision. Both the young people were sad to go away. Only now did Jensine fully realize the beauty of the landscape round her, for, after all, in the end she had made it her ally. Up here, she reflected, the dangers of the world were obvious, ever in sight. In Copenhagen life looked secure, but might prove to be even more redoubtable. She thought of her pretty house, waiting for her there, with lace curtains, chandeliers and linen cupboards. She could not at all tell what life within it would be like.

The day before they were to sail they were staying in a small village, from where it was six hours' drive in a cariole down to the landing-place of the coast steamer. They had been out before breakfast. When Jensine sat down and loosened her bonnet, the string of pearls caught in her bracelet, and the pearls sprang all over the floor, as if she had burst into a rain of tears. Alexander got down on his hands and knees, and, as he picked them up one by one, placed them in her lap.

She sat in a kind of mild panic. She had broken the one thing in the world that she had been afraid of breaking. What omen did that have for them? "Do you know how many there were?" she asked him. "Yes," he said from the floor, "Grandpapa gave Grandmama the string at their golden wedding, with a pearl for each of their fifty years. But afterwards he added one every year, at her birthday. There are fifty-two. It is easy to remember; it is the number of cards in a pack." At last they got them all collected and wrapped them up in his silk handkerchief. "Now I cannot put them on till I get to Copenhagen," she said.

At that moment their landlady came in with the coffee. She observed the catastrophe and at once offered to assist them. The shoemaker in the village, she said, could do up the pearls for them. Two years ago an English lord and his lady, with a party, had travelled in the mountains, and when the young lady broke her string of pearls, in the same way, he had strung them for her to her perfect satisfaction. He was an honest old man, although very poor, and a cripple. As a young man he had got lost in a snowstorm in the hills, and been found only two days later, and they had had to cut off both his feet. Jensine said that she would take her pearls to the shoemaker, and the landlady showed her the way to his house.

She walked down alone, while her husband was strapping their boxes, and found the shoemaker in his little dark workshop. He was a small, thin, old man in a leather apron, with a shy, sly smile in a face harassed by long suffering. She counted the pearls up to him, and gravely confided them into his hands. He looked at them, and promised to have them ready by next midday. After she had settled with him she kept sitting on a small chair, with her hands in her lap. To say something, she asked him the name of the English lady who had broken her string of pearls, but he did not remember it.

She looked round at the room. It was poor and bare, with a couple of religious pictures nailed on the wall. In a strange way it seemed to her that here she had come home. An honest man, hard tried by destiny, had passed his long years in this little room. It was a place where people worked, and bore troubles patiently, in anxiety for their daily bread. She was still so near to her school books that she remembered them all, and now she began to think of what she had read about deep-water fish, which have been so much used to bear the weight of many thousand fathoms of water, that if they are raised to the surface, they will burst. Was she herself, she wondered, such a deep-water fish that felt at home only under the pressure of existence? And her father, her grandfather and his people before him, had they been the same? What was a deep-water fish to do, she thought on, if she were married to one of those salmon which here she had seen springing in the water-falls? Or to a flying-fish? She said good-bye to the old shoemaker, and walked off.

As she was going home she caught sight, on the path in front of her, of a small stout man in a black hat and coat who walked on briskly. She remembered that she had seen him before; she even believed that he was staying in the same house as she. There was a seat by the path, from which one had a magnificent view.

The man in black sat down, and Jensine, whose last day in the mountains it was, sat down on the other end of the seat. The stranger lifted his hat a little to her. She had believed him to be an elderly man, but now saw that he could not be much over thirty. He had an energetic face and clear, penetrating eyes. After a moment he spoke to her, with a little smile. "I saw you coming out from the shoemaker's," he said. "You have not lost your sole in the mountains?" "No, I brought him some pearls," said Jensine. "You brought him pearls?" said the stranger humorously. "That is what I go to collect from him." She wondered if he were a bit deranged. "That old man," said he, "has got, in his hut, a big store of our old national treasures—pearls if you like—which I happen to be collecting just now. In case you want children's tales, there is not a man in Norway who can give you a better lot than our shoemaker. He once dreamed of becoming a student, and a poet—do you know that?—but he was hard hit by destiny, and had to take to a shoemaker's trade."

After a pause he said: "I have been told that you and your husband come from Denmark, on your wedding trip. That is an unusual thing to do; these mountains are high and dangerous. Who of you two was it who desired to come here? Was it you?" "Yes," said she. "Yes," said the stranger. "I thought so. That he might be the bird, which upwards soars, and you the breeze, which carries him along. Do you know that quotation? Does it tell you anything?" "Yes," said she, somewhat bewildered. "Upwards," said he, and sat back, silent, with his hands upon his walking-stick. After a little while he went on: "The summits! Who knows? We two are pitying the shoemaker for his bad luck, that he had to give up his dreams of being a poet, of fame and a great name. How do we know but that he has had the best of luck? Greatness, the applause of the masses! Indeed, my young lady, perhaps they are better left alone. Perhaps in common trade they cannot reasonably purchase a shoemaker's sign board, and the knowledge of soling. One may do well in getting rid of them at cost price. What do you think, Madam?" "I think that you are right," she said slowly. He gave her a sharp glance from a pair of ice-blue eyes.

"Indeed," said he. "Is that your advice, on this fair summer day? Cobbler, stay by your last. One should do better, you think, in making up pills and draughts for the sick human beings, and cattle, of this world?" He chuckled a little. "It is a very good jest. In a hundred years it will be written in a book: A little lady from Denmark gave him the advice to stay by his last. Unfortunately, he did not follow it. Good-bye, Madam, good-bye." With these words he got up, and walked on. She saw his black figure grow smaller amongst the hills. The landlady had come out to hear if she had found the shoemaker. Jensine looked after the stranger. "Who was that gentleman?" she asked. The woman shaded her eyes with her hand. "Oh, indeed," said she. "He is a learned man, a great man, he is here to collect old stories and songs. He was an apothecary once. But he has had a theatre in Bergen, and written plays for it, too. His name is Herr Ibsen."

In the morning news came up from the landing-place that the boat would be in sooner than expected, and they had to start in haste. The landlady sent her small son to the shoemaker to fetch Jensine's pearls. When the travellers were already seated in the cariole, he brought them, wrapped in a leaf from a book, with a waxed string round them. Jensine undid them, and was about to count them, but thought better of it, and instead clasped the string round her throat. "Ought you not to count them?" Alexander asked her. She gave him a great glance. "No," she said. She was silent on the drive. His words rang in her ears: "Ought you not to count them?" She sat by his side, a triumphator. Now she knew what a triumphator felt like.

Alexander and Jensine came back to Copenhagen at a time when most people were out of town and there were no great social functions. But she had many visits from the wives of his young military friends, and the young people went together to the Tivoli of Copenhagen in the summer evenings. Jensine was made much of by all of them.

Her house lay by one of the old canals of the town and looked over to the Thorwaldsen Museum. Sometimes she would stand by the window, gaze at the boats, and think of Hardanger. During all this time she had not taken off her pearls or counted them. She was sure that there would at least be one pearl missing. She imagined that she felt the weight, on her throat, different from before. What would it be, she thought, which she had sacrificed for her victory over her husband? A year, or two years, of their married life, before their golden wedding? This golden wedding seemed a long way off, but still each year was precious; and how was she to part with one of them?

In the last months of this summer people began to discuss the possibility of war. The Schleswig-Holstein question had become imminent. A Danish Royal Proclamation, of March, had repudiated all German claims upon Schleswig. Now in July a German note demanded, on pain of federal execution, the withdrawal of the Proclamation.

Jensine was an ardent patriot and loyal to the King, who had given the people its free constitution. The rumours put her into the highest agitation. She thought the young officers, Alexander's friends, frivolous in their light, boastful talk of the country's danger. If she wanted to debate the crisis seriously she had to go to her own people. With her husband she could not talk of it at all, but in her heart she knew that he was as convinced of Denmark's invincibility as of his own immortality.

She read the newspapers from beginning to end. One day in the *Berlingske Tidende* she came upon the following phrase: "The moment is grave to the nation. But we have trust in our just cause, and we are without fear."

It was, perhaps, the words "without fear" which now made her collect her courage. She sat down in her chair by the window, took off her pearls and put them in her lap. She sat for a moment with her hands folded upon them, as in prayer. Then she counted them. There were fifty-three pearls on her string. She could not believe her own eyes, and counted them over again; but there was no mistake, there were fifty-three pearls and the one in the middle was the biggest.

Jensine sat for a long time in her chair, quite giddy. Her mother, she knew, had believed in the Devil. At this moment the daughter did the same. She would not have been surprised had she heard laughter from behind the sofa. Had the powers of the universe, she thought, combined, here, to make fun of a poor girl?

When she could again collect her thoughts, she remembered that before she had been given the necklace, the old goldsmith of her husband's family had repaired the clasp of it. He would therefore know the pearls, and might tell her what to believe. But she was so thoroughly scared that she dared not go to him herself, and only a few days later she asked Peter Skov, who came to pay her a visit, to take the string to him.

Peter returned and told her that the goldsmith had put on his spectacles to examine the pearls, and then, in amazement, had declared that there was one more than when he had last seen them. "Yes, Alexander gave me that," Jensine interrupted him, blushing deeply at her own lie. Peter reflected, as the goldsmith had done, that it was a cheap generosity in a lieutenant to make the heiress he had married a rich present. But he repeated to her the old man's words. "Mr. Alexander," he had declared, "shows himself a rare judge of pearls. I shall not hesitate to pronounce this one pearl worth as much as all the others put together." Jensine, terrified but smiling, thanked Peter, but he went away sadly, for he felt as if he had annoyed or frightened her.

She had not been feeling well for some time, and when, in September, they had a spell of heavy, sultry weather in Copenhagen, it left her pale and sleepless. Her father and her two old aunts were upset about her and tried to make her come and stay at his villa on the Strandvej, outside town. But she would not leave her own house or her husband, nor would she, she thought, ever get well, until she had come to the bottom of the mystery of the pearls. After a week she made up her mind to write to the shoe-maker at Odda. If, as Herr Ibsen had told her, he had been a student and a poet, he would be able to read, and would answer her letter. It seemed to her that in her present situation she had no friend in the world but this crippled old man. She wished that she could go back to his workshop, to the bare walls and the three-legged chair. She dreamed at night that she was there. He had smiled kindly at her; he knew many children's tales. He might know how to comfort her. Only for a moment she trembled at the idea that he might be dead, and that then she would never know.

Within the following weeks the shadow of the war grew deeper. Her father was worrying over the prospects and about King Frederik's health. Under these new circumstances the old merchant began to take pride in the fact that he had his daughter married to a soldier, which before had been far from his mind. He and her old aunts showed Alexander and Jensine great respect.

One day, half against her own will, Jensine asked Alexander straight out if he thought there would be war. "Yes," he answered quickly and confidently, "there will be war. It could not be avoided." He went on to whistle a bit of a soldier's song. The sight of her face made him stop. "Are you afrightened of it?" he asked. She considered it hopeless, and even unseemly, to explain to him her feelings about the war. "Are you frightened for my sake?" he asked her again. She turned her head away. "To be a hero's widow," he said, "would be just the part for you, my dear." Her eyes filled with tears, as much of anger as of woe. Alexander came and took her hand. "If I fall," he said, "it will be a consolation to me to remember that I have kissed you as often as you would let me." He did so now, once more, and added: "Will it be a consolation to you?" Jensine was an honest girl. When she was questioned she tried to find the truthful answer. Now she thought: Would it be a consolation to me? But she could not, in her heart, find the reply.

With all this Jensine had much to think of, so that she half forgot about the shoemaker, and, when one morning she found his letter on the breakfast table, she for a minute took it to be a mendicant's letter, of which she got many. The next moment she grew very pale. Her husband, opposite her, asked her what was the matter. She gave him no reply, but got up, went into her own small sitting-room, and opened the letter by the fireplace. The characters of it, carefully printed, recalled to her the old man's face, as if he had sent her his portrait.

"Dear young Danish Missus," the letter went.

"Yes, I put the pearl onto your necklace. I meant to give you a small surprise. You made such a fuss about your pearls, when you brought them to me, as if you were afraid that I should steal one of them from you. Old people, as well as young, must have a little fun at times. If I have frightened you, I beg that you will forgive me all the same. This pearl I got two years ago, when I strung the English lady's necklace. I forgot to put the one in, and only found it afterwards. It has been with me for two years, but I have no use for it. It is better that it should be with a young lady. I remember that you sat in my chair, quite young and pretty. I wish you good luck, and that something pleasant may happen to you on the very same day as you get this letter. And may you wear the pearl long, with a humble heart, a firm trust in the Lord God, and a friendly thought of me, who am old, here up at Odda. Good-bye.

"Your friend, Peiter Viken."

Jensine had been reading the letter with her elbows on the mantelpiece, to steady herself. As she looked up, she met the grave eyes of her own image in the looking-glass above it. They were severe; they might be saying: "You are really a thief, or if not that, a receiver of stolen goods, and no better than a thief." She stood for a long time, nailed to the spot. At last she thought: "It is all over. Now I know that I shall never conquer these people, who know neither care nor fear. It is as in the Bible; I shall bruise their heel, but they shall bruise my head. And Alexander, as far as he is concerned, ought to have married the English lady."

To her own deep surprise she found that she did not mind. Alexander himself had become a very small figure in the background of life; what he did or thought mattered not in the least. That she herself had been made a fool of did not matter. "In a hundred years," she thought, "it will all be one."

What mattered then? She tried to think of the war, but found that the war did not matter either. She felt a strange giddiness, as if the room was sinking away round her, but not unpleasantly. "Was there," she thought, "nothing remarkable left under the visiting moon?" At the word of the visiting moon the eyes of the image in the looking-glass opened wide; the two young women stared at one another intensely. Something, she decided, was of great importance, which had come into the world now, and in a hundred years would still remain. The pearls. In a hundred years, she saw, a young man would hand them over to his wife and tell the young woman her own story about them, just as Alexander had given them to her, and had told her of his grandmother.

The thought of these two young people, in a hundred years' time, moved her to such tenderness that her eyes filled with tears, and made her happy, as if they had been old friends of hers, whom she had found again. "Not cry quarter?" she thought. "Why not? Yes, I shall cry as high as I can. I cannot, now, remember the reason why I would not cry."

The very small figure of Alexander, by the window in the other room said to her: "Here is the eldest of your aunts coming down the street with a big bouquet."

Slowly, slowly Jensine took her eyes off the looking-glass, and came back to the world of the present. She went to the window. "Yes," she said, "they are from Bella Vista," which was the name of her father's villa. From their window the husband and wife looked down into the street.

THE INVINCIBLE

SLAVE-OWNERS

"CE PAUVRE JEAN," said an old Russian General with a dyed beard on a summer evening of 1875 in the drawing-room of a hotel at Baden-Baden. "This poor Jean. He is really an excellent fellow, quite decidedly a most excellent person. You know Jean, of course, the waiter at my table, the oldest waiter of the hotel? Well, I shall tell you what a good fellow he is. I am in the habit of taking, every morning, a nectarine with my coffee —a nectarine, mind you, no peach or apricot for me—but it must be really good, ripe, yet not over-ripe. This morning, now, Jean came up and spoke to me. He was white, I assure you; the man was as white as a corpse. I thought that he had been taken ill. 'Your Excellency,' he says, 'it is terrible,' and then he can say no more. 'What is terrible, my friend?' I ask. 'Is there a European war?' 'No,' he says, 'but it is terrible; something awful has happened. Your Excellency, there are no nectarines to be had today.' And at that two big tears do roll down his cheeks. Yes, he is a good fellow."

The person to whom the General spoke was a young Dane, named Axel Leth, a good-looking and well-dressed young man, who did not talk much himself, and for that reason was often chosen as a listener by the people of the watering place who had something to say.

As the General had finished his story an old English lady came up and joined the group. For her benefit the Russian repeated the tale of Jean and the nectarine. The Englishwoman listened with the expression of scorn and contempt with which she received all communications at this time of the day.

"*A qui le dites-vous?*" she asked. "Jean? I knew him before you ever did. Nine years ago he cut his thumb on a carving-knife while serving me a chicken, and I myself bandaged it for him. He would not let me do it. He was genuinely indignant and shocked that

127

I should take trouble about him. I honestly believe that the fool would have preferred to lose his thumb. He would go through fire and water for me ever since, of course, would die for me, in fact."

She did not wait for any answer from the General, but turned to young Leth and gave him a little smile to emphasize her indifference to the Russian. "I promised you last night," she said, "to tell you more of the review at Munich." Axel, who had been brought up by his grandmother and had been taught to pay elderly ladies attention, put on an expectant face.

"To me," said the old lady, "it was particularly affecting. Because I understand King Ludwig. The swan-hermit! A French poet has addressed him: *'Seul roi de ce siècle, salut!'* That accurately expresses my own feelings. To me his solitude at Neuschwanstein is exquisite and majestic, sublime. He cannot live at Munich. He cannot breath the air polluted by the crowd, nor bear the rank smell of it. He cannot enjoy art in the presence of the profane, so at the Residenz Theatre performances are often commanded for him alone. He is a true aristocrat. To the High Order of the Defenders of the Immaculate Conception of the Blessed Virgin, of which he is grand master, no candidate is eligible who cannot prove his sixty-four quarterings. But at Neuschwanstein, high above the common world, the King is happy. In that mountain air and silence he wanders, dreams and meditates. There he feels near God."

"He is not very popular, I am told," said the General airily.

"Who told you?" returned the Englishwoman with hauteur. "No one, surely, who has been to Munich. The emotion of the crowd waiting to see their King was touching to me. Few of them had seen him before; he shows himself so rarely. When he appeared, on a white horse, a storm of enthusiasm broke. It was as if the hearts were running forth to him, like a wave. Tears were streaming down these rough, tanned faces of artisans and labourers; children were lifted in hard dirty hands so that he should see them; coarse voices were breaking to the general cry of 'Long live the King.' An unforgettable day."

The General said nothing, and Axel, glancing at him, saw his face change. He was gazing with surprise and exultation towards the door. From its expression the young man guessed that an unknown, pretty woman had come in. The eyes of the English lady took the same direction, her old face, too, immediately altered. Axel turned round. Two women, whom till now he had never seen at the resort, evidently a young lady of the best society with her *dame de compagnie* or governess, had entered the room.

The first, who at once captured the attention of the assembly, was a very young beauty of such freshness, that it was as if she was sweeping with her, into the closely furnished, velvet-hung room, a sea breeze or a summer shower, and Axel remembered a reviewer's remark about a young German actress: 'She enters the stage with a wild landscape at her heels.' The astonishment and admiration which her loveliness aroused were, at the next moment, accompanied by a little smile of wonder or mockery, because her slender, forceful, abundant figure was dressed up, two or three years behind her age, in the short skirt of a schoolgirl, and she wore her hair down her back. The clothes gave her a curious likeness to a doll, and inspired in onlookers the sentiment of humourous tenderness with which one looks at a big, beautiful doll.

The girl was in herself rather tall than short, a high-stemmed rose. Indeed it looked as if she had, at the moment when her Maker was holding her up for contemplation, slid through His mighty hand, and in this movement had all her young forms gently pushed upwards. The slight calves of her delicate legs—in white stockings and neat little shoes—were set high up, so was the immature fullness of the hips, while the knees and thighs, which, in her quick walk, showed through the flounces of her frock, were narrow and straight. Her young bosom strutted just below the armpits, high above a slim waist. Her milk-white throat was long and round, strangely dignified and monumental in one so young. Her hair itself seemed averse to the law of gravitation. Behind the ribbon that held it back from the forehead it streamed out almost horizontally. This rich hair was of a rare colour, a pale, coraline red, with no yellow in it, such as is found in sea-shells. The girl's fair, smooth, rosy face had not a lie in it, no grain of powder or paint, and not a single wrinkle. The eyes, outlined by the thin black streak of the eyelashes, were set in it without a line, like two pieces of dark-blue glass. Her cheekbones were a little high, the nose, too, had an upward tilt. But by far the most striking feature in the face was the mouth, a thick, sullen, flaming mouth, like a red rose. Looking at it one might well imagine the whole straight, proud figure to exist only in order to carry this fresh, presumptuous mouth about the world.

She was dressed with precise neatness in a white muslin frock with a pink sash. She had a black velvet ribbon round her throat, but no ornament whatever. She walked quickly, in a defiant, disdainful gait, magnificently vital, as if at the same time, and with all her might, giving and holding back herself to the world. Axel, the dreamer, in his mind quoted a poem that he had read only a short time ago:

> D'un air placide et triomphant,
> Tu passes ton chemin, majestueuse enfant.

The lady who followed at the girl's heels was a distinguished person in black silk, with a thin gold watch chain down her narrow bust, and blue glasses. She was severe in all her lines, the model governess or duenna. Still she had something of her own, a cat-like suppleness of movement, and a quiet, grave determination. The two together made a picturesque group, and to accentuate the unity of it, the elder woman's austerely plaited hair had in it a faded reflection of the red within the girl's floating locks. It was as if the artist had found a little of the colour left upon his pallet and had been loath to waste such a glorious mixture.

"Nom d'un chien," said the General to Axel.

After supper he again came up to him, with two roses in his old cheeks, rejuvenated by the quickened circulation of his imagination.

"I can let you have," he said, "a few facts about our beauty." At that he gave her name, which, he explained, belonged to a very old family, and added a row of details about its history and connections. The girl's name was Marie, but her governess called her Mizzi. Mizzi's father, he believed, had been a famous gambler. He had, he was told, lately married a second time. "One does not need to be told that," the General went on, "the child is obviously the victim of a jealous stepmother—at that time of life when the venom in women inevitably strikes in and poisons their system —who would give her ratbane if she dared to, but has sent her off here instead, with that female Jesuit as a jailer. What do you think, my friend, does she birch her? It is both a deadly sin and a joke to dress up that young woman as a child; she would wear a tiara before any other woman in the room. What a walk! And what innocence! All the same she is furious with us all, and will get her own back. I wish I were your age."

There had been music in the drawing room; a lady had sung, and an elderly German gentleman had played a fugue by Bach. But as the clock on the mantelpiece struck ten, the governess gave the girl a glance and a few low, respectful words. Mizzi rose at once, like a soldier on parade. On her way to the door she dropped her little handkerchief. Two young men, one in black and one in uniform, threw themselves upon it. But Mizzi did not as much as look at them. It was the lady companion who demurely took it from them and thanked them with a ceremonious little bow, before she held the door open to the girl, let her pass before her, and was gone.

Late in the evening Axel went out on the terrace, smoked a cigar and looked at the lights of the town, and then up at the stars. He often did so.

The cadence of the lively conversation in the drawing-room was still in his ears, and he reflected that human talk is a centrifugal function, ever in flight outwards from what is on the talker's mind. He only knew the people of the resort from their conversations together; consequently he did not know them at all; neither did they know him. He was told by the other guests of the hotel that the General had been suspected of poisoning his wife. Of that he would not talk. But when he was alone, in his bed and his dreams: was the old General sincere, an honest murderer? He tried to imagine one after another of his acquaintances —the General, the old Englishwoman—asleep, such as they probably were at this hour. The idea was melancholy to him, and he took his thoughts off them again.

He turned them to the young girl, whom he had seen for the first time today. She too would be asleep now, and would be rosy in her sleep, fresh as her linen, with her eyelids firmly closed and the red hair spread over her pillow, grave, sleeping in the manner of a child, to whom sleep is a task, an earnest occupation. He thought of her for a long time, and felt that he might do so without offending her; it was not otherwise than a gardener walking in a rose garden by night. She was free now, to wander where she chose, and he wondered what she would be dreaming of. "Could I fall in love with her?" he asked himself. He had been in love before; that had even, in part, brought him to Baden-Baden, and he was so young that he believed he could never love again. But he wished that he were her brother, or an old friend, with a right to help her, if ever she would turn to him for help. He had been depressed, ashamed of himself, for being ill and in necessity of going to a watering place. In the night air on the terrace it seemed to him that there was hope and strength in the world still. It was as if a friend of his were asleep in the hotel behind him, and when she woke up the two would understand each other.

"And then," he thought sadly, "we shall probably part and go each our own way without ever having spoken together. Life is like that."

Within a few days the bees and butterflies of the watering place were humming round the new fair, fragrant rose, and the thin black prop to which it was tied. The difficulty of approach, and something pathetic in Mizzi's own figure, called upon the daring and chivalry of the courters. Each felt like Saint George with the dragon and the captive princess. The situation would have held infinite promise of piquancy if it had been possible to lure the princess into joining her partisans and playing a trick on the dragon. But it was found that she was unswervingly loyal to her duenna, and that not a smile, not a glance could be obtained behind Miss Rabe's back. The governess' distinguished figure took on an appalling aspect. Of what secret power was she possessed to hold a vigorous young person so completely in submission?

The old English lady took the wiser course, and graciously patronized the governess. Her strategy brought her a surprise.

She was genuinely struck with Miss Rabe's tact, talents and excellent principles, and proclaimed to all the world that this was the one governess within a thousand. She was also rewarded for her trouble by being for two or three days the most important person in the park of the Casino, for she could now introduce people to Mizzi. In this enterprise she unfolded the whole craft of an ancient *entremetteuse* of society, and for every favour counted herself paid in compliments and attentions. On account of their old friendship, Axel was the first young man whom she smilingly presented to the girl.

Axel, with some wonder and self irony, fell in love with Mizzi. It was a variety of love new to himself, more contemplative than possessive. He was even pleased to see her surrounded by admirers, since nothing becomes a pretty girl like success, and since she accepted the homage of the resort's *jeunesse dorée* with so much simplicity and dignity, as if she took their competitive zeal to be the normal manner of young men with a maiden, she only allowed her own vitality to swell a little within this her true element. His feelings also had in them an imaginative moment; he would often, dreamily, set the girl against a background of a book or a song or a familiar place in Denmark.

One thing within her in particular enchanted him—that she did blush so easily and deeply, for reasons of her own and incomprehensible to him. It was never a compliment or an ardent glance, nor a squeeze of her slim fingers at the end of a waltz, which called forth her blush. She looked her wooers quietly in the eyes, even when they themselves blushed and stuttered. But sometimes, while she sat by herself, listening to the music in the park, or while an old gentleman of the hotel entertained her with a discourse on politics, a slow, vehement flame would mount and spread all over her face, from the collar-bone to the roots of her hair, and make it glow and burn—as if she had been standing below a crimson church window—until the fire again slowly sank back and died out. It was in itself a pretty and unusual spectacle. But to Axel it was much more: a symbol and a mystery, a manifestation of her being, a mute avowal, more significant than any declaration. What forces within her own nature did the simple and strong creature suspect or dread to make all her blood change place at the apprehension?

His fancy played with the girl's blushes. He imagined her happy, spoiled, in the harmony of a home of her own, and wondered whether she would colour there in the same way. Over her needlework in a window, or on a walk with her husband, pausing to gaze at the view, would she suddenly redden like a morning sky? He thought: "What more divine, proud, generous, honest compliment could a newly married husband receive from his wife than this silent, unwilled rising of her blood?" It was dangerous as well. To an old husband it would be alarming; to a vain or weak man it might bode perdition. He was well aware of the hazard, since he himself, until he met her, had felt weak and worthless. And if, after five or ten years of married life, a husband should catch his wife blushing so deeply and silently at her own thoughts? What a summons, he thought, on the whole nature of a man— in a name mightier than that of the King.

At times he believed that his young girl would colour at a particularly conventional remark in the conversation, as if she were ashamed of the pretence and falsity of her surroundings. At that he rejoiced, for he had himself suffered by the sham of his world. He thought then: This fresh peach of a girl has got a ruthless respect for the truth; she is horrified at our frivolous mode of living—and longed to talk to her of the ideas that occupied his own mind.

All these were pleasing meditations. But there were other notions connected with Mizzi which made him heavy at heart. It happened, as in his mind he was moving the maiden about in the woods and the rooms of his home at Langeland, that the figure of Miss Rabe would accompany her, and refuse to leave the picture. The misgivings which that dark figure awoke in him were harder to deal with than the chimera of his day dreams, inasmuch as they were of a practical and palpable nature. For he might, he reasoned, fell the dragon and carry off Mizzi. It would be a sweet and glorious venture; it was what his rivals were all dreaming about. But he was a wise young man and looked deeper than they. When he rode away, was he sure that he would not be carrying off Miss Rabe on the pommel of his saddle?

He was an observer; it had amused him to find that the pretty girl had not lived a day, and probably was incapable of living a day, without an attendant at her heels. She had never opened a door herself, nor pulled out a chair at table or picked up her handkerchief when she dropped it, nor put on her own hat. Her absurd childish clothes, like her own dainty person, were exquisitely arranged and kept by someone else. When one day her sash became undone she tried to fix it, blushed and stood motionless until Miss Rabe hurried up and tied the bow for her. She must be, he reflected, dressed and undressed like a doll. Her helplessness was like that of a person without hands. Her whole existence was based upon the constant, watchful, indefatigable labour of slaves. Miss Rabe was the silent and omnipresent symbol of the system; therefore he dreaded her.

Axel was a wealthy young man, heir to a pleasant place in Denmark and in his own country a good match. But he was not rich according to the standard of the world in which he moved here. He decided, sadly, that he could not give his wife the slaves which to her were a necessity of life. He wondered whether her own freedom would fully indemnify her for their loss, whether his personal love and care would make up for their service. Or would she, within his own house, so to say within his arms, yearn for Miss Rabe herself? This was a fatal thought. Besides, he distrusted and condemned the principle. It was sweet, both droll and pathetic when represented, in Mizzi's person, in one otherwise obviously ready to meet her destiny. But it was in itself contrary to his idea of a dignified human existence.

Many of his rivals could offer her the kind of life to which she had been brought up. There was a Neapolitan Prince amongst them, and a young Hollander of great wealth, who owned, he was told, estates in the East Indies. The latter he liked, and reflected that he was better-looking than himself. Sometimes he believed that Mizzi thought so too.

He was a conscientious young man; he weighed these matters in his mind in sleepless hours. If only, he thought as he turned his head on the pillow, Mizzi would for once pick up her glove, or arrange the bouquets that he brought her, and put them in water. But she just gracefully placed them on a table, and Miss Rabe put them in water.

There was a ball given at the hotel on a Saturday night; an orchestra played the waltzes of Strauss. Axel danced with Mizzi. She looked like a flower, and he told her so. They also spoke of the stars, and he told her that there were philosophers who held them to be inhabited by live creatures, like the earth. As they were again about to take the floor they found themselves close to the Russian General. He was gazing at a waltzing couple.

"Now, consider, my young friends," said the General, "what a strange animal is man, and how with him the half is ever more than the whole. Here are now"—and he gave the names. "They are married a fortnight; the wedding was in all the papers. They are Romeo and Juliet! Their families have an ancient feud, and for a long time opposed the marriage. They are now on their honeymoon, at a castle in the hills, fifteen miles away. They are at last alone, free to give themselves up to the fruition of their love. And what do they do? They drive fifteen miles to dance together here because there is a fine orchestra and a good floor, and they are both famous waltzers. Some people hold that dancing is the foretaste or the substitute of love-making. Mark you, it may as well be said to be the essence of it. The half is more than the whole. But it will be so," the General added proudly, "solely to the aristocratic mind. The bourgeois might come here from vanity. A young peasant and his wife after the first waltz would exchange the ballroom for the hayloft."

Here Axel and Mizzi danced out. As everything delighted Axel tonight, he also thought the General's little lecture charming. He imagined himself and Mizzi on their honeymoon in the hills, and coming to dance at the hotel because the half is more than the whole. In the midst of the waltz he found that Mizzi was looking at him, or, as with Mizzi it was not the eyes which counted most, he found her face and mouth turned straight upon him. The face was all alive, resolute, as assertive as a challenge. But as the dance was over, and he led her back to her seat by the old English lady at the other end of the ballroom, she told him in a low, gentle voice that she and Miss Rabe were leaving Baden-Baden on Thursday. The information cast Axel down from the summit of happiness; for a moment the glittering room was dark to him. Then he reasoned that he still had three days left.

About an hour's walk from the watering place, in the hills and the pine forest, there stood a little wooden summer house, built in a romantic style, like a watch tower, with a battlement at the top. The stairway leading up to the roof was so decayed that nobody ventured upon it, but Axel, in passing it, had reflected that there would be a fine view from up there. To this place, on Sunday, he drove out in a cab to collect his thoughts in solitude. The afternoon was so perfectly still, so golden, that he felt as if he had found his way into a picture, some classic Italian painting, that suited him well. The fresh turpentine smell of the pines heightened the illusion. When he had sent his droschke back and ascended to the top of the tower, he was disappointed in the view; the trees had grown up so high that they hid it. But looking up he saw the blue summer sky streaked with thin white clouds. Up on the platform there was a table and a couple of chairs, much worn with sun and rain. It seemed like a dream to sit up so high and the world infinitely far away. As he looked over the battlement he saw a roe gracefully walk out of the wood, across the road, and into the bracken of the other side. On the green sward below him there was a rustic seat. He took off his hat.

He had sat for a while in deep thought, from time to time taking his pencil and writing a few words, when from the forest path he heard voices which slowly came nearer. Two women were talking, but the talk was broken by the one of them sobbing pitifully, like a lost child, like Gretl in the dark wood and in the witch's power. A few tearful words reached him out of the storm of woe. It was Mizzi's voice. He got up. He would have rushed to her aid, and might have thrown himself from the parapet, if he had not at the next moment caught in her sobs a querulous, plaintive tone, such as he would never have expected to hear from Mizzi, like that of a child demanding to be comforted and petted. For a second he was in a storm of jealousy; then he wondered if Mizzi, in the woods, was confiding in some girl friend from the hotel. He would have liked to get away, but it was too late, now that he had heard her weep. Perhaps, he thought, they will walk on. But they had stopped, and he gathered that they were seating themselves on the bench below. It was a strange, highly dramatic staging. He sat above them like a bird of prey, lurking over a pair of doves. He could not help listening.

"But if you love him, sweet, sweet little sister," said the one, "that is no misfortune. He loves you. They all love you and think you lovely."

It was Miss Rabe's voice. But it was a voice new to him, many years younger than he had heard it before, more sonorous and freer. It came from the speaker's heart. At the same time it was very tired.

After a silence Mizzi answered. This long pause was, all through the conversation, repeated before each of her phrases. "No," she said, and her voice too was changed, free, coming from the heart; it was also, like the elder woman's, tired. "I do not love him. One does not love a dupe, a gull. How can one love the people whom one is fooling? I am fooling them all, Lotti. I do not love any of them. No, not one."

"All the same, my darling," said Miss Rabe, who out here in the wood seemed to be called Lotti, "you would be unhappy if they did not love you."

A pause. Then Mizzi said: "Yes, they admire me. Because they believe that I am like them—safe, rich, used to all the good things of life. Yes, he admires me, he thinks I am like a flower, so fine and sweet and pure. He thinks that I know nothing of the world. If he knew how much I know about it, would he love me? No, not he."

"He will never know," said Lotti.

"No, of course not," said Mizzi. "The fool." Then after a pause she went on: "But if he knew? If he was told that I have gone to market to buy cabbage and have taken it home in a basket? If he was told that I feed the chickens and clean the chicken house? If he knew that I hang up washing!"

Axel reckoned that, now that they were seated, they would not look up. He peeped over the battlement. They sat with their backs to him, tenderly clinging to one another. Mizzi had her head upon Lotti's shoulder; her hat lay on the seat; her marvellous hair half covered the other's slim back.

"You have some little pleasure here, all the same," said Lotti. "You danced last night. I wish I could have danced."

"Yes," said Mizzi haughtily and maliciously. "Are you not soon tired of being Miss Rabe?

"And my clothes," broke out Mizzi, in a voice hoarse with despair, "I am too big for them. Next year they will be altogether impossible. Where will I show myself then? I shall have to sink into the ground, when, then, I have no mantilla, no hat with ostrich feathers, no gown with a train on it, as other women have. They are so romantic, all of them!" she cried scornfully. "They think that I have got a string of pearls, earrings, bracelets, and that my stepmother is just wickedly keeping them from me. If they only knew that I have not got any of them, not a single one." She burst into tears.

"You will be lovelier in yourself, next year, in any case," said Lotti.

"How I hate you," said Mizzi. "How I despise you, when you coax me as if I were a baby. You might as well say that I should be lovelier without any clothes at all."

"Oh, Mizzi," said Lotti.

"Yes," said Mizzi, "I know. It is a dreadful thing to say. But you might as well say that. I wish I were dead."

She sobbed as if her heart was breaking. Lotti fondled her and said: "Do not cry." But it had no effect on Mizzi. At last she said: "Let us die together, Lotti. The world is too horrible. Somewhere it will be different, somewhat different. Think of how big the world is, with all the stars in it. The scientists believe that there are people on them, just as on the earth. I feel that it will be a little better there." After a long pause she said: "That Papa must spend all that money at the Casinos!"

"Papa had to keep up his reputation," said Lotti.

"Yes," said Mizzi, in a faint voice. "Poor Papa."

Again they sat for a long time without talking. Then Lotti spoke, with a quiver in her voice, as if she herself realized the temerity of her statement: "Perhaps," she said, "if Axel Leth knew everything he would love you all the same."

This time Mizzi's reply, in a low, harsh voice, came without delay. "I could not bear it," she said. "I would rather die!"

A few minutes later she said: "Come. Let us go away. People might come and see that we have not even had a cab to bring us here."

"I shall tell them that the doctor has ordered you to take walks," said Lotti.

Nevertheless they soon after got up and walked away down the path.

When he had seen them disappear into the green pine forest closely entwined, Axel laid his arms on the table and his head on his arms. Later he did not know whether, within his own arms, he had laughed or wept.

He lay there for nearly an hour. Then he sat up, put his elbow on the table and his chin in his hand, and thought the situation over.

He had a good sense of art. The two tragic sisters in the wood, their red locks emblazed by the sun, in their very contortions had been so harmonious that he saw them as a classic group, two maidenly Laocoöns, locked in one another's arms, and in the deadly coils of the serpent. Never again would he see them separated. Mizzi might twist round her indignant and affrighted young face to him for a moment, but her embrace, her bosom was for Lotti. The idea of making love to one of the two was as absurd, as scandalous, as that of making love to one of the Siamese twins. The rings of the serpent themselves held them together. His last thought before he got up was this: That it was a good thing, a thing for which one should be thankful to Providence, that it had been he, and not one of the other young men from the watering place who had happened to overhear the conversation in the wood. They might have put down the Laocoön sisters as a pair of adventuresses who had come to the hotel to captivate a rich husband. Such a thing was as far as possible from their minds. They had come to Baden-Baden, as birds of passage come to their places, according to the seasons of the year, because at this time one was at Baden-Baden, or at a similar place. If they had not been here they would now have been at some other watering place. And wherever they had been, since they had to be somewhere, their situation and their problem would have remained the same. He walked away slowly, a wiser person than he had come.

In the evening there was much affliction at the hotel over Mizzi's near departure. A young officer, Axel believed, proposed to her that night. The old English lady questioned Miss Rabe on their plan of travel. They were going home, the governess explained, by Stuttgart. The young Hollander here remarked that he himself was going to Stuttgart, might he have the honour of accompanying the ladies so far? The Italian Prince, who had been lost in lamentations, at once exclaimed that he, too, had got business in Stuttgart, and might he share the honour? At this Miss Rabe and Mizzi exchanged a short glance, then accepted. Otherwise Mizzi herself was radiant tonight, her colour heightened, as if she was carried forth on the wave of general woe. She seemed older than before. In the course of the evening Axel two or three times found her eyes on his face, but they did not speak together.

In the morning Axel went into town and bought a large bouquet of roses for Mizzi. On the card he wrote Goethe's lines:

> *Die Sterne, die begehrt man nicht,*
> *Man freut sich ihrer Pracht.*

He had meant to write more, to express his grief at not seeing her again. But he did not do so, for he was averse to telling a lie. In the afternoon while everyone in the hotel was away in the hills on a farewell picnic to Mizzi, he left word that he had been called to Frankfurt for a week, and took the train to Stuttgart.

He had been to Stuttgart before, on his way to Italy. At his old hotel he got the address of a tailoring firm in the town, and here he ordered a long coat, and a whole outfit for a servant, to be ready the next day. He also bought a hat, and had a small cockade set in it. He knew the colours of Mizzi's family from a game of forfeits.

When, before, he had been to the town, he had visited the theatre in the company of a friend, and had even been introduced behind the scenes. He now looked up the dresser of the theatre, and confided to him that the matter turned on a wager of great importance: he must be done up in the role of an elderly, respectable family-servant. The old stager, an Italian, fell in with the scheme as if his own life hung on it, and immediately broke off his client's explanations with a row of inspired suggestions. He walked round him to study his face and figure from all sides.

On Thursday morning, when Axel had fetched his livery from

the tailor, he found his whole attire brilliantly thought out. The Italian's wife, evidently initiated, came in to help her husband with the finishing touches. Axel had his hair whitened, with two little mutton-chops attached, his face delicately tanned and a few wrinkles drawn on it, his eyebrows done up. It was all exquisitely done. The two artists, in the end, were carried away with pride. As, on their invitation, he glanced into the long looking-glass, he had a slight shock, so unfamiliar was the figure within it to himself. Here stood, hatted and gloved, a venerable, trusted, self-respecting old servant.

He went back to his hotel, taking trouble to walk slowly. He practised his part in the streets of Stuttgart, and made up his experiences. He found that he was more nervous about his role in the presence of the porter of the hotel and the cabman than with the ladies and gentlemen. At the hotel he ordered rooms and dinner, with flowers upon the dinner table, for two ladies. Before noon he was back at Baden-Baden.

When, later in life, he thought his adventure over, he was surprised that he had been so calm and certain about it. It was a grey day; a light shower fell, as if, at Baden-Baden, nature herself wept to see Mizzi go. Nobody seemed in the least to doubt the old servant's genuineness. At the hotel he modestly introduced himself to the porter as Frantz, Mizzi's servant, and asked him to let his lady know that Frantz had arrived and that he was waiting for her orders in the hall.

A hotel boy took the message upstairs, and within a minute Mizzi herself came down the stairs, in a grey dust-coat and a childish straw bonnet tied under the chin, so that they met at the foot of the stairs, where he stood with his hat in his hand. She came down quickly, light of foot, but somewhat alarmed, her eyes wide open. She stopped dead at the sight of him, as if she had seen a ghost. She took him in, he felt, from head to foot; she noticed the travelling rug on his arm, and the cockade in his hat. He saw her change colour and grow deadly white; her mouth itself faded away, so that they thought she was going to fall. But with an effort she held herself up straight, came down the last two steps and stood face to face with him. At that moment two ladies of the hotel rushed in from outside, put down their little umbrellas and shook their ample skirts in order, complaining about the rain. They ran up to the girl with tender laments. "So you are leaving us today, you sweet child," they cried. They gave Axel's figure a glance and asked: "Is that your servant?" "Yes," said Mizzi, quite white and bewildered with trembling lips. "You have had him up to travel with you?" the lady asked. "That is wise. It is unpleasant to women to travel alone." Now over Mizzi's head, at the top of the stairs, Axel caught sight of Miss Rabe. "He looks a nice old person," said the lady. "What is his name?" "Frantz," said Mizzi.

All the watering place went to see Mizzi off. Her cab was filled with bouquets. Axel followed in a cab with all the luggage. He had before taken the ladies' tickets and reserved their seats, and he now helped them into the train. A little girl from the hotel, who had made friends with Mizzi, burst into tears and gave her a big lovely rose. Mizzi bent to kiss the child, her hair tumbling over her face, and fastened the rose at her bosom. From his own carriage window Axel saw the white handkerchiefs waving as the train glided out of Baden-Baden.

All that day he moved and spoke quietly, like a person who knows himself to be the instrument of destiny. Even the near separation from Mizzi, which he felt like a physical pain, seemed, strangely, to steady him, and to hold him to his purpose. He talked a little with his fellow-passengers and lent a hand to a young woman with a baby and two heavy baskets. A workman gave him a newspaper, and a heated lecture on politics.

Twice Mizzi looked at him. As the train stopped at a small station she got out and walked a little with one of her cavaliers of Baden-Baden, who held the umbrella over her. The other remained by the carriage door with Miss Rabe, since she would not venture out in the drizzle. There were some children selling fruit by the fence. Mizzi's companion ran to buy, swiftly handing the umbrella to Axel. So here they were, close together and, so to say, alone. Mizzi did not take away her eyes, but let them tell him what she thought of him. He winced before her glance. She might well have struck him, he thought. She would have killed him if she could, for she was furious and without fear or misgiving. But she was held back from raising her voice to him, even from looking at him for more than a second or two, by a sacred symbol, mightier than herself: by the cockade in her colours on his hat. When Miss Rabe called to her, she let him walk by her, with the umbrella, all the length of the platform.

During that walk of perhaps a hundred steps, the relation between Axel and Mizzi ripened and set. As they stopped, it was cast in its final and unalterable mould. The figure of Axel Leth was gone, and Frantz, the servant, had taken his place.

Axel realized and understood, the umbrella in his hand—with reverence, since he was now in livery—that the slave-owner's dependency upon the slave is strong as death and cruel as the grave. The slave holds his master's life in his hand, as he holds his umbrella. Axel Leth, with whom she was in love, might betray Mizzi; it would anger her, it might sadden her, but she was still, in her anger and melancholy, the same person. But her existence itself rested upon the loyalty of Frantz, her servant, and on his devotion, assent and support. His treachery would break the integrity of her being. If she were not, at any moment, sure that Frantz would die for her, she could not live. If, he went on in his mind, in her own house a lover annoyed her, if a jealous adorer made a scene, she would ring for Frantz, and ask him to see her guest out, and the frantic lover, who would have braved a father and a husband, would be prostrate before the power of Frantz, and follow him without a word.

Back in his own carriage Axel thought: "If now there was to be a railway accident, she would think of my safety first of all."

In Stuttgart the ladies were altogether in the hands of their old servant. He went with them to the hotel, and the porter at once recognized him and handed him their keys.

But as now the understanding between the three was established and confirmed, Axel also guessed the immediate reason for the sisters' alarm and dread of him. They believed that he meant to follow them to their journey's end, to run them, so to say, to earth. Their own plan would be to go away in the early morning, before anybody knew, and they trembled like two birds in a snare as they saw their freedom of disappearance threatened. Nothing had been further from his thoughts, and he grieved that they should think so ill of him. So when he had seen their luggage brought up, and found everything to be in order, he respectfully asked Miss Rabe if she had any more orders for him, as otherwise he would set out on his home journey tonight, in order to be able to receive the ladies on their arrival. He watched the deep relief in her face as she let him go. Mizzi at the moment had her back to him, but he felt that a great movement ran through her too; still she neither turned nor said a word.

He stood down in the hall, alone—and from this evening it dated that to him the hall was ever the central room of a hotel, the place where things went on. His task was completed, and he ought to go.

But everything, he thought, could not be ended here; there must be something left, a word or a glance; he must see her once more, when she should come down for dinner. As people passed into the dining room he gazed through the door, and noted with content that there were flowers on their table. The two gentlemen of Baden-Baden had come into the hall too; they were to dine in the same room as the ladies, although they had not dared to ask to join them at their table. They were waiting to accompany them in. At last the two sisters came down the stairs and Axel reflected that, in spite of all their woes, they were looking strangely, pathetically happy and at ease, in harmony with life. They went in, pleasantly. So now he had seen her once more, and might go forth into the rain.

He was already opening the front door when Mizzi's low, clear voice called him back. "Frantz," she said. She had come out from the dining room and was standing in the midst of the hall. There was no confusion or vexation about her now. In spite of her clothes she looked so grownup, wholly in the grand style, like a martyr. "Here is the letter, Frantz," she said, and handed him an envelope. As he took it, their fingers met. He had kissed her hand many times, and had had his arm round her in the waltzes, but no touch had been as significant as this fugitive, momentary contact.

Axel went from the hotel to the rooms of the theatrical dresser, where his clothes had been kept for him. The old man was not in, but his wife with a skilfull hand undressed and washed him, the while discreetly inquiring if he had won his bet. Yes, he said, he had won it. When the painful process was over, she turned him round to the glass. Here was Axel Leth back, such as he was, of no consequence to any human being, and here was Frantz gone forever. Where was Axel Leth to go? He might go anywhere! But he went to Frankfurt, out of a vague respect for the truth.

As he had Frantz's clothes packed he took out the envelope. The letter, too, belonged to Frantz, and he had no real right to open it, but it might be that it contained a message for Axel Leth, through Frantz. There was a rose in it, a little faded, but still soft and moist, the rose that the child had given Mizzi at the station of Baden-Baden.

When Axel came back to Baden-Baden the place was still grieving a little for Mizzi, although the melancholy would soon be dispersed by new arrivals. Axel decided that his cure was finished and fixed a day for his return to Denmark. The old English lady was the most faithful of Mizzi's friends, and twice took him out for a drive, to talk of her. She was determined that he had proposed and been refused, and now took pleasure in turning the knife in his wound. She praised the girl as a great lady in the bud, a maiden brought up on the high principles of the old world, and undefiled by any low contact, a rose, a young swan. One could not be certain, with the present state of politics, and the rebelliousness of youth itself, whether, in a hundred years, there would still be such real ladies in the world, worthy of the worship of men, and how would man, poor unstable creature, get on then? And what skin! And what pretty legs!

In the solitude of the terrace, Axel once wept over the emptiness of the world. Still he preserved his resigned, fatal state of mind.

On the second day after his return he walked up to a small waterfall in the hills. The day was grey after a week's rain, the forest roads were moist, the rush of water was like a song, an elegy, the voice of the still, wet woods, and the smell of the water was almost quenchingly fresh. He sat there and thought of Mizzi.

What would become, he thought, of the two sisters, who had been so honest as to give life the lie, the partisans of an ideal, ever in flight from a blunt reality, the great, gentle ladies, who were incapable of living without slaves? For no slave, he reflected, could more desperately sigh and pine for his enfranchisement than they did sigh and pine for their slave, nor could freedom, to the slaves, ever be more essentially a condition of existence, the very breath of life than their slaves were to them.

Very likely next year the parts would be interchanged; Lotti would be the slave-owner and Mizzi the slave. Lotti might then become an invalid lady of rank, in a bath-chair, since that role could be played without the jewels or feathers, the want of which Mizzi had deplored in the woods. And Mizzi would be the companion, demure in the plain attire of a nurse, patient under the whims of her mistress. It was good to think that they might still, then, in the forest, weep in each other's arms, and kiss like sisters.

He kept his eyes upon the waterfall. The clear stream, like a luminous column amongst the moss and the stones, held its noble outline unaltered through all the hours of day and night. In the midst of it there was a small projecting cascade, where the tumbling water struck a rock. That, too, stood out immutable, like a fresh crack in the marble of the cataract. If he returned in ten years, he would find it unchanged, in the same form, like a harmonious and immortal work of art. Still it was, each second, new particles of water hurled over the edge, rushing into a precipice and disappearing. It was a flight, a whirl, an incessant catastrophe.

Are there, in life, he thought, similar phenomena? Is there a corresponding, paradoxal mode of existing, a poised, classic, static flight and run? In music it exists, and there it is called a Fuga:

> *D'un air placide et triomphant,*
> *Tu passes ton chemin, majestueuse enfant.*

THE DREAMING CHILD

IN THE FIRST HALF of the last century there lived in Sealand, in Denmark, a family of cottagers and fishermen, who
were called Plejelt after their native place, and who did not seem
able to do well for themselves in any way. Once they had owned a
little land here and there, and fishing-boats, but what they had
possessed they had lost, and within their new enterprises they
failed. They just managed to keep out of the jails of Denmark, but
they gave themselves up freely to all such sins and weaknesses—
vagabondage, drink, gambling, illegitimate children and suicide—
as human beings can indulge in without breaking the law. The old
judge of the district said of them: "These Plejelts are not bad
people; I have got many worse than they. They are pretty, healthy,
likable, even talented in their way. Only they just have not got the
knack of living. And if they do not promptly pull themselves together I cannot tell what may become of them, except that the rats
will eat them."

Now it was a queer thing that—just as if the Plejelts had been
overhearing this sad prophecy and had been soundly frightened by
it—in the following years they actually seemed to pull themselves
together. One of them married into a respectable peasant family,
another had a stroke of luck in the herring-fishery, another was
converted by the new parson of the parish, and obtained the office
of bell-ringer. Only one child of the clan, a girl, did not escape its
fate, but on the contrary appeared to collect upon her young head
the entire burden of guilt and misfortune of her tribe. In the course
of her short, tragic life she was washed from the country into the
town of Copenhagen, and here, before she was twenty, she died in
dire misery, leaving a small son behind her. The father of the child,
who is otherwise unknown to this tale, had given her a hundred
rixdollars. These, together with the child, the dying mother handed
over to an old washerwoman, blind in one eye, and named Madame

155

Mahler, in whose house she had lodged. She begged Madame Mahler to provide for her baby as long as the money lasted, in the true
spirit of the Plejelts, contenting herself with a brief respite.

At the sight of the money Madame Mahler got a rose in each
cheek; she had never till now set eyes on a hundred rixdollars, all
in a pile. As she looked at the child she sighed deeply; then she
took the task upon her shoulders, with what other burdens life had
already placed there.

The little boy, whose name was Jens, in this way first became
conscious of the world, and of life, within the slums of old Copenhagen in a dark backyard like a well, a labyrinth of filth, decay
and foul smell. Slowly he also became conscious of himself, and
of something exceptional in his worldly position. There were other
children in the backyard, a big crowd of them; they were pale and
dirty as himself. But they all seemed to belong to somebody; they
had a father and a mother; there was, for each of them, a group of
other ragged and squalling children whom they called brothers and
sisters, and who sided with them in the brawls of the yard; they
obviously made part of a unity. He began to meditate upon the
world's particular attitude to himself, and upon the reason for it.
Something within it responded to an apprehension within his own
heart: that he did not really belong here, but somewhere else. At
night he had chaotic, many-coloured dreams; in the day-time his
thoughts still lingered in them; sometimes they made him laugh,
all to himself, like the tinkling of a little bell, so that Madame
Mahler, shaking her own head, held him to be a bit weak in his.

A visitor came to Madame Mahler's house, a friend of her youth,
an old wry seamstress with a flat, brown face and a black wig. They
called her Mamzell Ane. She had in her young days sewn in many
great houses. She wore a red bow at the throat, and had many
coquettish, maidenly little ways and postures. But within her

sunken bosom she had also a greatness of soul, which enabled her to scorn her present misery in the memory of that splendour which in the past her eyes had beheld. Madame Mahler was a woman of small imagination; she did but reluctantly lend an ear to her friend's grand, interminable soliloquies. After a while Mamzell Ane turned to little Jens for sympathy. Before the child's grave attentiveness her fancy took speed; she called forth, and declaimed upon, the glory of satin, velvet and brocade, of lofty halls and marble staircases. The lady of the house was adorned for a ball by the light of multitudinous candles; her husband came in to fetch her with a star on his breast, while the carriage and pair waited in the street. There were big weddings in the cathedral, and funerals as well, with all the ladies swathed in black like magnificent, tragic columns. The children called their parents Papa and Mamma; they had dolls and hobby-horses to play with, talking parrots in gilt cages, and dogs that were taught to walk on their hind legs. Their mother kissed them, gave them bonbons and pretty pet-names. Even in winter the warm rooms behind the silk curtains were filled with the perfumes of flowers named heliotrope and oleander, and the chandeliers that hung from the ceiling were themselves made of glass in the shape of bright flowers and leaves.

The idea of this majestic, radiant world, in the mind of little Jens merged with that of his own inexplicable isolation in life into a great dream, or fantasy. He was so lonely in Madame Mahler's house because one of the houses of Mamzell Ane's tales was his real home. In the long days, when Madame Mahler stood by her wash-tub, or brought her washing out into town, he fondled, and played with, the picture of this house and of the people who lived in it, and who loved him so dearly. Mamzell Ane, on her side, noted the effect of her *épopée* on the child, realized that she had at last found the ideal audience, and was further inspired by the discovery. The relation between the two developed into a kind of love-affair; for their happiness, for their very existence they had become dependent upon each other.

Now Mamzell Ane was a revolutionist, on her own accord, and out of some primitive, flaming visionary sight within her proud, virginal heart, for she had all her time lived amongst submissive and unreflective people. The meaning and object of existence to her was grandeur, beauty and elegance. For the life of her she would not see them disappear from the earth. But she felt it to be a cruel and scandalous state of things that so many men and women must live and die without these highest human values—yes, without the very knowledge of them—that they must be poor, wry and un-elegant. She was every day looking forward to that day of justice when the tables were to be turned, and the wronged and oppressed enter into their heaven of refinement and gracefulness. All the same she now took pains not to impart into the soul of the child any of her own bitterness or rebelliousness. For as the intimacy between them grew, she did in her heart acclaim little Jens as legitimate heir to all the magnificence for which she had herself prayed in vain. He was not to fight for it; everything was his by right, and should come to him on its own. Possibly the inspired and experienced old maid also noted that the boy had in him no talent for envy or rancour whatever. In their long, happy communications, he accepted Mamzell Ane's world serenely and without misgiving, in the very manner—except for the fact that he had not any of it—of the happy children born within it.

There was a short period of his life in which Jens made the other children of the backyard party to his happiness. He was, he told them, far from being the half-wit barely tolerated by old Madame Mahler; he was on the contrary the favourite of fortune. He had a Papa and Mamma and a fine house of his own, with such and such things in it, a carriage, and horses in the stable. He was spoiled, and would get everything he asked for. It was a curious thing that the children did not laugh at him, nor afterwards pursue him with mockery. They almost appeared to believe him. Only they could not understand or follow his fancies; they took but little interest in them, and after a while they altogether disregarded them. So Jens again gave up sharing the secret of his felicity with the world.

Still some of the questions put to him by the children had set the boy's mind working, so that he asked Mamzell Ane—for the confidence between them by this time was complete—how it had come to pass that he had lost contact with his home and had been taken into Madame Mahler's establishment? Mamzell Ane found it difficult to answer him; she could not explain the fact to herself. It would be, she reflected, part of the confused and corrupt state of the world in general. When she had thought the matter over she solemnly, in the manner of a Sibyl, furnished him with an explanation. It was, she said, by no means unheard of, neither in life nor in books, that a child, particularly a child in the highest and happiest circumstances, and most dearly beloved by his parents, enigmatically vanished and was lost. She stopped short at this, for even to her dauntless and proven soul the theme seemed too tragic to be further dwelt on. Jens accepted the explanation in the spirit in which it was given, and from this moment saw himself as that melancholy, but not uncommon, phenomenon: a vanished and lost child.

But when Jens was six years old Mamzell Ane died, leaving to him her few earthly possessions: a thin-worn silver thimble, a fine pair of scissors and a little black chair with roses painted on it. Jens set a great value to these things, and every day gravely contemplated them. Just then Madame Mahler began to see the end of her hundred rixdollars. She had been piqued by her old friend's absorption in the child, and so decided to get her own back. From now on she would make the boy useful to her in the business of the laundry. His life therefore was no longer his own, and the thimble, the scissors and the chair stood in Madame Mahler's room, the sole tangible remnants, or proof, of the splendour which he and Mamzell Ane had known and shared.

At the same time as these events took place in Adelgade, there lived in a stately house in Bredgade a young married couple, whose names were Jakob and Emilie Vandamm. The two were cousins, she being the only child of one of the big shipowners of Copenhagen, and he the son of that magnate's sister—so that if it had not been for her sex, the young lady would with time have become head of the firm. The old shipowner, who was a widower, with his widowed sister, occupied the two loftier lower stories of the house. The family held closely together, and the young people had been engaged from childhood.

Jakob was a very big young man, with a quick head and an easy temper. He had many friends, but none of them could dispute the fact that he was growing fat at the early age of thirty. Emilie was not a regular beauty, but she had an extremely graceful and elegant figure, and the slimmest waist in Copenhagen; she was supple and soft in her walk and all her movements, with a low voice, and a reserved, gentle manner. As to her moral being she was the true daughter of a long row of competent and honest tradesmen: upright, wise, truthful and a bit of a pharisee. She gave much time to charity work, and therein minutely distinguished between the deserving and the undeserving poor. She entertained largely and prettily, but kept strictly to her own milieu. Her old uncle, who had travelled round the world, and was an admirer of the fair sex, teased her over the Sunday dinner-table. There was, he said, an exquisite piquancy in the contrast between the suppleness of her body and the rigidity of her mind.

There had been a time when, unknown to the world, the two had been in concord. When Emilie was eighteen, and Jakob was away in China on a ship, she fell in love with a young naval officer, whose name was Charlie Dreyer, and who, three years earlier, when he was only twenty-one, had distinguished himself, and been decorated, in the war of 1849. Emilie was not then officially engaged to her cousin. She did not believe, either, that she would exactly break Jakob's heart if she left him and married another man. All the same, she had strange, sudden misgivings; the strength of her own feelings alarmed her. When in solitude she pondered on the matter, she held it beneath her to be so entirely dependent on another human being. But she again forgot her fears when she met Charlie, and she wondered and wondered that life did indeed hold so much sweetness. Her best friend, Charlotte Tutein, as the two girls were undressing after a ball, said to her: "Charlie Dreyer makes love to all the pretty girls of Copenhagen, but he does not intend to marry any of them. I think he is a Don Juan." Emilie smiled into the looking-glass. Her heart melted at the thought that Charlie, misjudged by all the world, was known to her alone for what he was: loyal, constant and true.

Charlie's ship was leaving for the West Indies. On the night before his departure he came out to her father's villa near Copenhagen to say good-bye, and found Emilie alone. The two young people walked in the garden; it was moonlit. Emilie broke off a white rose, moist with dew, and gave it to him. As they were parting on the road just outside the gate, he seized both her hands, drew them to his breast, and in one great flaming whisper begged her, since nobody would see him walk back with her, to let him stay with her that night, until in the morning he must go so far away.

It is probably almost impossible to the children of later generations to understand or realize the horror and abomination which the idea and the very word of seduction would awake in the minds of young girls of that past age. She could not have been more deadly frightened and revolted had she found that he meant to cut her throat.

He must repeat himself before she understood him, and as she did so the ground sank beneath her. She felt as if the one man amongst all, whom she trusted and loved, was intending to bring upon her the supreme sin, disaster and shame, was asking her to betray her mother's memory and all the maidens in the world. Her own feelings for him made her an accomplice in the crime, and she realized that she was lost. Charlie felt her wavering on her feet, and put his arms around her. In a stifled, agonized cry she tore herself out of them, fled, and with all her might pushed the heavy iron gate to; she bolted it on him as if it had been the cage of an angry lion. On which side of the gate was the lion? Her strength gave way; she hung on to the bars, while on the other side the desperate, miserable lover pressed himself against them, fumbled between them for her hands, her clothes, and implored her to open. But she recoiled and flew to the house, to her room, only to find there despair within her own heart, and a bitter vacuity in all the world round it.

Six months later Jakob came home from China, and their engagement was celebrated amongst the rejoicings of the families. A month after she learned that Charlie had died from fever at St. Thomas. Before she was twenty she was married and mistress of her own fine house.

Many young girls of Copenhagen married in the same way—*par dépit*—and then, to save their self-respect, denied their first love and made the excellency of their husbands their one point of honour, so that they became incapable of distinguishing between truth and untruth, lost their moral weight and flickered in life without any foothold in reality. Emilie was saved from their fate by the intervention, so to say, of the old Vandamms, her forefathers, and by the instinct and principle of sound merchantship which they had passed on into the blood of their daughter. The staunch and resolute old traders had not winked when they made out their balance-sheet; in hard times they had sternly looked bankruptcy and ruin in the face; they were the loyal, unswerving servants of facts. So did Emilie now take stock of her profit and loss. She had loved Charlie; he had been unworthy of her love; and she was never again to love in that same way. She had stood upon the brink of an abyss, and but for the grace of God she was at this moment a fallen woman, an outcast from her father's house. The husband she had married was kind-hearted, and a good man of business; he was also fat, childish, unlike her. She had got, out of life, a house to her taste and a secure, harmonious position in her own family and in the world of Copenhagen; for these she was grateful, and for them she would take no risk. She did at this moment of her life with all the strength of her young soul embrace a creed of fanatical truthfulness and solidity. The ancient Vandamms might have applauded her, or they might have thought her code excessive; they had taken a risk themselves, when it was needed, and they were aware that in trade it is a dangerous thing to shy danger.

Jakob, on his side, was in love with his wife, and prized her beyond rubies. To him, as to the other young men out of the strictly moral Copenhagen bourgeoisie, his first experience of love had been extremely gross. He had preserved the freshness of his heart, and his claim to neatness and orderliness in life by holding on to an ideal of purer womanhood, in the first place represented by the young cousin whom he was to marry, the innocent fair-haired girl of his own mother's blood, and brought up as she had been. He carried her image with him to Hamburg and Amsterdam, and that trait in him which his wife called childishness made him deck it out like a doll or an icon; out in China it became highly ethereal and romantic, and he used to repeat to himself little sayings of hers, to recall her low, soft voice. Now he was happy to be back in Denmark, married and in his own home, and to find his young wife as perfect as his portrait of her. At times he felt a vague longing for a bit of weakness within her, or for an occasional appeal to his own strength, which, as things were, only made him out a clumsy figure beside her delicate form. He gave her all that she wanted, and out of his pride in her superiority left to her all decisions on their house and on their daily and social life. Only within their charity work it happened that the husband and wife did not see eye to eye, and that Emilie would give him a little lecture on his credulity. "What an absurd person you are, Jakob," she said. "You will believe everything that these people tell you—not because you cannot help it, but because you do really wish to believe them." "Do you not wish to believe them?" he asked her. "I cannot see," she replied, "how one can well wish to believe or not to believe. I wish to find out the truth. Once a thing is not true," she added, "it matters little to me whatever else it may be."

A short time after his wedding Jakob one day had a letter from a rejected supplicant, a former maid in his father-in-law's house, who informed him that while he was away in China his wife had a liaison with Charlie Dreyer. He knew it to be a lie, tore up the letter, and did not give it another thought.

They had no children. This to Emilie was a grave affliction; she felt that she was lacking in her duties. When they had been married for five years Jakob, vexed by his mother's constant concern, and with the future of the firm on his mind, suggested to his wife that they should adopt a child, to carry forward the house. Emilie at once, and with much energy and indignation, repudiated the idea; it had to her all the appearance of a comedy, and she would not see her father's firm encumbered with a sham heir. Jakob held forth to her upon the Antonines with but little effect.

But when six months later he again took up the subject, to her own surprise she found that it was no longer repellent. Unknowingly she must have given it a place in her thought, and let it take root there, for by now it seemed familiar to her. She listened to her husband, looked at him, and felt kindly towards him. "If this is what he has been longing for," she thought, "I must not oppose it." But in her own heart she knew clearly and coldly, and with awe of her own coldness the true reason for her indulgence: the deep apprehension, that when a child had been adopted there would be no more obligation to her of producing an heir to the firm, a grandson to her father, a child to her husband.

It was indeed their little divergences in regard to the deserving or undeserving poor which brought upon the young couple of Bredgade the events recounted in this tale. In summer-time they lived in Emilie's father's villa on the Strandvej, and Jakob would drive in to town, and out, in a small gig. One day he decided to profit by his wife's absence to visit an unquestionably unworthy mendicant, an old sea-captain from one of his ships. He took his way through the ancient town, where it was difficult to drive a carriage, and where it was such an exceptional sight that people came up from the cellars to stare at it. In the narrow lane of Adelgade a drunken man waved his arms in front of the horse; it shied, and knocked down a small boy with a heavy wheelbarrow piled high with washing. The wheelbarrow and the washing ended sadly in the gutter. A crowd immediately collected round the spot, but expressed neither indignation nor sympathy. Jakob made his groom lift the little boy onto the seat. The child was smeared with blood and dirt, but he was not badly hurt, nor in the least scared. He seemed to take this accident as an adventure in general, or as if it had happened to somebody else. "Why did you not get out of my way, you little idiot?" Jakob asked him. "I wanted to look at the horse," said the child, and added: "Now, I can see it well from here."

Jakob got the boy's whereabouts from an onlooker, paid him to take the wheelbarrow back, and himself drove the child home. The sordidness of Madame Mahler's house, and her own, one-eyed, blunt unfeelingness impressed him unpleasantly; still he had before now been inside the houses of the poor. But he was, here, struck by a strange incongruity between the backyard and the child who lived in it. It was as if, unknowingly, Madame Mahler was housing, and knocking about, a small, gentle, wild animal, or a sprite. On his way to the villa he reflected that the child had reminded him of his wife; he had a reserved, as it were selfless, way with him, behind which one guessed great, integrate strength and endurance.

He did not speak of the incident that evening, but he went back to Madame Mahler's house to inquire about the boy, and, after a while, he recounted the adventure to his wife and, somewhat shyly and half in jest, proposed to her that they should take the pretty, forlorn child as their own.

Half in jest she entered on his idea. It would be better, she thought, than taking on a child whose parents she knew. After this day she herself at times dwelt upon the matter when she could find nothing else to talk to him about. They consulted the family lawyer, and sent their old doctor to look the child over.

Jakob was surprised and grateful at his wife's compliance with his wish. She listened with gentle interest when he developed his plans, and would even sometimes vent her own ideas on education.

Lately Jakob had found his domestic atmosphere almost too perfect, and had had an adventure in town. Now he tired of it and finished it. He bought Emilie presents, and left her to make her own conditions as to the adoption of the child. He might, she said, bring the boy to the house on the first of October, when they had moved into town from the country, but she herself would reserve her final decision in the matter until April, when he should have been with them for six months. If by then she did not find the child fit for their plan she would hand him over to some honest, kindly family in the employ of the firm. Till April they themselves would likewise be only Uncle and Aunt Vandamm to the boy.

They did not talk to their family of the project, and this circumstance accentuated the new feeling of comradeship between them. How very different, Emilie said to herself, would the case have proved had she been expecting a child in the orthodox way of women. There was indeed something neat and proper about settling the affairs of nature according to your own mind. "And," she whispered in her mind, as her glance ran down her looking-glass, "in keeping your figure."

As to Madame Mahler, when time came to approach her, the matter was easily arranged. She had it not in her to oppose the wishes of her social superiors; she was also, vaguely, rating her own future connection with a house that must surely turn out an abundance of washing. Only the readiness with which Jakob refunded her her past outlays on the child left in her heart a lifelong regret that she had not asked for more.

At the last moment Emilie made a further stipulation. She would go alone to fetch the child. It was important that the relation between the boy and herself should be properly established from the beginning, and she did not trust to Jakob's sense of propriety on this occasion. In this way it came about that, when all was ready for the child's reception in the house of Bredgade, Emilie drove by herself to Adelgade to take possession of him, easy in her conscience towards the firm and her husband, but, beforehand, a little tired of the whole affair.

In the street by Madame Mahler's house a number of unkempt children were obviously waiting for the arrival of the carriage. They stared at her, but turned off their eyes, when she looked at them. Her heart sank as she lifted her ample silk skirt and passed through their crowd and across the backyard. Would her boy have the same look? Like Jakob, she had many times before visited the houses of the poor. It was a sad sight, but it could not be otherwise. "The poor you have with you always." But today, since a child from this place was to enter her own house, for the first time she felt personally related to the need and misery of the world. She was seized with a new deep disgust and horror, and at the next moment with a new, deeper pity. In these two minds she entered Madame Mahler's room.

Madame Mahler had washed little Jens and watercombed his hair. She had also, a couple of days before, hurriedly enlightened him as to the situation and his own promotion in life. But being an unimaginative woman and moreover of the opinion that the child was but half-witted, she had not taken much trouble about it. The child had received the information in silence; he only asked her how his father and mother had found him. "Oh, by the smell," said Madame Mahler.

Jens had communicated the news to the other children of the

house. His Papa and Mamma, he told them, were coming on the morrow, in great state, to fetch him home. It gave him matter for reflection that the event should raise a great stir in that same world of the backyard that had received his visions of it with indifference. To him the two were the same thing.

He had got up on Mamzell Ane's small chair to look out of the window and witness the arrival of his mother. He was still standing on it when Emilie came in, and Madame Mahler in vain made a gesture to chase him down. The first thing that Emilie noticed about the child was that he did not turn his gaze from hers, but looked her straight in the eyes. At the sight of her a great, ecstatic light passed over his face. For a moment the two looked at each other.

The child seemed to wait for her to address him, but as she stood silent, irresolute, he spoke. "Mamma," he said, "I am glad that you have found me. I have waited for you so long, so long."

Emilie gave Madame Mahler a glance. Had this scene been staged to move her heart? But the flat lack of understanding in the old woman's face excluded the possibility, and she again turned to the child.

Madame Mahler was a big, broad woman. Emilie herself, in a crinoline and a sweeping mantilla, took up a good deal of room. The child was much the smallest figure in the room, yet at this moment he dominated it, as if he had taken command of it. He stood up straight, with that same radiance in his countenance. "Now I am coming home again, with you," he said.

Emilie vaguely and amazedly realized that to the child the importance of the moment did not lie with his own good luck, but with that tremendous happiness and fulfillment which he was bestowing on her. A strange idea, that she could not have explained to herself, at that, ran through her mind. She thought:

"This child is as lonely in life as I." Gravely she moved nearer to him and said a few kind words. The little boy put out his hand and gently touched the long silky ringlets that fell forward over her neck. "I knew you at once," he said proudly. "You are my Mamma, who spoils me. I would know you amongst all the ladies, by your long pretty hair." He ran his fingers softly down her shoulder and arm, and fumbled over her gloved hand. "You have got three rings on today," he said. "Yes," said Emilie in her low voice. A short, triumphant smile broke upon his face. "And now you kiss me, Mamma," he said, and grew very pale. Emilie did not know that his excitement rose from the fact that he had never been kissed. Obediently, surprised at herself, she bent down and kissed him.

Jens' farewell to Madame Mahler at first was somewhat cere-monious in two people who had known each other for a long time. For she already saw him as a new person, the rich man's child, and took his hand tardily, her face stiff. But Emilie bade the boy, before he went away, to thank Madame Mahler because she had looked after him till now, and he did so with much freedom and grace. At that the old woman's tanned and fur-rowed cheeks once more blushed deeply, like a young girl's, as by the sight of the money at their first meeting. She had so rarely been thanked in her life. In the street he stood still. "Look at my big, fat horses!" he cried. Emilie sat in the carriage, bewil-dered. What was she bringing home with her from Madame Mahler's house?

In her own house, as she took the child up the stairs and from one room into another, her bewilderment grew. Rarely had she felt so uncertain of herself. It was, everywhere, in the child, the same rapture of recognition. At times he would also mention and look for things which she faintly remembered from her own childhood, or other things of which she had never heard. Her small pug, that she had brought with her from her old home, yapped at the boy. She lifted it up, afraid that it would bite him. "No, Mamma," he cried, "she will not bite me, she knows me well." A few hours ago—yes, she thought, up to the moment when in Madame Mahler's room she had kissed the child—she would have scolded him: "Fie, you are telling a fib." Now she said nothing, and the next moment the child looked round the room and asked her: "Is the parrot dead?" "No," she answered, wondering, "she is not dead; she is in the other room."

She realized that she was afraid both to be alone with the boy, and to let any third person join them. She sent the nurse out of the room. By the time Jakob was to arrive at the house she listened for his steps on the stairs with a kind of alarm. "Who are you waiting for?" Jens asked her. She was at a loss as how to designate Jakob to the child. "For my husband," she replied, embarrassed. Jakob on his entrance found the mother and the child gazing in the same picture-book. The little boy stared at him. "So it is you who are my Papa!" he exclaimed, "I thought so, too, all the time. But I could not be quite sure of it, could I? It was not by the smell that you found me, then. I think it was the horse that remembered me." Jakob looked at his wife; she looked into the book. He did not expect sense from a child, and was soon playing with the boy and tumbling him about. In the midst of a game Jens set his hands against Jakob's chest. "You have not got your star on," he said. After a moment Emilie went out of the room. She thought: "I have taken this upon me to meet my husband's wish, but it seems that I must bear the burden of it alone."

Jens took possession of the mansion in Bredgade, and brought it to submission, neither by might nor by power, but in the quality of that fascinating and irresistible personage, perhaps the most fascinating and irresistible in the whole world: the dreamer whose dreams come true. The old house fell a little in love with him. Such is ever the lot of dreamers, when dealing with people at all susceptible to the magic of dreams. The most renowned amongst them, Rachel's son, as all the world knows, suffered hardships and was even cast in prison on that account. Except for his size, Jens had no resemblance to the classic portraits of Cupid; all the same it was evident that, unknowingly, the shipowner and his wife had taken into them an amorino. He carried wings into the house, and was in league with the sweet and merciless powers of nature, and his relation to each individual member of the household became a kind of aerial love affair. It was upon the strength of this same magnetism that Jakob had picked out the boy as heir to the firm at their first meeting, and that Emilie was afraid to be alone with him. The old magnate and the servants of the house no more escaped their destiny—as was once the case with Potiphar, captain to the guard of Egypt. Before they knew where they were, they had committed all they had into his hands.

One effect of this particular spell was this: that people were made to see themselves with the eyes of the dreamer, and were impelled to live up to an ideal, and that for this their higher existence they became dependent upon him. During the time that Jens lived in the house, it was much changed, and dissimilar to the other houses of the town. It became a Mount Olympus, the abode of divinities.

The child took the same lordly, laughing pride in the old shipowner, who ruled the waters of the universe, as in Jakob's staunch, protective kindness and Emilie's silk-clad gracefulness. The old housekeeper, who had often before grumbled at her lot in life, for the while was transformed into an all-powerful, benevolent guardian of human welfare, a Ceres in cap and apron. And for the same length of time the coachman, a monumental figure, elevated sky-high above the crowd, and combining within his own person the vigour of the two bay horses, majestically trotted down Bredgade on eight shod and clattering hoofs. It was only after Jens' bed hour, when, immovable and silent, his cheek buried in the pillow, he was exploring new areas of dreams that the house resumed the aspect of a rational, solid Copenhagen mansion.

Jens was himself ignorant of his power. As his new family did not scold him or find fault with him, it never occurred to him that they were at all looking at him. He gave no preference to any particular member of the household; they were all within his scheme of things and must there fit into their place. The relation of the one to the other was the object of his keen, subtle observation. One phenomenon in his daily life never ceased to entertain and please him: that Jakob, so big, broad and fat, should be attentive and submissive to his slight wife. In the world that he had known till now bulk was of supreme moment. As later on Emilie looked back upon this time, it seemed to her that the child would often provoke an opportunity for this fact to manifest itself, and would then, so to say, clap his hands in triumph and delight, as if the happy state of things had been brought about by his personal skill. But in other cases his sense of proportion failed him. Emilie in her boudoir had a glass aquarium with goldfish, in front of which Jens would pass many hours, as silent as the fish themselves, and from his comments upon them she gathered that to him they were huge—a fine catch could one get hold of them, and even dangerous to the pug, should she happen to fall into the bowl. He asked Emilie to leave the curtains by this window undrawn at night, in order that, when people were asleep, the fish might look at the moon.

In Jakob's relation to the child there was a moment of unhappy love, or at least of the irony of fate, and it was not the first time either that he had gone through this same melancholy experience. For ever since he himself was a small boy he had yearned to protect those weaker than he, and to support and right all frail and delicate beings in his surroundings. The very qualities of fragility and helplessness inspired in him an affection and admiration which came near to idolatry. But there was in his nature an inconsistency, such as will often be found in children of old, wealthy families, who have got all they wanted too easily, till in the end they cry out for the impossible. He loved pluck, too; gallantry delighted him wherever he met it, and for the clinging and despondent type of human beings, and in particular of women, he felt a slight distaste and repugnance. He might dream of shielding and guiding his wife, but at the same time the little cool, forbearing smile with which she would receive any such attempt on his side to him was one of the most bewitching traits in her whole person. In this way he found himself somewhat in the sad and paradoxical position of the young lover who passionately adores virginity. Now he learned that it was equally out of the question to patronize Jens. The child did not reject or smile at his patronage, as Emilie did; he even seemed grateful for it, but he accepted it in the part of a game or a sport. So that, when they were out walking together, and Jakob, thinking that the child must be tired, lifted him on to his shoulders, Jens would take it that the big man wanted to play at being a horse or an elephant just as much as he himself wanted to play that he was a trooper or a mahout.

Emilie sadly reflected that she was the only person in the house who did not love the child. She felt unsafe with him, even when she was unconditionally accepted as the beautiful, perfect mother, and as she recalled how, only a short time ago, she had planned to bring up the boy in her own spirit, and had written down little memoranda upon education, she saw herself as a figure of fun. To make up for her lack of feeling she took Jens with her on her walks and drives, to the parks and the zoo, brushed his thick hair, and had him dressed up as neatly as a doll. They were always together. She was sometimes amused by his strange, graceful, dignified delight in all that she showed him, and at the next moment, as in Madame Mahler's room, she realized that however generous she would be to him, he would always be the giver. Her sisters-in-law, and her young married friends, fine ladies of Copenhagen with broods of their own, wondered at her absorption in the foundling—and then it happened, when they were off their guard, that they did themselves receive a dainty arrow in their satin bosoms, and between them began to discuss Emilie's pretty boy, with a tender raillery as that with which they would have discussed Cupid. They asked her to bring him to play with their own children. Emilie declined, and told herself that she must first be certain about his manners. At the New Year, she thought, she would give a children's party herself.

Jens had come to the Vandamms in October, when trees were yellow and red in the parks. Then the tinge of frost in the air drove people indoors, and they began to think of Christmas. Jens seemed to know everything about the Christmas-tree, the goose with roast apples, and the solemnly joyful church-going on Christmas morning. But it would happen that he mixed up these festivals with others of the season, and described how they were soon all to mask and mum, as children do at Shrovestide. It was as if, from the centre of his happy, playful world, its sundry components showed up less clearly than when seen from afar.

And as the days drew in and the snow fell in the streets of Copenhagen, a change came upon the child. He was not low in spirits, but singularly collected and compact, as if he were shifting the centre of gravitation of his being, and folding his wings. He would stand for long whiles by the window, so sunk in thought that he did not always hear it when they called him, filled with a knowledge which his surroundings could not share.

For within these first months of winter it became evident that he was not at all a person to be permanently set at ease by what the world calls fortune. The essence of his nature was longing. The warm rooms with silk curtains, the sweets, his toys and new clothes, the kindness and concern of his Papa and Mamma were all of the greatest moment because they went to prove the veracity of his visions; they were infinitely valuable as embodiments of his dreams. But within themselves they hardly meant anything to him, and they had no power to hold him. He was neither a worldling nor a struggler. He was a Poet.

Emilie tried to make him tell her what he had in his mind, but got nowhere with him. Then one day he confided in her on his own account.

"Do you know, Mamma," he said, "in my house the stairs were so dark and full of holes that you had to grope your way up it, and the best thing was really to walk on one's hands and knees? There was a window broken by the wind, and below it, on the landing, there lay a drift of snow as high as me." "But that is not your house, Jens," said Emilie. "This is your house." The child looked round the room. "Yes," he said, "this is my fine house. But I have another house that is quite dark and dirty. You know it, you have been there too. When the washing was hung up, one had to twine in and out across that big loft, else the huge, wet, cold sheets would catch one, just as if they were alive." "You are never going back to that house," said she. The child gave her a great, grave glance, and after a moment said: "No."

But he was going back. She could, by her horror and disgust of the house, keep him from talking of it, as the children there by their indifference had silenced him on his happy home. But when she found him mute and pensive by the window, or at his toys, she knew that his mind had returned to it. And now and again, when they had played together, and their intimacy seemed particularly secure, he opened on the theme. "In the same street as my house," he said, one evening as they were sitting together on the sofa before the fireplace, "there was an old lodging-house, where the people who had plenty of money could sleep in beds, and the others must stand up and sleep, with a rope under their arms. One night it caught fire, and burned all down. Then those who were in bed did hardly get their trousers on, but ho! those who stood up and slept were the lucky boys; they got out quick. There was a man who made a song about it, you know."

There are some young trees which, when they are planted, have thin, twisted roots and will never take hold in the soil. They may shoot out a profusion of leaves and flowers, but they must soon die. Such was the way with Jens. He had sent out his small branches upwards and to the sides, had fared excellently of the chameleon's dish and eaten air, promise-crammed, and the while he had forgotten to put out roots. Now the time came when by law of nature the bright, abundant bloom must needs wither, fade and waste away. It is possible, had his imagination been turned on to fresh pastures, that he might for a while have drawn nourishment through it, and have detained his exit. Once or twice, to amuse him, Jakob had talked to him of China. The queer outlandish world captivated the mind of the child. He dwelled with the highest excitement on pictures of pig-tailed Chinamen, dragons and fishermen with pelicans, and upon the fantastic names of Hongkong and Yangtze-kiang. But the grown-up people did not realize the significance of his novel imaginative venture, and so, for lack of sustenance, the frail, fresh branch soon drooped.

A short time after the children's party, early in the new year, the child grew pale and hung his head. The old doctor came and gave him medicine to no effect. It was a quiet, unbroken decline: the plant was going out.

As Jens was put to bed and was, so to say, legitimately releasing his hold upon the world of actuality, his fancy fetched headway and ran along with him, like the sails of a small boat, from which the ballast is thrown overboard. There were, now, people round him all the time who would listen to what he said, gravely, without interrupting or contradicting him. This happy state of things enraptured him. The dreamer's sick-bed became a throne.

Emilie sat at the bed all the time, distressed by a feeling of impotence which sometimes in the night made her wring her hands. All her life she had endeavoured to separate good from bad, right from wrong, happiness from unhappiness. Here she was, she reflected with dismay, in the hands of a being, much smaller and weaker than herself, to whom these were all one, who welcomed light and darkness, pleasure and pain, in the same spirit of gallant, debonair approval and fellowship. The fact, she told herself, did away with all need of her comfort and consolation here at her child's sick-bed; it often seemed to abolish her very existence.

Now within the brotherhood of poets Jens was a humorist, a comic fabulist. It was, in each individual phenomenon of life, the whimsical, the burlesque moment that attracted and inspired him.

To the pale, grave young woman his fancies seemed sacrilegious within a death-room, yet after all it was his own death-room.

"Oh, there were so many rats, Mamma," he said, "so many rats. They were all over the house. One came to take a bit of lard on the shelf—pat! a rat jumped at one. They ran across my face at night. Put your face close to me, and I will show you how it felt." "There are no rats here, my darling," said Emilie. "No, none," said he. "When I am sick no more I shall go back and fetch you one. The rats like the people better than the people like them. For they think us good, lovely to eat. There was an old comedian, who lived in the garret. He had played comedy when he was young, and had travelled to foreign countries. Now he gave the little girls money to kiss him, but they would not kiss him, because they said that they did not like his nose. It was a curious nose, too—all fallen in. And when they would not he cried and wrung his hands. But he got ill, and died, and nobody knew about it. But when at last they went in, do you know, Mamma— the rats had eaten off his nose!—nothing else, his nose only! But people will not eat rats even when they are very hungry. There was a fat boy in the cellar, who caught rats in many curious ways, and cooked them. But old Madame Mahler said that she despised him for it, and the children called him Rat-Mad."

Then again he would talk of her own house. "My Grandpapa," he said, "has got corns, the worst corns in Copenhagen. When they get very bad he sighs and moans. He says: 'There will be storms in the China Sea. It is a damned business; my ships are going to the bottom.' So, you know, I think that the seamen will be saying: 'There is a storm in this sea; it is a damned business; our ship is going to the bottom.' Now it is time that old Grand-papa, in Bredgade, goes and has his corns cut."

Only within the last days of his life did he speak of Mamzell

Ane. She had been, as it were, his Muse, the only person who had knowledge of the one and the other of his worlds. As he recalled her his tone of speech changed; he held forth in a grand, solemn manner, as upon an elemental power, of necessity known to everyone. If Emilie had given his fantasies her attention many things might have been made clear to her. But she said: "No, I do not know her, Jens." "Oh, Mamma, she knows you well!" He said: "She sewed your wedding-gown, all of white satin. It was slow work—so many fittings! And my Papa," the child went on and laughed, "he came in to you, and do you know what he said? He said: 'My white rose.'" He suddenly bethought himself of the scissors which Mamzell Ane had left him, and wanted them, and this was the only occasion upon which Emilie ever saw him impatient or fretful.

She left her house for the first time within three weeks, and went herself to Madame Mahler's house to inquire about the scissors. On the way the powerful, enigmatical figure of Mamzell Ane took on to her the aspect of a Parca, of Atropos herself, scissors in hand, ready to cut off the thread of life. But Madame Mahler in the meantime had bartered away the scissors to a tailor of her acquaintance, and she flatly denied the existence both of them and of Mamzell Ane.

Upon the last morning of the boy's life Emilie lifted her small pug, that had been his faithful playmate, onto the bed. Then the little dark face and the crumpled body seemed to recall to him the countenance of his friend. "There she is!" he cried.

Emilie's mother-in-law and the old shipowner himself had been daily visitors to the sick-room. The whole Vandamm family stood weeping round the bed when, in the end, like a small brook which falls into the ocean, Jens gave himself up to, and was absorbed in, the boundless, final unity of dream.

He died by the end of March, a few days before the date that Emilie had fixed to decide on his fitness for admission into the house of Vandamm. Her father suddenly determined that he must be interred in the family vault—irregularly, since he was never legally adopted into the family. So he was laid down behind a heavy wrought-iron fence, within the finest grave that any Plejelt had ever obtained.

Within the following days the house in Bredgade, and its inhabitants with it, shrank and decreased. The people were a little confused, as after a fall, and seized by a sad sense of diffidence. For the first weeks after Jens' burial life looked to them strangely insipid, a sorry affair, void of purport. The Vandamms were not used to being unhappy, and were not prepared for the sense of loss with which now the death of the child left them. To Jakob it seemed as if he had let down a friend, who had, after all, laughingly trusted to his strength. Now nobody had any use for it, and he saw himself as a freak, the stuffed puppet of a colossus. But with all this, after a while there was also in the survivors, as ever at the passing away of an idealist, a vague feeling of relief.

Emilie alone of the house of Vandamms preserved, as it were, her size, and her sense of proportion. It may even be said that when the house tumbled from its site in the clouds, she upheld and steadied it. She had deemed it affected in her to go into mourning for a child who was not hers, and while she gave up the balls and parties of the Copenhagen season, she went about her domestic tasks quietly as before. Her father and her mother-in-law, sad and at a loss in their daily life, turned to her for balance, and because she was the youngest amongst them, and seemed to them in some ways like the child that was gone, they transferred to her the tenderness and concern which had formerly been the boy's, and of which they now wished that they had given him even more. She was pale from her long watches at the sick-bed; so they consulted between them, and with her husband, on means of cheering and distracting her.

But after some time Jakob was struck with, and scared by, her silence. It seemed at first as if, except for her household orders, she found it unnecessary to speak, and later on as if she had forgotten or lost the faculty of speech. His timid attempts to inspirit her so much appeared to surprise and puzzle her that he lacked the spirit to go on with them.

A couple of months after Jens' death Jakob took his wife for a drive by the road which runs from Copenhagen to Elsinore, along the Sound. It was a lovely, warm and fresh day in May. As they came to Charlottenlund he proposed to her that they should walk through the wood, and send the carriage round to meet them. So they got down by the forest-gate, and for a moment their eyes followed the carriage as it rolled away on the road.

They came into the wood, into a green world. The beech trees had been out for three weeks, the first mysterious translucence of early May was over. But the foliage was still so young that the green of the forest world was the brighter in the shade. Later on, after midsummer, the wood would be almost black in the shade, and brilliantly green in the sun. Now, where the rays of the sun fell through the tree-crowns, the ground was colourless, dim, as if powdered with sun-dust. But where the wood lay in shadow it glowed and luminesced like green glass and jewels. The anemones were faded and gone; the young fine grass was already tall. And within the heart of the forest the woodruff was in bloom; its layer of diminutive, starry, white flowers seemed to float, round the knotty roots of the old grey beeches, like the surface of a milky lake, a foot above the ground. It had rained in the night; upon the narrow road the deep tracks of the wood-cutters' cart were moist.

Here and there, by the roadside, a grey, misty globe of a withered dandelion caught the sun; the flower of the field had come on a visit to the wood.

They walked on slowly. As they came a little way into the wood they suddenly heard the cuckoo, quite close. They stood still and listened, then walked on. Emilie let go her husband's arm to pick up from the road the shell of a small, pale-blue, bird's egg, broken in two; she tried to set it together, and kept it on the palm of her hand. Jakob began to talk to her of a journey to Germany that he had planned for them, and of the places that they were to see. She listened docilely, and was silent.

They had come to the end of the wood. From the gate they had a great view over the open landscape. After the green sombreness of the forest the outside world seemed unbelievably light, as if bleached by the luminous dimness of midday. But after a while the colours of fields, meadows and dispersed groups of trees defined themselves to the eye, one by one. There was a faint blue in the sky, and faint white cumulus clouds rose along the horizon. The young green rye on the fields was about to ear; where the finger of the breeze touched it it ran in long, gentle billows along the ground. The small thatched peasants' houses lay like lime-white, square isles within the undulating land; round them the lilac-hedges bore up their light foliage and, on the top, clusters of pale flowers. They heard the rolling of a carriage on the road in the distance, and above their heads the incessant singing of innumerable larks.

By the edge of the forest there lay a wind-felled tree. Emilie said: "Let us sit down here a little."

She loosened the ribbons of her bonnet and lay it in her lap. After a minute she said: "There is something I want to tell you," and made a long pause. All through this conversation in the wood she behaved in the same way, with a long silence before each phrase—not exactly as if she were collecting her thoughts, but as if she were finding speech in itself laborious or deficient.

She said: "The boy was my own child." "What are you talking about?" Jakob asked her. "Jens," she said, "he was my child. Do you remember telling me that when you saw him the first time you thought he was like me? He was indeed like me; he was my son." Now Jakob might have been frightened, and have believed her to be out of her mind. But lately things had, to him, come about in unexpected ways; he was prepared for the paradoxical. So he sat quietly on the trunk, and looked down on the young beech-shoots in the ground. "My dear," he said, "my dear, you do not know what you say."

She was silent for a while, as if distressed by his interruption of her course of thought. "It is difficult to other people to understand, I know," she said at last, patiently. "If Jens had been here still, he might perhaps have made you understand, better than I. But try," she went on, "to understand me. I have thought that you ought to know. And if I cannot speak to you I cannot speak to anyone." She said this with a kind of grave concern, as if really threatened by total incapacity of speech. He remembered how, during these last weeks, he had felt her silence heavy on him, and had tried to make her speak of something, of anything. "No, my dear," he said, "you speak, I shall not interrupt you." Gently, as if thankful for his promise, she began:

"He was my child, and Charlie Dreyer's. You have met Charlie once in Papa's house. But it was while you were in China that he became my lover." At these words Jakob remembered the anonymous letter he had once received. As he recalled his own indignant scouting of the slander and the care with which he had kept it from her, it seemed to him a curious thing that after five years he was to have it repeated by her own lips.

"When he asked me," said Emilie, "I stood for a moment in great danger. For I had never talked with a man of this matter. Only with Aunt Malvina and with my old governess. And women, for some reason, I do not know which, will have it that such a demand be a base and selfish thing in a man, and an insult to a woman. Why do you allow us to think that of you? You, who are a man, will know that he asked me out of his love and out of his great heart, from magnanimity. He had more life in him than he himself needed. He meant to give that to me. It was life itself; yes, it was eternity that he offered me. And I, who had been taught so wrong, I might easily have rejected him. Even now, when I think of it, I am afraid, as of death. Still I need not be so, for I know for certain that if I were back at that moment again, I should behave in the same way as I did then. And I was saved from the danger. I did not send him away. I let him walk back with me, through the garden—for we were down by the garden-gate—and stay with me the night till, in the morning, he was to go so far away."

She again made a long pause, and went on: "All the same, because of the doubt and the fear of other people that I had in my heart, I and the child had to go through much. If I had been a poor girl, with only a hundred rixdollars in all the world, it would have been better, for then we should have remained together. Yes, we went through much."

"When I found Jens again and he came home with me," she took up her narrative after a silence, "I did not love him. You all loved him, only I myself did not. It was Charlie that I loved. Still I was more with Jens than any of you. He told me many things, which none of you heard. I saw that we could not find another such as he, that there was none so wise." She did not know that she was quoting the Scripture, any more than the old shipowner had been aware of doing so when he ordained Jens to be buried in the field of his fathers and the cave that was therein —this was a small trick peculiar to the magic of the dead child. "I learned much from him. He was always truthful, like Charlie. He was so truthful that he made me ashamed of myself. Sometimes I thought it wrong in me to teach him to call you Papa."

"By the time when he was ill," she said, "what I thought of was this: that if he died I might, at last, go into mourning for Charlie." She lifted up her bonnet, gazed at it and again dropped it. "And then after all," she said, "I could not do it." She made a pause. "Still if I had told Jens about it, it would have pleased him; it would have made him laugh. He would have told me to buy grand black clothes, and long veils."

It was a lucky thing, Jakob reflected, that he had promised her not to interrupt her tale. For had she wanted him to speak he should not have found a word to say. As now she came to this point in her story she sat in silence for a long time, so that for a moment he believed that she had finished, and at that a choking sensation came upon him, as if all words must needs stick in his throat.

"I thought," she suddenly began again, "that I would have had to suffer, terribly even, for all this. But no, it has not been so. There is a grace in the world, such as none of us has known about. The world is not a hard or severe place, as people tell us. It is not even just. You are forgiven everything. The fine things of the world you cannot wrong or harm; they are much too strong for that. You could not wrong or harm Jens; no one could. And now, after he has died," she said, "I understand everything."

Again she sat immovable, gently poised upon the tree-stem. For the first time during their talk she looked round her; her gaze ran slowly, almost caressingly, along the forest scenery.

"It is difficult," she said, "to explain what it feels like to under-stand things. I have never been good at finding words, I am not like Jens. But it has seemed to me ever since March, since the Spring began, that I have known well why things happened, why, for instance, they all flowered. And why the birds came. The generosity of the world; Papa's and your kindness too! As we walked in the wood today I thought that now I have got back my sight, and my sense of smell, from when I was a little girl. All things here tell me, of their own, what they signify." She stopped, her gaze steadying. "They signify Charlie," she said. After a long pause she added: "And I, I am Emilie. Nothing can alter that either."

She made a gesture as if to pull on her gloves that lay in her bonnet, but she put them back again, and remained quiet, as before.

"Now I have told you all," she said. "Now you must decide what we are to do."

"Papa will never know," she said gently and thoughtfully. "None of them will ever know. Only you. I have thought, if you will let me do so, that you and I, when we talk of Jens—" She made a slight pause, and Jakob thought: "She has never talked of him till today"—"might talk of all these things, too."

"Only in one thing," she said slowly, "am I wiser than you. I know that it would be better, much better, and easier to both you and me if you would believe me."

Jakob was accustomed to take a quick summary of a situation and to make his dispositions accordingly. He waited a moment after she had ceased to talk, to do so now.

"Yes, my dear," he said, "that is true."

ÁLKMENE

MY FATHER'S ESTATE lay in a lonely part of Jutland, and I was his only child. When my mother died he did not care to send me away to school, but when I was seven years old he took on a tutor for me.

My tutor's name was Jens Jespersen; he was a theological student and, I believe, the most honest man I have known in my life. He was himself the son of a poor village parson; he had had to work hard to get on to the University of Copenhagen, and there the professors had been expecting great things from him. But his health had suffered during his years of study, and for that reason he had, already five years ago, left town and taken on the job as a teacher in the country.

Under his direction I took to books more willingly than I had ever thought I would, and was quite happy both at school and in the company of our keepers and grooms. And so I managed to gather a little knowledge of mathematics and of the classics, as well as of horses and game.

Two years later my father went off to a watering place, took me with him, and left me at a school in Holstein; but after an equal span of time he again fetched me back. During my absence our old, drunken parson of the estate had died, and my father had presented the living to my former tutor. He was now settled in the parsonage and had married the girl to whom he had been engaged for five years. From then on I continued my lessons by riding down to the parsonage every day. I also sometimes stayed there over a night or two.

The parsonage was a ramshackle old place, and the people within it were poor, for the living was but small, and my old teacher still had heavy debts from his student days to pay off. All the same, it was a joyous place, because the parson was so happily married. His wife's name was Gertrud. She was twelve years younger than her husband, but twelve years older than I, so that she sometimes seemed to be the contemporary of the clergyman, and sometimes of the schoolboy. She was a big young woman, who was not considered pretty by the parish, for she had a broad face, and in summer she was as freckled as a turkey's egg. But she had clear, bright eyes—so that when in Homer I read about the lively-glancing maiden Chryseis, I thought of her—and rich reddish hair. I remember the first time that I realized how well I liked her. One summer evening a party of young people from the neighbourhood were gathered at the parsonage and were playing hide-and-seek all over the house. I had hidden in a small lumber room in the attic. While I was there the parson's wife came rushing in, and without seeing me squeezed up behind the door. She stood there, all out of breath from her run up the stairs, and placed a finger upon her lips. Then a moment after she must have bethought herself of a better hiding-place; she swept from the room and was gone. I thought it very pretty in her to behave so neatly and gaily when she believed that she was all alone.

One summer we had a distinguished visitor at the parsonage, a friend of the parson's student's days, although older than he, and now a professor at the Royal Opera, or Ballet, of Copenhagen; I do not remember which. He also visited the manor, played on our old piano, and quite enchanted my father, as he did everybody. Once he and I were alone in a room of the parsonage; he was standing by the open garden door and was looking at the parson's wife, who picked up apples under the trees. "It is indeed a priceless thing," he said, more to himself than to me, "that this young woman should be held by the good people of Hover parish to be lacking in looks. It is true that her head is but roughly modelled. But were she living in the great world, where ladies are more liberal in showing their charms, she would be the idol of the one sex and the envy

of the other. For such a living, breathing Venus I have not set eyes
on in my life. Why, she outshines Henrietta Hendel-Schutz in her
'Morgenscenen.' Would she then," he went on, "still make our
godly parson such a model wife? To women with a plain face and
a divine body, virtue must at times appear strangely paradoxical."
This was perhaps a frivolous discourse to hold before a young boy;
still I do not remember his words to have left any such impression
with me. They only seemed to make it clear to me why I should
feel so well in Gertrud's company.

But in the course of the next year the parson's happy household
became overhung by a black and horrible shadow. The gentle
young housewife from time to time would appear deadly pale, red-
eyed with weeping, turned to stone, and would shrink from her
husband as in dread or hatred. I was alarmed and grieved at the
sight. I thought that the parson showed her but inadequate sympathy in her misery, and the situation to me was both mysterious
and woeful.

One day the parson, in his study, was taking me through a chapter in Genesis. When he came to the verse in which Rachel says
to Jacob: "Give me children or else I die," he laid down the book
and said: "Rachel was a good woman, but she had little patience
with her husband or with the Lord. You will in this house have
seen, Vilhelm, how hard the lot of childlessness comes to a woman.
My heart bleeds for my wife, and yet I fear that I am lacking both
in Christian compassion and in knowledge of the nature of woman-
kind. For she is a better Christian than I am, and all the same she
will storm and rage against the Lord, and refuse to bow her heart
to His will. I do not believe that I myself should ever be capable of
grieving so vehemently, and so persistently, over a misfortune in
which I was altogether without guilt. Although," after a moment
he added gravely, his hands folded, "God alone knows. It is a wise

man who can say of himself: Of such a thing I could never be capable." These last words of his I remembered, and they came back to me, later, in a sad and bloody hour.

Again after a while he said, with a little smile: "The good man Jacob, however, was, in Jewry, in a position to prove to his wife that the fault lay not with him."

I was thus enlightened on Gertrud's sorrows. Still the state of things was somewhat enigmatical to me, since I could not comprehend that anybody should desire children so ardently as to die from want of them.

In those days the mail came but twice a month, and a letter was a rare event. One day in October the parson had a letter from Copenhagen. He turned it in his hands, informed me that it came from his friend the professor, and wondered what he could well have to write. But when he had read the letter through twice, he said: "I shall give you leave for the afternoon, for this gives me so much to think about that I will make but a poor teacher." A few days after, it happened that we were out in the stable together, to look at a sick cow, for the parson always held that I had a good hand with animals, while he himself knew but little about them. When we had doctored the cow, he stood on in thought, and in the dim stable he told me what was on his mind. "I think, Vilhelm," he said, "that your mother must have been a woman of good sense, for you have a level head, and that you did not inherit from the Squire. Now I am going to tell you what I have spoken of to no one else. The Scripture has it that wisdom may be found in the mouths of children."

The professor, he said, wrote to him that he had, by some strange adventure, got on his hands a little girl of six, singularly and tragically situated in life, so that indeed she might be named Perdita after the heroine of Shakespeare's tragedy. The nativity of this child he must never disclose. It was, he wrote, no wonder that the sight of a homeless and friendless child to him should call forth the picture of his friend's happy household, wherein only a child was lacking. But he would now in no way persuade the parson to take on the girl; under the particular circumstances this would even be unseemly. He only stated that, should any Christian man or woman have pity on her, and take her as their own, they would never be interfered with by any relation or connection of the child. "And one more thing I feel it my duty to set down"—he finished the letter— "If no one can be found to take this child, her fate will, by the nature of things be highly uncertain and perilous and, in fact, I know of no human being who does more completely and pathetically answer to the proverbial saying of the brand to be snatched from the fire." He gave the name of the child; it was Alkmene.

I listened to all this, and said that it sounded like a tale out of a book. "Yes," said the parson. "And very likely is. For my old friend is a man of few scruples. One of those dancing and singing mamzells of Copenhagen may have sought his help to rid herself of an inopportune child, and there he goes: inventing, fabulating, weeping even, to play a trick on his simple friend, the village parson. Alkmene, now," he went on, "will that really be the name of the child? When I was a young student, and dreamed of becoming a poet, I wrote an epic called 'Alkmene' and he knows of it, for I read it to him." I quoted the *Iliad,* and said: "Nor Alkmene of Thebes . . ." "Who bore me Heracles, a child staunch of heart," the parson finished the verse for me. "Yes. He means to call me back to Olympus."

"Vilhelm," he said after a while, "I shall tell you something, which I do not believe I could recount to a grown-up person. It is absurd and will make you laugh, still to me it has once been dead earnest. I have told people that I left Copenhagen on account of my health. But it was not only that. I went because I had there fallen into temptation, yea, into sin. It was not vice, or weakness either, but that graver wickedness by which the angels fell. I was working too hard in Copenhagen and had little to eat, and no natural diversions. I sat with my books, and did not speak to any human being for months. And it came to this with me: that I firmly believed myself to have been chosen by the Lord for great things; yes, I held that in the whole world all was done by the Lord with a view to my soul and my destiny. When the old mad King died I thought: 'How does the Lord mean this to affect me?' and when later the Emperor Napoleon was beaten by the Russians, at Moscow, I said to myself: 'Now that man is gone who would have turned the eyes of the world from such great things as the Lord means me to accomplish.' It was a good thing that my condition became clear to me before it was too late. I saw, with great fear, that I was on the brink of the abyss of insanity, and that I must save myself at any cost, at the cost of my studies. When, here, I came to live in the country once more, with good, simple people, my mind regained its balance. And later on my dear wife set me right. But even here, Vilhelm, even here, the old temptation has come back to me. When I have sat by the death-beds of my parishioners, and have listened to their confessions—and you will sometimes hear awful things from these peasants—and when, rightly, I should be concerned with the soul of the poor sinner only, I have sat and wondered: Why does the Lord place these things on my path? Does he mean to try my faith, by confronting it with the powers of darkness?

"Now my old friend here a long time ago guessed most of this matter. He once took an interest in me, and believed in my talents; he was disappointed when I ran away from Copenhagen. Is his letter not, now, a small revenge, or a joke, on me? It brings back to me the great town, and the whole sphere of the theatre, which once meant much to me. The name of Alkmene itself rings with an echo of the Greek world, with its gods and nymphs, and of my old ambition as a poet. During these last days I have reflected, as once up in my garret: What is the Lord doing to me? Does he hold that my life has been too easy, and that I stand in need of temptation? Yes, I have met again with that young, wild, distracted student, who ten years ago walked the streets of Copenhagen. And all the time I am well aware that I should be concerning myself with other things, as with the idea of the happiness of my wife. And first and foremost perhaps with the fate of this poor child, Alkmene."

I do not remember that I made any comment to the parson's speech. While he talked I reflected that I myself did reason much in the manner that he had described. But while it was unreasonable in him, in me it was legitimate, since I was the Squire's son, and here at Nørholm, at least, things were done for my sake and in my interest. That night I dreamed of the child Alkmene. I met her in a field, and the big A in her name shone like silver.

A fortnight later the parson's wife fell on my neck and told me that she and her husband had decided to take, as their own, a little girl from Copenhagen—for all the world as if she had been confiding to me that she was with child. About the secrecy of the child's birth she did not speak. Later on she gave out to a few friends that the child was her cousin's, an officer's widow, and I believe that there was indeed such a person.

It was some time before travelling accommodations could be found for the child. The parson jestingly spoke of these months as his wife's period of pregnancy. She was very happy and gentle with us all, but often strangely moved. Whenever she and I were alone, she talked of the child, and pictured how she was to be like a small sister to me. "And how, Vilhelm," she whispered, "would you like to fetch a little wife at Hover parsonage?" The idea was ridiculous to me, and had the child been her own, Gertrud would never have hit upon it either. After Alkmene had come, however, she did never again mention it, for then, I believe, she could not bear to think that the child might ever leave her, were it to marry the King's son.

At last, late in December, the child was to arrive in Vejle from Copenhagen, and the parson went in to fetch her. I had been to the parsonage that day, to get some books. While I was there the wind rose, and such a wild blizzard began that I did not ride home, but stayed for the night where I was. From time to time the parson's wife and I went outside to look at the weather. The air was thick with snow; it ran along the earth like smoke, and lay so deep on the stone steps that it was hard to open the door. It was the first time that Gertrud and I were ever alone in the house. She began to talk to me of her childhood. Her father, she said, was a big cattle-dealer out westward, who worked hard and did well, until, in the state bankruptcy in 1813, he lost his money. When he was told that all his savings were worth but fifty rixdollars, the cattle-dealer's heart broke; from then he was sunk in melancholia. His wife, to save her family, then began sheep farming, and Gertrud, the eldest of nine children, and by then eleven years old, became her assistant in the work. It was a hard life. "But what better thing," said Gertrud, "can be found on our earth than that hard, honest work which God set us there to do? We should not question." Gertrud's heart was still with the sheep. She became eager to impart her knowledge of them to me, and I learned much about lambing and shearing while we waited on this evening of the snowstorm.

Just past midnight we heard sleigh-bells, and ran to open the door to our travellers, who stumbled from the sledge all white with snow. They had been stuck in the snow drifts seven times since leaving Vejle. The parson bore the child in, and set her on the floor by the stove. She was wrapped in a large cloak. As he pulled off her cap her fair, short hair rose with it, like a flame above her head and I recalled the professor's words of the brand to be snatched from the fire. I also reflected that my good pulpiteer and his wife would never, between them, have produced a child of such strange, striking, noble beauty. Her small face, with its grandly swung eyebrows, was as white as marble from cold and fatigue. Gertrud knelt down before her, folded her hands in her own to warm them, and patted her cheek. She blushed like a rose, trembled and smiled. "Have you had a cold journey, my poor lamb?" she asked. The pale child neither advanced nor withdrew; she stood up straight and took in the room, and the people within it, with wide-open, grave, light eyes. "And what will your name be, now, my pretty chick?" Gertrud went on. "Alkmene," said the child.

When Gertrud had made her drink a cup of hot milk, she carried her in her arms into the bedroom. Through the door we heard her prattling and cooing to the child, and once or twice the little girl's low, clear voice. In a while Gertrude came and stood in the door-way, she could not speak, for she was crying. "Oh, Jens," she said at last to her husband, "she has got no shift on." Then again she closed the door. The parson was warming a jug of coffee and rum on the stove. "The old fox," he said to me, and laughed. "He reads women's hearts like a book. He may well have pulled the child's shift off with his own hands, to move the heart of my poor wife."

This Christmas, as I was now fourteen, my father gave me a gun. I was out every day shooting, following the game-track in the snow, and except for my lessons I did not see much of the people in the parsonage. But whenever Gertrud could catch me, she would talk of Alkmene. They called the child Alkmene at first, but Gertrud thought the name outlandish, so they shortened it to Mene, and by this name the child of the parsonage became known by the neighbourhood. I remember when, that summer, there was a clergyman's meeting at the parsonage, that an old pastor from Randers got hold of the name, and exclaimed: "Mene mene tekel upharsin!" But neither the parson nor his wife liked the joke.

To Gertrud the child was wonderful from the beginning; she held her spellbound by everything she did. The first thing she told me about her was that she seemed to be altogether without fear. Neither the bull nor the gander frightened her; she liked them best of all the farm animals. She climbed the ladder to the ridge of the barn, when they were rethatching it after the snowstorm. Gertrud was uneasy about this trait in the child. Together with the missing shift it set her fancy running; she imagined that the little girl had been so forlorn as to know of no risk in life. Perhaps she even hit on the truth. So she made it her first duty as a mother to teach her child, as in the fairy-tales, to know fear. She next confided to me that Mene did not seem to know truth from untruth. She did not tell tales in her own interest, but things to her looked different from what they did to other people, often in the most surprising way. If Gertrud had been alone with the child she could never have minded, for she had the peasants' love of fables and inventions, but she knew that her husband judged these things differently, and endeavoured, with patience and perseverance, to correct the child's failings. Alkmene was highly extravagant, too; she took but little care of her things and would often lose or even give away what Gertrud with great trouble had got together for her. This shocked and hurt Gertrud; she took it much to heart, and at times could not help thinking the child off her head. Still something about it impressed her as well; she had seen, or heard of, great people behaving in such a way.

When in the spring I came to the parsonage more frequently, I found it an idyl, such as one reads about in books. I think that this year and the following to my friend Gertrud were the most blissful of her life. The child called the parson and his wife Father and Mother, and after a while she seemed to have forgotten the time before she came to them, and to hold herself to belong to the parsonage. Gertrud would not let the child out of her sight, and Mene too, although she never liked to be fondled or petted, swerved round her mother neatly, like a kid with the roe. As if she had been trained by the professor himself she manifested a genuine adoration of Gertrud's beauty. She often talked of it, and she strung beads for necklaces for her, and in summer made a hundred garlands of flowers for her pretty hair. Gertrud had never before been admired for her looks; nor would the parson, I think, ever have made an inventive lover. This grave and graceful courtship was a new thing to her, and although to us she laughed at it, I saw that it delighted and enchanted her. The parson taught Mene to read and write, for she had none of these accomplishments. He found her quick of apprehension, and so in every way the three together made a happy group.

Although at first I laughed at all the fuss made over a little girl from Copenhagen, after a while Alkmene and I came to pass a good deal of our time together. It began when she begged leave to go with me when I was out shooting or fishing. She was so swift of eye and movement that it was like having a small cute dog with you. Here I learned that the fearless girl was scared in the face of death. The first time that I picked up a dead bird, still warm in my hands, she was sick with horror and disgust. But she would catch snakes and carry them in her hand. And she had a fancy for all wild birds, and learned to know of their nests and eggs. Then it was pleasant to hear her, in summer, imitate and answer the ring-dove and the cuckoo in the woods.

We did thus become friends in a way, I believe, unusual with a big boy and a small girl. We were indeed much like sister and brother, such as the parson's wife had wished us to be, and still, I think, not quite in the way she had wanted. When Gertrud spoke of the girl as a wife for me, I had thought the idea laughable. Even at fourteen I understood enough of the world to decide that a parson's daughter was no fit match for me. Later on, as she grew up so pretty, one might imagine that I should have dreamed of seducing the sweet lass of the parsonage. But that was as far from my mind as marriage. Our friendship was always chaste, and I do not remember that I did ever as much as take her hand. We quarrelled badly at times, such as friends, or brothers and sisters, will do, although we none of us quarrelled with our people at home, and once she did even, in anger, throw a stone at me. But the chief feature of our relation was a deep, silent understanding, of which the others could not know. We seemed, both of us, to be aware that we were like one another, in a world different from us. Later on I have explained the matter to myself by the assumption that we were, amongst the people of our surroundings, the only two persons of noble blood, and that hers was possibly, even by far, the noblest. In this manner, too, our companionship was mainly of the woods and the fields; it became suspended, or latent, when we were back in the house.

It was a curious trait in our friendship that I should so often dream of Alkmene, even when in the day I had not given her a thought. In my dreams she frequently disappeared, and was lost. One might imagine that these dreams, in the end, would have inspired me with a real fear of losing her. But it was not so; on the contrary, and to my own peril, they convinced me that, even when she appeared to be gone and away, she would be sure to come back when the day dawned.

Both as a child and a girl Mene was wonderfully light of movement. If she only lifted an arm to smooth her hair, it was a thing to make one gape, so favourable and faultless was it. And when she skipped in the woods she made me think of a roe, or of a fish that leaps in a brook. Later I have seen some famous dancers in the great theatres, but for sweetness and harmony of motion none of them to my mind could touch the girl in the parsonage. I saw this from the beginning, but I do not think that the others ever noticed it; to Gertrud it was just part of the general excellence of the child. My father, however, remarked upon it. Now in the parsonage all dancing was prohibited. Moreover, to Gertrud, the art of the dance was somehow connected with the theatre and with the child's early years, of which she was very jealous, so that she would not hear or think of them. Alkmene, then, was never allowed to dance. But the parson taught her many other things. For a while he even set himself to teach her Greek, at which, he told me, she was quite extraordinarily quick. She could recite verses from the Greek comedies and tragedies.

During the next years Alkmene twice tried to run away from the parsonage. The first time, on a day in March, when the snow was just off the ground, she walked straight south across the fields, and had gone more than twelve miles before the parson's cowman, who was sent out in search that way, caught up with her and brought her home. Gertrud had believed the child drowned; her distress had been pitiful. She now clasped the girl to her bosom, stared at her, and kept on asking her why she had done them this great grief. The next day, when she thought that she was alone with the child, I heard her again question her: "Why did you run away? Why did you leave us?" And still she got no answer.

Two years later, when she was eleven, the girl again ran off, and this time gave her parents a still worse fright. For there had been a band of gypsies in the village; they had left the night before with their caravan, and had gone across the moors west of my father's land, and it was clear that Mene had gone after them. These people had a bad name in the country; it was believed that they had killed a pedlar a year ago. This time it was I who rode out and brought home the girl. I had by then finished my lessons with the parson. I had also travelled, but I still frequently came down to the parsonage.

It was a hot day in midsummer; there was a quivering air and great mirages over the moors. Twice I believed that I saw the girl in the vast landscape, when it was but a stack of peat. At last I caught sight of her small figure far away. She walked on quickly; after a while she began to run. It made me laugh, on my horse, as I was so sure that she could not escape me. Still there was something sad in the picture as well. As I came up to her I did not stop her, but for a while rode on side by side with her. She kept on hastening forth. She was bareheaded, very white, her face was wet with sweat. She could not keep pace with the horse. As a black-cock ran out of the heather in front of her and took to the wing with much noise, she stumbled and stood dead still. I felt sorry for her. I thought she was going to cry. "Give me your horse, Vilhelm," said she, "then I shall still catch up with them." "No," I said, "you are to come back. But I shall let you ride, and I will walk." Not a word said she. So I lifted her into the saddle.

It was a still day. I began to sing, and in a little while Alkmene joined in in her clear voice. We sang many songs, and in the end an old folk-song of a mother lamenting her dead child. I said: "You frighten your people, you fool, when you run away." She said: "Why will they not let me go?" I sang another verse and then said: "People are different. Look at my father now; nothing that I do will be right to him, and I am ever in his way. But your folks love you, and think you just a glorious girl, if you will only agree to stay with them." Alkmene was now silent for a long time; then she asked: "What about the children, Vilhelm, who do not want to be loved?"

We got back late. The summer moon rose, although the sky was still quite light. As we came to my father's land we crossed a barley field. The corn grew but sparsely in the sandy soil, but all over the field there was such a multitude of yellow marigolds that it seemed to reflect the moon in it, like a lake.

Gertrud, before I went, had made her husband promise to beat the child this time, but it was all forgotten when they got her back. Yet the mother, still very white with fear, could not becalm herself. She said: "You love these wicked people better than us, you would rather be with them than with your father and me. Do you not know that they would have killed you and eaten you?" Alkmene looked at her, her light eyes wide open. "Would they have eaten me?" she asked. Gertrud believed that she was mocking her. "Oh, you hard child!" she cried.

By the time when Mene was to be confirmed, two problems rose to the people of the parsonage. First, the parson found that he had never seen the child's certificate of baptism, and could not be sure that she had ever really been baptized. He wrote to the professor, but had to wait for the reply, for the old man had left Copenhagen, and had got a high office in a German court. When at last the letter came, the professor would do no more than give his word of honour that the girl was baptized. The parson, now, did not know whether to confirm the girl without more ado, or to baptize her himself, privately, first, to make sure. His wife told me that the dilemma caused him many sleepless nights. He said to me: "Some theologians hold baptism to be but a symbol. God help us all, symbols are mighty things. I myself may have handled great symbols too lightly." It was from this time that he gave up teaching the girl Greek. In the end, however, he took his wife's advice, and confirmed Mene together with the other children of the parish.

But at the confirmation class Mene met with other girls, and listened to their talk. And here, now, the parson and his wife found reason to believe that she heard rumours of how she was not their own child. Alkmene herself did not speak of it; somebody had overheard the girls' conversation. The parson weighed the matter in his mind, and one day, in my presence—really, I believe, because he feared to open the subject when he was alone with his wife— he told her that he meant to deal openly with the girl, and to tell her the truth. Gertrud at once turned upon him. I had not seen her so hard with him since the time before Mene came. It was as if she had forgotten that she was not really the girl's mother, and now held him to be wilfully bereaving her of her own child. "Nay," said the parson, "but I am to lay my hand on the child's head in the name of the Lord. What if, at that moment, in her heart she knows me to be deceiving her?" Gertrud stood up. "And do you want to take her from me altogether?" she cried. "Have you not seen, then, that she already hates and fears me? If now she is to be taught that I am not her mother, I shall have no means to hold her; she will wholly despise me and turn her back on me!" The parson sat dumb before her accusation. Still, as she spoke, I believe that we both realized that she was right. During these two last years Alkmene had altered and hardened towards her mother; at times she showed her a strange distrust, revolt and hostility. At last the parson said: "Dear wife, it might have been better if we had never taken on this task, but had sat here in our parsonage peacefully, an aging, childless couple." Gertrud stared at him, quite bewildered. "But we have laid our hand on the plough," he went on. "We must now carry through the work, according to our light." Gertrud began to cry. "Do as you think best," she said, and left the room.

But as I was going away she lay in wait for me. She took my hand, looked me in the face and said: "Vilhelm, you are my child's friend. Will you do something for me? Watch her, good Vilhelm. When her father will have spoken to her, note how it affects the poor child, and tell me what she says to you about it. For God help us, she will say nothing to me." It seemed to me a sad and affecting thing that Gertrud should thus turn to me for help, for she had till now held that no one but herself knew or understood her daughter. So I promised to do as she asked me.

Still a fortnight or so later on she said to me: "God is merciful, Vilhelm, or Jens is a wise man. Behold, since he has spoken to the child she is changed. She has come back to me, and keeps to me as sweetly as when she was a small girl. I myself feel young with it. I happened to look into the mirror today. You may laugh, but it was the face of a young woman that I saw there. I do not know why, but I feel, now, that this good and kindly conformity between us is going to last as long as we live." She quite forgot to question me on the matter, as she had said she would. "But is it not strange," she added after a while, "that she has not asked a single question about her real father and mother? She does not know that we could not have answered her."

To me Alkmene never spoke of her enlightenment. But I think that the parson, in the course of their talk, may have mentioned the professor's name, for one day she asked me if I knew him. I told her that I had seen him. "I should like," she said, "to see him, too, some time."

Gertrud complained to me that Mene was heedless about her clothes, and would take no more care of her Sunday gown, which she herself had made for her, than of her little faded week-day frocks. But one day the girl happened to hear our old housekeeper speak of my mother's fine gowns that were all locked up in a big chest in the attic, because my father would not see them, nor let anybody else wear them. She then gave me no peace until, on a day when my father was out, I broke open the chest for her and took out the clothes. She spread them out one by one and sat for a long time gazing at them; in the end she asked me to give her one. This was a dress of thick green silk with a yellow pattern to it. When I see it now it looks to me somewhat like a lime-tree in bloom. I laughed at her and asked her whether she meant to put it on to go to church. "No," she said, but she would wear it some time.

A little later, on a June evening, Gertrud had been baking fresh bread, and Alkmene begged leave of her to go with me—for I was then home for the summer holidays—and bring some to old Madame Ravn, the widow of our late parson, who lived on the other side of the village. But when we came out on the road, she told me that she did not mean to go to Madame Ravn at all; she would put on her silk gown, and we would go for a walk in the wood and the fields. She kept the gown in a cottage near by, with a woman who had before been working at the parsonage, but had been sent away because she drank. She went in there and soon came out again in the green and yellow frock. She had not put up her hair or washed her hands, yet I do not think that I have ever seen anyone more royal or at ease than she was then.

We walked in the woods, and she did not speak much. Her frock was a little too long for her, and she let it trail on the ground. I told her of my new horse that I had then just bought, and of a quarrel I had had with my father. If we had met people there they must have wondered and laughed at encountering a girl so magnificently dressed upon a forest path. All the same it somehow seemed natural that she should walk here like that. The wood was fresh. Where the low sun fell into it the foliage was all green and yellow like her gown, and as she walked the silk made a small chirping noise, like a late bird in a tree. We came upon a fox on the path, but we met no human beings.

When the sun was just above the horizon we came out in the fields. Here there was an exceeding high hill. We walked to the top of it, and from there had a great view to all sides over the golden plains and moors, and the glory of them. Alkmene stood quite still and gazed at it all. Her face was as clear and radiant as the air. After a while she drew a deep sigh of joy, and I reflected what ludicrous creatures girls are, who will be made happy by standing on the top of a hill in a silk gown. Later we sat down and ate the bread that Gertrud had meant for the old widow. It was still warm from the oven. Ever since, when I taste fresh bread, I am reminded of that evening and the hill.

As we came home to the parsonage, after Alkmene had again changed her clothes in the cottage, we found Gertrud by a tallow-candle with her glasses on, before a high pile of the girl's white stockings that were to be darned. She had done a good many already, but I thought that if she were to finish them all she must sit up late into the night. She smiled at us and wanted us to tell her of Madame Ravn. Alkmene stood behind her and looked at her and at the stockings, and it seemed to me that she was growing very white. "Let me help you to darn the stockings, Mother," she said. "No, my puss," said Gertrud, and snuffed the candle. "You have been a long way and ought to go to bed."

In the autumn of that same year a thing happened to me that came to have some influence on my life. A girl in the village, whose name was Sidsel and who was, by the way, daughter to the woman in whose cottage Alkmene had fetched her silk frock, had a baby that died and fathered me with the child. I did not believe her to be right, for she was no model of virtue. Still people would talk about it. My father said to me: "The child is dead, and Sidsel is to marry the keeper. But you shall not play the fool in your own village, while you wait for the wench in the parsonage to be big enough for you. Go up now to your uncle at Rugaard, in Djursland, for six months. His daughter is two years older than you, and will some day be a rich girl. In any case, you can there learn something about farming; it is time that you get that into your head." This last part of the lecture was unfair to me, for till now my father had but laughed, and called me a peasant, whenever I took any interest in the farm-work on the estate, which was then in a bad way.

I did not mind going away, but I wondered what the people in the parsonage were thinking of me. The parson would be sadly disappointed, for all his life he had preached against the licentiousness of his parish, and since I had been his pupil for such a long time, he had come to look on me as his own work. Gertrud might forgive me, for she was a country girl, and used to country ways, but she would take pains to keep the matter from Mene, and might also try to hold the girl herself away from me.

One afternoon when my father had gone to Vejle, I was in the library taking out some books, when the door was opened and Alkmene stood in the doorway. Our library turns north; she had the sun behind her, and her hair shone like a flame. She asked me: "Is it true what they are telling about you and Sidsel?" I was surprised to see her, for she had never before come to the manor alone. But she asked so forcibly that I had to answer. "Yes," I said. She cried out: "How dare you, Vilhelm!" Now it was a queer thing that I had for some time felt a grudge against the girl, as if, in what happened to me, she were at fault. As now she began to speak in the very words of the grown-up people, with a heavy heart I asked her to leave me alone. But she did not listen; she came into the room, her face all aflame with agitation. "How dare you?" she cried once more. I then remembered that with her you could generally take the words to mean just what they said. I realized that she was asking me a question, to be enlightened, such as she often did. I could not help laughing. "Perhaps," I said, "it does not take as much courage as it will seem to a girl." She looked at me, gravely and proudly. "You will be going to hell now, do you not think so?" she said. "They all tell me to go there," I said. "My father has turned me out of the house; your people will not speak to me. You and I, Alkmene, might remain friends for the time we have got left." "Has your father turned you out?" she asked. "Have you no home now? Then I shall come with you. We can go on the high roads together. And then," she added, and drew her breath deeply, "I shall do something, so that we shall not have to beg. I shall learn to dance." "Nay," I said, "I am going to my uncle at Rugaard." At that she grew very pale. "Are you going to your uncle?" she said. "I thought that they had chased you out in the wide world. I thought that nobody had ever done such a bad thing as you have done." All the time I was getting happier about things. "Why," I said, "you, who have read about the Greek gods, will know that such things have happened before in the world." "No," she said, "they will not let me read those books any more. They will not tell me anything. What am I to do now?" At that moment I saw clearly that she and I belonged to one another and I came near to ask her: "Will you wait for me until I come back, Alkmene? Then nobody shall part us again." But I thought of how young she was, and it seemed to me that the moment was not well chosen. She stood before me and wrung her hands. "Will you," she asked, "write to me? No," she interrupted herself, "it is only in books that people ever get a letter. But if you do a terrible thing once more, will you write of it to me?" "I shall come back in six months," I said. "Do not forget me, Alkmene." "No," she said, "I cannot forget you. You are my only friend. Do not forget Alkmene, Vilhelm." At that she was gone, as suddenly as she had come. A few days later I went to Rugaard.

Of my life at Rugaard I shall not write, since this is a story about Alkmene. The country seats in Djursland lie close to one another. I met many young people of my own age, and did not often think of people or things at home. But here also I dreamed about Alkmene.

When I had been at Rugaard for three months I had a letter from my father, who complained about his gout, and told me to come back. I did not give it much attention until I got another letter of the same kind; then I went home.

The first question that my father asked me was whether I had been making love to my cousin at Rugaard. He seemed pleased when I told him: "No," and rubbed his hands. "There are things going on here in your old district," he said; "there are great changes at the parsonage." I asked him what he meant, and he answered: "You had better go down and find out for yourself. These people were always such friends of yours." The next day I walked down to the parsonage.

The parson was alone in the house; his wife and daughter had gone on a sick-visit. He had changed, even as my father had said. He was grave, much occupied with his own thoughts, and I reflected that this was how he would have looked in those young days of his that he had told me of. He had forgotten all about the sad matter of Sidsel and greeted me kindly. After we had talked of other things for some time he said: "You ought to know, Vilhelm, what has come to us here, at your old parsonage," and went on to recount the happenings to me.

The old professor, his friend, had written him, shortly after my departure, to let him know that his adopted daughter had—by what ways, as usual, he could not or would not tell—come into an inheritance, just as if she had entered, he wrote, the wonder-cave of our immortal Oehlenschlager's *Aladdin*. In loyalty, he wrote on —the professor was always great on loyalty—to the first bargain between them he would endeavour no persuasion, but would leave to his friend to decide whether, on behalf of the girl, he would accept or refuse the fortune.

The parson said that he had thought the question over before he had taken his decision. "And it is a queer thing," he remarked, "that in what concerns our girl, my wife and I never seem to see eye to eye. Gertrud would not take the money. Now if it had been a smaller amount, it is possible that the arguing would have been all the other way round; she might then have been happy to see the girl secured in life, while I should have preferred to leave her as she was, of our own circumstances, a village parson's daughter. As it is, the greatness of the heritage frightens my poor wife." The parson here gave me the figure very precisely; it was over three hundred thousand rixdollars. "Gertrud cannot but feel that such a pile of gold must needs spring from a demonic source. To me, too, it has become a different thing."

He sat for some time in thought. "I have never," he said, "eagerly desired money. It did not even enter into the dreams of my youth. Other things I have craved and prayed for, but gold held no temptation to me. But in this case it takes on a new aspect; it becomes a symbol. I have seen it," he went on. "I went to Copenhagen, and there, in the bank, the gold was shown to me. I touched it. It lies dormant there, awaiting the hand which is to turn it into reality.

How much good can one not do, with a fortune like that, in this world? Mark, Vilhelm," he said, "I ignore not the power of Mammon. As I touched it, I recognized the danger which is in gold. But if it is to be, here, a trial of strength between God and Mammon, should I decline to take on the championship of the Lord?"

I asked the parson if Alkmene knew of her good luck. Yes, he answered, she had been told. She was a child still; it made but little impression on her; from her manner she might have known of it all her life. The work then was the more sacred to him, as he was undertaking it on behalf of a child. Indeed, he added, he had known from the first that through Alkmene some great task might come to him. "And when I am dead," he said, "I shall live on in her good works, for there is great strength in the lass, Vilhelm."

His speech gave me much to think about. It made me laugh to myself. I reflected that I did, perhaps, know Alkmene better than her father did.

My father, when I came home, questioned me eagerly on my visit, and I told him most of what the parson had told me. "And did you," he asked, "demand the girl in marriage?" "No," I said. "You are a fool," said my father. "A fortune like this compensates for the obscurity of her birth; it does, in some way, throw a new light upon it. You may well, in return, give her your name." As I did not answer him, he began to hold forth on the merits of the girl, like a horsedealer with a horse, and I was surprised to learn how well he had observed her, the while I believed him never to have given the parson's child a thought. In the end, although I rarely spoke my mind to him, I told him that I should think it highly inelegant in me to come and propose to Alkmene, on the news of her inheritance, when I had never before given her people reason to believe that I would do so. My father repeated that I was a fool, and in our discussion got very heated. At last he declared that if I were imbecile enough to refuse my chance, he himself would ask the girl to marry him.

I am ashamed to tell he really did so, and in a very silly manner. He had the team of four, which was seldom used, harnessed, and drove down to the parsonage to ask for Alkmene's hand. What happened in the interview I do not know. I doubt if my father did ever succeed in making clear to the parson and his wife the errand on which he came. But even after his failure my father kept on going through those improvements and embellishments of the estate, which might be worked with the girl's money. By all this he so much tired and annoyed me that I went away again without having seen Gertrud or Alkmene.

The next piece of news which I received from my home was that the parson had died. For many years his health had been weak; the journey to Copenhagen in the middle of winter had much exhausted him. There he caught a cold that developed into pneumonia. At his funeral I was struck by the deep grief of all his parish over their shepherd. Gertrud, in her great sorrow and distress, told me of his patience during the illness, and of how, on his deathbed, he had seemed to have a sudden and splendid revelation, and cried out that now he understood the ways of the Lord. She showed me a newspaper that had been sent her from Copenhagen. It contained an obituary of her husband, and was so strong in its praise of his character, on the role which, had he had ambition, he might have played on the stage of the world, and on his talents as a young man that it surprised even me, who held so high an opinion of him. The article was unsigned, but both she and I took it to have been written by his old friend, the professor.

After some months, during her year of grace at the parsonage, Gertrud went away to stay with a sister of hers, who was ill. My father, at the same time, had gone to Pyrmont for his gout. Alkmene was alone at the parsonage, as I at the manor. She then sent me a message and asked me to come down to see her.

She was now fifteen years old, tall for her age, but slight, and much like herself when she had first come to the parsonage. She said to me: "Do you remember, Vilhelm, that you once promised me that if ever I asked you to do me a great service, you would do it?" I recalled the occasion, and asked her what it was she wanted of me. "I want to go to Copenhagen," said she, "and you must take me. It shall be done now, while my mother is away. But I only want to stay there for a day." Now this was not easy to carry out. With the journey there and back, we should have to be away for a week, and nobody must find out. But Alkmene was determined to go, and, as I had once promised, I could not now refuse to help her. I also thought of what a sweet adventure it would make. So I did as she asked. She first went to friends in Vejle, and there, one early morning, I joined her at the stopping place of the coach. Luckily, neither in Vejle nor later did we meet, amongst the passengers, anybody we knew.

It was the month of May. The country through which we drove was freshly unfolded and green; the woods gave gentle, delicate shade. In the early mornings it was cool and dewy, but the larks were already in the sky. When we stopped at Sorø, in the spring evening we heard the nightingale. As now I look back upon the journey, I believe that I must by then have made up my mind to make Alkmene my wife, if she would have me, for I was most careful of her good name. Wherever we went I gave out that the pretty girl was my sister, and there was nothing in our manner to make people doubt my words. But my heart was filled with more pleasure and excitement than a brother's. I reflected that I had never been happy till now. I pictured to myself how in the future

we would often travel together. The girl took in the swiftly changing scenery as eagerly as a child. The sea in particular, as on the
second day in sunshine and a light breeze we crossed the Great
Belt, set her beside herself with wonder and exultation. The mys-
teriousness of our destination only, and at times something in her
face, caused me a vague uneasiness.

I had been to Copenhagen more than once. I had, before we
arrived, fixed on the hotel where we would stay. It was a quiet
place. We came to the town in the afternoon. The girl looked at
the people in the streets and at the women's dresses, but she did not
say much.

When we had had our evening meal at the hotel, I asked her to
let me know why she had come to Copenhagen. She then took
from her bag the newspaper which, after the parson's death, Gertrud had shown me, and said: "That is what I have come for."
Upon the last page there was a paragraph about a notorious murderer named Ole Sjælsmark, who was to have his head cut off on
the common north of Copenhagen. The paper told that the public
would be given access to the execution. It also gave the date and the
hour of the execution, and it was the next morning.

As I read this a great fear took hold of me. I saw and understood
clearly that the forces amongst which I had been moving were
mightier and more formidable than I had guessed, and that my
own whole world might be about to sink under me. I said to the
girl: "Such a thing would be terrible to watch. Many people hold
that it is a barbaric custom to let the crowd make an entertainment
for themselves out of a man's suffering and death, however horrible
are the things he has done." "No," said she, "it is not an entertainment. It is a warning to the people who may be near to doing the
same thing themselves, and who will be warned by nothing else.
Now the sight of this man's death will hold them from becoming

like him. My father," she went on, "once read to me a poem about a girl who had her head cut off. I remember what she said. It goes like this:

> *"Now over each head has quivered*
> *The blade that is quivering over mine.*

"For God alone knows all," she said. "And who can say of himself: of this deed I could never have been guilty?"

In the early morning Alkmene and I drove out to the North Common, a long way. By the scaffold a great crowd was already gathered, mostly rough and common people, but there were many women amongst them, and some had even brought their children. As we worked our way through the throng, they stared at the graceful, deadly pale girl on my arm. But then again they turned their eyes to where, in their midst, the dreadful structure was raised above the ground, with the executioner and his assistant already waiting.

When the cart, with the doomed man and the prison chaplain in it, came along, slowly, over the heads of the people, Alkmene trembled so heavily that I put my arm round her, and, although I was myself terrified and sad, it gave me a sweet content. The murderer sat with his face towards us. For a moment I thought that his eyes were seeking the face of the girl. The chaplain mounted the scaffold with him, and there took his hand and spoke to him, before he made him kneel in front of the block, and himself stood back to let the executioner take his place. A moment later the axe fell.

I thought that Alkmene would sink to the ground, but she kept upon her feet. The crowd now thronged round the scaffold, many of them dipping bits of cloth in the blood, which is held by the common people to cure the falling sickness, but we went away.

I had not slept that night, and the awful sight had made my hair rise on my head. I supported the girl, but I did not find a word to say to her. On our way back, while the day became clearer, I remembered the plans which, on our journey, I had made to show Alkmene the town, and I laughed at myself for being such a pitiful figure, a dunce. Still I said to her that before we went away—for I had promised to take her back that same evening—we ought to see the King's palace. So when we had left our cab at the hackney stable, we went there on foot. I could not help seeing how well she walked in the street, how graceful and grandly she carried herself in her little village dress and bonnet. And when we stood before the palace, and she gravely gazed up at it, I reflected that she had been born to live in a place like that.

While we stood there, an old man came along with a big bouquet in his hand, gazed at the girl as he passed, and, when he had walked on a bit, turned and came back to pass her and gaze at her again. I recognized him, although he was very old and crooked, and was also now dyed and painted, for it was the professor. I saw him following us at some distance, through the streets, and as we entered the hotel he kept standing before it, looking at the windows. I thought: "He is now going to deliver his bouquet, to whomever it is meant for, and then he will come back. But then, according to my promise to her, we shall have gone."

It happened that at the hotel I met a man I knew, who told me of a ship leaving for Vejle that same evening. I thought that it would be the easier to travel by sea, and I also was loath to pass, backwards, the very road by which we had come to Copenhagen. So when we left the hotel we took the way to the harbour.

It was a fine spring evening with a gentle southern wind as we sailed up the Sound. We sat on the deck and watched the coast; we saw a few lights spring up both on the Danish and the Swedish coast, and we kept sitting there most of the clear night. Alkmene had taken off her bonnet and tied a shawl round her head. When we had sailed past Elsinore and the castle of Kronborg, the moon came up.

I said to her: "I thought that you and I might have kept together all our lives, Alkmene." "Did you think that?" said she. "It is late to speak of these things now." "There was never really anything to make me doubt," said I, "that it might be so." "Nay," said she, "I have learned now that there are so many ways of looking at things. You, you speak about my life now. But before, when it was time, you did not try to save it." "But I want to ask you a question," I said. "Have you not known that I loved you all the time?" "Love?" she said. "They all loved Alkmene. You did not help her. Did you not know, now, all the time, that they were all against her, all?" I thought her words over for a while. "To me it was a joke," I said, "a thing of fun. Nay, I think that I did even feel sorry for them. It never occurred to me but that you were the stronger." "Yes, but it was not so," said she. "They were the strongest. It could not be otherwise when they were so good, when they were always right. Alkmene was alone. And when they died, and made her watch it, she could stand up against them no longer. She could see no way out, but she must die, too." She sat very still, and she looked small upon the ship's deck. "And can you not," she asked me "not even now say: 'Poor Alkmene'?" I tried to, but it would not come to me. "Will you remember," I at last asked her, "that I am your friend?" "Yes," said she, "I shall always remember that you took me to Copenhagen, Vilhelm. That was good of you."

I brought her back two days later, and nobody in the parsonage guessed but that she had been with her friends in Vejle all the time.

A short time afterwards, my father wrote to me to join him in Pyrmont, as he was ill and dared not undertake the journey home alone. It seemed to me that I had nothing to do at Nørholm; so I went. At Pyrmont my father and I each had a letter from Gertrud, who communicated to us her decision to leave the parsonage before the end of her year of grace. For her daughter had bought land in the west country, with a small farmhouse to it, to keep sheep there. Gertrud was no great letter writer. To my father she wrote humbly and gratefully. But in my letter I read, between the lines, an appeal for enlightenment: why had things gone the way they had? There was also, there, a dumb anguish, as if she were, in her heart, frightened at leaving her home, and at going out in the world, alone with her daughter. I did not see that I could set her at rest. I wrote back, thanked her for many years' kindness to me, and said good-bye.

I have not much more to tell in this story about Alkmene.

Sixteen years after our journey to Copenhagen, it happened that a matter of business took me out westwards, to the district where Alkmene's farm lay. My road ran close to it. I thought that I might call in, and turned off by the narrow, rough road to the house.

I drove through a wide, lonely landscape, with moors, bogs and long hills. It was a day in late August; the clouds hung low; it had rained, but towards evening a wind rose, and the sunset was fine. On my way I met a bullock-cart, loaded high with sacks, and reflected that it would be Alkmene's wool. The farm, when I came there, had a big barn and some stables, with a number of tall stacks round it. The house itself was a long, low, thatched building. All was neatly kept, but very poor. An old man and some children stared at me, as if it was a rare thing to see a visitor here. As I drove up before the door, a peasant woman, in bare feet, with a small shawl round her head, came out through the stable door, and it was Gertrud herself.

Gertrud had aged. She no longer had her slim waist or rounded bosom, but was square like a stack of firewood. Her bony face was tanned, as if all her small freckles had run into one, and she had lost a tooth or two. But she was still light-footed and clear-eyed, an upright, genial old farm wife.

In the lonely house any visitor might have been welcome, but Gertrud was as pleased to see me as if I had been her son. She was alone on the farm, she told me. Alkmene had driven to Ringkøbing with wool, and to put money into the savings bank—indeed, I ought to have met her on the road. She took me into the best room, which was obviously never used, and went to make coffee, the which she did solemnly fetch from a secret small box behind the chest. While I was alone I looked round. Everything here was clean, but very poor. I thought of the past, and of the girl I had then known, and a kind of dread came upon me.

Over our coffee Gertrud and I talked of old days. She had a keen memory for people and places, but the events had become blurred to her. She confused their succession, as if she had not talked or thought of them for a long time. She asked me if I had married. I told her that I had been engaged to my cousin at Rugaard, but that after my father's death we had agreed to break off the engagement.

Afterwards we got on to the farm and the sheep. She asked my advice on a sick lamb, recalling how I had doctored the cow in the parsonage. She and her daughter were doing well, she said, after the first few years in which they had made mistakes and had been cheated. They had increased their stock, and every month Alkmene went to Ringkøbing and put money into the savings bank. But they were still working hard, from sunrise to night, and allowing no waste at all. They had but poor help from the old man who was their only farm hand. Gertrud became animated as she talked about the sheep; she had two roses in her cheeks, and she made use of a bold, straight language, which I had not heard from her before. I reflected that the sheep and the landscape here would have taken back Gertrud to her childhood and early youth, and that I was, in reality, speaking to the young country lass, whom my old tutor had fallen in love with. In this way, too, her daughter with her had taken the place of her mother, so much that she might even, when her back was turned, play a small trick on her with the secret box and the coffee.

I had heard much of Alkmene's parsimony. During these sixteen years the rich woman on the lonely farm had become a kind of myth to the country, and people were a little afraid of her; they held her to be mad. Everything round me here went to confirm the rumours. I saw, then, how old we had all grown; the world seemed to me an infinitely sad place, and I fell to wonder both bitterly and amusedly whether Gertrud might not, in the innocence and activity of her nature, find good meaning, and something to do, in hell as well.

I asked Gertrud what they were going to do with all the money that they were collecting from month to month. Gertrud swept off my question indulgently as if I had been a child. "It would have been a good thing to my poor father, had he had that money in the savings bank, would it not?" she asked. When after a while I came back to it, she took upon herself to preach a little to me: "The world, surely, is a dangerous place, Vilhelm," she said, "and what better thing will we find in it than that hard, honest work which the Lord has set us here to do? We should not question."

Still my remark had touched a theme to which she had perhaps herself, without speaking, given consideration. She became thoughtful and after a time she confided to me that Mene was too sparing on her own behalf. She was kind to her mother; I must not but think so, but she was so hard on herself.

Gertrud looked up at me, the net of fine wrinkles in her face contracted. Her eyes for a moment shone the brighter with two small tears. She took my hand and pressed it. "Vilhelm," she said. "Do you know? She has got no shift on!"

THE FISH

I N THE WINDOW within the fathom-thick wall a small
star stood, shining, in the pale sky of the summer night. The
restfulness of this star made the King's mind restless; he could
not sleep.

The nightingales, which all evening had filled the woods with
their exuberant, rapturous singing, were silent for a few hours
round midnight. There was no sound anywhere. But from the
groves round the castle came, through the open window, the scent
of fresh, wet foliage; it bore all the woodland-world into the
King's alcove. His mind wandered, unhindered and aimless,
within that silvery land: he saw the deer and the fallow-deer
lying peacefully amongst the big trees, and in his thoughts, without bow or arrow, and without any wish to kill, he walked up
quite close to them. Here, maybe, the white hind was now grazing,
which was no real hind, but a maiden in hind's slough, with hoofs
of gold. Farther on, in the depths of the forest, the dragon was
asleep in a valley, his terrible, scaly neck under his wing, his
mighty tail stirring faintly in the wet grass.

The King's mind was strangely moved and upset; a sadness
was upon it, and yet he felt as strong as never before. It was as if
his own strength lay heavily upon him, and weighed him down.

The King thought of many things, and called to mind how,
ten years ago, when he was seventeen, in the town of Ribe he
had met with the Wandering Jew. He had been told by Father
Anders, his confessor, that the old outlaw of twelve hundred
years had come to Ribe, and had sent for him. But when the
ancient, crooked, earth-coloured Ahasuerus, in the black caftan,
fell upon his face before him, that terrible wrath that had filled
his heart against the man who had mocked the Lord again withdrew from it; he stood and looked at him, struck with wonder.
"Are you the Cobbler of Jerusalem?" he asked him. "Yes, yes,

I am that," the Jew answered and sighed deeply. "I was once a cobbler in Jerusalem, that great city. I made shoes and sandals for the rich burghers, and for the Romans as well. Once I made a pair of slippers for the wife of Pontius Pilate, the Governor, that were set all over the toe with chrysoprases and roses."

Now the King felt again, as if no time had passed and as clearly as that day in Ribe, the infinite loneliness of the old Wanderer. But tonight things had been turned about and had become real to him in a new sense: he was himself Ahasuerus. How many people, since then, had died around him! Gallant knights had fallen in battle, gay friends of his youth had disappeared, fair ladies—they were all gone, like tunes played on a lute. He remembered the old king's fool, with the little bells on his cap, and how merrily he had jumped up and down on the table while he mimicked the great lords of the court. Now it was many years since he had died, and many years, even, since the King had thought of him. Often he had met the gaze of the hunted, jaded stag, as he set his knife in its heart and turned it round; tears had run from the animal's limpid eyes. But the King could not tell, he did not know, if he himself were ever to die.

A light breeze ran through the grass and the crowns of the trees outside. The tapestries by the window rustled gently; in the dark he could not distinguish the figures of men and beasts on them, but he knew that they would be moving as if their procession was advancing along the wall.

The King's thoughts walked on, and found no content anywhere. He remembered how, in the old days, delight had filled his heart at the idea of hunting and dancing, of tournaments, of revenge, of his friends and of women. Slowly he went through it all. But where was he now to look for the wine which would make him glad? No human being had power to pour it out to him. He was as lonely in his kingdom of Denmark as he was in his sleep, in his dreams. Lately the King had fought a long and bitter struggle with his mighty vassals, and he had rejoiced in the thought of their humiliation; that had not been the rapture, the honey on the tongue of days gone, but it had still been to him a game worth playing. Now, in the profound, fresh, silent embrace of the night, and in the presence of that silver star, the trials-of-strength with his liegemen, such as they were, became to him but vanity, a pastime for a boy. The great forces within him cried out for mightier undertakings, and for a fuller task. He thought of the women of his court, the ladies with swans' necks, who trod the dance on his castle's floors. He liked well to see them dance and to hear them sing; he had once found pleasure in their fair bodies, when they were naked in his arms, but with none of them would his heart tonight lie down.

The King grieved for the sake of his dear soul, which he could not gladden. This burning love of his own soul belonged to his youth; it brought back spring nights of long ago. Then it had been but the yearning of an adolescent; now, that he knew the world, it ran all through him, a bitter ache. On the earth his soul had no friends. All other human beings, his peasants and barons, his soldiers and learned men, could find their equals, in whom to confide and with whom to rejoice, but who could cheer the soul of a king? The King lifted his thoughts to the Lord God in heaven. He must be as lonely as himself, lonelier maybe, inasmuch as he was a greater King.

Again he looked at the star, so high up, and pure as a diamond. "Ave Stella Maris," he sighed, "Dei mater alma." Amongst all the ladies who had walked on the earth, the Virgin alone would know and value his heart, and gracefully prize his adoration.

That old Jew, he reflected, must have seen the Virgin, and

might have described her to him, had he questioned him. If he himself had been born so many hundred years earlier, he too might have travelled to the Holy Land, and have seen Mary with his own eyes. Would the young King of Denmark, then, have been a rival to the old King of Heaven? "No, no, Lord," he whispered. "I should but have worn her glove on my helmet. I should but, my lance felled, have made my tall, grey, mail-clad horse walk by her ass, on that road to Egypt. You Yourself would have smiled down to me."

How perfect might not, the King thought, the understanding between the Lord and himself, how sweet and genial might not their concord be, if only they were alone on the earth, with no other human beings to dim the perception by their vanity, their ambition and their envy. "O Lord, it is time," the King thought, "that I should turn away from them, that I should throw off everybody that stands in the way of the happiness of my soul. Of that only will I think. I will save my soul; I will feel it rejoice once more."

At that moment it was to him as if a bell were ringing in the summer night, which no one but he could hear. Its waves of sound enclosed him, as the sea a drowning man. The King rose on his knees in his bed and lifted up his face. He knew and understood everything. He saw that his loneliness was his strength, for he himself was all the earth.

The sound withdrew. A long time after, as he lay still with his hands folded upon his breast, the King saw, by the paleness of the sky, that it was not long till morning. The star that he had first watched had moved upwards, to the window-frame. A cold current ran through the world, so that he drew the silken cover of his bed to his chin; the dew was falling. He heard the first three or four chirping notes of the yellow-hammer in the top of a tree;

soon the other birds would follow; in a little while he would hear
the cuckoo from the woods. The King fell asleep.

In the morning when his valets came to wake up and dress the
King, it rained. As the King now woke up, he had in his mind his
father's old Wendish thrall, Granze. Perhaps he had dreamed of
him in the last light sleep of the night, and the sound of the rain
had brought on the dream, for he had still in his ear the whisper
of waves running over pebbles. This old thrall's father had been
brought to Denmark from the island of Rugen, as a child, by the
great Bishop Absalon himself. In all his life he had known no one
of his own tribe. He was as old as the salt sea, but with the Wends,
the King reflected, years did not count as with Christian people;
they lived forever. Twenty years ago the thrall had been his own
best friend. They had passed many days by the seaside, and the
Wend had taught him to set bow-nets and to spear eels by torch-
light. Now they had not met for a long time. But he knew that the
old hermit was still alive, and dwelt in a hut by the sea. He would
ride down, he thought, and see the thrall once more. Granze had
been the beginning of his life, as he remembered it; it was befit-
ting that he should now come into it again. The Wend had knowledge of many things ignored by the King's Danish subjects.

All his thoughts of the night were in the King's mind; he was
strong, easy at heart and calm. But in the light of the day he did
not dwell upon them. He had done with musing, and knew his
way. Yes, he was himself the way, the truth and the life.

The King let his valet hang his heavy, richly folded, blue and
rust-coloured mantle, inwoven with leaves and birds, over his
shoulders. But while his page was buckling on his spurs, news
was brought him that the Priest Sune Pedersen had arrived from
Paris. This to the King seemed a good omen. He sent for him.
Sune Pedersen belonged to the Hvide family, a headstrong clan,

amongst which were many of the King's hardiest opponents. But
the King and Sune, when they were boys, had been taught their
letters together. Sune had stood half a head lower than the Prince,
but he had been his equal in archery, horsemanship and falconry,
and he was a quick, keen scholar. He was a loyal friend to his
friends and afraid of nothing. Now he had been away for five
years to study in Paris, and from time to time the King had been
told of his progress and fine prospects there.

Sune came in, still in his black travelling clothes, half clerical,
half cavalier, and bent his knee to the King, but the King lifted
him up, and kissed him on both cheeks. Sune Pedersen was an
elegant and frank young priest with white hands. His clothes sat
well on him; his small fresh red mouth wore a quiet and gay
smile. He had a melodious voice, and spoke in his old artless
Danish manner; only now and then he introduced a French word
in his speech. He began by complimenting the King on improvements in the churches of Denmark, and conveyed greetings from
great prelates in Paris. He was the bearer of a present to the King
from Matthew of Vendôme, a relic set in a chased gold cross, but
was to hand it over later, in the presence of the dignitaries of the
Church of Denmark.

As they talked, the King's first Scribe came in and brought him
a list of the lords and churchmen waiting to see him. The King
let his eyes run over the paper. These were the men who had
disturbed the peace of his soul, and who had set themselves against
the will of the King of Denmark. Why had he let it be so? A
faint pang ran through him, as if he had, at some time, given over
a noble horse to be ridden by a coarse groom. He stood for a
while sunk in thought. This paper catalogued a row of proud
Danish heads. All the same they could be bent, and all the same
they could fall. He handed the paper to the Scribe and sent word

by him that he would see nobody today; he would ride out. The Queen sent a message with her chamberlain; she was upset because her favourite lap dog was sick, and asked the King to come and look at it. The King replied that he would come the next day.

The King told Sune to ride with him. Sune had known Granze in old time, and smiled at the recollection. The King, too, smiled. The memories that he had in common with Sune, he reflected, were all bright, as if clearly illuminated; those connected with the Wend belonged to earlier days, when he had hardly been conscious of himself or of the world. They stirred dully in the dark, and smelled of seaweeds and mussels. The smile remained on his face as he let his thoughts wander on. If he was to have one of the two set to death, which head would have to fall—the old dark knaggy skull, or this young, gracefully tonsured head? He asked Sune whether he must produce an ambler for him to ride on. Sune replied that he would still venture himself on any horse from the King's stables. But he had brought fresh horses with him. He had not come straight from France, but had laid his way by Jutland, to visit his kinsmen. The King frowned, then smiled again. Soon the King and Sune were riding through the castle-court, and the gateway together, and the watchman upon the gallery blew his horn. Three of the King's grooms, Sune's servant and a dog boy, clattered behind them, and the King let his favourite stag-hound bitch, Blanzeflor, run by his stirrup.

They rode through the forest. In the dripping-wet woods, the young leaves were still soft and slack, silky, less like leaves than like petals, and drooping in the sweet forest-air like seaweeds in deep water. Under the tree-crowns the forest-road was filled with translucent clarity, and with the live, bitter fragrance of fresh foliage and flowers of maple trees and poplars. In the fine drizzling rain the birds sang on all sides; the stockdove was cooing in the high branches as they rode beneath them. Once a fox crossed the winding road in front of them, stopped a second and gazed at the riders, his brush on the ground, then slid off, like a small red flame extinguished in the wet ferns.

The King questioned Sune Pedersen on life in Paris, and Sune answered freely and gaily. The splendour of the university, he said, was perhaps not what it had been a hundred years ago, in the days of Abelard and Peter of Lombardy, but their spirit was still upon it, and shone from it. You could not, he went on, till you had been to Paris, fully know what it is to walk in light, in the illumination of the great sciences and arts. Also the independence of the university had lately been confirmed by the papal bull of Parens Scientiarum. He turned to talk of the King of France and his Court. King Philip was a mighty huntsman. Sune himself, with a noble young English priest, his friend, had been to the King's castle of St. Germain, and there had witnessed a hunt. He described in detail the run, the horses and the hounds. And the French ladies, he said, were as bold in the saddle as the men. Was it true, the King asked him, what was said of the loveliness of those ladies of France? Yes, Sune replied, for as much as an ecclesiastic could tell him of it, they were lovely, noble, pious and accomplished, as sweet as melodies in their talk and manners. Above them all shone young Queen Mary of Brabant, a white lily. She had much influence with the King, her husband, and was, so everyone hoped, going to break down the scandalous power of Pierre la Brosse, on whom the King lavished land and honours. Pierre paid him back in an ill way, for it was believed that he had tried to poison young Prince Louis, the King's eldest son.

"Such is the way of the world," said the King. "Loyalty is a rare thing for a king to find, if it exists at all." "Yes, indeed, that is so, my lord," said Sune. "What loyalty will the King of France find as long as he favours a bondsman, his father's barber, before his born lieges?"

Again Sune talked of the churches of Paris. He described to the King the Sainted Chapel that had been built by King Louis. It was in very truth saintly and glorious, like paradise. A sadness fell upon Sune himself as he spoke. He broke off his narration and rode in silence. This green wood of Sealand—he had seen it in his dreams many times, and had thought it lovelier than all the cathedrals of France. Yet now that he was riding through it once more, in the gentle rain, his heart misgave him; he yearned for Paris and for something that was not here. He repeated: "Like paradise."

"Tell me, Sune," said the King, "is it by the will of the Lord that mankind cannot be happy, but must ever be longing for the things which they have not, and which, maybe, are nowhere to be found? The beasts and the birds are at ease on this earth. May it not, then, be good enough for the human beings whom God has set within it: the peasants who complain of their hard lot, the great lords, who do never get enough, and the young priests who sigh for paradise, in the green woods? Might not man—might not, after all, one man out of them all—be in such understanding with the Lord as to say: 'I have solved the riddle of this our life. I have made the earth my own, and I am happy with her'?"

"My lord," said Sune, and while he spoke he patted his horse's neck, "that is the old cry of mankind. For a thousand years men have lamented to God in heaven: 'You have made the earth, O Lord, and you have made man, but you know not what it is to be one of us. We cannot reconcile the conditions of the earth with the nature of our hearts, such as You Yourself have created them within us. We do not find here the peace, or the justice, or the happiness, for which we yearn. It is an everlasting schism and we can bear it no longer. Impart to us, at least, Your plan with the world and with ourselves, give us the solution to the riddle of this life.' They caught the ear of the Lord. He meditated upon their complaint, and He asked the good angels, who are sent everywhere to watch the ways of man: 'Is it indeed as hard on my people of the earth as they make it out?' The angels answered: 'It is indeed hard on Your people of the earth.' The Lord thought: 'It is unsafe to rely on the statement of servants. I have taken pity on man. I will go down and see for myself.' And God assumed the shape and likeness of man, and went down to earth. At that the good angels rejoiced, and said to one another: 'See, the Lord has taken pity on man. Now he will at last show these poor ignorant and unwitty mortals the way to be prosperous, happy and in harmony there, even as we are in our heaven. Now we shall see, on our ways on earth, no more tears.' Thirty-three years passed by, which to the inmates of paradise are but as one hour. Then the Lord again ascended to his throne, and called his angels around him. They came flying from all sides, eager for news. The Lord looked younger than they had ever seen Him, resplendent and grave; as He lifted his hand to speak, the angels saw that it was pierced through. 'Aye, I have come back from the earth, my angels,' He said, 'and I now know the conditions and modes of man; no one knows them better than I. I had taken pity on man, and resolved to help him. I have not rested until I had fulfilled my promise. I have now reconciled the heart of man with the conditions of the earth. I have shown this poor and unwitty creature the way to become reviled and persecuted; I have shown him how to get himself spat upon and scourged; I have taught him how to get himself hung upon a cross. I have given to man that solution of his riddle, that he begged of me; I have consigned to him his salvation.' "

The King at first had not listened, for he was riding in his own thoughts. As Sune advanced in his tale, however, he listened with half an ear, and laughed in his heart. Not in vain, he reflected, had Sune visited his kinsmen, his own great liegemen at Møllerup and Hald: the little young divine, his schoolfellow, meant to prove to the King of Denmark that humility is a godlike virtue. This was the way of your friends: they rode by your side, but had their own designs in their hearts. But Sune's voice, as he talked, was sweetly modulated, mellifluous and measured, pleasant to the ear of the King. He thought: "Nay, I shall do Sune no harm. On the contrary, I shall not let him go back to Paris, but shall keep him with me, so that he may tell me such tales as I hear from no one else. I shall keep both him and Granze with me, and both shall serve me!"

"Still," the King said thoughtfully, as Sune had finished his tale, "the Lord did not, to my mind, try His hand sufficiently on the conditions of man. Why did he stay only with carpenters and fishermen? Once He was down here, He might have tried the circumstances of a great lord, yes, of a king. He cannot be said to have full knowledge of the earth as long as He has not ridden a horse. Is it possible that He may have, at the time, forgotten, that He had himself created the horse, the deer, iron, sweet music, silk?"

As they had ridden on, the wood had become lower and sparer round them; the oaks and maples were succeeded by thin, wind-crooked birch trees. Here and there in the glades the heather grew, and in the end the road became but a sandy path. The rain had ceased. They came to the end of the wood and cantered over grassland with a few scattered and gnarled thorn trees. Two ravens, walking sedately on the short grass, flew up in front of the horsemen. Before them lay a row of irregular low downs; they rode up on them, and came in view of the open sea.

The King reined up his horse and looked out. The full, salt, moist breath of the sea met his face and embraced him. It was saturated with the rank smell of sea-thong; he drew it in deeply, and wondered why he had not come here for such a long time. For a few minutes he thought of nothing but the sea.

The day was dim, but the world was filled, like a glass bell, with vague, blurred light, and with the incessant, songful murmur of the sea: a powerful, low rushing from the depths far out—strangely unreal in the still day, but a strong wind had been blowing for three or four days before—a sweet prattle near by, where the waves ran up on the stones and the gravel. It was these sounds that the King had heard in his dream. All round the horizon the sea and the sky played together, unsteadily and beguilingly. Towards the west the sea was lead-coloured, darker than the sky; to the east it was lighter than the air itself, nacreous, like a luminous mirror. But to the north the sea and the sky joined without the faintest line of division, and became but the universe, unfathomable space. Far out, the light of the sun stole through the amorphous, blind clouds, and where it caught the sea, the surface of it glimmered like silver, as if innumerable shoals of fish were playing on the water. Half way out to the horizon a flight, a wedge of wild swans drew a white line, like a pearly breaker of the air, across the pale field of view.

One of the King's men was to point out the hut of the thrall to him, but the hut was small and similar in colour to the seashore. He only caught sight of it by the thin column of blue smoke rising from its conical roof. Outside it, Granze's short, broad, dark boat lay, and as they rode down the dunes they saw the owner of it all, Granze himself, in the water to his knees, wading ashore, and dragging a weight, a heavy catch of fish, after him. When he saw the horsemen coming towards him, the old thrall stopped and shaded his eyes with his hand to gaze at them, then again occupied himself with his catch. He had trussed up his goatskin frock to the waist, and the young men could not help laughing at the sight of him, so little human was his crooked, dark nakedness. He waded on land, shaggy and flat-footed, snorted like a water-dog and placed on the sand the big fish he trailed; then he let down his frock to his ankles. He stood dead still and waited for his visitors. As they came close to him, Sune's horse gamboled and came up in front of the King's horse. Granze did not look at the King, but laid his hand on Sune's foot.

"Is it you who have come here, Sune, kinsman of Absalon?" he said. "I thought that you were dead." "Nay, not dead yet, by the grace of God," said Sune smiling, and quieted his horse. Granze looked at him. "You came near to it, though, seven full moons ago," he said. "Yes, that is so," said Sune gravely. Granze stood a moment silent; then he chuckled. "A woman cooked a nice dish for you," he tittered, "and put ratsbane in it. Did she take you for a rat, little Sune? If the rats would go into the holes that God made for them, people would not poison them." Sune had grown pale. He sat on his horse without a word.

The King drove his horse on to his old thrall. The gold in his frock, his sword-hilt and saddle-cloth glinted. "Do you not know me, Granze, Gnemer's son?" he asked the thrall. "Aye, I know you, Prince Erik," the Wend said solemnly, "although you are paler than you were last time. I knew you already when you were on the top of the down." He looked the King full in the face a long time. "Hail," he cried, "you are welcome, my master, when you honour your father's good, faithful thrall by coming to him.

Come, drink with Granze. You will have the same good brew as you had here the other day, or better. And I have caught a big fish early this morning. I shall fry it for you. I am smoking fish in my house, but I will make you a fire out on the stones. You sit down and eat with Granze once more."

He dived into his hut, and came out with a full black goatskin on his shoulder. "Call off your dog, my master," he cried, as the bitch followed him and sniffed at his legs, and he changed feet quickly, as if he was treading water. "She is fine, very strong. Surely she helps you well to catch the deer. But the dogs of great people never like the thralls." He lifted the black, greasy skin to the King's mouth, where he sat on his horse. "Drink," he said. The King had forgotten the brew, which he had long ago tasted in the Wend's hut. Now the flavour at once brought back many pictures of Granze jabbering and dancing under its effect. It burnt his tongue and sent a sweet satisfaction through his veins. Granze held the jar up to Sune, then set the spout to his own mouth, lay back his head and emptied the skin. "Now we are friends," he said. "Now what we dream and scheme may differ, but the water that we make will be the same."

Now the King had meant to question Granze on the future, but he no longer found that it was needed. It seemed to him that he and Granze were akin, more than any other two men in the land —the thrall, who had been taken away from his home and had never seen any of his own people, and the King, who found no equal anywhere around him. Lonelier than the others they were, but wiser as well; the secret powers of the world recognized them and yielded obedience to them.

"You are a mighty man here, Granze," he said, "and have the world to yourself as far out as you can see. You are as good a saint in a way as the old hermits who withdrew to the desert, as the man who stood on the column to worship God. Only it is not the Lord God whom you serve, but your own old, black, wooden pictures inside your hut, which I remember well."

"No, no," said Granze quickly, and looked to Sune for support. "Granze has been watered, Granze has been instructed and has forgotten nothing. I know of her who gave birth, and still kept her maidenhead, like your glass windows that the sun goes through and does not break. Also of the man who was swallowed and again vomited up by the fish. Look!" he cried and solemnly crossed himself. Sune said in Latin: "Though thou shouldst bray a fool in a mortar amongst wheat, yet will not his foolishness depart from him."

Sune leaped from his horse, and held the stirrup to the King. The King's men also dismounted, and led the horses off. The King's valet spread a cloak over a stone for him to sit on.

Granze brought out fire in a basin, charcoal and a long spit. He sat on his heels upon the sand and made the fire with care and skill, the while, on and off, watching his guests through the smoke. He held up a stick of black, hard and sticky peat, and said: "This was a tree growing in the soil before there was a hen in the land to lay an egg." "It is a long time ago," said the King, "and I do not remember the tree." "Nay, I should not remember it either, if I were you," said Granze. "But with us Wends it is a different thing. What has happened to our father's father, and to those old men, who were mould when he was suckled by his mother, we still keep in our mind; we recall it whenever we want. You, too, have the lusts and the fears of your fathers in your blood, but their knowledge you have not; they did not understand how to put that in when they were begetting a child. That is why each of you has to begin anew, from the beginning, like a new-born mouse fumbling in the dark.

"In those old days," he recounted, "many things had life which are now lifeless. The mossy, rotten old logs in the forest and the swamps could talk. I myself have not heard it, but I have heard one of them snore in its sleep as I passed it on the narrow path at night. The big stones at the bottom of the sea came on land upon full-moon nights, shining wet, hung with sea-thong and mussels; they ran a race, and copulated, on the shore.

"Men had to fell the trees of big woods to make themselves ploughland. Hey, that was sour work. My two hands here did not do the work, and still they are knotted with it; should not my mind keep the knots as well? The tree-fellers made themselves a low cover to sleep in by the root of a tall fir tree, and they were very tired; they grew as small as wood-mice by their little fire by night. Then the storm came, seated itself in the top of the fir and sang: 'Snow-fields, stone-fields, wasteland, grey walking waves. Very wide is the world, without end is it!' The song ran down the fir stem and wailed: 'Full-fed am I with flight, sated with distance, weary, weary am I with wandering. When will my course be ended?' And all of a sudden the storm itself came sliding down, pushed its head into the hut, and roared: 'Ho ho! You little men! You rats, you lice, I might blow you out over the big cold ocean. Where would you be then?'—and whiffed smoke and ashes into their faces, and was gone."

The King sat with his chin in his hand and looked out over the water. He had laid by his cap, his long chestnut hair fell over his gold neck-chain. The seashore stretched out to both sides of him, bone-white, strewn with shells. Here nothing grew; here the earth had given up living or breeding; everything was nobly barren and waste. It was the end, and the beginning, of the world. He thought of the ships which, through centuries, had sailed from the coasts of Denmark. They had hoisted strong sails, and spears and swords had glinted aboard. From there King Canute had sailed to England, and Valdemar to Estonia; Bishop Absalon had launched his boats to chastise the Wendish pirates. These fairways led to great battles and conquests. The triumphs over men and nations were high pursuits. Still they were over and done with. The Kings, his fathers, were dead and even forgotten, and there was more than a war-song in the whispering of the waves: an endless course, infinity itself. Paradise, which Sune had spoken of, perhaps began where the sea and the sky met in front of him.

Granze's face blushed brick-red from the drink. He said to the King: "Now I shall tell you why I was afraid to speak to you when I first saw you. As you came over the downs you had a shining ring round your head, such as your holy pictures have. Where did you get that?"

The fire was now burning bright. Granze rose from it, and dragged along the big fish. He stuck his thick fingers through the gill-openings, and lifted it up before him. It was almost the length of his own stumpy body. "A fish for a great lord," he said, "for those who wear a shining ring round their heads. It has swum a long way to meet you." He took up a knife and wiped it on his frock. Laying the fish on the sand, he cut it up and plunged his hands into it to draw out the entrails.

Sune said to the King: "Look, my lord. The Wend has indeed not forgotten the ways of his fathers. Just like that, I believe, did the priests of Swantewit go through their human sacrifices. He is happy now. It is a strange thing," he added, "about happy human beings, and the matters which make them so. Food may do it, and blood, the sight of their children. Dancing, in women, may do it, too."

On this open seashore Sune's voice was not as gently modulated as it had been in the King's room. It had in it a quivering, eager note, like the breaking voice of a boy. Granze, made bold by his own brew, grinned back at him.

Suddenly the thrall stopped in his activity and stood still; his face grew dull and blank. He drew out his red right hand, held it up and stared at it. He spat on it, wiped it on his frock, and again stared.

"Ho!" he cried, his voice as deep as a bull's with surprise. "The fish carries a gift in his belly. He has brought a ring for you through the deep sea. Has not Granze, then, caught you the right fish?" He again spat on his fingers and rubbed them carefully on his goatskin frock.

Sune ran and took the ring from the thrall; he bent one knee to the King and handed it to him. "All hail, King of Denmark," he cried. "The elements themselves swear allegiance to you. They bring forth their treasures, as they did to King Polycrates."

The King drew off his embroidered glove, and let Sune set the ring on his finger. "I have unlearned the wisdom of our school days," he said. "How goes the story of King Polycrates?"

"Polycrates," Sune said, "was King of Samos, and was known for his good fortune. When he proposed an alliance to King Amadis of Egypt, this King, alarmed by his prosperity, made it a condition that Polycrates should checker it by relinquishing some treasure. So Polycrates threw into the sea a seal, the finest of his jewels. But the next day he received in a present a large fish, and in its belly the ring was found. When Amadis had news of this, he declined all alliance with King Polycrates."

"And what happened to King Polycrates?" the King asked.

"Some time after," Sune continued, "Polycrates visited Orontes, the Governor of Magnesia. His daughter, warned by a dream, begged him not to go, but he did not listen to her." "And what then?" asked the King. Sune said: "At Magnesia King Polycrates was put to death."

"But I," said the King, after a moment, "have not complied to sacrifice to the fates, to checker my luck." "No," said Sune, smiling, "your ring is a free gift from the fates; they pay obedience to you on their own accord. Yours will be a different tale to write down in books." "Then tell me," said the King, "by the comradeship of your childhood, what significance do you give to it?" "My Lord," said Sune, now grave, "I know this: that events attain significance from the state of mind of the men to whom they happen, and no outward event is the same to two men. You are my King and my Sovereign, but you are not my penitent. And I do not know your mind."

The King sat for a little while in silence. "When Granze found the ring, and cried out to me," he said, "I had my thoughts with King Canute of Denmark. You never forget a tale, Sune. You will remember how the sea did not obey King Canute, when he ordained her." "Yes, I know the tale, my lord," said Sune. "King Canute himself called forth the incident, to put his flatterers and eye servants to shame, and he was never a greater King than at that hour." "Nay," said the King. "But if the sea had obeyed him? If it had obeyed him, Sune?"

There was a long silence.

He held up his hand. "The stone in the ring," he said, "is blue, like the sea." He stretched out his hand to Sune to see.

Sune lifted up the King's fingers respectfully, but stood for such a long time dead still, gazing at them, that the King asked him: "What are you looking at?" Sune released the King's hand, and let his own hand fall. "As God lives, my lord," he said in a low, clear voice, "this is such a strange thing that I hardly dare speak to you of it. When last I saw a ring like this, it sat on the hand of my kinswoman, the wife of your Lord High Constable Stig Andersen." "Upon her hand?" the King said. "Yes," said Sune, "in very truth, upon her right hand." "What is her name?" the King asked him. "Ingeborg," answered Sune.

"How can that be?" the King asked. "No, my lord, I know not," said Sune. "I was staying with her husband at Møllerup, in the country of Mols, just lately, a week ago, as I came from France. We sailed together in a boat out to a small island, Hielm, not far from the coast, which belongs to her husband. It was a clear, sunny day, the sea was blue, and the Lady Ingeborg let her hand trail in the water. Her fingers were slim and smooth; the ring was too large for them, and I told her to be careful, lest she should lose it in the sea, for, I said, she would not get another like it." The King looked at the ring and smiled. "So Granze's fish," he said, "has come across the sea from our country of Mols."

After a while he said: "I have heard much of the beauty of your kinswoman, but I have never seen her for myself. Is she indeed so fair?" "Yes, she is indeed very fair," said Sune.

Before the eyes of the King's mind rose the picture of the boat in blue water and a gay breeze, with the young black priest in it, and the fair lady, in silk and gold, her white fingers playing in the ripples, and underneath them the big fish swimming in the dark-blue shadow of the keel. "Why did you tell your kinswoman that she would not get another ring like this one?" he asked Sune. Sune laughed. "My lord," he said, "I have known my kinswoman since she was a child. I have taught her to play chess, and the lute, and we have jested together many times. I said to her, in jest, that she must take good care of her ring, for she would not get another blue stone which was so like her own eyes." The King said: "It is gracious and courteous in the Lady Ingeborg to send me her ring by the fish. I shall wear it until I can give it back to her."

"It is a curious thing," he added after a moment, "when fair women wear jewels, these mate themselves with some part of their face or body. Pearls seem to be only another expression of the fairness of their neck and breasts, rubies and garnets of their lips, finger-tips and nipples. And this blue stone, you tell me, is like the lady's eyes."

Granze had gone back to his fire, but from there he had watched the talk, and kept his eyes on the one face or the other. He cried out to the King: "Now the fish has swum, and has been caught, now it is fried and ready to serve. It remains but for you to eat it; your meal is here for you."

King Erik of Denmark, surnamed Glipping, was murdered in the barn of Finnerup, in the year of 1286, by a party of rebellious vassals. According to the tradition and the old ballads, the murderers were headed by the King's Lord High Constable, Stig Andersen Hvide, who killed King Erik in revenge, because he had seduced his wife, Ingeborg.

PETER AND

ROSA

ONE YEAR, a century ago, spring was late in Denmark. During the last days of March, the Sound was ice-bound, and blind, from the Danish to the Swedish coast. The snow in the fields and on the roads thawed a little in the day, only to freeze again at night; the earth and the air were equally without hope or mercy.

Then one night, after a week of raw and clammy fog, it began to rain. The hard, inexorable sky over the dead landscape broke, dissolved into streaming life and became one with the ground. On all sides the incessant whisper of falling water re-echoed; it increased and grew into a song. The world stirred beneath it; things drew breath in the dark. Once more it was announced to the hills and valleys, to the woods and the chained brooks: "You are to live."

In the parson's house at Søllerød, his sister's son, fifteen-year-old Peter Købke, sat by a tallow candle over his Fathers of the Church, when through the rustle of the rain his ear caught a new sound, and he left the book, got up and opened the window. How the noise of the rain rose then! But he listened to other, magic voices within the night. They came from above, out of the ether itself, and Peter lifted his face to them. The night was dark, yet this was no longer winter gloom; it was pregnant with clarity, and as he questioned it, it answered him. And over his head, called the music of wandering life in the skies. Wings sang up there; clear flutes played; shrill pipe-signals were exchanged high up beyond his head. It was the trekking birds on their way north.

He stood for a long time thinking of them; he let them pass before the eyes of his mind one by one. Here travelled long wedges of wild geese, flights of fen-duck and teal, with the shell-duck, for which one lies in wait in the late, warm evenings of August. All the pleasures of summer drew their course across the sky; a migra-

251

tion of hope and joy journeyed tonight, a mighty promise, set out to many voices.

Peter was a great huntsman, and his old gun was his dearest possession; his soul ascended to the sky to meet the soul of the wild birds. He knew well what was in their hearts. Now they cried: "Northward! Northward!" They pierced the Danish rain with their stretched necks, and felt it in their small clear eyes. They hastened away to the Northern summer of play and change, where the sun and the rain share the infinite vault of heaven between them; they went off to the innumerable, nameless, clear lakes and to the white summer nights of the North. They hurried forth to fight and to make love. Higher up, in the lofts of the world, perhaps big swarms of quail, thrush and snipe were on the move. Such a tremendous stream of longing, on its way to its goal, passed above his head, that Peter, down on the ground, felt his limbs ache. He flew a long way with the geese.

Peter wanted to go to sea, but the parson held him to his books. Tonight, in the open window, he slowly and solemnly thought his past and his future over, and vowed to run away and become a sailor. At this moment he forgave his books, and no longer planned to burn them all up. Let them collect dust, he thought, or fall into the hands of dusty people fit for books. He himself would live under sails, on a swinging deck, and would watch a new horizon rise with each morning's sun. As he had taken this resolution he was filled with such deep gratitude that he folded his hands upon the window-sill. He had been piously brought up; his thanks were dedicated to God, but they strolled a little on their way, as if beaten off their course by the rain. He thanked the spring, the birds and the rain itself.

Within the parson's house death was zealously kept in view and lectured upon, and Peter, in his survey of the future, also took the sailor's end into consideration. His mind dwelled for some time on his last couch, at the bottom of the sea. Soberly, his brows knitted, he contemplated, as it were, his own bones upon the sand. The deep-water currents would pass through his eyes, like a row of clear, green dreams; big fish, whales even, would float above him like clouds, and a shoal of small fishes might suddenly rush along, an endless streak, like the birds tonight. It would be peaceful, he reflected, and better than a funeral at Søllerød, with his uncle in the pulpit.

The birds travelled forth over the Sound, through the stripes of grey rain. The lights of Elsinore glimmered deep below, like a fragment of the Milky Way. A salt wind met them as they came out beyond the open water of the Kattegat. Long stretches of sea and earth, of woods, wasteland and moors, swept south under them in the course of the night.

At dawn they sank through the silvery air and descended upon a long file of flat and bare holms. The rocks shone roseate as the sun came up; little glints of light came trickling upon the wavelets. The rays of the morning refracted within the duck's own fine necks and wings. They cackled and quacked, picked and preened their feathers, and set to sleep, with their heads under their wings.

A few days later, in the afternoon, the parson's daughter Rosa stood by her loom, at which she had just set up a piece of red and blue cotton. She did not work at it, but looked out through the window. Her mind was balancing upon a thin ridge, from which at any moment it might tumble either into ecstasy at the new feeling of spring in the air, and at her own fresh beauty—or, on the other side, into bitter wrath against all the world.

Rosa was the youngest of three sisters; the two others had both married and gone away, one to Møen and one to Holstein. She was a spoilt child in the house, and could say and do what she liked, but she was not exactly happy. She was lonely, and in her heart she believed that some time something horrible would happen to her.

Rosa was tall for her age, with a round face, a clear skin and a mouth like Cupid's bow. Her hair curled and crisped so obstinately that it was difficult for her to plait it, and her long eyelashes gave her the air of glancing at people from an ambush. She had on an old, faded blue winter frock, too short in the sleeves, and a pair of coarse, patched shoes. But the ease and gracefulness of her young body lent to the rough clothes a classical and pathetic majesty.

Rosa's mother had died at her birth, and the parson's mind was fixed upon the grave. The daily life of the parsonage, even, was run with a view to the world hereafter; the idea of mortality filled the rooms. To grow up in the house was to the young people a problem and a struggle, as if fatal influences were dragging them the other way, into the earth, and admonishing them to give up the vain and dangerous task of living. In her own way Rosa meditated upon death as much as Peter. But she disliked the thought of it; she was not even allured by the picture of paradise with her Mother in it, and she trusted that she would live a hundred years still.

All the same during this last winter she had often been so weary of, so angry with her surroundings that in order to escape and punish them she had wished to die. But as the weather changed she too had changed her mind. It was better, she thought, that the others should all die. Free from them, and alone, she would walk over the green earth, pick violets and watch the plovers flitting low over the fields; she would make pebbles leap on the water, and bathe undisturbed in the rivers and the sea. The vision of this happy world has been so vivid with her that she was surprised when she heard her father scolding Peter in the next room, and realized that they were both still with her.

This spring Rosa had a particular grudge against fate. She felt it strongly, yet she did not like to admit it to herself.

Peter, her orphan cousin, had been adopted into the house nine years ago, when both he and Rosa were six years old. She could still, if she wanted to, recall the time when he had not been there, and remember the dolls, which, with the arrival of the boy, had faded out of her existence. The two children got on well, for Peter was a good-natured creature and easy to dominate, and they had then had many great adventures together.

But two years ago Rosa grew up taller than the boy. And at the same time she came into possession of a world of her own, inaccessible to the others, as the world of music is inaccessible to the tone-deaf. Nobody could tell where her world lay; neither did the substance of it lend itself to words. The others would never understand her, were she to tell them that it was both infinite and secluded, playful and very grave, safe and dangerous. She could not explain, either, how she herself was one with it, so that through the loveliness and power of her dream-world she was now, in her old frock and botched shoes, very likely the loveliest, mightiest and most dangerous person on earth. Sometimes, she felt, she was expressing the nature of the dream-world in her movements and her voice, but she was then speaking a language of which they had no knowledge. Within this mystic garden of hers she was altogether out of the reach of a clumsy boy with dirty hands and scratched knees; she almost forgot her old playfellow.

Then last winter Peter had suddenly, as it were, caught her up. He became the taller of the two by half a head, and this time Rosa reflected with bitterness he would remain so. He became so much stronger than she that it alarmed and offended the girl. On his own he began to play the flute. Peter was of a philosophical turn of mind, and, seven or eight years ago, when the two were walking together, he had often held forth to Rosa on the elements and order of the universe, and on the curious fact that the moon, when quite young and tender, was let out to play at the hour when the other children were put to bed, but that when she grew old and decrepit she should be chased out early in the morning, when other old people like to stay in bed. But he had never talked much in the presence of his elders, and when Rosa ceased to take an interest in his enterprises or reflections, he had withdrawn into himself. Now lately he would, uninvitedly, and before the whole household, give venture to his own fancies about the world, and many of them rang strangely in Rosa's mind, like echoes of hers. At such moments she fixed her gaze hard on him, seized by a deep fear. She could no longer, she felt, be sure of her dream-world. Peter might find the "Sesame" which opened it, and encroach upon it, and she might meet him there any day.

It was to her as if she had been betrayed by this boy whom she had treated kindly when he was a child. His figure began to bar her outlook and to deprive her of air within her own house, to which he had really no right. From the talk of the grown-up people Rosa had guessed Peter to be an illegitimate child. This fact, if he had been a girl, would have filled her with compassion; she would have seen her playmate in the light of romance and tragedy. Now, as a boy, he came in for his part of the perfidy of that unknown seducer, his father. During the months of the long winter she had sometimes found herself wishing that he might go to sea, and there meet with sudden death before, through him, worse things should happen to her. Peter was a wild, foolhardy boy, she was free to hope.

Of all these strong emotions within the girl's bosom Peter knew nothing at all. In his own way he had loved Rosa from the time when he first came into the parson's house; amongst the people there she was the only one in whom he had confidence. He had

suffered by her capriciousness, and yet he somehow liked it well, as
he liked everything about her. Of late he was sometimes disappointed when he found it impossible to rouse her sympathy in such
things as mattered to him; he then even deemed her a little shallow
and silly. But on the whole, human beings, their nature and their
behaviour to him, played but a small part in Peter's sphere of
thought, and there ranged only just above books. The weather,
birds and ships, fish and the stars, to him were phenomena of far
greater moment. On a shelf in his room he kept a barque that he
had carved and rigged with much preciseness and patience. It
meant more to him than the good-will or displeasure of anybody in
the house. From the beginning, it is true, the barque had been
named *Rosa,* but it would be difficult to decide whether this was
meant to be a compliment to the ship or to the girl.

The girl Rosa did not weave, but looked out through the window.
The garden was still winterly bare and bleak, but there was a faint
silvery light in the sky; water dripped from the roof and from the
boughs of every tree; and the black earth showed in the garden-
paths where the snow had melted away. Rosa beheld it all, as grave
and wistful as a Sibyl, but in reality she thought about nothing.

The parson's wife, Eline, came into the room with her small son
by the hand. The parson's wife had been his housekeeper till he
married her, four years ago, and the gossips of the parish thought
that she had been more. She was only half her husband's age, but
she had worked hard all her life and looked older than her years.
She had a brown, bony, patient face and was light of foot and
movement, with a soft voice. Her life with the parson was often
burdensome to her, for he had soon again repented of his infidelity
to the memory of his first wife, who was his own cousin, a dean's
daughter and a virgin when he married her. In his heart he did not,
either, recognize the peasant woman's son as equal to his daughters.

But Eline was a simple creature, anchored in the resigned philosophy of the peasant; she aspired to no higher position in the house than that which she had held there from the beginning. She left her husband in peace when he did not call her, and was a handmaid to her pretty stepdaughter.

Rosa in all divergencies in the household sided with the wife. She was fond of her little brother, and had instated him in the parsonage as the one person besides herself entitled to have his own ways in everything—in manner of a monarch who acclaims another: "Brother, Your Majesty." But the child did not lend itself to be spoilt. In this house, overhung by the shadow of the grave, the other young people strove to keep alive; only the youngest inhabitant, the small, pretty child, seemed to fall in quietly with its doom, to withhold himself from life and to welcome extinction, as if he had only reluctantly consented to come into the world at all.

The parson's wife sat down demurely on the edge of a chair, and let her industrious hands rest in her lap upon her blue apron.

"No, your father will not buy the cow," she said and sighed a little. "They would sell that brindled cow at Christiansminde for thirty rixdollars. She is a fine cow, to calve in six weeks. But your father was angry with me when I asked him for it. For how do I know, he says, but that the day of judgment and the return of Christ may be nearer than anybody suspects? We should not hoard up treasures in this world, he says. Still," she added and sighed again, "we could do with the cow over the summer, in any case."

Rosa frowned, but she could not collect her thoughts sufficiently to be really angry with her father. "He will have to buy her in the end," she said coldly.

A butterfly that had kept alive through the winter and had wakened with the first rays of spring was fluttering towards the light, beating its wings on the window-pane as in a succession of little, gentle fingertaps. The child had kept his eyes on it for some time; now, in a great, steady glance he imparted his discovery to Rosa.

"My brother," said Eline, "went to have a look at the cow. She is a good cow, and gentle. I could milk her myself."

"Yes, that is a butterfly," said Rosa to the child. "It is pretty. I will catch it for you."

As she tried to take hold of it, the butterfly suddenly flew up to the top of the window. Rosa pushed off her shoes and climbed onto the window-sill. But up there, above the world, she realized that the prisoner wanted to get out, and to fly. She remembered the white butterflies of last summer, flitting over the lavender borders in the garden; her heart became light and great, and she felt sorry for the captive. "Look, we will let her out," she said to the boy. "Then she will fly away." She pushed the window open and wafted off the butterfly. The air outside was as fresh as a bath; she drew it in deeply.

At that moment Peter came up the garden-path from the stable. At the sight of Rosa in the window he stood dead still.

Since on the night of the rain he had resolved to run away to sea his heart had been filled with ships: schooners, barques, frigates. Now Rosa, in her stockinged feet, with the skirt of her blue frock caught back by the cross-bar of the window, was so like the figure-head of a big, fine ship that for an instant he did, so to say, see his own soul face to face. Life and death, the adventures of the seafarer, destiny herself, here stood straight up in a girl's form. It dawned upon him that long ago, when he was a child, something similar had happened to him, and that the world did then hold much sweetness. It is often the adolescent, the being just out of childhood, who most deeply and sadly feels the loss of that simple and mystic world. He did not speak; he was uncertain of how to address a figure-head, but as he stared at her she looked back at him, candidly and kindly, her thoughts with the butterfly. It seemed to him then as if she were promising him something, a great happiness; and within a sudden, mighty motion he decided to confide in her, and to tell her all.

Rosa stepped down from the window and into her shoes, at ease with the world. She had made a butterfly happy; she had made a child happy and a boy—were it only the silly boy Peter—all in a movement, and with a glance. They knew now that she was good, a benefactress to all living creatures. She wished that she could have stayed up there. But as this could not be, and as she saw Peter remaining immovable in the same place before her window, she went out and stood at the garden door.

The boy flushed as he saw her so close to him. He came up to her and took hold of her wrist, beneath the scanty sleeve. "Rosa," he said, "I have got a great secret which nobody in the world must know. I will tell it to you." "What is it?" asked Rosa. "No, I cannot tell it here," said he. "Others might overhear us. All my life depends upon it." They looked at each other gravely. "I shall come up to you tonight," said Peter, "when they are all asleep." "Nay, they will hear you, then," said she, for her room was upstairs, in the gable of the house, and Peter's below. "No. Listen," he said, "I shall set the garden-ladder up to your window. Leave it open to me. I shall get in that way." "I do not know if I will do that," said Rosa. "Oh, do not be a fool, Rosa," cried the boy. "Let me come in. You are the only one in the world whom I can trust." When they were children, and had been planning some great enterprise, Peter sometimes came to Rosa's room at night. She bethought herself of it, and for a moment there was in her heart, as in his, a longing for the lost world of childhood. "Maybe I will do it," she said, as she freed her arm of his grip.

The night was misty, but this was the first night after the equinox in which one felt the sweet lengthening of daylight. Peter sat still till he had seen the lamp put out in the parson's room; then he went out. He rocked the ladder to the gable wall, raised it to Rosa's window, and scratched his hand in the effort. When he tried the window, it was unfastened, and his heart began to beat. He swung himself into the room, and slowly and noiselessly crossed the floor. In the dark he ran his hand over the bed to make sure that the girl was in it, for she neither stirred nor said a word. Then he sat down on the bed, and for a while he was as silent as she.

The prospect of opening his mind to a friend, who would not interrupt him or laugh at him, rendered him as pensive and grateful as when he had listened to the trekking birds. He remembered that it was a long time, years perhaps, since he had talked like this to Rosa. He did not know whether the fault lay with her or with him; in either case it seemed a sad thing. Now, he reflected, it would be difficult to him to express himself. When in the end he spoke the words came tardily, one by one.

"Rosa," he said, "you must try to understand me, even if I speak badly." He drew in his breath deeply.

"I have been wrong all my life, Rosa," he said, "but it has not been made clear to me till now. You know that there are people in the world called atheists, terrible blasphemers, who deny the existence of God? But I have been worse than they. I have injured God and have done Him harm; I have annihilated God."

He spoke in a low, stifled voice, with long pauses between the phrases, hampered by his own strong emotion, and by his fear of waking up the people in the house.

"For you see, Rosa," he said, "a man is no more than the things he makes—whether he builds ships, or makes clocks or guns or even books, I dare say. You cannot call a man fine, or great, unless what he makes is great. It is so with God as well, Rosa. If the work of God does not glorify him, how can God be glorious?—And I, I am the work of God.

"I have looked at the stars," he went on, "at the sea and the trees, and at the beasts and birds, too. I have seen how well they come in with the ideas of God, and become what he means them to be. The sight of them must be satisfactory and encouraging to God. Just as when a boat-maker builds a boat, and she turns out a smart, sea-worthy boat. I have thought, then, that the sight of me will make God sad."

As he paused to collect his thoughts he heard Rosa draw her breath gently. He was thankful to her because she did not speak.

"I saw a fox the other day," he took up his theme, after a long silence, "by the brook in the birch-wood. He looked at me, and moved his tail a little. I reflected, as I looked back at him, that he does excellently well at being a fox, such as God meant him to be. All that he makes or thinks is just foxlike; there is nothing in him, from his ears to his brush, which God did not wish to be there, and he will not interfere with the plan of God. If a fox were not so, a beautiful and perfect thing, God would not be beautiful and perfect either.

"But here am I, Peter Købke," he said. "God has made me, and may have taken some trouble about it, and I ought to do him honour, as the fox does. But I have crossed his plans instead; I have worked against him, just because the people by me, such people as are called your neighbours, have wished me to do so. I have sat in a room for years and years, and have read books, because your old father wishes me to become a clergyman. If God had wished me to be a clergyman, surely He would have made me like one; it would even have been a small matter to him, who is almighty. He can do it when He wants, you know; He has made many clergymen. But me He has not made that way. I am a slow learner; you know yourself that I am dull. I have become so stale and hard that I feel it in my own bones, an ugly thing to have in the world, in reading these Fathers of the Church. And in that way I have made God stale and ugly as well.

"Why must we try to please our neighbour?" he went on thoughtfully, after a pause. "He does not know what is great; he cannot invent the fine things of the world any more than we can ourselves. If the fox had asked people what they wanted him to be, if he had even asked the King, a poor thing he would have become. If the sea had asked people what they wanted her to be, they would have made but a muddle of her, I tell you. And what good can one do to one's neighbour, after all, even if one tries? It is God to whom we must serve and please, Rosa. Yes, even if we could only make God glad for a moment that would be a great thing.

"If I speak badly," he said after a silence, "you must believe me all the same. For I have thought about these things for a very long time, and I know that I am right. If I am no good, God is no good."

Rosa agreed with most of what he said. To her the surest proof of the magnificence of Providence was the fact that she was there, Rosa, by the grace of God lovely and perfect. As to his view of her neighbour, she was not certain. She held that she might do a great deal to her neighbour. Neither do men light a candle—Rosa—and put it under a bushel, but on a candlestick, and she giveth light unto all that are in the house. Still, if Peter could speak in this way, he was a companion in the house, and might, surprisingly, be of use to her some time. She smiled a little on her pillow.

"And yet," said Peter, in such a great outburst of passion that against his own will his voice rose and broke, "I love God beyond everything. I think of the glory of God before anything else."

He became afraid that he had spoken too loud and kept perfectly still for a few minutes.

"Move in a little, can you," he said to the girl, "so that I can lie there too? There is room enough for both of us."

Without a sound Rosa withdrew to the wall, and Peter lay down beside her. The boy never washed more than strictly needed, and smelled of earth and sweat, but his breath was fresh and sweet in the dark, close to her face.

With the horizontal position calm came to him, and he spoke less wildly. "And all this," he said very slowly, "has come about only because I have not run away."

"Run away?" said Rosa, speaking for the first time. "Yes," said he. "Yes. Listen. I shall run away to sea, to be a sailor. God means me to be a sailor; that is what He has made me for. I shall become a great sailor, as good as any He has ever made. To think of it, Rosa! That God made those great seas, and the storms in them, the moon shining on them—and that I have left them alone and have never gone to see them! I have sat in that room downstairs and stared at things six inches off my nose. God must have disliked looking my way.

"Nay, imagine now, Rosa," he said after a while, "imagine only, just in order to understand what I say, that a flute-maker did make a flute, and that nobody did ever play on it. Would not that be a shame and a great pity? Then, all at once, someone takes hold of it and plays upon it, and the flute-maker hears, and says: 'That is my flute.'" He once more drew in his breath deeply, and there was a long silence in the bed.

"But," said Rosa in a small, clear voice, "I have often wished that you would go to sea."

At this unexpected and amazing expression of sympathy, Peter became perfectly still. He had a friend in the world, then, an ally.

For a long time he had failed to value his friend rightly; he had even held her to be light-headed and frivolous. And the while she had been faithful, she had thought of him, and had guessed his needs and his hopes. In this calm and fresh hour of the spring night, the sweetness of true human intercourse was, for the first time, mysteriously, revealed to him. In the end he timidly asked the girl: "How did you come to think of that?" "I do not know," said Rosa, and really at this moment she had forgotten why she had wanted Peter to go to sea.

"Will you help me to run away, then?" he asked, lowly and giddily. "Yes," said she, and after a while: "How am I to help you?"

"Listen," he said, and eagerly moved a little closer to her. "It is at Elsinore that I will get my ship. I know of a ship, the *Esperance*, the captain Svend Bagge, that lies at Elsinore now. She would take me. But I can not get to Elsinore! your father would not let me go. Only you might tell him that you want to go to see your God-mother there, and that you do not care to travel alone, and then he might let me come with you.

"And when we are there, Rosa, when we are at Elsinore I shall go aboard the *Esperance* before anybody can know of it. I shall be on the North Sea before they get scent of it, and nearing Dover, England, Rosa. Some day I shall round the Horn." He had to stop; he had too much to tell her, now that at last he had got himself under sail. "But I can stay here all night," he thought. "I can easily stay here till morning."

Rosa did not answer at once; it was as well that he should be kept in suspense a little and learn to appreciate her help. "You have thought it all out very precisely," she said at last, with a bit of irony. He thought her words over. "No," he said. "No, I did not exactly think it out. It all came to me on its own, suddenly. And do you know when? When I saw you standing in the window." He was shy of telling her that she had looked like the figure-head of the *Esperance* itself, but there was so much joyful triumph in his whisper that Rosa understood without words.

After a minute she said: "Many ships go down, Peter. Most sailors are drowned in the end." He had to fetch his mind back from the picture of her in the window before he could speak. "Yes, I know," he said. "But all people are to die some time, you know. And I think that to be drowned will be the grandest death of all." "Why do you think that?" asked Rosa, who was herself scared of water. "Oh, I do not know," said he, and after a moment: "It will be, perhaps, because of that great lot of water. For when you come to think of it, there is really nothing dividing the one ocean from the other. They are all one. When you drown in the sea, it is all the seas of the world that take you. It seems to me that that is grand." "Yes, it may be," said Rosa.

Peter, in talking of the oceans, had made a great gesture and had struck Rosa's head. He felt her soft, crispy hair towards his palm, and beneath it her little hard, round skull. Once more he became very still. Against his own will his fingers fumbled over her head and played with and stroked her hair. He drew his hand back, and after a minute he said: "Now I must go." "Yes," said she. He got out of the bed and stood beside it in the dark. "Good night," he said. "Good night" said the girl. "Sleep well," said Peter, who had never in his life wished anybody to sleep well. "Sleep well, Peter," said Rosa.

Peter came down the ladder in such a state of rapture and bliss that he might as well have gone the other way, heavenwards, to those well-known stars which were now hidden behind the mist. The causes of his agitation were, on the one hand, his flight and his future at sea, and on the other: Rosa. Under ordinary circumstances the two ecstasies would have seemed to be incompatible. But to-

night all elements and forces of his being were swept together into
an unsurpassed harmony. The sea had become a female deity, and
Rosa herself as powerful, foamy, salt and universal as the sea. For
a moment he thought of reclimbing the ladder. His soul, indeed,
went up, and once more embraced Rosa in the transport of glorious
fellowship. His body would have followed it if he had not, be-
wilderedly, realized that he did not know what to do with it, once
he got it there. So he sat down on the lowest rung of the ladder, his
head in his hands, in mystic concord with all the world.

After a time his thoughts began to adjust themselves. There was,
after all, a distinction in his attitude towards the universe round
him and that towards the girl above him.

In regard to the world, mankind in general and his own fate, he
was from now on the challenger and the conqueror. They would
have to give themselves up to him; if they struck he would strike
back, and he would take from them what he wanted. On their side,
everything was clear as daylight, bright as metal or the surface of
the sea, shining with danger, adventure, victory.

But towards Rosa all his being went forth in a tremendous
motion of munificence and magnanimity, in the desire to give. He
had no earthly riches with which to reward her, and even if he had
possessed all the treasures of the world he would have forgotten
them now. It was something more absolute which he meant to
yield up to her; it was himself, the essence of his nature, and at the
same time it was eternity. The offering, he felt, would be the highest
triumph and the utmost sacrifice of which he was capable. He could
not go away until it had been consummated.

Would Rosa understand him then, would she receive him, and
accept his gift? As slowly his mind swung from marine adventures
and exploits to the girl, he saw that on her side everything lay in
a solemn and sacred darkness, such as would be found, he thought,

in the deep waters of the oceans, off sounding. It seemed that he did not know her, as she knew him. His thoughts, even, could not get quite close to her, but were held back, every time, as by an unknown law of gravitation. His wild, overwhelming longing to beatify her, and this new, strange unapproachableness of her figure in his imagination kept him awake, in his own bed, till morning. He remembered Jacob, who had wrestled all night with the angel of God. Only here he somehow appropriated to himself the part of the angel, and reversed the cry of the Patriarch's heart. His soul called out to Rosa: "Thou shalt not let me go except I bless thee."

In her room upstairs, Rosa, a little while after Peter had left her, turned to her side, her cheek upon her folded hands and her long plait on her bosom, such as she used to do in the evening, when she meant to fall asleep. But she felt, wonderingly, that tonight she would not sleep at all. She had read about people passing a sleepless night, but as a rule they were either miscreants or rejected lovers, and it was, she reflected, a curious thing that one might be sleepless with content and ease as well. She kept on thinking of the hour that Peter had passed in her bed. A faint scent of his hair lingered on the pillow. She would not for all the world have moved any closer to the place where he had lain, but remained squeezed up against the wall, as she had been while he was there.

All, she repeated in her thoughts, had come to him on its own, suddenly, when he saw her standing in the window. She vaguely remembered that she had, not long ago, distrusted her old play-mate, and had meant to refuse him access to her own secret world. "You are a silly girl, Rosa," she whispered, as when she had been scolding her dolls. The idea of his strength, which had alarmed her, was now pleasing to her mind. She recalled an incident of which she had not thought for many years. A short time after Peter had first come to the house he and she had had a great fight.

She had pulled his hair with all her might while, with his tough boy's arms round her, he had tried to fling her to the floor. She laughed at the memory, with her eyes closed. Peter, when he climbed down the ladder, had failed quite to shut the window behind him. The night-air was cold in the room. Half an hour after Peter had gone Rosa fell into a sweet, quiet sleep.

But towards morning she had a terrible dream, and woke up with her face bathed in tears. She sat up in bed, her hair sticking to her wet cheeks. She could not recollect the dream in full; she only knew that within it she had been let down and deserted by someone, and left in a cold world, from which all colour and life were gone. She tried to chase off the dream by turning to the world of realities, and to her daily life. But as she did so she remembered Peter, and the fact that he was running away to sea. At that she grew very pale.

Yes, he was running away, that was his thanks to her for letting him come into her bed, and for liking him, since last night, better than other people. She went through their night talk, sentence by sentence. She had meant to be sweet to him—before she went to sleep had she not, in her fancy, stroked his thick, glossy hair, which once she had pulled, smoothed it and twisted it round her fingers? But he was going away all the same, to far places, where she could not follow him. He did not mind what became of her, but left her here, forlorn, as in her dream.

In two or three days he would be gone. He would see the house no more, nor the garden, nor the church. He would not even hear the Danish language spoken, but some strange tongue, incomprehensible to her. And he would not think of her; she would have gone from his mind. Gone, gone, she thought, and bit her hair that was wet with salt tears.

She was now, according to her promise, going to speak to her father, and to get leave for herself and Peter to go to Elsinore. After a while an idea rose to the surface of her mind. How easily could she not make all his great plans void? If she did tell her father of his project, there would be no ships in Peter's life, no rounding of the Horn, no drowning in the water of all the oceans. She sat in her bed, crouching on the thought, like a hen on her eggs. Till now, it seemed to her, she had managed to keep things at a distance; today they were drawing in upon her, touching her, as she hated things to do, pressing her breast. In the end she got up and put on her old frock.

Rosa very rarely begged her father for anything. He would give her what she asked, for the reason, she had been told, that she was so like her mother, after whom she was named. But she did not like to assume, in this way, the part of a dead woman; she wanted to be herself, the young Rosa. So she might sometimes apply to him on behalf of Eline or of her child, but for herself she would not do it. Still, today she needed the support of both Father and Mother. Some time ago, to amuse herself, she had put up her hair after the fashion of her mother's hair in her small portrait. Now, in front of the little dim mirror she again carefully did it up in the same way. Then she went down to her father's room.

She came out from it again with a blank face, like a doll's, and for some time stood quite still outside the room. She had her handkerchief in her hand, with a small pile of money tied up in it, the purchase price of the cow, which the parson had given her, and told her to hand over to Eline. He had been so deeply moved during their talk together, that he had even covered his face at the idea of his nephew's ingratitude, and again lifted it, marked by tears. As she was about to go, he took her hand and looked at her.

To the parson it was a constant burden and grief that he could not quite believe in the dogma of the resurrection of the body, on which, all the same, he must preach from his pulpit, for he distrusted and feared the body. The young girl, he thought, would not be tormented by any such doubts. And indeed the flesh that he touched was fresh and clean; one might imagine that it would be admitted to paradise. He had sighed deeply, counted up the money and laid it in her cool, calm hand. To Rosa all ideas of purchase and sale were, for some reason, displeasing. She took it reluctantly, and so unconcernedly that the old man had reminded her to tie it up in her handkerchief. Now, outside the door, she put the bundle into the pocket of her skirt.

She wanted to strengthen herself in the conviction that she was behaving normally and reasonably, and decided that she would go down to the kitchen, to have her breakfast. On the steps down she heard lively voices in there, and in the kitchen she found the whole household gathered round a fish-wife from the coast, who brought fish for sale in a creel upon her back.

These fisherwomen were a brisk, hardy race; they would walk twenty miles, heavy-laden, in all kinds of weather, and come home to cook and darn for a husband and a dozen children. They were quick-witted, great newsmongers and at home in every house, and they preferred their roving outdoor profession to that of the peasant woman, tied up in the stable or by the churn, and to that of the parson's wife. Emma, the fish-wife, had placed her creel on the floor and herself upon the chopping-block. She was drinking coffee from a saucer and giving out the news of the neighbourhood, laughing at her own tales. The lump of candy in her mouth, her scarcity of teeth and the broad dialect of her talk—mixed up with Swedish, for she was a Swede by birth as were many of the fishermen's wives along the Sound—made it difficult to follow her tales. But the children of the parsonage could speak the dialect themselves, when they wanted to. She broke off her story to nod to the parson's pretty daughter, and Rosa took her own cup of coffee to the chopping-block, to hear the news.

Peter caught sight of the girl, and saw or heard nothing else. After a while he came up and stood close to her, but he did not speak. When the talk and laughter were loud in the kitchen, Rosa said, without looking at him: "I have talked with my father. I may go to Elsinore, and you can come with me. Now that the snow is thawing we can go with the waggoners. We may even go today." At her news the boy grew pale, as she herself had done when, in the early morning, in bed, she had thought of him. After a long time he said: "No. We cannot go today. I shall come up to your room again tonight; there is something more that I have to tell you. I can come, can I not?" he asked. "Yes," said Rosa. Peter went away, to the other end of the kitchen, and came back again. "The ice is breaking up," he said. "Emma has seen it this morning. The Sound is free." Emma, for the benefit of the girl, repeated her report. All winter the fishermen had had to walk a long way out on the ice, to take cod with a tin bait. Now the ice was breaking; the open water was in sight. In a few days they would have their boats afloat once more.

"I shall go down to see it," said Peter. Rosa glanced at his face, and then could not take her eyes off it again—it was so strangely solemn and radiant—and he knew, she thought, nothing at all of what she did know. "Come with me, Rosa," he exclaimed in a great, happy seizure, as if he could not let her out of his sight. "Yes," said Rosa.

The little boy, when he heard that they were going to see the ice break up, wanted to come with them. Rosa lifted him up. "No, you cannot come," she said to him. "It is too far away for you. I shall tell you about it when I come back." The child gravely put his hands to her face. "No, you will never tell me," he said. Eline tried to hold back the girl, and told her that it was too far away for her as well. "Nay, I want to go far away," said Rosa. She put on an old cloak, and a pair of scabby furred gloves that belonged to her father, and went out with Peter.

As they came out of the house they saw that the snow was gone from the fields, but that all the same the world was lighter than before, for the air was filled with blurred, resplendent clarity. It almost blinded them. They strove to get up their eyelids against it. To all sides they heard the sound of dripping and running water. The walking was heavy; the melting snow had made the road slippery. Peter set off at a quick pace, and then had to wait impatiently for the girl, who in her old shoes slid and stumbled on the path. She caught up with him, warm with the exertion, and giddy, like himself, with the air and the light.

He stood still. "Listen," he said, "that is the lark." They kept immovable, close to one another, and did indeed hear, high over their heads, the incessant, triumphant jingle of a lark's song, a rain of ecstasy.

A little farther on, in the forest, they came upon a couple of wood-cutters, and Peter stopped to talk with them while he chose and cut a long stick for himself and one for Rosa, from two young beeches. An old man looked at Rosa, asked if she was the parson's girl at Søllerød, and remarked on how much she had grown. It was rare that the children of the parsonage had talk with outside people. Now, with Emma and the old wood-cutter, Rosa felt the world to be opening up to her.

Peter had walked on in a state of blissful intoxication, with the sea before him and dragging him like a magnet, and with the girl so close in his track. After his talk with the wood-cutters he had to go on speaking, but could not possibly find words for his own course of thought, so he began to tell her a story.

"I have heard a story, Rosa, you know," he said, "of a skipper who named his ship after his wife. He had the figure-head of it beautifully carved, just like her, and the hair of it gilt. But his wife was jealous of the ship. 'You think more of the figure-head than of me,' she said to him. 'No,' he answered, 'I think so highly of her because she is like you, yes, because she is you yourself. Is she not gallant, full-bosomed; does she not dance in the waves, like you at our wedding? In a way she is really even kinder to me than you are. She gallops along where I tell her to go, and she lets her long hair hang down freely, while you put up yours under a cap. But she turns her back to me, so that when I want a kiss I come home to Elsinore.' Now once, when this skipper was trading at Tranke-bar, he chanced to help an old native King to flee from traitors in his own country. As they parted the King gave him two big blue, precious stones, and these he had set into the face of his figure-head, like a pair of eyes to it. When he came home he told his wife of his adventure, and said: 'Now she has your blue eyes too.' 'You had better give me the stones for a pair of earrings,' said she. 'No,' he said again, 'I cannot do that, and you would not ask me to if you understood.' Still the wife could not stop fretting about the blue stones, and one day, when her husband was with the skippers' corporation, she had a glazier of the town take them out, and put two bits of blue glass into the figure-head instead, and the skipper did not find out, but sailed off to Portugal. But after some time the skipper's wife found that her eyesight was growing bad, and that she could not see to thread a needle. She went to a wise woman, who gave her ointments and waters, but they did not help her, and in the end the old woman shook her head, and told her that this was a rare and incurable disease, and that she was going blind. 'Oh, God,' the wife then cried, 'that the ship was back in the har-bour of Elsinore. Then I should have the glass taken out, and the jewels put back. For did he not say that they were my eyes?' But the ship did not come back. Instead the skipper's wife had a letter from the Consul of Portugal, who informed her that she had been wrecked, and gone to the bottom with all hands. And it was a very strange thing, the Consul wrote, that in broad daylight she had run straight into a tall rock, rising out of the sea."

While Peter told his tale they were walking down a hill in the wood, and in the descent Rosa felt something gently knocking against her knee. She put her hand in her pocket, and touched the handkerchief with the money in it that she had forgotten to give to Eline. She ran her fingers over it; there ought to be thirty coins there. The figure rang familiar to her mind. Thirty pieces of silver, the purchase-price of a life. She had sold a life, she thought, and had done what Judas Iscariot did once do.

The idea had perhaps been in her mind vaguely for some time, ever since she had looked at Peter in the kitchen. As now she put it into words to herself, it hit her with such awful strength that she thought she must fall headlong down the hill. She wavered on her feet, and Peter, in the midst of his story, told her to hold on to him. She heard what he said, but she could not answer, and his voice to her seemed to be followed by a dead silence. Although she kept on trudging at the boy's heels, she heard neither their footsteps nor the sounds of the wood, but moved on like a deaf person.

So now it had come, she thought, what all her life she had feared and waited for. Here, at last, was the horror which was to kill her.

She did not exactly feel the catastrophe, or the ruin, to have been brought on her by her own fault; she had not it in her to feel so, but in all calamities would be quick to put the blame on somebody else. But she accepted it in full as her personal lot and portion. It was her fate and her doom; it was the end of her.

The name of Judas stuck in her ear, and kept on ringing there with terrible force. Yes, Judas was her equal, the only human being to whom she could really turn for sympathy or advice; he would show her her way. So strongly did the idea take hold of her that after a minute she looked round, bewildered, for a tree, such as Judas had found for himself. They were walking through a glade in the forest, where only a few tall beech-trees grew here and there, and, as she gazed about her, a buzzard, the first she had seen that year, loosened itself from a high branch and majestically sailed farther into the wood, with a silver glimmer on its broad, tawny wings. Judas, Rosa reflected, had kissed Christ when he betrayed him; they must have been such good friends that it came natural to them to kiss each other. She had not kissed Peter, and now they would never kiss, and that was the only difference between her and the accursed apostle.

She did not see the wood round her, or the pale sky above her. She was once more back in her father's room, and at the moment when she had denounced Peter to him. The parson had spoken to her of his youth and had told her how in Copenhagen he had been assistant to the prison chaplain. There he had learned, he said, that a prison is a good, a safe place for human beings to be in; he himself still often felt that he might sleep better in a prison than in any other place. Some of the wrongdoers, he told her, had tried to break out; he had pitied their short-sightedness, and had felt it to be to their own good when they were captured and brought back. Then, a moment before with a sigh he took up the money and gave it to her, he had looked her in the face and said: "But you, Rosa, you do not want to run away; you will stay with me." Rosa had gazed round the room; then, it had seemed to repeat the same words. It was a poor room, sparsely furnished, with a sanded floor; people laughed, she knew, at the thought that it was a clergyman's study. Yet this room belonged to her; she had known it all her life. Why should anyone, she had thought, disown and desert it any more than she did? Now she had sided with that room, with the prison, with the grave, and had closed the doors of them on her. For she had not guessed it, then, to be her fate that, if Peter was a prisoner, she herself would no more be free. She remembered the open window of last night, after Peter had gone from her, and the fresh darkness round her pillow. She had closed that window too. She had closed all the windows in the world on her, and never again would she stand in an open window, and let everything come to Peter, on its own, at the sight of her.

Slowly she returned to the world of reality round her, to the wet brown wood, the curves of the road and Peter's figure upon it, bareheaded, with a big old muffler round his neck. She did not quite like him, for through him her misery had come, and if he had not been there she would still have walked in the woods, beautiful, content and proud. But it was impossible to her to think of anything upon the earth but him. He stalked on lightly, a strong, straight boy, his head filled with dreams. It was as if she were tied to him with a rope, and were being dragged along after him, a bent, decrepit old woman, so much older than he as to be grieving, as to be weeping over his youth and simplicity.

They again came to the top of a hill, from where there was a view over the lower parts of the wood, blue with the spring mist. Peter stopped, and stood for a minute in silence.

"Do you remember, Rosa," he said, "that when we were small we came here to gather wild raspberries? In many years, when we are old people, we shall come back here again. Perhaps then everything will be changed, the wood all cut down, and we shall not know the place. Then we will talk together of today."

It was, once more, the mystic melancholy of adolescence, which will take in, at the very height of its vitality and with a grave wisdom that soon again vanishes, both past and future: time itself, in the abstract. Rosa listened to him, but could not understand him. The past she had destroyed, and she shrank from the future with horror. All that she had got in the world, she thought, was this one hour, and their walk to the sea.

In a short time they came to a steep brink, grown with straggly fir trees, and had the Sound straight in front of them.

It was a rare and wonderful sight. The ice was breaking up; a little way out from the coast it still lay solid, a white-grey plane. But already at a short distance from land, clear of the ground and dissipated into floes and sheets, it was gently rocking and swaying, and slowly turning with the current beneath it. And outside the irregular, broken white line, was the open sea, pale blue, almost as light as the air, a mighty element, still drowsy after its long winter-sleep, but free, wandering on according to its own lustful heart, and embracing all the earth.

There was hardly any wind, but in the air a faint rustle, like a low, joyful chatter, where the sheets of ice rubbed against one another, and thronged to get afloat.

Peter had not touched Rosa since he had played with her hair in bed; now for a second he seized her hand, and in his warm palm she felt a stream of energy and joy. Then in a few long leaps he rushed down the brink and out on the ice, and she ran after him.

If Rosa had been ten or twenty years older she might at this moment have died or gone mad with grief. Now she was so young that her despair itself had vigour in it, and bore her up. Since she had only this one hour of life left to her, she must, within it, enjoy, experience and suffer to the utmost of her capacity. She bounded on the ice as swift as the boy.

To Rosa the supreme wonder and delight of the scenery lay in the fact that everything was wet. Things had lately been dry and hard, unyielding to the touch, irresponsive to the cry of her heart. But here all flowed and fluctuated, the whole world was fluid. Near the shore there were patches of thin white ice that broke as she trod on them, so that she had to wade through pools of clear water. Her shoes soon got soaked; as she ran the water sprinkled over her skirt, and the sense of universal moisture intoxicated her. She felt as if, within a minute or two, she herself, and Peter with her, might melt and dissolve into some unknown, salt flow of delight, and become absorbed into the infinite, swaying, wet world. She seemed to see their two figures quite small upon the white plane. She did not know that her pale face became radiant as she ran on.

Here on the ice Peter waited for her patiently, and kept close to her, more collected and with more weight to him than when on the road he had been swept forward by the wild longing of his soul. They walked or ran side by side. Rosa thought: "I have gone to sea with Peter, after all." She made him stop a moment.

"Nay, Peter," she said. "Look, we are going to Elsinore now. That tall packing of ice out there is Godmother's house. And that one farther out, you know, that is the harbour."

They made straight for her Godmother's house. On the way to it Peter said: "Is it not a strange thing about the sea, Rosa? You may look out over it as over a prairie, all the horizon round. And then, just by turning your eyes, you may look down into it as well, all the way to the bottom of it, and it holds back nothing from you. People sometimes say that the sea is treacherous and the earth trustworthy. But the earth closes itself up to one. There may be anything, just below your feet—a buried treasure, the treasure of one of the old pirates—and you can have no idea of it. And as to the air—you may gaze up into it, but you will never know how it looks from the outside. The sea is a friend."

They stopped at Rosa's Godmother's house, sat down on it, and tried to make out places along the wide, hazy coastline. Two trees formed a landmark above the fishing village of Sletten; they were palmtrees upon a coral island. A glint in the air, from the copper roof of Kronborg Castle, far up north, was the first gleam of the white cliffs of Dover. To the south, a mile away, there were people out on the ice, like themselves; they would be wild men, cannibals, whom they must avoid. "Yes," thought Rosa, "why would he not content himself with such journeys as these? Then we might have been happy."

As they walked farther they had, from time to time, to straddle over deep cracks in the ice, which shone green as glass; the ice was more than two feet thick. Once Rosa imagined that she felt the ground faintly moving under her, and got a strange sensation that something or someone, a third party, had joined in their sea adventure, but she said nothing to Peter. They kept running and leaping, always side by side. "Now," Rosa cried out, "we are at the harbour of Elsinore!"

The breath of the sea here came straight into their warm, flushed faces. There was a southerly current on the still day, the sheets of ice before them were slowly travelling north.

By the coast of Sealand the wind rarely goes round north from east to west, but it will blow a long time from the east with rain and foul weather, then change and go southeast and south, to finish up in the west and let the air clear up. Sometimes a calm follows, and, while the wind dozes, the Sound slowly fills with slackened sails from many countries, like loose goose-down blown together to one side of a pond. Peter and Rosa thought of the ships they had seen gathered here in summer weather.

Now there were tuffed ducks swimming in the pale water, themselves so similar to it in colour that they could only be distinguished by their black necks and wings, an irregular, shifting group of little dark specks upon the waves.

"Yes," Peter said slowly, "now we are at the harbour of Elsinore. And that," he added and pointed ahead, "is the *Esperance*. She is riding at anchor, but she is ready to put to sea." The *Esperance* was a large floe of ice, fifty feet long, and separated from the ice on which they stood by a long crevice. "Am I to board her now, Rosa?"

Rosa crossed her arms on her breast. "Yes, we will go aboard now," she said. "We shall be in the North Sea before anyone has got the scent of it, and near England. And then some day we will go round the Horn." Peter cried: "Are you coming aboard with me?" "Yes," said Rosa. "And sailing with me" he asked, "all the way, to the South Pole, are you?" "Yes," said she. "Oh, Rosa," said Peter, after a pause.

They strode on to the ice floe, and Peter took Rosa's hand and held it. They were both tired with their run on the ice, and pleased to stand still on deck.

Peter looked in front of him, his face lifted. But the girl, after a time, turned her head to see what her native coast of Sealand would look like from so far out. Then she saw that the crevice between the floe and the land-ice had widened. A clear current of water, six feet wide, ran where they had walked. The *Esperance* had really put to sea. The sight terrified Rosa; she wanted to shriek out loud, and run.

She did not shriek, though. She stood immovable, and her hand did not even tremble in Peter's hand. For within the next moment a great calm came upon her. That fate, which all her life she had dreaded, and from which today there was no escape—that, she saw now, was death. It was nothing but death.

For a few minutes she alone was aware of the position. She did not think much; she stood up straight and grave, accepting her destiny. Yes, they were to die here, she and Peter, to drown. Peter now would never know that she had let him down. It did no longer matter, either; she might, quite well, tell him herself. She was once more Rosa, the gift to the world, and to Peter, too. At the moment when she collected her whole being to meet death, Rosa did not grieve for herself. But she mourned, sadly, for the sake of the world, which was to lose Rosa. So much loveliness, so much inspiration, so many sweet benefactions were to go from it now.

Peter felt the slight swaying of the ice-sheet, spun round, and saw that they were adrift. His heart gave two or three tremendous throbs; he shifted his grip from the girl's arm to her elbow, and swung her with him to the edge of the floe. He saw, then, that he might possibly jump the channel, but that Rosa could not do it. So he again dragged her back a little, and looked round. There was clear water to all sides. The people whom they had seen on the ice were no longer in sight. The two were alone with the sea and the sky.

Bewildered and trembling the boy tore at his hair with one hand, still holding her elbow with the other. "And I myself begged you to come with me!" he cried out.

After a moment he turned round towards her, and this was the first time since they had come out of the house that he looked at her. Her round face was quiet; she gazed at him beneath the long eyelashes as from an ambush.

"Now we are sailing straight to Elsinore," she said. "It is better than that we should go home first, do you not see?"

Peter stared at her, and slowly the blood went up in his face, till it was all aflame. Their danger, and his own guilt in bringing her here, vanished and came to nothing before the fact that a girl could be so glorious. As he kept looking at her, all his life, and his dreams of the future, passed before him. He remembered, too, that he was to have come up to her room that night, and at the thought a swift, keen pain ran through him. Yet this was more wonderful than anything else.

"When we come to Elsinore," Rosa said, "where the Sound is narrow, the captain of the *Esperance* himself will see us, and fetch us on to his ship, do you not think?"

The boy's heart was filled to the brim with adoration. He felt the light wind in his hair and the smell of the sea in his nostrils, and the movement of the water, which terrified Rosa, intoxicated him. It was impossible that he should not hope; it could not be that he should not have faith in his star. It seemed to him, at this moment, that for a long time, perhaps for the length of his whole life, he had been lifted from one ecstasy into another, and that this might well be the crowning miracle of it all. He had never been afraid to die, but he could not, now, give room to the idea of death, for he had not before felt life to be so mighty. At the same time, just as dream and reality seemed, on the floe, to have become one, so did the distinction between life and death seem to have been done away with. Dimly he guessed that this state of things would be what was meant by the word: immortality. So he did no more look ahead or behind; the hour held him.

He let go his grip on Rosa's arm, and again looked round. He went to pick up their walking-sticks which they had flung away as they came onto the *Esperance*. He was some time boring a hole in the ice with his knife, so as to make fast his stick in it, and in tying his big old red handkerchief to the top of the stick. Now it would serve them as a flag of distress, and be seen from far off. He tied the knife to Rosa's stick with a bit of cord from his pocket, to turn it into a boathook—if ever the current would bear them close to the land-ice he might get a grip on to it with the hook. Rosa looked on.

With the raising of the flag their floe became a different thing to the others round them, a ship, a home on the water for him and her. It was not cold; a silver light had come into the sky. A curious idea ran through Peter's head; he wished that he had brought his flute, to play to her as they sailed, for till now she had never cared to hear him.

In his pocket he had a bottle with gin in it. He dug it up, and asked Rosa to drink from it. It would do her good, he said, and he would himself have some after her. Rosa strongly disliked the smell of gin, and had before been angry with Peter for drinking it. Now, after hesitating a little, she consented to taste it, and even to drink of the bottle, for they had no glass. The few drops that she swallowed made her cough, and brought tears into her eyes, but when again she recovered her breath she said: "Gin is not really a bad thing, after all." For Peter's sake she even had another draught, which warmed her all through and brightened all the world to her. Peter then had a pull at the bottle himself, and set it down on the ice.

Peter pulled off his coat and muffler, and wrapped them around Rosa, crossing the muffler over her breast, and she let him do so without a word. "Why have you put up your hair today?" he asked her. Rosa only shook her head in reply; it would take too long to explain. "Let it hang down," he said. "Then the wind will blow in it." "Nay, I cannot get my arms up, with your muffler on," said Rosa. "Can I take it down?" he asked. "Yes," said she.

Peter with skilled fingers, trained at the rigging of the barque *Rosa,* undid the ribbon that held up her hair as she stood patiently, with her head a little bent, close to him. The soft, glossy mass of hair loosened and tumbled down, covering her cheeks, neck and bosom, and, just as he had foretold, the wind lifted the tresses, and gently swept them against his face.

At that moment suddenly, without any warning, the ice broke

beneath their feet, as if they had stepped on a hidden crack in it, and their combined weight had made it give way. The break threw them on to their knees, and to each other. For a minute the ice still bore them, a foot below the surface of the water. They might have saved themselves, then, if they had separated and struggled on to the two sides of the crack, but the idea did not occur to either of them.

Peter, as he felt himself flung off his balance, and the ice-cold water round his feet, in one great movement clasped his arms round Rosa and held her to him. And at this last moment the fantastic, unknown feeling of having no ground under him in his consciousness was mingled with the unknown sense of softness, of her body against his. Rosa squeezed her face into his collar-bone, and shut her eyes.

The current was strong; they were swept down, in each other's arms, in a few seconds.

A CONSOLATORY TALE

CHARLES DESPARD, the scribe, walked into a small café in Paris, and there found a friend and compatriot dining sedately at a table by the window. He sat down face to face with him, drew a deep sigh of relief and ordered an absinthe. Till he had got it and tasted it he did not speak, but listened attentively to a few commonplace remarks from his companion.

It snowed outside. The wayfarers' footsteps were inaudible upon the thin layer of snow on the pavement; the earth was dumb and dead. But the air was intensely alive. In the dark intervals between the street lamps the falling snow made itself known to the wanderers in a multitudinous, crystalline, icy touch on eyelashes and mouth. But around the gas-lit lantern-panes it sprang into sight, a whirl of little, transilluminated wings, which seemed to dance both up and down, a small white world-system, like a hectic, silent, elfish bee-hive. The Cathedral of Notre Dame loomed tall and grim, a rock, slanting upward infinitely into the blind night.

Charlie had just had a great success with a new book, and was making money. He was not good at spending it, for he had been poor all his life, and had no expensive tastes, and when he looked at other people to learn from them, the ways in which they were getting rid of their earnings most often seemed to him silly and insipid. So he left his wealth in the hands of the bankers, as with people mysteriously keen on and experienced in this side of existence, and was himself generally short of cash. By this time his wife had gone back to her own people, and he had no regular establishment, but travelled about. He felt at home in most places, but still had in his heart a constant, slight nostalgia for London, and his old life there.

He was silent now, and shy of human society, subject to that particular sadness which is expressed in the old saying: *omne animal post coitum triste.* For to Charlie the pursuit of writing, and that of love-making, were closely related. It would happen to him to hear a tune, or smell a scent, and to say to himself: "I have heard this tune, or smelled that scent before, at a time when I was either deeply in love, or at work on a book; I cannot call to mind which. But I remember that I was then, at the height of my vitality, pouring forth my being in harmony and ecstasy, and that everything seemed to be, unwontedly and blissfully, in its right place." So he sat by the table like a man with whom a love-affair has just come to its end, chilled and exhausted, with a strong sense of the emptiness and vanity of all human ambitions. All the same, he was pleased to have met his friend, with whom he was always in good understanding.

Charlie was a small, slight man, and looked very young for his years, but his convive was smaller than he, and of indefinable age, although the poet knew him to be ten or fifteen years older than he. He was so neatly made, with delicate hands, feet and ears, finely chiselled features, a noble little mouth, a fresh complexion and a melodious voice, that he might have passed as a miniature model of the human figure made for a museum. His clothes were well cut and decorous; his high hat lay on a shelf behind him, above his coat and umbrella.

His name was Æneas Snell, or so he called himself, but in spite of his easy and debonair manner his origin and past life were obscure even to his friends. He was said by some to have been a cleric, and unfrocked at an early stage of that career. Later in life he had become a doctor of skin diseases, and had done well in the profession. He had travelled much in Europe, Africa and Asia, and knew many cities and men. No great events, either fortunate or sad, seemed ever to have come to him personally, but it had been his fate to have strange happenings, dramas and catastrophes take place where he was. He had been through the plague in Egypt and in the service of an Indian Prince during the mutiny, and he was secretary to the Duke of Choiseul de Praslin at the time when this nobleman murdered his wife. At the present moment he acted as bailiff to a great parvenu of Paris. His friends sometimes wondered that a man of so much talent and experience should all his life have felt content in the service of other people, but Æneas explained the case by pointing to the phlegm or passivity of his nature. He could not, he said, on his own find sufficient reason for doing a thing ever to do it, but the fact that he was being asked or told to do so by somebody else was to him quite a plausible reason for taking it on. He did well as a bailiff and had his employer's confidence in everything. Something in his carriage and manner suggested that by taking on this work he was conferring an honour both on himself and on his master, and this trait strongly appealed to the rich French gentleman. He was a pleasant companion, an attentive, patient listener and a skilful raconteur; he would not let his own person play any big role in his tales, but he would tell even his strangest story as if it had taken place before his own eyes, which indeed it might often have done.

When Charlie had drunk his absinthe, he became more communicative; he leaned his arm on the table and his chin in his hand, and slowly and gravely said: "Thou shalt love thy art with all thy heart, and with all thy soul, and with all thy mind. And thou shalt love thy public as thyself." And after a while he added: "All human relationships have in them something monstrous and cruel. But the relation of the artist to the public is amongst the most monstrous. Yes, it is as terrible as marriage." At that he gave Æneas a deep, bitter and harassed glance, as if he did see, in him, his public incarnated.

"For," he went on, "we are, the artist and the public, much against our own will, dependent upon one another for our very existence." Here again Charlie's eyes, dark with pain, fired a deadly accusation at his friend. Æneas felt the poet to be in such a dangerous state of mind that anything but a trivial remark might throw him off his balance. "If it be so," he said, "has not your public made you a pleasant existence?" But even these words so bewildered Charlie that he sat in silence for a long time. "My God," he said at last, "do you think that I am talking of my daily bread—of this glass, or of my coat and cravat? For the love of Christ, try to understand what I say. Nay, we are, each of us, awaiting the consent, or the co-operation of the other to be brought into existence at all. Where there is no work of art to look at, or to listen to, there can be no public either; that is clear, I suppose, even to you? And as to the work of art, now—does a painting exist at which no one looks?—does a book exist which is never read? No, Æneas, they have got to be looked at; they have got to be read. And again by the very act of being looked at, or of being read, they bring into existence that formidable being, the spectator, the which, sufficiently multiplied—and we want it multiplied, miserable creatures that we are—will become the public. And so there we are, as you see, at the mercy of it." "In that case," said Æneas, "do show a little mercy to one another." "Mercy? What are you talking about?" said Charlie, and fell into deep thought. After a long pause he said, very slowly: "We cannot show mercy to one another. The public cannot be merciful to an artist; if it were merciful it would not be the public. Thank God for that, in any case. Neither can an artist be merciful to his public, or it has, at least, never been tried.

"No," he said, "I shall explain to you how it does stand with us. All works of art are beautiful and perfect. And all of them are, at the same time, hideous, ludicrous, complete failures. At the moment when I begin a book it is always lovely. I look at it, and I see that it is good. While I am at the first chapter of it it is so well balanced, there is such sweet agreement between the various parts, as to make its entirety a marvellous harmony and generally, at that time, the last chapter of the book is the finest of all. But it is also, from the very moment it is begun, followed by a horrible shadow, a loathsome, sickening deformity, which all the same is like it, and does at times—yes, does often—change places with it, so that I myself will not recognize my work, but will shrink from it, like the farm wife from the changeling in her cradle, and cross myself at the idea that I have ever held it to be my own flesh and bone. Yes, in short and in truth, every work of art is both the idealization and the perversion, the caricature of itself. And the public has power to make it, for good or evil, the one or the other. When the heart of the public is moved and shaken by it, so that with tears of contrition and pride they acclaim it as a masterpiece, it becomes that masterpiece which I did myself at first see. And when they denounce it as insipid and worthless, it becomes worthless. But when they will not look at it at all—*voilà,* as they say in this town, it does not exist. In vain shall I cry to them: 'Do you see nothing there?' They will answer me, quite correctly: 'Nothing at all, yet all that is I see.' Æneas, if the case of the artist be so with his public, it is not good to paint or to write books.

"But do not imagine," he said after a time, "that I have no compassion with the public, or am not aware of my guilt towards them. I do have compassion with them, and it weighs on my mind. I have had to read the Book of Job, to get strength to bear my responsibility at all." "Do you see yourself in the place of Job, Charlie?" asked Æneas. "No," said Charlie solemnly and proudly, "in the place of the Lord.

"I have behaved to my reader," he went on slowly, "as the Lord behaves to Job. I know, none so well, none so well as I, how the Lord needs Job as a public, and cannot do without him. Yes, it is even doubtful whether the Lord be not more dependent upon Job than Job upon the Lord. I have laid a wager with Satan about the soul of my reader. I have marred his path and turned terrors upon him, caused him to ride on the wind and dissolved his substance, and when he waited for light there was darkness. And Job does not want to be the Lord's public any more than my public wishes to be so to me." Charlie sighed and looked down into his glass, then lifted it to his lips and emptied it.

"Still," he said, "in the end the two are reconciled; it is good to read about. For the Lord in the whirlwind pleads the defense of the artist, and of the artist only. He blows up the moral scruples and the moral sufferings of his public; he does not attempt to justify his show by any argument on right and wrong. 'Wilt thou disannul my judgment?' asks the Lord. 'Knowest thou the ordinances of heaven? Hast thou walked in the search of the depth? Canst thou lift up thy voice to the clouds? Canst thou bind the sweet influence of the Pleiades?' Yes, he speaks about the horrors and abominations of existence, and airily asks his public if they, too, will play with them as with a bird, and let their young persons do the same. And Job indeed is the ideal public. Who amongst us will ever again find a public like that? Before such arguments he bows his head and foregoes his grievance; he sees that he is better off, and safer, in the hands of the artist than with any other power of the world, and he admits that he has uttered what he understood not." Charlie made a pause. "The Lord did the same thing to me, once," he said gravely, sighed and went on: "I have read the Book of Job many times," Charlie concluded, "at night, when I could not sleep. And I have slept badly these last months." He sat silent, lost in remembrance.

"But all the same I wonder," he said after a long pause, "what is the meaning of the whole thing. Why may we not give up painting and writing, and give the public peace? What good do we do them, in the end? What good, in the end, is art to man? Vanity, vanity, all is vanity."

Æneas by this time had finished his dinner, and was quietly sipping his coffee. "Monsieur Kohl, my principal," he said, "is himself a dilettante of pictures, and keen to make a gallery in his hotel. But as he has no real knowledge of painting, and no leisure to learn about it, the selection of his pictures used to vex and trouble him. Now, however, I have on his behalf gone round to the painters, one by one, and have asked each of them to sell me the one picture which, out of all he has ever painted, he personally holds to be the best. Our gallery is growing, and it is going to be very fine."

"He is wrong," said Charlie gloomily. "The artist himself cannot say which is his finest work. Even if your artists be honest people, and you have not foisted upon you the picture which they cannot sell to anybody else—such as you deserve to have—they cannot tell." "No, they cannot tell," said Æneas. "But a collection of pictures, each of which has been picked by the painter as the finest he has ever painted, may well, in the end, tickle the curiosity of the public, and fetch its price at a sale."

"And you yourself," said Charlie bitterly, "you go on the errand of a rich dilettante from one artist to another. But you have never, upon your own, painted a picture, or bought one. When, in time, you quit this world of ours, you might as well not have lived." Æneas nodded his head. "What do you nod your head at?" asked Charlie. "At what you are saying," said Æneas. "I might as well not have lived."

Charlie had now rid himself of the restlessness and chagrin that had beset him as he first came into the café, and he felt that it would be pleasanter to listen than to go on speaking. He also found that he was hungry, and ordered dinner. By the time when he had finished his soup he leaned back in his chair, glanced round the room as if he saw it for the first time, and in a low and languid voice, like that of a convalescent, said to Æneas: "Can you not even tell me a story?"

Æneas stirred his coffee with his spoon, and picked up the sugar left on the bottom of the cup. He put the napkin to his small mouth, folded it and laid it on the table. "Yes, I can tell you a story," he said. He sat for a minute or two, ransacking his memory. During that time, although he kept so quiet, he was changed; the prim bailiff faded away, and in his seat sat a deep and dangerous little figure, consolidated, alert and ruthless—the story-teller of all the ages. "Yes," he said at last, and smiled, "I can tell you a consolatory story," and in a sweet and modulated voice he began.

When I was a young man, I was in the employ of an esteemed firm of carpet dealers in London, and was by them designated to travel to Persia, there to buy up a consignment of ancient carpets. But by the dispensations of destiny I became, for two years, during a period of political unrest and intrigue, when the English and the Russians vied for the greater influence with the Persian Court, physician in ordinary to the ruler of Persia, Mahommed Shah, a highly deserving Prince. He suffered great distress from erysipelas, a disease against which I had been happy enough to find a cure. The present Shah, Nasrud-Din Mirza, was then heir-apparent to the throne.

Nasrud-Din was a lively young Prince, keen on progress and reform, and of a willful and fantastic mind. He was ambitious to know the conditions and circumstances of his subjects, from the highest to the poorest, and gave himself or his surroundings no rest in this pursuit. He had studied the tales of the Arabian Nights, and from this reading he fancied for himself the role of the Caliph Haroun of Bagdad. So he would often, in imitation of this classical histrionic, all by himself, and in the disguise of a beggar, a peddler or a juggler, wander through his town of Teheran, and visit the market-places or the taverns of it. He listened to the talk of the labourers, water-carriers and prostitutes there, in order to get from them their true opinion on the office-holders and placemen, and upon the custody of justice in the kingdom..

This caprice of the Prince caused much alarm and distress to his old Councillors. For they thought it an untenable and paradoxical state of things that a Prince should be so *au fait* with the doings and sentiments of his people, and one quite likely to upset the whole ancient system of the country. They represented to him the dangers to which he exposed himself, and the injustice that, in his intrepidity, he was doing to the realm of Persia, which might thus wantonly suffer the saddest bereavement. But the more they talked the keener Prince Nasrud-Din became upon his fancy. The ministers then had recourse to other measures. They took care that he should be, wherever he went, secretly followed by armed guards; they also bribed his valets and pages to discover in what disguise he would go, and to what part of the city he would betake himself, and often the beggar or the prostitute with whom the Prince entered into talk had been pre-instructed by the judicious old men. Of this Nasrud-Din knew nothing, and the Councillors dreaded his wrath, should he find out, so that even amongst themselves they kept silent upon their wiles.

Now it came to pass, by the time when I was at Court, that the old High Minister Mirza Aghai one day sought audience with the Prince, and solemnly imparted to him news of a strange and sinister nature.

There was, he said, in the town of Teheran a man, in face, stature and voice so like the Prince Nasrud-Din that the Queen, his mother, would hardly know the one from the other. Moreover, the

stranger in all his ways minutely imitated and copied the manner
and habits of the Prince. This man had for some months been
walking through the poorest quarters of the city, in the disguise of
a beggar, similar to that which the Prince was wont to wear, had
seated himself by the gates or the walls, and there questioned and
held forth to the people. Did not the fact, the old Minister asked,
prove the danger of the Prince's sport? For what would lie behind
it? The mystificator was either a tool in the hands of the Shah's
enemies, set by them to sow discontent and rebellion amongst the
populace, or he was an impostor of unheard temerity, working
upon some dark scheme of his own, and possibly nurturing the
horrible plan of doing away with the heir to the throne, and of
passing himself off to the people as the Prince. The old man had
let all the foes of the Royal House pass muster in his mind. Before
him had then risen the shadow of a great lord, cousin to the Shah
and decapitated in a rebellion twenty years ago, and he remembered to have heard that a posthumous son had been born to the
outlaw's name. This youth, Mirza Aghai reflected, might well endeavour to revenge his father, and to get his own back. He begged
his young lord to renounce his excursions until such time as the in-
triguer should have been seized and punished.

Nasrud-Din listened to the Chamberlain's proposal and played
with the silken tassels of his sword-knot. What, he asked, did this
strange plotter, the double of himself, tell the people, and what impression had he made upon them? "My lord," said Mirza Aghai,
"What exactly he has told the people I cannot report, partly because
his sayings seem to be deep and twofold, so that those who have
heard them do not remember them, and partly because he really
does not say much. But the impression which he has made is sure
to be very profound. For he is not content to investigate their lot,
but has set himself upon sharing it with them. He is known to

have slept by the walls on winter nights, to have lived upon the leavings which the portionless paupers have spared to him, and, when they had nothing to give, to have kept fast for a whole day. He frequents the cheapest prostitutes of the city in order to convince the poor of his compassion and fellow-feeling. Yes, to insinuate himself with the lowest of your townfolk, under your favour, he keeps company with a girl who, in the tavern of a market-place, gives performances with a donkey. And all this, my Prince, within your effigy."

The Prince was a gay and gallant young man; it amused him to vex the old, cautious men of his father's Court, and Mirza Aghai's tale to him contained the promise of a rare adventure. When he had thought the matter over, he told the Minister that he would not forego the chance of meeting his *doppelganger*. He would go himself to speak with him, and detect the truth about him. He forbade the old men to interfere with his plan, and this time took such precautions that it became impossible to them to impede or control him. In vain did Mirza Aghai beseech him to give up so perilous a project. The only concession which in the end they wrested from him was the promise that he would go about well armed, and that he would take with him one attendant in whom he could trust.

I was, just then, seeing much of the young Prince. For Prince Nasrud-Din had on his left cheekbone a mole, the size of a cherry. It was slightly disfiguring in itself, and it was naturally in his way when he wished to go about incognito. So after he had watched my cure of his father, the Shah, he called upon me to rid him of the nevus. The treatment was slow; I had time to entertain the Prince with the narratives that he loved, and I held, by the nature of things, a big bag of tales which belongs to our classic Western civilization, and were new to him.

The Prince was also afraid of growing fat, so that at times he

would eat very little. The Queen, his mother, who thought that he
had never been more lovable than when, as a baby, he had been fat,
took much trouble with the purveyors and the chefs of the royal
household, to make them bring and prepare such rare dishes as
might tempt her son's appetite. Now she saw that when I was relat-
ing my stories to him the Prince would sit long over his food, and
she graciously entreated me to keep him company at table. I told
the Prince as much as I could remember of the *Divina Commedia,*
and of a few of Shakespeare's tragedies, together with the whole
of the *Mysteries of Paris,* by Eugene Sue, that I had read just before
I left Europe. During our talks on such works of art I gained his
confidence, and when by this time he was to choose a companion
in his secret expeditions he asked me to go with him.

He took pleasure in having me dressed up as a Persian beggar,
in a big cloak and slippers, and with a flap over one eye. Each of us
kept a poniard in his belt and a pistol in his breast; the Prince made
me a present of my poniard, which had a silver hilt, set with tur-
quoises. The old Minister Mirza Aghai then approached me, and
promised me his gratitude and a permanent and lucrative office at
Court should I, in the end, succeed in turning the mind of Nasrud-
Din from his caprice. But I had no faith in my power to turn the
mind of a Prince, nor had I any wish to do so.

We thus wandered through the streets and the slums of Teheran,
during some evenings of early spring. On the terraces of the Royal
Gardens the peach trees were already in blossom, and in the grass
there were crocus and jonquils. But the air was sharp and the night
frost not far away.

Within the city of Teheran the evenings of this season are wonderfully blue. The ancient grey walls, the planes and olive trees in
the gardens, the people in their drab garments and the long, slow

files of heavy-laden camels coming home through the gates—all seem to float in a delicate mist of azure.

The Prince and I visited strange places, and made the acquaintance of dancers, thieves, bawds and soothsayers. We had various long discussions on religion and love, and many times we also laughed together, for we were both young. But for a while we did not find the man on whose track we walked; neither did we, anywhere, hear much of him. Still we knew the name by which he called himself, which was the same as the Prince had used as a beggar. And in the end, one evening, we were guided by a small boy to a market-place, close to the oldest gate of the town, where, we were told, the plotter by this hour was wont to seat himself. By the well of the place the bare-legged child stopped, and pointed to a small figure sitting on the ground at some distance. He gave us a clear, steady glance, said: "I will go no farther," and ran off.

We paused for a moment, and felt our knives and pistols. It was a poor and vile square; narrow streets led to it; the houses were pitiable and decayed; the air filled with nauseous smells; the ground broken and dusty. The ragged inhabitants of the streets had come from their work, and in the last hour of daylight were lounging and chatting in the open, or drawing water from the well. A few of them were buying wine by the counter of an open tavern, and we did so too, asking for the cheapest that the innkeeper had to sell, since we were ourselves beggars tonight. As we drank, we kept an eye on the man upon the ground.

There was an old crooked fig tree growing out from a creek in the wall, and he sat beneath it. No crowd surrounded him, as we had been led to expect. But while I watched him I saw the wayfarers slacken their pace as they passed him. One and another amongst them stood still and exchanged a few words with him before they walked on, and each of them seemed to turn his face half away from the beggar, and to hold himself, in his nearness, with reverence and awe. As slowly I took in the whole scene before me, I thought it to be in some way unusual and striking. The place was as low and miserable as any I had walked through in the town, yet there was dignity in the atmosphere of it, and a stillness as of anticipation and confidence. The children played together without fighting or crying, the women prattled and laughed lowly and gaily, and the water-drawers waited patiently for one another.

The innkeeper was talking with a donkey driver, who had brought him two big baskets of fresh beans, cabbage and lettuce. The donkey driver said: "And what do you imagine that they will be dining on at the palace tonight?" "On what will they be dining?" said the innkeeper. "That is not easy to tell. They may be having a peacock, stuffed with olives. They may eat carps' tongues, cooked in red wine. Or they will be partaking of a fat-rumped, cinnamon-stewed sheep." "Yes, by God," said the ass driver. We smiled at the description of these extraordinary dishes, which were obviously dainties to the poor. Prince Nasrud-Din paid for his wine, draped his mendicant's cloak over his head, and without a word went forth and seated himself a little way from the stranger. I took the place next to him, by the wall.

The man for whom we had so long searched, and of whom we had talked so much between us, was a still person; he did not lift his eyes to look at the newcomers. He sat on the earth with his legs crossed, his head bent, and his folded hands resting on the ground in front of him. His beggar's bowl stood beside him, and it was empty.

He had on a large cloak, like that which the Prince wore, only more tattered and patched. It had a hood to it, which partly covered his head, but while he sat so quiet, his eyes downcast, I had time to study his face. It was true that he bore a likeness to the

Prince. He was a dark, slight young man, a few years older than Nasrud-Din, of such age as the Prince would assume in his role of beggar. He had long, black eyelashes, and a small thin black beard, similar to the beard which the Prince used to put on with his beggar's disguise, only it was really growing on his face. Upon his left cheekbone he had a brown mole, the size of a cherry, and I saw, because I had experience in that matter, that it was put on artificially, with skill. As to his countenance and manner, he was in no way like the daring and dangerous conspirator whom I had expected to meet. His face was peaceful, so that indeed I do not remember to have set eyes on a more serene human physiognomy. It was also singularly vacant of shrewdness, or even of much intelligence. That dignity and collectedness which, a moment ago, I had been surprised to find in the market-place around him, were repeated within the figure of the man himself, as if these qualities were concentrated in, or issuing from, the ragged and lean beggar's form. Perhaps, I reflected, there are few things which will impart as great dignity to a man's appearance as the air of complete content and self-sufficiency.

When we had thus sat together in silence for a while, it happened that a poor funeral procession came along, on its way to the burial ground outside the walls, the corpse on a litter and covered with a cloth, a few mourners following it, and some idlers of the street strolling behind. As they caught sight of the beggar under the fig tree, they again seemed to be seized with some kind of fear or veneration; they swerved a little in their course as they passed, but they did not speak to him.

When they had gone by, the beggar lifted his head, gazed at the air before him, and in a low and gentle voice said: "Life and Death are two locked caskets, each of which contains the key to the other."

The Prince started as he heard his voice, so like was his mode of speaking, even to a slight snuffle within it, to his own. After a moment, he himself spoke to the stranger. "I am a beggar like you," he said, "and have come here to collect such alms as merciful people will give me. Let us not waste our time while we wait for them, but talk about our lives. Is your life as a beggar of so little value to you that you would be content to exchange it for death?" The beggar seemed unprepared for so energetic an address. He did not answer for a minute or two, then gently wagged his head and said: "Not at all."

Here an old poor woman came staggering across the square towards us, approaching the beggar in the shy and submissive manner of the others, turning her face away as she spoke to him. She was pressing a loaf of bread to her bosom, and as she stopped she held it out to him in both her hands. "For the mercy of God," she said, "take this bread and eat it. We have seen that you have sat here by the wall for two days, and have had nothing to eat. Now I am an old woman, the poorest of the poor here, and I think that you will not refuse alms from me." The beggar softly lifted his hand to reject the gift. "Nay," he said, "take back your bread. I will not eat tonight. For I know of a beggar, my brother in mendicancy, who sat by the town wall for three full days, and was given nothing. I will experience myself what he did then feel and think." "Oh, God," sighed the old woman, "if you will not eat the bread I shall not eat it myself either, but I shall give it to the cart-bullocks which come in by the gate, and are tired and hungry." And with that she staggered away again.

When she had gone, the Prince once more turned to the beggar. "You are wrong," he said. "No beggar of the town has sat by the wall for three days and has been given nothing. I have asked for alms myself, you know, and have never been without food even for the length of a day. The people of Teheran are not so hard-hearted nor so indigent as to let the meanest of beggars starve for three days." To this the beggar answered not a word.

It was now growing colder. The great space above our heads was still glass-clear and filled with sweet light; innumerable bats had come out from holes in the wall and were noiselessly cruising within it, high and low. But the earth and everything belonging to it lay in a blue shadow, as if it had been finely enamelled with lazulite. The beggar drew his old cloak round him and shivered. "It would be better for us," I said, "to seek a little shelter in the gate itself." "Nay, I shall not go there," said the beggar. "The gate-keepers chase away beggars from the gate with a bastinado." "You are wrong once more," said the Prince. "I, who am a beggar myself, have sought shelter in the gates, and no gate-keeper has ever told me to go away. For it is the law that poor and homeless people may sit within the gates of my city, when the traffic of the day is done."

The beggar for a minute thought his words over; then he turned his head and looked at him. "Are you the Prince Nasrud-Din?" he asked him.

Prince Nasrud-Din was startled and confused by the beggar's straight question; his hand went to his knife, as my hand to my own. But after a second he haughtily looked him in the face. "Yes, I am Nasrud-Din," he said. "You must know my face, since you have counterfeited it. You must have followed me for a long time, and closely, in order to assume my part in the eyes of my people with so much skill. I have known about your game, too, for some time. Your motive for playing it, only, I do not know. I have come here tonight to learn it from your own lips."

The beggar did not answer at once; then again he shook his head. "Heigh-ho, my gentle lord," he said. "May you rightly say so, when

I have donned that very attire and semblance, which you yourself think most dissimilar to your own, and most likely to conceal you, and to beguile the people of your town? Might not I as justly charge you yourself with having, in your greatness, mimicked my humble countenance, and embezzled my beggar's appearance? Aye, it is true that I have once seen you, at a distance, in your mendicant's clothes, but I have learned more from those who followed and watched you. It is true, too, that I have made use of the likeness that God deigned to create between you and me. I have profited by it to be proud, and grateful to God, where before I was cast down. Will a Prince blame his servant for that?"

"And whom," asked the Prince with a penetrating glance at the beggar, "do the people of the market-place and the streets believe you to be?" The beggar threw a quick, furtive glance round him to all sides. "Hush, my lord, speak low," he said. "The people of the market-place and the streets dare not for their lives let me know who they believe me to be. Did you not see them turning away their heads and cast down their eyes as they passed by or spoke to me? They know that I will not be known; they are afraid that, if ever I find out who they believe me to be, my wrath against them shall be so terrible that I shall go away, never to come back to them."

At these words the Prince coloured and became silent. At last he said gravely: "They all believe you to be Prince Nasrud-Din?" The beggar for a moment showed his white teeth in a smile. "Yes, they believe me to be Prince Nasrud-Din," he said. "They think that I have got a palace to live in, and may go back there whenever I wish. They believe that I have got a cellar filled with wine, my table laid with rich food, my chests filled with garments of silk and fur."

"Who, then," the Prince asked, "are you, who have been made

proud and thankful to God in playing to be me?" "I am what I look," said the beggar. "I am a beggar of Teheran. As such I was born. My mother was a beggarwoman, and she thrashed the profession into me before I weighed as much as a cat. I have asked for alms in the streets, and by the walls of the city all my life." "What is your name, beggar?" the Prince asked. "I am named Fath," said the beggar.

"And have you not," the Prince asked after a silence, "planned to get into that palace of which you speak, upon the strength of the likeness between you and me?" "No," said Fath. "Have you not endeavoured," the Prince asked again, "to gain influence and power with the people and to serve your ambition by means of that likeness?" "No," said Fath. He sat for a while in thought; then he said: "No. I am a beggar, and may be clever in the trade of a beggar. But about the other things I know not, and I care for none of them. I should be sadly troubled if I were to deal with them. I have gained power over the people, that is true, and it is likely that they would do what I wish, but what would I wish them to do?"

"What have you been doing, then," asked the Prince, "after you had so cleverly studied my looks and ways and had made the people of Teheran believe that you are Prince Nasrud-Din?" "I have," said Fath, "been asking for alms in the streets, and by the walls of the city." He looked at the Prince, and exclaimed: "What have you done to the mole on your cheek?" The Prince held his hand to his cheek. "I have had it removed," he said. Fath lifted his own hand to his cheek. "The people will not like that," he said gravely.

"But wherefore do you slander my people," asked the Prince, "and make out the lot of the beggars of my town harder than it is? Why did you tell that a beggar had sat for three days by the wall, and had received nothing, and that you yourself wished to know what he felt thereby?" "As God lives," said Fath, "it is no slander, but the truth." "Who," the Prince asked him severely, "was the beggar who was so cruelly treated?" "My lord, it was I, myself," said Fath, "in the days before I had seen you."

"But now tell me, for that I do not understand," said the Prince, "why you will accept nothing from the townsfolk by this time, when you have brought them to offer you the best they have got? Why did you refuse the loaf of bread which the old woman took to you and send her away so sad?" Fath thought his words over. "Good, my lord," he said. "With your permission, I perceive that you know but little about beggary. You, I suppose, all your life have had as much as you wanted to eat. If I take what they offer me, how long will they go on offering it? And how long will they believe, then, that I have got, in my palace, the richest food, and all the delicacies of the world, from the east to the west?"

The Prince was silent for a while; then he began to laugh. "By the tombs of my fathers, Fath," he said, "I took you for a fool, but now I think that you are the shrewdest man in my kingdom. For see, my courtiers and my friends demand from me offices, distinctions and gold, and when they have got them they leave me in peace. But a beggar of Teheran has harnessed me to his waggon, and from now on, awake or asleep, I shall be labouring for Fath. If I conquer a province, if I shoot a lion, if I write a poem, or if I marry the daughter of the Sultan of Zanzibar—it will all be one: it will all serve to the greater glory of Fath."

Fath looked at the Prince beneath his long eyelashes. "It may be said," he said, "and now you have said it. But I may hold, as against that, that you yourself have made Fath, and all there is of him. You did not, when you walked the streets as a beggar, endeavour to be any wiser or greater, any nobler or more magnanimous than the other beggars of the town. You made yourself just one of them, and took good care not to differ from them in any way, in order to hoax your people, and to listen, unobserved, to their talk. Therefore, now, I am no more than a common beggar either. Awake or asleep I am but the beggar's mask of Prince Nasrud-Din." "That, too, may be said," said the Prince.

"I beseech you, Prince," Fath went on solemnly, "to conquer provinces, to kill lions, to write poems. I have seen to it that the name of Prince Nasrud-Din, and that the renown of his loving-kindness, have been great with the paupers of Teheran. See to it now that the name of Fath, and his reputation for gallantry and wit, be great amongst the Kings and the Princes. As you kill a lion, remember that the heart of Fath rejoices at your bravery. And when you have married the Sultan's daughter, how highly will not the people think of you, as they still watch you sitting by the wall, all through the cold night, in order to share their hard lot. How highly will they not think of you when, to partake of the sorry fate of the poorest, you still sit down and talk with the prostitutes of these streets." "Do the prostitutes of these streets," the Prince asked, "embrace you with ardour, now, and shiver with ecstasy in your arms? Come, you ought to tell me, since I myself know nothing about it, and since their shiverings are in some way my own due." "Nay, I cannot tell you," said Fath. "I know no more about it than you do. I dare not embrace them; they are wise, and may know the embrace of a great lord." "So you stand in awe of my women, Fath?" said the Prince. "You, who showed no fear when I denounced myself to you." "My lord," said Fath, "man and woman are two locked caskets, of which each contains the key to the other."

"Hold out your hands, Fath," said the Prince, and as the beggar did so he lifted his mendicant's wallet from his belt and emptied it into the outstretched hands. Fath kept the coins in his palms, and looked at them. "Is that gold?" he asked. "Yes," said the Prince. "I have heard of it," said Fath. "I know it to be very powerful."

He hung his head, and sat for a long time, mournfully, in deep silence. "I see now," he said at last, "why you have come here to-night. You mean to put an end to my grandeur. You will have me sell my honour, and my great name with the people, for this mighty and dangerous metal." "No, by my sword," said the Prince, "I had no such thing in my mind." "What am I to do with the gold, then?" Fath asked. "Indeed, Fath," said the Prince, some-what embarrassed, "that is a question which I have not been asked before. If you have no use for it yourself, you may give it to the poor of the market-place." Fath sat still, gazing at the gold. "I might," he said, "like the man in the tale of the forty thieves, ask for the loan of a beggar's bowl, and when I give it back by mistake leave a piece of gold at the bottom of it, so as to convince the people of my opulence. But my lord, it would do myself, or them, no good. They would want more, and more than you have given me, and more than you could ever give me. They would no longer love me, as they do now, and no more believe in my compassion, or in my wisdom. Take it back, the beggar begs you. The gold is better with you than with me."

"What can I do for you, then?" the Prince asked. Fath thought his words over, and his face lightened up, like the face of a child.

"Listen, my great lord," he said. "There is one scene which I have often pictured to myself; you can make it come true if you want to. Some day let the finest regiment of your horsemen ride through the market-place, your captain at the head of it. Then I shall seat myself in the place, and when they come I shall not move, or get out of their way. So command your captain, as he sees me, to pull up his horse in great surprise and dread, and to stop the whole regiment, in order that they shall not touch me; yes, to stop it so suddenly that the fiery horses all rear at it. But command him further, when I make a sign with my hand, to ride on, and over me, all the same—only tell him to use a little caution, so that the horses shall not hurt me. This is what you can do for me, my lord."

"What wild fancy of yours is that, Fath?" the Prince asked and smiled. "It has never happened that my horsemen have ridden over one of the people in the streets, or in the market-place." "Yes, it has happened, my lord," said Fath; "in that way my mother was killed."

The Prince sat for some time in thought. "Vanity, vanity, all is vanity," he said in the end. "I have before now, at Court, learned much about the vanity of men. But I have learned more from you, a beggar, tonight. It seems to me, now, that vanity may feed the starving, and keep warm the beggar in his ragged cloak. Is it so, Fath?" "You see, my lord," said Fath, "it will be written in the books, in a hundred years, that Nasrud-Din was such a Prince, and ruled his kingdom of Persia in such a way, that his poorest subjects did hold their vanity fully gratified as they starved, in their beggars' cloaks, by the walls of Teheran."

The Prince once more draped his cloak about him and drew it over his head.

"I shall go back now," he said. "Good night, Fath. I should have liked to come here again, on an evening, to talk with you. But in the end my visits would ruin your prestige. I will see to it that you shall sit in peace, from now, by your wall. And God be with you."

As he was about to go, he stopped. "One more word, before I go," he said with some hauteur. "It has come to my ear that you visit the woman who, in the tavern of the market-place, gives performances with a donkey. It is well that the people should learn of my wish to know their conditions, and even to share them with them. But you are taking a great liberty with our person when you make us tread, so to say, in the footsteps of an ass. From tonight you must see the woman no more." I had not guessed this particular instance in the beggar's scheme to have impressed itself so deeply on the Prince's mind; now I saw that it had shocked and offended him, and that he felt Fath to have made light of things really great and elevated. But then he was not only a Prince, but a young man.

At his word Fath looked highly bewildered and dismayed; he gazed down and wrung his hands. "Oh, my lord," he cried, "this command of yours comes hard on me. The woman is my wife. It is by the gains of her craft that I live."

The Prince stood for a long time looking at him. "Fath," he said at last, in a very gentle and royal manner, "when, in the matter between you and me, I give in to you in everything, I cannot myself say whether it be from weakness, or from some kind of strength. Tell me, my beggar of Teheran, what in your heart you hold it to be." "My master," said Fath, "you and I, the rich and the poor of this world, are two locked caskets, of which each contains the key to the other."

As we walked back in the late evening I felt that the Prince was thoughtful and disturbed in his soul. I said to him: "You will, Your Highness, tonight have learned something new as to the greatness and the power of Princes." Prince Nasrud-Din did not answer me for a while. But when we had come out of the narrow, evil-smelling streets and were entering the richer and statelier quarters of the city, he said: "I shall no more walk in my town in disguise."

In this way we came back to the Royal Palace about midnight, and had supper there together.

Here Æneas finished his story. He leaned back in his chair, took out cigarette-paper and tobacco, and rolled himself a cigarette.

Charlie had listened to the tale observantly, without a word, his eyes on the table. At the silence of his friend he looked up, like a child waking from its sleep. He remembered that there was tobacco in the world, and after Æneas' example he slowly rolled and lighted a cigarette. The two small gentlemen, each at his side of the table, smoked on in peace, and gazed at the faint blue tobacco smoke.

"Yes, a good tale," said Charlie, and after a little while added: "I shall go home now. I believe that I shall sleep tonight." But when he had come to the end of his cigarette he, too, leaned back in his chair thoughtfully. "No," he said. "Not a very good tale, really, you know. But it has moments in it that might be worked up, and from which one might construct a fine tale."

LONDON FIELDS
by Martin Amis

Two murders in the making: the first, of a femme fatale intent on goading one of her lovers into killing her, and the other, that of Earth itself.

"An uninhibited high-energy performance...[Amis] is one of the most gifted novelists of his generation." —*Time*

Fiction/Literature/0-679-73034-6

POSSESSION
by A. S. Byatt

An intellectual mystery and a triumphant love story of a pair of young scholars researching the lives of two Victorian poets.

"Gorgeously written...dazzling...a tour de force."

—*The New York Times Book Review*

Fiction/Literature/0-679-73590-9

THE WOMAN WARRIOR
by Maxine Hong Kingston

"A remarkable book...As an account of growing up female and Chinese-American in California, in a laundry of course, it is anti-nostalgic; it burns the fat right out of the mind. As a dream—of the 'female avenger'—it is dizzying, elemental, a poem turned into a sword." —*The New York Times*

Nonfiction/Literature/0-679-72188-6

MATING
by Norman Rush
WINNER OF THE NATIONAL BOOK AWARD FOR FICTION

A female American anthropologist of high intellect and grand passion, at loose ends in Botswana, finds love with Nelson Denoon, a charismatic intellectual who is rumored to have founded a secretive and unorthodox utopian society in a remote corner of the Kalahari Desert.

"A complex and moving love story...breathtaking in its cunningly intertwined intellectual sweep and brio...a major novel."

—*Chicago Tribune*

Fiction/Literature/0-679-73709-X

Available at your bookstore or call toll-free to order: 1-800-793-2665.
Credit cards only.